A NECESSARY DARKNESS

SUSAN CATALANO

This is a work of fiction. Names, characters, businesses, places, events and incidents are either the products of the author's imagination or used in a fictitious manner. Any resemblance to actual persons, living or dead, or actual events is purely coincidental.
No part of this book may be reproduced, scanned or distributed in any printed or electronic form without permission. All rights reserved.

Cover artwork and design: Christian Catalano

Copyright © 2016 Susan Catalano
All rights reserved.
ISBN-10: 1532864337
ISBN-13: 978-1532864339

DEDICATION

For my husband
For believing

1 DEVIL

She wiped at the dribble of spit sliding down her cheek as another landed on her skirt. She didn't reprimand those who spat or hurled insults or looked upon her with loathing. She deserved every ounce of their condemnation. More than a few were here solely due to her hysterical accusations. So Susannah Sheldon allowed the disdain of the accused to follow her through the damp, stinking dungeon that had been their home for many months.

A tentative smile played upon Tituba's lips as Susannah approached. A tightness gripped Susannah's chest at the sight of the disheveled woman—a friend who'd only meant to provide a bit of entertainment, something to make their dull days a bit brighter. And Susannah and the others had turned Tituba's friendship into a dark, evil thing.

"Missy Sheldon," Tituba said.

Susannah couldn't stop her lips from turning up into a weak smile. She put her hands on the bars that separated them. "Tituba."

Tituba lifted herself from the floor with some difficulty, her movements stiff and awkward as she took the few steps that brought her directly in front of Susannah. "What you doing here?"

"Have you heard?" Susannah asked.

Tituba studied Susannah a moment, eyes glittering with knowledge.

"You *have* heard."

"Haven't heard nothing," Tituba said, nodding once. "I know."

"What do you know?"

"They gone. Vanish. Poof," Tituba said with a flourish of her hand.

Susannah nodded. "I saw it with my own eyes. The plank was pulled out from beneath them and they started to fall. Before the noose could tighten, Merry and William disappeared into thin air."

"He took 'em."

Susannah frowned. "God?"

"Pffft. Not God."

Tituba stared at Susannah with her dark, piercing eyes. They conveyed an unspoken truth. Susanna's hand flew to her mouth as she shook her head back and forth.

"Uh huh. He came saw me," Tituba said. "Saw you too."

Tears streamed down Susanna's face. *That evil being, the Tall Man. Of course he took them.* After stirring up chaos at the last witch trial, it was clear the Tall Man wanted William for his own. "But why?"

"Master Darling got something he want. Why else?"

"What, Tituba? What does he have?"

Tituba stared at her for a moment. Finally, she said in a grave tone, "He have light, Missy Sheldon. And what do darkness want more than light? Hmm?"

Minutes. Hours. Days. William had no way of knowing how much time had passed since Merry had leapt back through her colors. The surrounding darkness afforded no context by which to judge the passage of time. No waning shadows or hint of dawn. Its blackness was complete.

He stumbled through the dark for a while, hands searching

for some form of egress—a crack in the wall, a tunnel, a door. At some point, he succumbed to exhaustion. His limbs became leaden weights, every step a labor, and he collapsed against the rough walls, making a bed of the dirt beneath him. His dreams were the same as his surroundings, filled with nothing but blackness.

He awakened covered in sweat, the chill of sleep offering little relief in the oven-like cave. Thirst and hunger gnawed at him. His neck throbbed where the noose had so recently tightened around it.

William resumed his search, pressing his hands against the stone wall, inch by inch, so as not to miss the slightest puff of air or drift of sunlight. He believed he was still in the area where Merry's colors had taken her away. Thankfully, she'd made it into the colors. He hoped she'd made it back to Liz and Sophie. There was no guarantee in which direction of time the colors would take her, but at least she was far from this hell.

A low chuckle sounded behind him.

At first he thought the corpse hands were back, reaching toward him, poised to land on him at any moment. But the sound was too singular. The chuckle came again and with it a churning in his chest as the curse inside him responded. He knew then who was with him in the dark.

He pressed his back against the wall, wishing it would absorb him. Steady footsteps made their way toward him, but William's focus turned to steadying the internal beast that yearned to consume him in the presence of its master. Two red orbs shone through the darkness as the Tall Man's visage appeared. William's uneven breathing was the only sound between them until the Tall Man spoke in his deep, gravelly voice.

"And what would you do if you escaped?"

William said nothing, gritting his teeth against the surge of need emanating from the mark at its master's voice.

A teasing smile played upon the Tall Man's lips. "Would you go to her?"

William forced himself to hold his gaze steady as he stared into the Tall Man's unnatural crimson eyes. William's fear was nothing against the innate urge to protect the love he held for Merry. It didn't matter that it would no longer be realized. He'd not allow such evil to taint the memories of what they'd shared.

Even the mark couldn't penetrate his determination and soon a calm came over him, the dark receding. Did he imagine it or was the Tall Man's countenance blemished by a moment of uncertainty? If so, it didn't last. The Tall Man came closer, cool and assured, eyes level with William's.

"Tell me, William. Was it your light or darkness that killed Jonathan Parish?"

The question caught William unawares. It was a good question, a powerful one. Light or dark, indeed. He'd killed a person. Someone he knew. He could let the lie stand as truth that Powder's hoof had delivered the death blow, but he knew it was his desire empowered by the Tall Man's mark that had landed the horse's hoof perfectly upon Jonathan's head. William had held the desire. He'd controlled the weapon. It was no accident Jonathan was dead. Still, the Tall Man's question stood. Was it William's light, his heart's unwavering love for Merry, or the mark and its penchant for mayhem that had driven him to end Jonathan's life?

William shuddered, wishing the sin away. But it was his to own. He, William Darling, was a killer. A murderer.

"Yesssssssss." Many voices hissed the word, paralyzing him.

The Tall Man disappeared, swallowed by the shadows. The sound of several - more than several - slithering creatures filled the room. A rolling wave of darkness emerged from the dim shadows, forging itself into a mass of snakes—hundreds of them. William stared in horror as they neared, their forked tongues flitting in and out of fanged mouths, their red eyes focused on him.

"William," they hissed.

He barely breathed.

Then one of the snakes darted toward him, sinking its fangs into his leg. William beat at the creature, yanking it from his flesh, its smooth body writhing and flipping back on itself as it tried to bite his arm. He flung it into the sea of snakes surrounding him. For a moment they stilled, their beady eyes watching. Calculating. Then, as though an order had been given, they surged, jaws open, flooding him with their vile venom. His screams were heeded by no one.

When it was done, they disappeared into the ground, the walls, the darkness, leaving William to surrender to the wretchedness of this unending nightmare. Agony and suffering in the form of a stuttering heartbeat and ragged breath filled the corner where he lay. His agony. His suffering.

Some time later, cautious steps headed William's way, and with considerable effort, he opened his eyes to the oppressive darkness, broken only by the spare light cast from a flickering torch on the wall. Through the gloom, a figure took shape. A woman. He didn't move at her approach—he couldn't. She knelt down beside him. Shining blonde hair swooped forward as Corinne lowered a tray onto the floor.

He followed her gaze as it trailed down his abused body. The wounds were already healing; William's skin begged to be scratched as they stitched together. Splotches of blood, some dried, some glistening in the meager torchlight, covered him like a bad art form. Corinne's gaze locked onto his.

"What do ye want?" William asked, his voice hoarse from the screams that had been torn from him.

"I brought you some food and water," Corinne answered, nodding toward the tray she'd set down.

A mirthless laugh escaped him. "Why bother? I'll die sooner without."

"Why would you think we want you dead?"

"Mayhap 'tis the torture and general mistreatment."

"My father likes to keep amused," she replied with a bored shrug.

Rage gripped William. The paralyzing venom allowed him only to grit his teeth. "You... your father... you are of the

Devil."

Tentatively, she reached out and touched first her fingertips, then her flattened palm, to his chest. William moaned as his skin burned beneath her hand. A knowing, gleeful smile spread across her lips. "It seems you're of the Devil now as well, William."

2 FOUND

"Quiet Maddie!" Mark Witmer shouted at his dog, again.

Ten minutes ago, he'd started with a calm "no bark" command. As the barking continued, his voice had grown louder and his commands more desperate. He left his desk, grabbed a couple of biscuits from the treat canister, and headed to the deck where Maddie, his fluffy, good-natured Bernese Mountain dog barked, transfixed by something only she could hear in the woods behind the house.

Mark opened the french doors and stepped out. "Maddie! No bark!" Still, the barking continued. "Treat," he said, tossing one to her, and then another when she didn't notice the first. Ignoring him was one thing, but she never ignored a treat. Mark squinted against the bright sunlight, following Maddie's focused gaze towards the woods. He saw nothing. Heard nothing.

"Quiet Maddie," he said, forcing calm into his voice. This tactic brought about the desired result, but it also emboldened her; she stopped barking and ran down the deck stairs. Mark shouted after her, but she kept running, disappearing into the woods.

"Ah, shit." Mark ran down the stairs, across the lawn, and

chased after her. He shouted her name, while following the leaf-crushing sounds she made as she bounded through the woods. A flash of black fur caught his eye, and he spun to the left, picking his way over protruding rocks and root-veined earth. After a few moments he slowed, realizing he couldn't hear her movements anymore.

"Maddie!"

Houses sat on either side of the shallow woods. The energetic shouts from a ballgame at the nearby Gallows Hill Park filtered through the trees. But, no barking. Mark continued in the direction he'd seen her last. Then Maddie barked. Not an aggressive bark, like she might use if she'd encountered a threat, but a desperate, urgent yelp. Mark's blood chilled. He ran as fast as he could, calling her name. The barking grew louder, and soon he came upon his dog, prancing on her front paws, head toward the sky.

Mark's mouth dropped open as he came to the slow realization that the air around him was filled with color. For one indulgent moment, he thought he'd found the fabled end of the rainbow. He stood enthralled as the colors twisted and spiraled upon sunlit dust until they faded completely.

"What the hell?"

Maddie bumped against his thigh with her big, boxy head. Still searching the sky for colors, he reached down and tousled her floppy ears. "Yeah, I guess that was bark-worthy, girl." At that, Maddie woofed, walked a few feet away, and whined.

Mark looked down and his heart thumped an extra beat. He crouched beside his dog, legs quivering as he looked upon the inert body of a young woman, maybe twenty years old, lying on the forest floor. She was missing a sneaker, and her jeans and sweater were torn, dark bruises peering out from beneath them. Her sweater had risen up a bit, revealing a number of bruises bearing the distinct shape of fingers and hands. Many hands.

But what arrested his attention most was the violent red wound that ringed her neck. Someone had tried, or succeeded, to hang this girl. He reached out two shaking fingers and laid them on her neck, just beneath her jaw. He let out the breath he'd been holding as a weak pulse thudded beneath his fingers. The girl shuddered.

He touched her shoulder gently. "Hey, can you hear me?" Nothing. Maddie laid down beside her and whined. Mark pulled his cell out from his front pants pocket and dialed 911.

Her eyelids fluttered, allowing snippets of light to seep into her consciousness. She squinted against the brightness stabbing through the tall trees. Dried leaves scratched her neck; rocks poked her back and legs. A hammering agony pulsed through her body. She clamped her eyes shut against the torment. Fingers pressed against her shoulder. Her body rocked with tremors. Her throat tightened, and her neck screamed.

Mark Witmer paced beside the young woman's still form, Maddie remaining at her side.

The girl moaned.

"I think she's waking up," Mark said into the cellphone.

"Try to keep her from moving," the dispatcher said.

"Yeah, OK." He knelt down next to the young woman, and once again laid a gentle hand on her shoulder. "Hey, hey, shh... Stay still, OK? The ambulance is on the way. Should be here any..."

The girl's eyes shot open. She screamed as though her skin was being peeled from her body. Her eyes fixated on an invisible torturer. Mark lost his balance and fell backwards.

"Sir? What's happening?" the Dispatcher asked in a voice calmer than the situation warranted.

"I don't know, she started screaming, she's... oh, hey stop moving, please stay still."

"Sir, please try to keep her still."

"I am, I... please..." Mark put the phone down so he could use both hands to attempt to keep her still. She stopped screaming and straining against his hands, allowing him to ease her back to the ground. "That's good, you need to lay still. The ambulance is coming." She looked at him for a moment, her eyes searching for something, and then clamping shut. Mark scrambled for the phone and spoke as calmly as he could despite his hammering heart.

"She's awake. Where's the ambulance?"

"They just turned onto Witch Way, should be there any minute. Can she tell you anything? Her name? Address?"

"Hang on," he said, then touched the girl's cheek. Her eyes flew open. "Hey, it's OK. You're going to be all right. Can you tell me your name?"

She opened her mouth, then shut it.

"Don't you know your name?"

She stared into the sky as though it would give her the answer.

Mark's eyes fixed on the red marks encircling her neck. "Take it easy. You're injured."

She spoke, too low for him to hear. He leaned closer. She spoke again, barely a whisper, but this time he heard.

"Sir?" the dispatcher's voice came from the phone.

"Her name. She said her name is Molly."

The ambulance wailed in the distance.

3 MISSING

Liz cracked the door open and peered into Merry's room, empty of everything but shadows. The late afternoon sun somehow managed to add to the gloom rather than lift it.

"Hello?" Liz called out, knowing there'd be no answer, but still allowing herself to wish for one. She stepped inside the too quiet room and strolled through the sitting area, running her hand over the smooth, lifeless surface of the crystal ball upon the writing desk. She leaned down until her eyes were even with it.

"Where are you, Merry?" she asked. Nothing.

"Overgrown marble," Liz muttered. It had been two days since Merry had jumped through her colors off Liz's balcony to return to Salem Village. She cringed at the memory of the hysteria that had followed. Sophie had been inconsolable. Liz had been terrified. There was no telling if the energy from the rocks had been enough to get Merry back to 1692. She could be anywhere. Or nowhere.

However, a more haunting thought threatened Liz's mind. Today was September 24th, the day of the last witch hangings on Gallows Hill. The day history claimed Meredith Chalmers and William Darling were hanged. Liz's stomach churned at the thought.

She wandered to the closet, her gaze immediately falling upon the colonial garb Merry had been wearing when they'd first met. To the untrained eye, it might look like a costume worn by the many colonial performers on Salem's streets and venues. Certainly, she'd believed so the first time she'd seen it. She'd thought Merry worked at the Witch Museum, much to Merry's dismay. A hint of a smile tweaked her lips at the memory. She ran her hand down the coarse fabric and sighed.

Something on the floor caught Liz's eye. She plucked a polaroid photograph from beneath William's sneaker and did a double take. "What the?"

"Liz? Honey, you in here?"

Liz stepped out of the closet to find her mother peeking into the room. She held the photograph out as her mother entered. "Mom, look what I found."

Christine took the photo and studied it for a moment. "You found this in here?"

"In the closet. That's Uncle Robert, isn't it?"

"It is."

"Who's the girl next to him? She looks pretty friendly, if you know what I mean."

Christine sat down on the edge of the bed, her face paling.

"Mom? You OK?"

"Look at the date, Lizzie. August 21, 1984—the day Uncle Robert died."

Liz sat down next to her mother and they studied the photo together. "Do you know who the woman is?"

"No idea."

"She certainly looks like she was into Uncle Robert," Liz said. Not only into him, thought Liz, but wildly in love from the ecstatic look on her face.

"She does, doesn't she."

"He never mentioned her?"

Christine shook her head. "Aunt Helena was dead just shy of a year by this date."

"You think Uncle Robert was cheating on her?" Liz asked.

"We don't even know who this woman is. She could've been a friend."

Liz met her mother's eyes, challenging her to believe her own words.

"All right, yes. They don't look like they were only friends. But, I don't think he cheated on Helena. They must have met after she died." Christine flipped the photo over to see if there was anything written. "It doesn't matter now though, does it?"

"I guess not," Liz said, looking back at the closet for a moment. "Is Jonathan still here?"

"He hasn't left her side."

Liz pushed up from the bed and sighed. "I'll go check on him." Leaving her mother to mull over the mystery woman, Liz walked down the hall, past the library and staircase to Sidney's room, where she found Jonathan sitting in the chair beside Sidney's bed, holding her limp hand.

"Hey," she said as she shut the door.

"Hey," Jonathan replied.

Liz deposited a kiss on his cheek. She couldn't be mad at him any longer. Not after what he'd been through in the witch's circle and especially not after the attention he'd given Sidney since then. "How are you feeling?"

"I'm fine," he said, then lifted his casted arm. "Want to sign my cast?"

"Cute. You should go home. Get some rest."

"I'm fine," he repeated.

Liz sat on the end of the bed. "There's nothing you can do, Jonathan."

His smile faded as he looked back to Sidney. "What's wrong with her, Liz? You said it's not a coma. Why won't she wake up?"

"Jonathan, please," Liz said. "I told you, I don't know. The doctors don't even know."

Jonathan frowned. "You're leaving something out again, like you did when I told you about the witches disappearing with William at the circle."

Liz walked to the dresser and picked up the TV remote.

"There's no record of a William Darling that fits his description, so I guess I made him up too, huh?"

Liz refused to look at Jonathan. She wanted to tell him the truth. All of it. With Merry gone a couple of days now, she was scared. She'd exhausted all the possible reasons why Merry and William were still missing. None of them were good. She could use a friend. She clicked on the television hanging on the wall across from Sidney's bed.

She flicked through a few channels before landing on a local news station that showcased a shiny, young reporter who looked wholly unimpressed as he broadcasted the news of the witch's disappearances.

"The police think I made the whole thing up," Jonathan said. "Apparently I'm devious enough to break my own arm and give myself a concussion. Not to mention make the earth move."

Tell him, Liz.

"Lizzie, please. I feel like I'm losing my mind. I can't talk to anyone about what I saw because they'll think I'm crazy. *I* think I'm crazy."

Liz sighed. She stared at Jonathan and Sidney's linked hands. "You're not crazy, Jonathan."

Jonathan dropped Sidney's hand and sat up straighter.

"But, you might think I am after what I tell you." With that, Liz launched into the story of Merry and William and how they had time traveled from the seventeenth century to escape the Salem witch trials, only to succumb to the witches in current-day Salem. To Jonathan's credit, he only asked a few questions about Merry's magical abilities and listened intently as Liz described how she'd gone back in time to find William.

"I guess I should be relieved I didn't hallucinate William's disappearance, but it feels even worse now."

Liz paced the room. "Tell me about it."

They both gazed upon Sidney, lying like a fallen angel upon her bed, her white-blonde hair fanned out on the pillow like a glowing halo.

"So, she's unable to wake up because she's stuck in that

place."

"Nurya," Liz said.

Jonathan's gaze locked onto Liz's. "She's not stuck though. She *likes* it there."

Liz's lips pressed together, her cheek twitched. "Yeah."

"Even if she wanted to, she can't come back. Not until the others are returned or the light is restored or some other fairytale."

"Jonathan."

Jonathan drummed his fingers poking out of the end of the cast against his leg. "I'm not making fun, Liz. I'm frustrated."

"We all are. When we went to Nurya, I was so sure we'd be able to finally bring Sidney back. But, now, well, it seems more impossible than ever."

Jonathan shook his head. "Not impossible. It was possible for all those other things to happen."

They shared silence for a moment, then Jonathan spoke. "It'll happen. We'll get Sidney back."

Liz walked over to the window seat and pushed aside a few rocks to sit down. She wanted to believe Sidney would come back.

"What's with the rocks?" Jonathan asked.

Liz picked up a milky white chunk of rock and tossed it into a box, sending it clanking against others. "It's my rock collection. I was sorting through it while keeping Sidney company earlier."

"Seriously, what's with the rocks?"

"I was trying to figure out what kind they are and why some affect Merry one way and some another way and some not at all."

"Any theories?"

Liz picked up a paperback book and held it out to Jonathan. "Maybe. According to this book, each type of rock has it's own properties in the magical realm."

"Did you say magical realm?" Jonathan asked, tugging at the book. Liz pulled it back from him.

"I got it from Sidney's store. Witch stuff."

Liz picked up a striated, gleaming brown stone. "This Tiger's Eye? It's supposed to bring self-confidence and good luck." She shuffled through a few nondescript rocks. "These likely have no effect on Merry, as far as enhancing or diminishing her powers." Liz picked up another rock, split open to reveal a brilliant blue crystal center. "But, this one, this geode, is like the stone Merry took when she jumped. It gave her colors strength. Like a shot of energy."

She tossed it to Jonathan for a closer look.

"I still don't understand how it works," he said, poking at the bumpy crystal interior.

"Me neither, but Merry's powers are rooted in the elements. For you and me these rocks are rocks. Nothing more. For Merry, they're part of what makes her tick. Whatever their power, it's multiplied exponentially for her."

Jonathan pointed at a black, shining chunk of rock. "What about that one?"

"This one used to be part of the bench outside. Merry touched it, and it burst into a thousand pieces, most much smaller than this. It took her powers away."

"Is that the only one that can do that? Take them away?"

Liz shook her head. "I don't know."

"It's her kryptonite."

Liz grimaced. "Superman? Really?"

"And that's what? Crazy?" Jonathan grinned.

"OK, I have to give you that. This is serious though. As out there as it seems."

"Oh, it's out there," Jonathan said. "I mean I never thought... hey, are you crying?"

Liz wiped at her eyes, her face reddening. She stood to leave, but Jonathan reached out and grabbed her hand as she walked past him. "It's going to be all right, Lizzie."

A fat tear fell off her cheek. Liz tugged at her hand, but Jonathan held fast.

"You're not alone."

"I just," she said, her words heavy with tears. "They've been gone two days, Jonathan. Today is... today is..."

"I know what today is," he said, saving her from having to say the words out loud.

"What if they're—" Liz never finished her sentence, her cell phone interrupting their melancholy with its upbeat ringtone. Liz dug her phone out of her pocket. Sophie's name flashed across the screen. Seconds later, she and Jonathan were headed to Salem.

4 RETURN

Sophie gazed upon her bruised and broken granddaughter, afraid to touch her. Tears blurred her vision for a moment before forging a path down her cheeks. A gentle hand touched her shoulder.

"She looks worse than she is. Her outlook is good," the nurse said.

Her outlook is good. *What did that mean exactly?* Would she be the same woman when she awoke, or would her psyche be as bruised as her body appeared? Sophie didn't voice her concerns, she only thanked the nurse, Karin, and asked for some privacy.

"Merry," she said, once Karin left the room. "What happened to you?" More tears spilled, plunking onto the coverlet that was wrapped tightly around Merry's still form. She remained silent, sleeping, her body hard at rest as it attempted to repair the damage that had been done to it.

Sophie's private moment with Merry didn't last long. The door whooshed open and before the hydraulics pulled it shut again, a commotion followed the incursion. She heard the nurse's stern speech about family visitors only and the familiar voice of Liz claiming to be Merry's sister.

"And, I suppose this is her brother?" Karin asked.

Sophie shook her head and wiped at her tears. Her heart lifted at the thought of Liz. She hadn't realized how much she needed her until she heard her joyful sound. She pulled the door open to find Liz and Jonathan, released from the hospital only yesterday, arguing with Karin.

"It's OK," Sophie said. "They can come in."

"Are you sure?" Karin asked.

"Yes, I'm sure," Sophie answered as Liz lunged into her open arms.

Karin smiled and left them.

"How is she?" Liz asked.

Sophie hesitated, then said all she could think to say. "Her outlook is good."

"Yeah?" Liz asked. "What the hell does that mean?"

Sophie laughed. Liz stepped around her, gasping at the sight of her friend and ran to her bedside, taking a limp hand in her own.

Jonathan's face paled. "My God, did they hang her?"

They all stared at the angry red mark circling her neck.

"The doctor said that... that there was an attempted hanging, but the rope was too loose. It caused a fair amount of bruising though. They took x-rays and did an MRI when she was brought in. There's no other damage. It looks a lot worse than it is," Sophie said. *Damn, I sound like that silly nurse. But what else is there to say?*

"Sophie," Liz said. "It happened, didn't it? She and William were hanged."

Sophie's eyes darted toward Jonathan.

"It's OK, I told him everything," Liz said. Then upon seeing the alarmed look on Sophie's face, added, "I had to."

"Do you believe it? The time travel?" Sophie asked Jonathan.

Jonathan tilted his head, eyebrows raised. "After what I saw? Yeah, I guess I do. Obviously, a lot more is possible in this world than I ever thought."

"Than any of us thought," Liz said.

"I think back on it, and William, he never seemed to... I don't know... belong. He spoke like he was from another time. He didn't know common information, and reacted to some objects as though seeing them for the first time. I never thought the reason would be because he *was* from another time." He studied Merry's resting form. "Now, Merry... she had me fooled."

Liz rolled her eyes. "That's because you're a guy."

Sophie laughed, grateful for the respite from the despair that threatened to swallow her up. "I'm so glad you two came. This is all so..."

Liz rubbed Sophie's shoulder as she shuddered against a fresh wave of tears.

Jonathan clapped his hands together. "So, Merry's here, but..."

Liz sat down hard on the chair beside the bed. "Oh God, William has to be alive. What if they hanged him?"

Sophie watched her granddaughter's friends torment over the what-if's and cleared her throat. "He's not dead."

"How do you know?" Liz asked, then her eyes widened. "You had a vision!"

Sophie shrugged. "I had it before any of this happened, even before William disappeared, but I wasn't sure what it meant."

"Sophie, what did you see?"

"William was hurt. Badly. And Merry couldn't fix him." The anguish on Liz's face pained Sophie. "He made her leave him behind."

"She wouldn't do that. She'd never leave him," Liz said.

"Even I know that," Jonathan said.

"No, she wouldn't," Sophie said. "Unless she had no choice."

Merry heard people talking. Their words made little sense. Perhaps her own internal noise prevented her from comprehending. The pain riddling her body had its own voice, and it screamed inside her. Her sluggish mind paid no attention to her will, and after a few moments of trying to open her eyes, she gave up.

She focused on the voices outside her body. Hanged. *Hanged.* The word repeated, lingered. A phantom rope ringed her neck as though it were still there. *But why had someone tried to hang her?* She couldn't remember anything before that moment and the memories that came after were filled with darkness and pain. *What had happened to her?*

Again, she tried to push herself to consciousness. The voices outside became louder than the pain inside. Light danced beyond her lids, colors behind them. Strength zoomed through her numb limbs and woolly mind. She opened her eyes.

Someone screamed in surprise.

Merry attempted to turn toward the sound, but the unyielding collar around her neck, along with the pain at the attempt to move, prevented cooperation.

"Don't move, honey."

An older woman with concerned eyes stepped into her field of vision, looking down on her with relief. She exuded a motherly air, and it made Merry feel instantly safe. Another face popped into view, this one belonging to a woman around her age.

"How do you feel?" the woman asked.

Her voice came out in a whisper. "Hurts."

"Oh honey, they have your pain meds on a timer, but I can check with the nurse to see if they can up the dosage," the older woman said, reaching across her to press a button above the bed.

"Please," she said, a tear slipping from the corner of one eye and tickling its way down the side of her face. The young woman reached out and wiped it away.

"I'm so glad you're back, Merry."

Merry? Was the girl calling her Merry? Her name was Molly. *Wasn't it?*

"Me too," came a deep voice, and Merry looked toward the end of the bed to find a young man in the room as well. She glanced at each one of the people standing in the room. They seemed genuinely concerned for her. She had no idea who any of them were.

"Who are you?" she asked. Before anyone could do anything more than register shock at her question, a nasally voice came out of the wall behind her asking what they needed.

"Stronger pain meds," Sophie answered.

"Is she awake?"

"Yes, and she says she's in pain." The voice in the wall said someone would be right down.

The older woman then looked down at her with a soft smile. "I'm your grandmother, Sophie. These are your friends, Liz and Jonathan."

Alarm announced itself on Liz's face. "What's going on, Sophie?"

Sophie sighed. "She doesn't remember anything. She only remembers her name is Molly."

Liz's mouth dropped open, her eyes bulged. She looked at Merry as though begging her to remember. "You really don't remember anything? William? Do you remember him?"

Merry didn't remember anyone called William, but for some reason that fact made her nervous and afraid.

Jonathan must have noticed something in her face because he asked, "Are you sure you don't remember William?"

"He was a big part of your life for many years," Sophie said.

They patiently awaited her answer as she tried sorting through her muddled brain for something. She finally gave up and asked, "Why can't I remember?"

The girl called Liz looked like she might cry at any moment.

"Let's try this a different way. What *do* you remember?" Sophie asked.

Merry rummaged through her head for an answer, coming up with little. But one unwanted image appeared in her mind. "There were hands. They were pulling me down." She shuddered at the memory.

"Who, honey?"

"I don't know. It was too dark to see. There..." Merry

stopped. Someone had been with her in the darkness. Sophie encouraged her to continue. "I think there was someone in the dark with me."

"Was it William?" Liz asked. "Was he there with you?"

Merry's heart began an erratic dance. "I don't know. It's only a dream."

Sophie spoke slow and measured. "In the dream, do you know what happened to the other person?"

For a single moment the image of hundreds of rotted corpses filled her mind.

"Merry," Liz said, then corrected herself. "Molly, are you OK?"

"They got him," she said, panic rising inside her. "The man who was in there with me, they took him."

"Uh, guys, maybe we should hold off on the questions for now," Jonathan said, nodding toward the monitor that drew spastic green lines across the screen.

The nurse entered then, bearing medication and a frown at the activity on the heart monitor. She allowed them to say their goodbyes before making them leave. Merry watched her visitors go, wishing she could remember who they were.

Over the next couple of days, Merry's body healed, the pain dissipating with each passing moment. Every night she dreamed of colors. Each morning, she grew stronger. And every day her unknown visitors came.

Sophie claimed she was her grandmother, Liz her best friend and Jonathan another friend. Though she couldn't remember them, they brought her comfort and, eventually, a sense of familiarity. The doctor said she'd suffered trauma, which could sometimes cause one to suppress memories of the event. In her case, she'd suppressed the last fifteen years. Before then, she'd been too young to remember much anyway.

Blood tests were done, confirming she was indeed Sophie's granddaughter, the girl who'd disappeared with her mother over fifteen years ago. When snippets of memory came, they contradicted her surroundings. She remembered cooking in a kettle over a fire in a hearth that was nearly as tall as she. She remembered horses and a gray-haired woman dressed in clothing from a time period so long ago there was no way she could call it a memory. Yet it felt like one. Then recollections of swimming in a pool and riding in a car jumped into her head, clashing with the memories of a time long ago, but neither felt wrong.

Merry turned her head as much as the stiff neck collar allowed, until her gaze found the window. The day was sunny, the blue sky cloudless. Heat shimmered on the metal window frame. *Out there.* Her life was out there, somewhere.

As much as she wanted to leave the confines of her hospital room, the thought of what lay outside these sterile walls intimidated her. She nearly welcomed their cold comfort when imagining the vastness of what lay before her: a life to live with no consideration of the past. All the while she felt as though something urgently needed her attention, that every minute she spent trying to relearn her own life meant someone else's would suffer.

She couldn't put reasoning to this notion, but it persisted just the same. Her anxiety made her edgy, jumpy. Her doctor prescribed a sedative, but she was afraid to take it after the first dose caused her dreams to take a dark turn. Bodiless hands reaching for her, pulling her into the dirt and decay from which they came. Someone followed her, causing her to pause. She always woke before she could see who haunted her dreams.

Merry pushed the dreams from her thoughts and focused on what she did know. She was Molly Rose Cooke, daughter of Summer Cooke and Devon Raynes, granddaughter of Sophie Cooke. Yet knowing names was of little help. Her story read like a tombstone, telling nothing of her life lived. She knew somewhere, a hair's breadth beyond her grasp, lay the truth of who she was.

5 THE TALL MAN'S GIFT

"Hey, I brought you something."

A smile lit Merry's face. Liz was her first visitor today. In all fairness, Sophie had spent the night in a cot next to her bed and had left only moments earlier to go home and shower.

"You look better. When do you get the collar off?"

Merry touched the padded collar that kept her neck still. "Probably tomorrow. There are no fractures, but they don't want me moving too much yet."

"Looks annoying."

Merry emitted a small laugh. "It is." Despite not remembering Liz, it felt good to have her near. Liz sat down in the chair next to her bed, a big smile on her face.

"So, what did you bring?" Merry asked.

Liz opened a box in her lap and plucked out two rocks. "These."

"You brought me rocks?"

"Well, when you say it like that, it sounds like a stupid thing to do."

"I didn't mean... er... thanks?"

Liz laughed. "OK, maybe it is stupid, but humor me. Hold out your hand. I want to try something."

Merry turned her hands palms up and watched as Liz gently placed a rock in each one. She looked expectantly at Merry who returned her look with one of confusion.

"Is something supposed to be happening?"

"Is it? Do you feel something?"

"I don't feel anything."

"Wait," Liz said, exchanging the rocks in her hands with two others from the box. "What about these? Anything?"

"No."

When Liz tried to put a third set of rocks in her hands, Merry dumped them on the bed. "Please stop putting rocks in my hands."

Frowning, Liz put the rocks back in the box. "I'm sorry. You think I'm crazy and maybe I am, but you have to trust me. This worked before."

"Before? Have I been hanged more than once?"

"No, no, I didn't mean that. You were... under the weather, and these rocks, well, not these because I don't have those anymore, but rocks like these helped make you feel better."

"How could a rock make me feel better?"

"I have no idea. It has something to do with how your body reacts to them. Can I try one more? Please?"

Merry sighed. *What difference could it make?* "Sure."

Liz pulled out a particularly glossy rock, this one smooth with what appeared to be a dark cross stained upon its caramel face.

"That's a pretty one."

"It's called a cross stone. I got it from Sidney's shop."

Merry had no clue who Sidney was or why she would have a shop filled with rocks, but she didn't voice her confusion. Liz dropped the stone in Merry's hand, and Merry gasped as the smooth stone touched her skin. Almost instantly, a wave of energy emanated from her palm, up her arm, and into her chest. It coursed like a warm river through her veins, muscles and bones, touching every inch of her body right down to her pinky toes. She shuddered and let the stone fall onto the bed.

"What was that?" she asked, the monitor picking up her

accelerated heart rate.

"Did it do something?"

"I think so. It felt... I feel stronger."

Liz smiled. "Good. Do you remember anything more?"

She wished she could say yes, but she knew as much now as she did two minutes ago. "Sorry, Liz."

To her credit, Liz's smile stayed intact, though Merry knew she was disappointed. Liz picked up the stone and placed it on the bed tray. "I'll leave this one here. Who knows? Maybe it will help with your healing."

"Liz? We were friends, right?"

"I'd like to think we are still friends."

"Of course. I simply meant that, even though I can't remember that we were friends, you could tell me what happened to me."

"But, I don't know. I wasn't..."

"I don't mean the hanging," Merry said. "I mean before that."

Liz's mouth clamped shut into a thoughtful frown. "Oh."

"You don't even have to go that far back. I just want to know why, how, I got into this situation."

"It's not that I don't want to tell you, Merry. I'm trying to be good here. Sophie thinks it's best to give you a little time, see if your memories come back on their own."

Merry opened her mouth to argue that it wasn't Sophie's choice to make; it wasn't her grandmother's decision as to when someone should tell her about her own past. But a huge yawn took her words, and she was suddenly overcome with a drowsiness that forbade coherent thought. She was used to feeling tired these days, but this was something wholly different. Her limbs grew incredibly heavy, weighing her down, as though gravity had increased ten-fold.

"Merry?"

Liz's voice reached her as though it traveled across a great distance. For the barest of moments, her worried face was replaced with another's. A woman of sharp, fierce features and long, straight blonde hair filled Merry's vision. Hers was a cruel beauty, twisted by purpose. A purpose that appeared solely focused on Merry.

"What do ye want?" Merry asked. But, the voice was deep, hoarse, and not her own. It came from a man beside her. The man was familiar to Merry, yet the broken form he presented was utterly foreign. Though it was dark, she plainly saw the misery in his eyes. Her mind reeled as she realized the man lay covered in his own blood. A scream built up inside her, making her lighter, lifting her limbs.

Though she wanted nothing more than this nightmare to end, she also wanted to stay to help this poor soul. For she knew the woman before him would do no such thing. Her fears were confirmed when the woman reached out to the man and lay her hand upon his chest, spreading a burning poison until Merry experienced his torment inside her own skin.

Her screams awoke her from the trance long enough to notice the alarm on Liz's face before she succumbed to the absolute exhaustion of the tortured man in her vision.

6 PASSAGE

Liz had fallen asleep nestled beside Sidney after her hospital visit with Merry, or Molly as she now wanted to be called. She didn't think she'd get used to that. Hopefully Merry would get her memories soon and be Merry again once and for all. Liz had divulged these thoughts to her unconscious cousin, told her how Merry had suffered some sort of seizure and how she'd screamed as though the pain was tearing her apart before she'd finally passed out. With some guilt, she admitted her attempt to stir Merry's colors with the stones, wondering out loud if that may have caused the seizure. Sidney didn't pass judgment.

Someone had left a light on in the hallway, and it was sneaking beneath Liz's eyelids. The clock on the night table said it was 1:27a.m. She should go back to her room anyway— maybe her mother had left the light on so she'd find her way back to her own bed. Liz placed a kiss on Sidney's cheek and gently pushed some hair from her face, before leaving the bed.

"Night, Sid," she said to the silent room.

Part way down the darkened hallway, she paused. The reason she'd come out here in the first place was because she'd thought the lights were on. Yet, here she stood in the dark, nothing to be seen or heard but the night around her.

Something wasn't right. It was too still. As though she'd been lured out here and now someone waited for her. She started backing toward Sidney's room, ready to run in and lock the door behind her when a soft glow illuminated the doorway of her parent's room.

Fear turned to hope.

Liz took a tentative step toward the light. It stayed strong. She continued with soft treads down the hallway, now curious why she was the beneficiary of an Illuminator's guidance. When she stood before the bedroom door, the glow pulsated, then receded, inviting her in.

Liz leaned her ear against the door. Her father's not-so-subtle snores broke the quiet of night. Liz turned the door handle and eased the door open as silently as possible. The light picked up its glow near her mother's purse and then dove inside it. She crept past her sleeping parents and with fingers for eyes, rummaged inside the purse, past a wallet, eyeglasses, a tissue pack, and then her fingers landed on something soft and velvety. Liz's eyes widened as she realized what her hand had landed on. She pulled the pouch from the purse and crept out of the room, not stopping until she'd reached her own.

Flicking on the light, Liz sat on her bed and dumped the contents of the red, velvet sack. It held one item. An insignificant game piece to most, but to her, this Monopoly token, the Iron, was a passkey to another world. Well, not in her hands, specifically. In her hands, the most she could hope for was to pass go and collect $200. But in Sidney's hands, the small token brought Nurya to life. Liz shuttered, she didn't care if she never stepped foot in the so-called land of light again.

Liz hurried back to Sidney's room. The room was dark, but Sidney's hands glowed. Liz didn't need any further instruction to know what she needed to do. Sidney was trapped in Nurya, no longer able to go between worlds. There wasn't enough light to support her. But with this—this usually insignificant piece of metal—well, maybe it was the strength she needed.

Reaching down, Liz took one of Sidney's hands and placed the iron token in her upturned palm as she'd seen her mother do at the hospital. She curled Sidney's fingers around the piece, then stepped back. The glow became so bright that Liz had to turn her head away from the sudden glare.

When the light dimmed, she turned on the lamp beside Sidney's bed and, curious, uncurled her cousin's fingers to find the token had disappeared.

"Hold out your hand."
"Luke."
Luke sighed. "Do it."
Sidney extended her hand, palm up, and just before opening it, realized something was *in* it.

Luke grinned as she opened her hand. "Just what the doctor ordered."

Sidney peered at the object sitting atop her palm and smiled. It was her father's token, the Monopoly game piece that had become his key to other dimensions, Nurya being one of them. The fact that her body laid in a suspended state at Iron House, while her essence remained in Nurya had weakened her in both realms. She could barely lift her head, let alone rescue William. In her current state, The Tall Man would be the only one to benefit from what light she had left.

Not to mention, the luxury of time was not theirs. William was in danger not only of losing his life, but also of giving the power of his light over to an entity that desired only darkness. She couldn't let all the sacrifices that came before him go to waste. Now, perhaps there was a way.

Still smiling, she looked up at Luke. "For a kid, you're pretty smart."

"Technically, I'm 56 years old," Luke said, looking proud all the same.

"Yeah, well, you look great for your age. So how did you get it?"

"Led your cousin right to it. I think she figured it out once I brought her back to your room."

"What about..."

"Merry wasn't there."

"Oh," Sidney said. She stared at the iron, feeling stronger simply from the few seconds she'd been holding it. "She's not with him either."

"Her colors are weak. If she were near, I would've known. She's definitely not at Iron House."

"I've made such a mess. If Merry had her colors, we'd..." Sidney didn't finish her sentence. She needed to stay positive, to believe what they were about to do would work. Luke, however, had no problem voicing her fears.

"We'd have a better chance," he said.

She looked at him. He'd been sixteen when he'd died, and even though he'd since existed in Nurya for forty years, at that moment he looked more like a scared child than the Illuminator he was.

"You don't have to come," Sidney said.

Luke snorted, the scared child disappearing beneath his arrogance. "Right. You'd last about a minute out there against the dark. Even with that token."

He was right, of course. Tethered to both her human form and this pseudo iridescence, she didn't have full strength in either existence. And, because many Illuminators had either been extinguished or taken by the Tall Man during their fight to save William, the light and power of Nurya had been severely diminished, leaving Sidney unable to choose one form over the other. It was either this torn survival or none.

"So, here's the plan," Luke said.

"Since when are you in charge?"

"Since I'm the only one who's been to the Tall Man's underworld."

They stared at one another for a moment, then Sidney said, "All right, Luke. What's our plan?"

7 BOUND

Sweat covered William's body despite the chill that permeated his cave-like prison. He flattened his body against the cool stone in an attempt to diminish the heat that consumed him, moving down the wall every few seconds in search of a cooler patch of rock. William pressed his chest as close as he could to the uneven surface, but the heat only expanded that much quicker, causing the rock to burn instead of cool.

His breath came in harsh spurts as though his body had forgotten the most basic of life-preserving functions. He forced himself to endure the pain and heat in silence, not wanting to give the Tall Man and his sick entourage any more satisfaction than they'd already taken from his plight. Truthfully, he wasn't sure if his throat could sustain one more scream.

With shaking fingers, William undid the remaining buttons on his shirt. He pulled the fabric aside and looked down, sucking in his breath at what he saw. What once was skin and muscle was now something foreign and corrupt.

The mark, when originally branded upon him by the Tall Man, had been known only to him at first—an internal injury invisible to the human eye. As it twisted and churned inside him, evidence of its existence pushed outward, bubbling his skin into raised black, vine-like scars. When Merry had caught a glimpse days or weeks earlier—he'd lost track of time—it had been a fiery pool of bubbling skin. Now the initial area had blackened and coagulated into a rough, dark scab which covered the entire left side of his chest. That wasn't the worst of it.

Rivulets of bubbling skin erupted and snaked from the blackened area, up his shoulder, across and down his torso. Some had already finished their reach and scabbed over as had the original site; others continued to spread like slow-rolling waves of flame.

Bile rose in his throat. The heat was too much—a pain like a thousand branding irons pressing into his flesh. William slid down the wall to a crouched position. Involuntary tears streamed down his face.

Focus, he told himself. *Focus on something good, something better.* For a moment, it worked. Images of Merry flooded his mind until he pushed them away, afraid to think of her lest the Tall Man steal his thoughts and use them against him. Or worse, against her.

The pain returned ten-fold. Hands clawed at his legs, and he almost welcomed their cool touch. A river of flame burst through his skin and fried his flesh, filling the air with the smell of his own burning body. William screamed.

"What's wrong?"

Merry clutched her chest. Her breath caught in her throat.

Karin came to her side, put a hand on her shoulder and leaned down to look into her face. "What is it, Molly?"

Her heart felt like it was on fire, no... like it was boiling. Heat flamed across her skin, consuming her. An image came to mind, something she'd dreamed of before—burnt and bubbling skin. A face appeared, and she cried out. This wasn't her pain.

Karin attempted to peel Merry's hand away from her chest, but Merry pushed her away. Agony bent her in half.

"Please," she whispered, tears streaming down her face. There was more than the physical pain. There was the impossible knowledge that the pain wasn't coming from within her, not from any wound she suffered. This pain was *shared*. Someone else's suffering had somehow become hers as well.

A needle pricked her skin. Karin attempted to push her back on the bed. Merry fought at first, but her limbs grew heavy and useless. Her hand slipped off Karin's arm and landed with a thud against the mattress. Pain ebbed into discomfort. Her breathing slowed, eyelids slipped shut. A rainbow bloomed against them, and Merry fell.

Down, down, colors swirling around her, delivering her to both ink-black darkness and blinding white light. Hands landed on her: at first cold and wrong, then warm and safe. The darkness faded, the light settled, and a familiar face appeared before hers. Merry studied the flawless features of the woman before her, the curl of her long, black hair, the way light emanated from her skin. She *knew* this woman. Yet, she couldn't remember her.

"Merry, you cannot stay."

She was so surprised the woman knew her that she didn't even correct her that her name was Molly, not Merry.

"You must leave," another spoke up. She looked at the golden, glowing figures in front of her, all the while sensing something sinister at her back.

Merry's skin tingled. She turned to look behind her despite the fear pulsing through her veins. As in a dream, the pull was too strong, the choice removed. Merry spun to find her nightmare come to life. Hands, grotesque and familiar, reached for her from murky shadows. Merry scuttled backwards into the light. Her breathing came hard and fast.

"What's happening?" she asked.

The golden woman laid a warm hand on her arm. "You've traveled back to the last place your colors took you."

Merry shook her head. "It's only a dream." She repeated the words over and over again beneath her breath, all the while taking in the hard-packed earth beneath her, above her, around her. Panic rose. *I'm buried alive*, she thought.

Someone moaned. It came from above. Merry looked up at the dirt ceiling. "What was that?"

"Listen to me," said the glowing woman who knew who she used to be. Then she clasped Merry's hands and glowed bright, then brighter until her skin looked like light itself. Merry shut her eyes against the glare. Words whispered in her mind. *Bring the light.* All the while, she was acutely aware of the moaning, the suffering, coming from above.

When the woman's light faded, when the sounds of slithering bodies moved closer, when wisps of blue and red and more colors surrounded her, Merry rose. She braced herself against the impact as she neared the dirt-ceiling, but it never came. One moment she was beneath the earth then she was atop it in a dark cave. The moaning stopped, replaced with harsh breaths emanating from a corner of the cave. She sighted a man, broken and suffering. His breathing halted altogether as he took in her presence.

She stared into his eyes, finding herself drawn to him. The man made a slight movement toward her, and her gaze fell to the blackened skin on his chest. Her fingers trailed down her own chest, mimicking the path of the fiery rivulets of bubbling flesh streaming from the man's wound. She recalled the burning pain she'd so recently suffered. Her gaze shot back to the blue eyes watching her. She'd found the owner of the pain.

She wanted his suffering to end. At the wish to rid him of his pain, ribbons of yellow slipped away from her outstretched arm and covered the man. His gaze never left her as the color seeped into his chest. His breathing evened out; the fire smothered itself, the black mark faded. He opened his mouth to speak, but all she heard were his grief-riddled shouts as the colors grew bold, insistent, and bore her away.

Her name died on his lips as the last wisps of color faded to black.

Several moments passed before he realized he was standing in the place Merry had stood seconds earlier. His pain was gone, his health returned. The black, festering mark that had burned itself into his skin left no trace of ever having been. She'd healed him. She'd sent her colors into him and eradicated the onslaught of the mark within.

William peered into the dark beyond where Merry had appeared, where, when not succumbing to the mark, he'd spent much of his time looking for an escape. He turned to look over his shoulder into the darkness behind him. He and Merry had landed in that part of the cave. He'd stayed away from it since. It was infested with corpses. Corpses that tried to bring him down into the earth with them.

Yet, he wondered. Could escape be found amongst the dead? Renewed energy and hope coursed through him, and he found himself turning around, walking into the dark home of the dead. William stopped when several hands pushed through the ground, sending dirt and rock tumbling as they reached for him. As close as they were, they didn't touch him and William continued walking. Had Merry's colors given him immunity from their touch? More hands emerged, keeping a distance and forming a guided path of sorts.

As he proceeded further into the darkness, his ability to see diminished without the mark. William dragged a hand along the rough stone wall to his right until it dropped onto a ledge. He explored along the landing and found it ended after about a foot. His hand hit another ledge. Then another. He'd found a staircase—a way out.

Continuing to use his hand as a guide, he made his way to the bottom step. The staircase ascended into a dim gloom. William climbed the rough-hewn steps with careful purpose, stopping on each to listen for anyone, or anything, that might be coming down them. About ten steps up, the stairs turned. William paused at the sight of a thin beam of light at the top. That strip of light meant freedom. His heart pounded at the daring thought that escape might be within his reach.

He forced himself not to run to it, employing his methodical approach until he stood before a rather unremarkable wooden door. He'd expected something much more substantial, impenetrable. William reached out with both hands and pushed against the door, surprised when his efforts received no resistance and the door swung outward.

And there his journey ended as he came face-to-face with the Tall Man in all his glorious anger.

Before his brain could tell him what a fool idea it was, William grabbed hold of the Tall Man and, knowing he had no chance of getting past him, spun him off the threshold, sending them both tumbling down the stairs and back into the dark abyss. They landed in two heaps.

William rolled to his side, groaning at the pain the movement caused, his breath hitching against what were surely broken ribs. As he lifted his head, a warm liquid trickled down his face, the copper tang of blood slipping past his lips. He pressed a hand against his skull to stem the bloody wound. The Tall Man lay prone mere inches away from him. In the moment between thought and action, the earth erupted, and William was surrounded by an army of the dead. Immediately, many hands pinned him to the ground, each clamoring for a piece of him. Slippery, decaying, and yet strong, they immobilized his legs, arms, and head.

The Tall Man rose with a creak of bones, and the report of one or two broken pieces snapping back together. He approached, knees crackling as he knelt behind William. His furious face stared down at him, a thick, black ring encircling the blood red irises, making them more disconcerting than ever. William refused the instinct to shut his own eyes against them, instead staring back with a gaze wholly as fierce. He struggled in futility against the hands that held him. The sounds of his strained breathing filled the dank space.

When the Tall Man spoke, his words inspired a spark of hope. "How did she get in?"

He didn't know. The Tall Man, the Devil, didn't know how a girl had slipped into his realm. How she'd soothed the mark inside of William.

"More importantly," William replied, "how did she get out?"

The Tall Man's eyes narrowed. William's smirk faded as his tormentor's lips lifted into a sardonic smile. A shadow grew as the Tall Man's long fingers drifted into view. William tracked his hand as it descended toward his chest. A fear-filled spasm gripped his heart. Any bravado he'd recently claimed left him as the Tall Man's hand settled against his chest and brought the subdued mark back to fiery life.

William gulped quick, shallow breaths in an effort to stem the screams yearning to erupt from his throat. He clenched his teeth and squeezed his eyes shut, forcing hot tears to stream from them. Robbed of physical escape, he scrabbled to keep hold of his mind. Heat flooded his veins, a thousand knives pricked his skin. He wouldn't forget, he promised himself. He wouldn't allow his true self to disappear, to be devoured by the abomination being forced upon him. He'd get his life back, he'd fight, he'd... a deep calm tugged at the edges of his mind, muddling his thoughts. He clung to the bits and scraps he could, disappearing with them as the Tall Man's mark consumed him.

8 DISAPPEARED

"That can't be good." Liz and Sophie broke into a run, their coffees sloshing against the cup lids, at the sight of nurses shouting in front of Merry's room. *Shouting nurses were never a good sign.*

Karin, the day nurse who usually cared for Merry, stood near the door, sending nervous glances into the room. Liz's stomach flip-flopped. She pushed past the nurse and into the room, afraid of what she might find. But there was only Merry, peacefully sleeping, the green lines and beeps of the monitor dutifully announcing life.

She breathed a sigh of relief and turned her attention back to Karin and the other nurses. Karin looked like she needed a hospital bed as much as Merry. The other two nurses were arguing.

"What happened?" Liz asked.

Karin spoke as though she couldn't quite comprehend how her words made it past her lips. "She disappeared."

"Don't say that," said the nurse closest to her. She was an older woman with steel gray hair. She moved closer to Karin, reaching out and placing a hand on her shoulder while addressing Sophie and Liz. "We were talking about how

Karin's been pulling some late-night shifts. It's not for everyone."

"Wait," Liz said, "I want to know what happened."

"Nothing happened. You can see Molly is fine."

"So you always stand outside a patient's door and shout?" Sophie asked.

Both nurses, whose nametags read Jackie and Lisa, exchanged glances. Karin shrugged Jackie's hand from her shoulder.

"I came into the room. Molly appeared to be in a great deal of pain. She was covering her chest, but the monitors were fine. It wasn't her heart. So I gave her a sedative."

"Karin..." Jackie started.

Sophie glared at the gray-headed woman. "Let her talk,"

"As soon as she went unconscious, she..." Karin hesitated briefly before continuing. "She disappeared."

Both Lisa and Jackie raised their eyebrows as if Karin's words proved their theory that she was over-worked. Liz knew better.

"Please go on," Sophie said. "What do you mean, she disappeared?"

"I turned my back no more than a few seconds to check the monitor and when I looked back, she was gone. Vanished."

"She probably took a walk down the hall," Lisa said.

"Or you imagined the whole thing," Jackie added.

This is where we came in, thought Liz. "You're sure she couldn't have left the room?"

"Look at her! She's unconscious. Even if she'd been able to get out of bed, I would've noticed her disconnecting from the machine. I looked for her down the hallway. Her room was never out of my sight. When I checked again, she was in her bed as though nothing had happened."

"Nothing did happen," Jackie said under her breath.

Liz sensed Sophie's eyes on her, but she resisted the urge to return her stare.

After the nurses diligently checked that Merry, aside from her original injuries, was in good health, Sophie and Liz closed the door to her room and waited for her to wake up. At some point, Sophie went down to the cafeteria to replenish their coffees, and it was then that Merry's eyes popped open.

She stared unseeing at the ceiling until Liz asked her how she was, and then swung her panicked gaze in Liz's direction. With frantic movements, she inspected her chest, her stomach, and her arms.

"What's wrong, Molly?"

Merry looked at her a moment, then burst into tears. Liz immediately went to her, placing a protective arm around her shoulder.

"Are you hurt?" she asked.

Unable to speak, Merry simply shook her head.

"What is it then? Did you dream something?"

Merry pulled away, dropping her head back, wincing at the movement, her hand going to her neck. "It was more than a dream. But, it was so... it couldn't have been real. It was too awful."

Liz moved away and sat down in the chair beside her bed. "You can tell me about it. If you want to."

She studied her for a moment. "You're going to think I'm crazier than I already am."

"No, I won't. You're not crazy, either. You're suffering from a trauma. There's a difference."

"It doesn't feel different," she answered. After a drink of water, she talked. She spoke slowly at first, hesitating in her descriptions of the colors and the people made of light, shooting worried glances at Liz with each fanciful admission, as though afraid Liz would jab her with a needle to quiet her deranged ramblings.

At the end of her recounting, Liz breathed a sigh of relief.

Merry frowned. "What?"

Liz couldn't tell Merry she was relieved to find out both Adina and William were alive. Or, in Adina's case, existed.

It was good information. Information she could've shared with Merry, but not Molly. So, she simply shook her head and said, "Nothing." Then she patted Merry's leg. "I'm glad you're all right."

The effort of her journey - be it dream or real - along with the retelling of it and the lingering effects of the sedative, soon wore Merry out. Liz left the room to allow her some rest, but her thoughts superseded her weariness.

Liz hadn't contested anything she'd said, hadn't suggested it was only a dream, and, in fact, had looked relieved after hearing what she'd had to say.

But Merry had overheard the nurses. She knew Karin thought she'd disappeared from the room. She knew she'd done exactly that. She'd gone to another place, a place of great darkness and great light. A place where people made of light knew who she was. A place where she healed a man and bore his cries at her departure.

This information had not fazed Liz, reinforcing the suspicion that she was holding something back. Merry let her head sink into the flattened pillow and closed her eyes. A staircase filled her mind. A booted foot echoed upon the stone steps. Exhaustion tunneled her vision to a pinprick, a hand on a door, a shiver in her soul, before a crimson glow granted her sleep.

9 SINKING

Sophie hustled along the cobblestone walkway, barely noticing the early Halloween enthusiasts who invaded Salem. It was easy to do, having endured the migration of zombies, monsters, witches, and other fantastical creatures that made their way to Salem every October for as long as she could remember. The worry over her granddaughter surpassed the delight she normally experienced at the sight of the imaginative participants of Salem's Haunted Happenings. No, this year, she had her own happening to deal with. *Merry, Molly, Merry... ugh.*

Fifteen years ago, her daughter and granddaughter had disappeared into thin air. Over a month ago, her granddaughter had returned from time itself. She'd grown up in Salem Village hundreds of years earlier, where innocent people were hung under suspicion of witchcraft. She was the only witch who'd escaped her hanging.

Now she was back in the century she belonged to, at least where she *should* belong. Why, then, did it feel so wrong? Sophie rung her hands together as she allowed the thought to enter her head. Molly didn't belong here anymore. Somewhere along her incredible journey, Molly was lost. As crazy as it seemed, Sophie simply wanted *Merry* back.

"Excuse me."

Sophie stepped aside for a rather large pirate to pass, his enormous, feathered hat bobbing as he made his way toward Pickering Wharf. "Aye, aye," she muttered.

She hadn't wanted to go home after leaving the hospital, anxious for a reprieve from her reporter-infested neighborhood. For days now, a slew of news teams had jammed up the street in front of her house with their vans and equipment, waiting for Sophie to tell them something they hadn't already learned from the doctors or police. As if she'd like nothing more than to interact with them.

Sophie continued to scurry through the streets of Salem, casting glances behind her as only the paranoid do. She noticed a man in a gray hoodie, face hidden, certain she'd seen him on Derby Street, as well. When he ducked into a shop across from the Wax Museum, Sophie dismissed him as a tourist. With one more survey of the area, she approached the Witch Trials Memorial, her gaze captured by the threshold made of inlaid granite blocks etched with words of defiance and desperation. Before Merry, Sophie had regarded these proclamations with sadness and had pitied those who'd allowed their strong beliefs to incite such a blindness to truth and a denial of humanity. After Merry, despair swept through her heart at the sight of the memorial. *Oh Lord—Help Me*; the carved words at her feet bled into her own dialogue. She stepped over them and walked to the stones that memorialized Merry's and William's part in this tragedy.

Merry had come here, had seen the fate that awaited them, and had turned her despair into purpose. Sophie hoped to do the same. With one last glance to make sure no one was paying attention to her, she leaned forward and touched her fingers to William's name and hoped for a vision. Nothing. She ran her hand across the carved name and the date and still nothing happened. *Who was she kidding?* She received visions, sure, but never on command. They jumped in her head when *they* wanted to, or revealed themselves on the surface of crystal balls whenever she neared. She didn't have the power to turn them on or off at will. Sophie squeezed her eyes shut and held her hand to the stone in one last delusional effort. All she saw were flashes of light begging her to relieve the pressure on her eyeballs. She straightened and blinked her vision back to normal.

At first, Sophie didn't register the rumbling, clunking, and thumping sounds behind her. Then, it was all she heard. She peered into the graveyard on the other side of the memorial as the sounds of stone crashing against stone echoed in the twilight. Other passersby stopped to look, squinting into the shadowy burial ground to see headstones falling into one another. Sophie leaned against the rock wall for a better look, snatching her hands back as it quaked beneath her touch. An eerie groan escaped the earth as it cracked open and swallowed several gravestones. The fissure widened, and several more gravestones tumbled into the earth sending up a plume of dirt and dust.

As others scrambled to distance themselves from the widening gap, Sophie froze in place. Screams erupted around her, people ran, someone tugged on her arm, giving up when she didn't budge, transfixed as she was on the spectacle before her. The earth continued to heave and devour gravestones. It rumbled and tossed three-hundred-year-old graves from its belly, while sucking others into its unfathomable maw.

However, more fascinating was the dirt that fell *up*.

While the hole dragged the earth downward, a mass of dirt spiraled upward into a maelstrom that defied gravity. Sophie shielded her eyes from the spit of dust and debris. Between the twilight and mayhem, it was getting harder to see. She tried to convince herself that those were not decaying hands reaching beyond the spinning walls of cemetery soil; that the form of a grossly tall man hadn't manifested itself from within the impossible cyclone. A streak of red wove itself into the frenzied wall of dirt, coalescing into two shining orbs. Sophie's breath caught.

Merry stood at the window of her hospital room, hands

bone-white as they clenched the ledge. Outside her window lay an innocuous parking lot, but Merry's vision was consumed by a scene that went well beyond the limitations of her sight. Her skin prickled with fear. She sensed danger. Evil. With that sense, came a vision of the threat.

Hands of the dead protected an evil emerging from the same earth meant to shelter those who'd rightfully made their way back to dust. Her nostrils flared at the abomination. Her need to protect both the living and the dead sprang from her like a visible force. Merry screamed, and the window shattered outward. Her palms pulsed with their own heartbeat. She looked down to find a translucent stream of color, red, pouring from her hands. She didn't know much about herself, but right then she knew to hold her hands out and send the color into the coming night. To Salem.

The Tall Man, for Sophie was certain the apparition could be none other, solidified and stepped one foot outside the barrier that held him.

Sophie stumbled backward as the walls and stone benches rattled from the approaching destruction. Not again, she thought. Few hanged had been afforded a proper burial, these stone benches were all that dignified a life snuffed out under false accusations. It was a meager right that attempted to assuage an inconceivable wrong. The memorial was *important*.

"Stop!" she shouted before sanity could prevent her. For one horrible moment, the Tall Man's eerie red gaze locked onto hers.

From the corner of her eye, Sophie saw a movement. A red stripe streaked across the sky, arcing downward, it's target clear. Sophie held her breath as the red beam struck the vortex. She ducked beneath Merry's stone bench as the earth erupted and rained down on the graveyard and memorial. A tombstone embedded itself in the ground in front of her shelter. Sophie screamed as an animated corpse landed mere inches away, dragging itself toward her before digging and scurrying beneath the earth. More screaming, more stampeding. Then silence.

The ground stilled. The sky resumed its innocuous descent into night. Little by little, sound returned—someone sobbing nearby, a distant siren, her own hampered breathing.

When certain nothing else, not tombstones or dead people, would fall from the sky, Sophie crawled out of her hiding place. She joined several others already standing at the edge of the depression in the middle of the cemetery. The sirens drew closer.

"Sinkhole," a man said. Others murmured their agreement and expounded on their experience. Sophie walked away, tears blurring her vision. The Tall Man was once again coming to Salem.

Merry watched the trail of red blaze through the sky, until it disappeared from sight. She turned her back to the window, sliding down the wall until she sat on the floor, hugging her knees to her chest. Thinking over what she'd done didn't make it anymore comprehensible. She inspected the palms of her hands. They looked absolutely normal. A minute ago, color had somehow come out of these hands. Red had seeped from her skin and then shot into the night under her guidance. Her thoughts. She'd *thought* to send the color and off it went.

An orderly and a nurse ran into the room, fussing over her, looking for cuts. There were none. All the glass had blown outward. Merry responded to the nurse's inquiries into her well-being with absent nods and grunts. The nurse called for a wheelchair and shouted instructions to move her to another room. Merry gently ran her fingers over her newly-revealed neck, hissing at the pain caused by the light touch. Once again she wondered why a person would try to hang her.

Perhaps she was someone else's threat.

10 FLIGHT

The roar started loud and crescendoed into stentorian heights. An inferno shot up from the chasm that consumed the space between the Tall Man's abode and the rest of his domain. Corinne grasped the hip-height stone rail of the long, narrow bridge as it shook and swayed. She screamed and sank to her knees, covering her head with her arms as flames soared past her on both sides of the bridge. The stone beneath her grew warm, then hot as the firestorm raged.

Her father's thunderous voice overtook the crackle and hiss of the blaze. Corinne shuddered. Uncertainty and fear replaced pride.

"Daughter."

Corinne looked up, shamed by the cowering form she presented. The Tall Man towered over her, fire surging all around him, licking at his form like a desperate lover. He fixed his eyes on her, locking their gazes. She had no comparison for the scorching rage, the fathomless evil roiling off the entity before her.

The Tall Man growled. "Bring him to me."

The earth trembled beneath William. His eyes fluttered

open. Sleep only came as a fitful respite from his damned existence. It dissolved as the earth shifted and heaved beneath him. He leapt up, the sudden movement ricocheting pain throughout his abused body.

The floor buckled beneath him, and William tumbled into the hands of the dead. Dirt spilled into his mouth, his eyes, his nostrils. He pummeled at unseen bodies, their flesh splitting like overripe fruit. The earth pressed in on him as they bore him away. He lost all perception but for the cold, rotted touch of his captors and the rumbling of soil as it moved around him. And then, like a babe leaving its mother, he burst through the earth's crust with a cry and a heavy draw of breath.

One by one, his senses returned. First, the feel of the hard floor beneath him, then the sight of Corinne crouched beside him, followed by the sound of his fate.

The footsteps were familiar ones, a purposeful heaviness in their approach. Each step brought dread to his heart. Yet, despite his fear and anger and desire to kill the very being that made them, there lived something inside him that yearned for its maker.

The Tall Man chuckled at the sight of his prisoner; the mocking sound echoed in the cavernous room, stirring something hard and cold within. William had not expected his foray into the dwelling of the Tall Man to be anything but horrific, yet another torture to bear. And he was not disappointed.

"Open your eyes, William," the Tall Man said.

To his shame, William realized that, like a child, he'd curled himself into a ball and shut his eyes as though the act could make him unseen by the evil that sought him. He opened his eyes and sat up. He'd been dragged out of the dungeons into what appeared to be a large ballroom, blindingly bright after the darkness of his prison. Everything sparkled, encouraged by the light provided by the many chandeliers in the room. Yet, it did nothing to alleviate the oppressive night pressing against the windows as though it wanted to enter and devour all within.

His gaze landed on the Tall Man, and he willed himself to keep it there. The end had finally come, and he welcomed it. Gone would be the torture, the unknowing, and the pain of enduring a life without Merry. Another figure came through the door at the far side of the room. At first, he thought it was a hallucination—he'd had many over the past few days—but as she neared and gave him that wicked smile of hers, he knew. The darkness inside him knew too.

William gaped at Vanessa standing tall and strong before him, unlike the broken pile of bone and flesh she'd been when he'd last seen her.

"How are you alive?" he managed to ask. "You were dead."

A small, knowing smile lifted Vanessa's lips. "Some must die before they can truly live."

The Tall Man paced. "You see, William, I have many gifts to give."

William absently rubbed his chest where the dark mark resided.

"Do you know what I have granted you?" the Tall Man asked.

"I asked for nothing."

"I don't believe that. Do you, Vanessa?"

"William doesn't realize how lucky he is."

The Tall Man smiled. "Oh, but you do, my sweet." He reached out and slid a bony hand down her cheek and circled her neck. With a snap of his wrist and a sharp crack, Vanessa's neck tilted back at an unnatural angle. He let go of her and she crumpled to the floor.

The Tall Man walked across the room where a tall-backed throne, spiked with thorny branches, awaited him. A squirming bed of snakes encircled the throne, slithering apart to line a path as the Tall Man approached. As soon as he sat down, flames erupted, their fiery tongues engulfing the seat, climbing and licking at the thorns, feeding on, but not consuming, the Tall Man as he fixed his red-eyed stare on William.

William's heart raced. He leapt up and scanned the room, contemplating crashing through a window and running off into the night. But, then a movement out of the corner of his eye caught his attention. Vanessa was rising from the floor as though she'd woken from a nap. With a simple push on her neck, she looked as though nothing had happened, as though she'd not been dead for the last few minutes. She sauntered over to the Tall Man and placed her hand in his offered one.

Then she turned to William and said, "Are you sure there's nothing you want? Nothing you desire more than life itself?"

He knew what they wanted him to say, to admit. But, he would not drag what was precious into their sordid world.

The Tall Man rose from his fiery perch. The snakes circled the throne once again as he stepped away. Flames dripped from the Tall Man and died upon the marble floor. He stopped before William, his face mere inches away. "I know your desires, William."

The Tall Man held his hand up, palm hovering near, but not touching, William's chest. The mark connected them. William's chest jutted out to meet the Tall Man's clawed hand, and for a moment William entertained the fantasy that he'd tear the mark out of him and set him free. But, the thought faded as the mark first grew warm, and then bloomed into an unbearable heat. William's back arched over nothing but air as the Tall Man molded his dark gift into something new.

"No!" shouted William. He wanted only one outcome and he wanted the Tall Man to know it. "Kill me!"

"You don't want that," answered the Tall Man.

Oh, you don't know, thought William. Death would certainly be a better alternative than to go on living in this state of mayhem, torture and decay. The heat continued to build until his entire body was aflame. William screamed as he burned beneath the Devil's hands. Suspended in space, he twisted and turned trying to get away from the force of the Tall Man's largesse.

At some point, his conscious thought ignored the agony being perpetrated upon his body and fled to memories of what had been. Stolen kisses in the meadow, the feel of Merry's warm hand in his, the way she looked at him as though he was all she needed in the world. Her body meshed with his, the sound of her sleep-filled breathing, her laughter, and her smile, turned up at one corner when she delivered one of her teasing remarks. All these experiences had once been his, and though the darkness grew, intent on consuming him, he forged a place in his heart that would never forget her. He'd hoped for one day to live out his life with Merry; he would have to be content to die having loved her at all.

The mark that lived and thrived inside him festered and spread as the Tall Man worked his fearsome magic. As the mark grew, it overcame William's need to be rid of it. Flames licked his flesh, warmed his desires, and a new William was forged—a William who was both man and something else. The screams faded, the heat ebbed, as he floated to the ground, weightless. Inconsequential yet all-powerful.

The Tall Man reached down and scooped up a handful of the soot that was William. Then he blew, sending the dust of his existence flying. The windows opened and the remainder swirled and rose from the floor, joining its predecessor.

And with that, William soared into the night.

The Tall Man watched his newborn take flight—a proud moment. He looked at the discarded human on the stone floor, now nothing more than a shell. Thought and purpose had flown upon the wind. Corinne appeared excited, eager to discover what resulted from this act. Contrarily, Vanessa sat stoic in the chair, looking like death warmed over if he did say so himself. The Tall Man chuckled. Dying must be so exhausting.

He lifted a hand and said, "Take him." The floor bulged and receded as though it was a great breathing beast. Hands poked through the surface, a few at first, soon growing to hundreds of dead, bloated, gray fingers, reaching out to cover William's body. Then, they slowly sank back through the floor, taking William with them.

11 GRANDMOTHER'S HOUSE

She was running. She knew it was a dream, knew what she was running from could never truly harm her, yet, she ran.

And it felt so wrong.

A wild display of colors swarmed her. Taking her breath. Giving her life. But, the life they gave left her empty and alone.

Merry awoke gasping for air. She clawed at her neck, igniting a spark of pain. She sat up, forced herself to take slow, steady breaths until the choking sensation passed.

When at last she could breathe, another horror assailed her. Her first instinct was to close her eyes against the shifting shadows at the foot of her bed, but she stopped herself. Closing her eyes would be akin to running away, and she couldn't do that again. So, she watched the shadows waiver and coalesce into what appeared to be a man on fire. Another man stood tall over him molding the flames, wrapping them around the screaming victim hovering before him.

The tall man turned toward her then, a pair of fiery red eyes in the darkness. They searched for her, but never settled upon her for at that moment both he and the tortured man disappeared into the shadows and another figure emerged. Merry drew a sharp intake of air as she realized she was looking at her own face. But, she was someone else.

This version of her held the hand and heart of her lover. She laughed, teased, and clung to him in the midst of passion. She was loved in a way that defied measure.

For a moment, her lover stood before her, whole and beautiful. Then the flames overtook him, charred his flesh, and reduced him to ash.

Merry screamed.

A loud bang and a swear came from across the hall. Light filled the room, and Sophie stood in the doorway. "What is it? Are you hurt?"

Merry's breath came fast and erratic. Her heart pounded. She fought the urge to cry. "I... I had a dream. A nightmare."

"Do you want to talk about it?" Sophie asked.

She didn't want to talk about it. She didn't want to ever think of it again. Instead, Merry pushed aside the covers and walked to the window. She carefully peeled back the curtain and peered out.

"They're still out there," Merry said.

"I expect they'll be there for days," Sophie said. "Shouldn't be allowed. No respect for privacy." She peered around Merry. "Smaller crowd though. I guess we have the sinkhole to thank for that." Sophie stepped away then, squeezing and twisting her hands.

"Is everything all right?" Merry asked.

A tentative smile flickered upon her lips as Sophie placed gentle hands on Merry's shoulders and gingerly pulled her back. "C'mon. Let's get away from the window."

Merry let Sophie guide her back to bed. "Thank you for what you did before."

After being discharged from the hospital that morning, they'd arrived at Sophie's house to find news trucks lining the street, all vying to capture the homecoming of Molly Cooke. With uncanny precision, Sophie had stopped the car, allowing Merry to leap out and get inside before anyone knew what had happened. While Merry watched from behind a curtained window, Sophie handled the onslaught of cameras and the reporters' questions, all the while slowly working her way to the back door.

"You handled it well," Merry said.

Sophie sat at the end of the bed. "Well, I had some practice about fifteen years ago, didn't I?"

Merry hadn't thought of that. "Was it like this?"

"It was worse actually. I mean, the media circus was similar. But, fifteen years ago I lost you. I lost my daughter. And I had no idea if I'd ever see either of you again. It was a horrible time."

"And now?"

"And now, you're home."

Home. If she was home, why did she feel like she belonged somewhere else?

"Believe me, it's better finding someone, than losing someone."

"My mother..."

"Is at peace," Sophie said, before she could finish her thought.

"You know what happened to her?"

Sophie stared into her lap. "You'll remember soon enough."

"You won't tell me?"

Sophie pursed her lips. "Give it some time, honey."

Time felt slippery, as though it were leaving her behind. Merry needed her memories if she wanted to catch up to the present. They seemed far away in Sophie's home, unattainable. She wished she'd gone with Liz to Iron House. She'd wanted to the moment Liz had suggested it. That must count for something. Must *mean* something.

Merry reached across the covers and took Sophie's hand in her own. This woman, her grandmother, had been by her side every day since she'd been found, and despite feeling as though she were in the wrong place, Merry cared for Sophie.

"Were we close? Before?"

Sophie sighed. She suddenly looked much older. "I only had a little bit of time with you. A few weeks. But, yes, I would say we were close... are you all right?"

Merry rubbed her neck with gentle strokes. The throbbing had returned. The screaming probably hadn't helped.

Sophie rose, the bed springs rising with her, and grabbed the pill bottle from the dresser. "You need your medication."

"Sophie."

But, her grandmother brooked no argument. She dumped a small pill in Merry's hand and passed her the bottle of water from the night table.

"I don't need this," Merry said.

"You don't think you do. But if you let the pain get a foothold, it will take more than one pill to get rid of it."

Merry grimaced, but placed the pill on her tongue and washed it down with a swig of water.

As she placed the water bottle back on the table, her gaze landed on the crystals on the night table. They were of varying shapes—an oval, a pyramid, and several oblong stones, their ends tapered to points. She lifted the pyramid-shaped one; its weight felt comfortable in her hand. The faintest of rainbows could be seen in its corners if held up to the light in the right way. She smiled. When she wasn't dreaming of burning men, she dreamed of colors.

"They're pretty," she said.

Sophie's smile faltered for the briefest of moments, but Merry noticed and immediately felt like she'd said something wrong.

Whether the medicine or the effort of trying not to make Sophie worry, Merry suddenly went from tired to exhausted. Lethargy drew a thick cloak around her thoughts until they took on a dream-like quality. Her thoughts centered upon the man again, focused on his chest that bubbled, then burned as the darkness inside him spread its disease. The crystal slipped from her hand. Someone called her name. It was enough to pull her away from the images that haunted her.

Sophie eased Merry down against her pillow.

"Are you all right?" she asked with worried eyes. Always worried eyes.

"I'm tired," Merry said, not sure if the words had made it

past her tongue.

Sophie pulled the blanket to her shoulders, her eyes stalling on the purple bruise around Merry's neck.

"I didn't feel anything," Merry said, though her assurance couldn't stop Sophie's tears.

Comforting, spicy smells wafted up from the kitchen, awakening Merry to a ravenous mood. She pushed the covers aside and stood, stretching like a cat. Carefully, she rotated her neck, easing some of the stiffness out of it. All in all, she felt better than she had in days. Sleeping in a real bed had done wonders for her. Perhaps tomorrow she'd be able to make it through a day without an early afternoon nap.

A twinkle of light drew her eye to the sparkling crystals beside the bed.

Odd, she thought. She was certain the crystals had been filled with colors last night, but now they were clear, no hint of color.

She picked up a crystal as she padded toward the window. She held tightly to it as she peeked around the curtain. Something about her mother's crystals both calmed and rejuvenated her. A full army of news trucks remained out front, a conglomerate of cameramen and reporters on the sidewalk. She wondered what they would do if she came out right now. *What questions would they ask? What answers could she possibly give?*

She gazed about the room that had once been her mother's, her eyes falling upon the photo albums on the dresser. She picked up a small one and flicked through the pages, not recognizing anyone. Only a few of the pockets held a picture in the next album. One, she recognized as her mother. They looked so much alike. The others were of her mother and a man, presumably her father. She'd have to ask Sophie.

Before heading downstairs, Merry picked up the larger album. Maybe if she and Sophie looked through them together, it would help to bring her memory back. She found Sophie in the kitchen, dumping a pot full of noodles into a colander in the sink. Another pan on the stove held the delicious aroma that had lured Merry downstairs.

"What are you cooking?" Merry asked.

Sophie jumped and turned around.

"Sorry."

"Not your fault," Sophie said, placing the now empty pot back on an unlit burner on the stove. "I'm a little on edge. Sit down, I've made some goulash."

Merry sat, watching as Sophie scooped some noodles into a bowl, then added gravy and meat from the pan on the stove. She placed it before Merry. "Eat up. It warms the soul."

Merry scooped some of the warm food into her mouth. "I believe you."

Sophie smiled and watched her eat, then made a bowl for herself. "Well, I guess it beats hospital food, anyway."

"No, Sophie, this is truly delicious." After a few more mouthfuls, Merry asked, "What happened at the sinkhole?"

After chewing her food for a minute, Sophie finally answered, "I told you, the earth opened up and swallowed a bunch of graves."

Merry stared into her bowl and poked at a carrot. "You were scared."

"Well, yeah. It was scary."

The carrot dipped beneath the gravy, then bobbed back to the surface. Merry glanced at Sophie, then back down to her food.

"What is it?" Sophie asked.

Merry wanted to talk to someone about what had happened at the hospital. When the nursing staff had informed Sophie about the window blowing out and reassured her Merry was unharmed, she'd barely asked any questions. And, the amused, even proud, smile that had slipped across Sophie's face had not gone unnoticed by Merry. Still, she wasn't sure it was something she could share with her grandmother. She wasn't even sure what *it* was.

Sophie covered Merry's hand with her own. "Molly?"

Merry pursed her lips, opened her mouth, and then pursed

her lips again. This was foolish. *Why give voice to what was surely hallucination?* She couldn't have *thought* the window into bursting into a million pieces. Colors certainly couldn't have poured from her hands. But though she tried to convince herself differently, she was certain she hadn't imagined the colors. She was also certain she shouldn't tell anyone. But, perhaps Sophie could tell her something.

"I hoped that maybe you could tell me more about myself. About... well, about why someone would want to hang me."

Sophie cleared her throat, then looked up at her, a small, apologetic smile on her lips. "I'll tell you Merry. I promise I will. But, not now, OK? Too much is getting thrown at you. Let's slow it down, OK?"

"Sophie, I'm fine. A noose apparently couldn't kill me. I'm sure whatever it is you have to tell me won't either."

Sophie patted her hand, but said nothing. Merry pulled her hand away.

"At least tell me about my family. You won't even tell me what happened to my own mother. What about my father? Do you know what happened to him? Why isn't he here?"

A stern resolve hardened Sophie's kind face. Merry wished she could make her tell her what she wanted to know. Knowing there was nothing to gain by pressing Sophie further at the moment, she instead turned her attention to the backyard and the world beyond the kitchen's bay window.

12 DUST

Missing. He was missing a piece of himself. Whatever the Tall Man had done to him had somehow split him into two versions of himself. On the one hand, he was here, in body, suffering in the bowels of the Tall Man's domain. His mind muddled and confused. But, he was out there too. Free as the night. Able to go anywhere.

And so he did. He flew across lakes and streams, over castles and shacks. He passed through clouds, and their cool crystalized particles meshed with his dusty being. He shook off their watery life as he emerged into a dawning sky. Boats bobbed in a harbor below, seagulls circled and dove, and he dove with them, skimming the sail of a ship, flitting by storefront windows. William skipped across rooftops, plummeted to the earth and rose again.

As his shadow passed over a man and dog on their early morning walk, William came upon a large hole in the ground—the sight tugged at him. He sank toward tumbled gravestones, dismantled coffins, and scattered bones all tossed together like a macabre stew. The taint of his master's touch lingered, but there was something else. A calling, bright and true. He lifted away, and drifted a short distance, settling upon a specific stone bench within the Memorial. His dusty existence filled the etched words, nearly erasing them altogether. The carved letters of Merry's name cradled and stilled him.

When the sun beamed upon the wall, he swirled into its warm embrace, spinning like glitter in a globe, and continued his journey. As though it were a beacon, William soared toward the last place he'd been happy. The sun carried him through the day, depositing him at his destination with slow release. There it sat before him. Majestic and welcoming. Iron House.

His presence coalesced outside the window of the room he'd shared with Merry. Inside, a figure moved about, and William's dusty self shivered and shimmered with anticipation. He pressed close to the glass. Like a broom against a dirty floor, disappointment swept him away as he realized the person in the room was Liz, and she was alone.

Frustration sent him on an aimless course. The wind dictated his path. When darkness fell, he drifted along the bank of a babbling brook, finally settling into a burnt, sunken piece of earth in the midst of a dark wood.

13 REVELATION

Liz found herself once again in Merry's room. The photo of Uncle Robert and the unknown woman lay atop the night table where she'd left it days before. She carried it with her into the closet, curious to see if she'd find any more photos like it. She knelt and searched the floor, but after lifting the few shoes Merry and William possessed and finding nothing, she sat back on her legs and decided it must have been the only photo. It was when she stood up that she saw it.

    On a shelf sat a black plastic bag, the opening of which hung over the edge, putting its contents in danger of spilling to the ground. The gold chain of a necklace dangled from the bag, edging its way to freedom. Liz pulled the bag down, the cross of the necklace untangling from the bag and falling into her hand. She dumped its contents on the bed. Only two items remained: a license and a red book with a rainbow heart on its cover. Someone's journal. She picked up the license first, finding the same woman from the photograph smiling up at her. She was definitely an 80's girl with big hair and a shiny hot pink jacket with shoulder pads to rival a football player. Aimee Donovan was her name; her address was in nearby Salem. Liz still didn't know who she was, but at least she had a way to find out.

Laying the license next to the photo and the necklace, Liz reached for the book and hoisted herself up onto the bed, settling in to read. She flipped through the journal, its pages filled with a fine script drawn by a careful hand. It was nothing like her own hasty scribble. Looking at it, she admitted she may have deserved those corrective taps with the ruler on her young hand as she'd struggled through a torture called cursive. She stopped at a page in the middle of the book and read a few of the perfect lines.

> On the day of the transcendence, we went to Iron House. To a beautiful library in a rounded turret. I could've lived there forever.

Liz stared at the words on the page, flipped to the page before and after. Read a few lines more. Still gripping the edges of the open book, Liz stared unseeing into the space before her. Whoever had written this book, this woman, Aimee Donovan, had been with Uncle Robert the night he died. Liz's heart thrashed erratically inside her chest as she continued reading, this time from the beginning.

April, 1985

> An extraordinary thing is about to happen. And, since I can't tell anyone, not that they'd believe me, I thought I'd at least write it down. So, here goes.

> It was mid-December when I first saw him. I had just stepped out of the front row of the choir and sang a few notes of my solo, when he came into the church through the side door, like he wanted to enter unnoticed. There was no chance of that! At least on my part. And by the faltering warbles of the chorus behind me, they'd noticed him too. He was handsome, blonde hair a little

long, but no mullet, thank goodness. Too many knuckleheads had adopted that god-awful look. This was a man, not a boy. His face was chiseled, though not in a stern way. There was warmth, especially in those blue eyes. Blue eyes that seemed to have locked onto my own. I realized I'd stopped singing and looked at the pastor, blushing. The man walked to the back of the church and sat down in a pew. I resumed the song, barely hearing the words coming out of my own mouth.

He came again on Sunday, and the Sunday after that. At first I thought I was imagining his eyes finding mine among the chorus, but when I stepped out for my solo, there was no imagining. His gaze fixed on mine and soon I wasn't singing to God or the parishioners. I was singing to him.

One afternoon, I found him waiting for me out by the holy font in the foyer after everyone left. All those Sundays, eyes locked on one another, it was like I knew Robert Kerrington before he even told me his name. He told me he was a recent widower and had a small daughter. His grief had driven him to the church and then he'd heard me, my voice.

"It made me believe there was good again," he'd said.

It didn't take long for me to fall in love with him. He wanted to keep our affair quiet; his family wouldn't understand how he could be with someone so soon after his wife's passing. He didn't want to add stress to his young daughter's world, which had so recently been turned upside down. I admit I liked it that way. Not having to share him with anyone. Not his child, not a disapproving family, not anyone.

There was only us.

Then I became pregnant. There were so many reasons to panic, but I was elated. I was surprised how happy the news made Robert. I soon found out why.

Which brings me to today and the reason for this journal.

I'm three months pregnant, tired, sick, and barely showing. I still haven't met Robert 's family. He hasn't made me one of them. But, there's a reason. A secret. He made me swear never to tell a soul, and I did swear even though I wanted to tell someone, anyone, after I heard it.

"I'm descended from a line of Illuminators," he told me. I can hear his voice, quiet and serious, as I write this.

At first, I thought he was playing a joke on me. I think I laughed a little. But, he didn't laugh, as he talked of an ancient race called Illuminators. They lived in a land called Nurya. Another dimension. I heard him say that word - dimension - and thought he'd lost his mind. Did he expect me to believe this tale? When he saw my doubt, he pulled out a small object. It was a monopoly game piece—the iron. That didn't help to dispel the crazy.

"What are you going to do with a game piece?" I asked.

"I'm going to prove it."

He took my hand, the token clutched in his other one and before I knew what was happening, the room dissolved in a bright light. I don't know how else to describe it. One minute we were in my living room, the next we were in a golden, green, dream-like place filled with glowing people, and a peace that I didn't think possible. Robert called it Nurya. One day he would be a part of it.

After only a few seconds, a bright flash returned us to my apartment. I think I stopped breathing for a moment. I was dizzy and stunned, and I had to lay down while Robert told me that those amazing glowing figures had been humans once. Just like him. Maybe even like me. People who'd been driven to do good, to help others. Perhaps even sacrificing themselves to save another. These humans had achieved a state of purity in body, mind, and spirit. Upon death, their uncompromised souls transformed into light.

"The Illuminators serve as a guide of sorts. Helping people find their way, choose the right path," Robert explained.

"Like a guardian angel?" I asked. Robert kissed the tip of my nose. I loved when he did that.

"That's a common comparison, but for the very human component." He gripped my arms. His eyes conveyed a disconcerting mix of sadness and determination, and he stared at me in a way that chilled my heart. Then he released me and paced the room like a trapped animal.

"What is it?" I asked.

He let out a resigned sigh. "Amy, there are some of us who are burdened with a much more odious task. Genetics decree that only male Illuminators can continue the line. It doesn't guarantee the child will become an Illuminator. Even the father may never mature into light. All those other human factors I mentioned come into play, of course. But, that's the path, and there are consequences."

"What are you saying?" I asked. Or thought. I'm not sure. I heard the answer though. Producing such a being causes its host, aka, mother, to age at a rapid pace and may result in compromised health. Even death.

Robert began to talk of the constant struggle to balance the light against a conquering darkness, but I'd zoned him out by then. Because after hearing his secret, after learning what he was, all I could think was that the child growing inside me was a child of light. And I was its host.

May 1985

I had an ultrasound. It's a boy. William will be his name. Robert is overjoyed. He would have been happy with a girl. But a boy... a boy can carry on the line.

For several days I tried to pretend the secret was still untold. I have to admit, at least to myself on this sheet of paper, that I'm scared. Terrified, actually. Though a wonderful and fantastic world has been revealed to me, I know my part in it is a throw away. This child I carry has the potential to become an Illuminator, but I am nothing in their world. I am a host. I provide a service. I can never be part of their world. But, I believe in God and I believe in good. And, Robert is good personified. I have a role to fill. I have a purpose.

The Illuminator numbers are dwindling. Because only males can carry on the line, they have little chance of increasing those numbers any time soon. The balance between light and dark is compromised. An entity had gotten a foothold during the Salem Witch Trials and continued to perpetuate his evil through the centuries. World events proved how off-kilter the balance between light and dark was. But, Robert says there is a way to restore stability. He has a plan, and it involves a huge sacrifice.

MINE

With his light, Robert thinks he has one chance to send our unborn child and me back in time to the seventeenth century. William's light could strengthen the number of Illuminators in that time and truly bring an enlightenment to pass.

I screamed at Robert. I begged. "Why William? Why not your daughter? Why must my unborn child and I be asked to sacrifice so much?"

He held me while I cried.

As luck would have it, aside from Robert, our unborn son will be the only other male Illuminator. Only males can produce more light. Only our son can save the light.

June 1985

I love Robert. I love his eyes, his laugh, his arms around me. I love his love.

And, I will love this child he's given me. William. I can't wait to see his tiny hands, his face, his light.

What Robert has asked of me is impossible. Terrifying.

I love him. I will do this. No matter what it takes.

Today, Robert presented me with a wardrobe straight out of Colonial New England. He had the clothing made by a local costume designer. The care that went into putting such authenticity into these garments brings home the seriousness of the path my life and the life of my son will soon take.

I'm on edge. No, that doesn't even begin to describe how I feel. The day grows closer to my travel through time. God, that sounds crazy.

To make our adventure more interesting, Robert revealed another small hitch. I will need to trade places with someone from the seventeenth century. An Illuminator will facilitate the exchange. Timing will be everything, because If I get stuck in time without a trade, both William and I will die.

July 1985

Today is my last day in the twenty-first century—that is if all of this isn't some grand joke. But Robert wouldn't do that to me. To us.

This morning, I ate at my favorite breakfast place in town, ordered a full meal of pancakes, eggs, and bacon and drank nearly a pot of coffee. I'm not sure when I'll eat like that again. When I'll have coffee again. I'm like an inmate on death row. My requests: a full breakfast, a hot bath, and for Robert to make love to me one last time.

The first two went off without a hitch. The last was bittersweet. There was passion and love and so much that was good about it. But, I'd be lying if I said that every second wasn't tinged with sadness and the awareness of loss.

Those last moments in Robert's arms, his warm skin against mine, I won't ever forget.

July - year unknown

I'm writing this days after the transcendence. T-Day.

Robert is dead.

He's dead, and I can't do this. I can't!

I have to write this down.

My hand is shaking.

My heart is broken.

On the day of the transcendence, we went to Iron House. To a beautiful library in a rounded turret. I could've lived there forever.

In fact, I made one last plea to live our lives within those walls. But, when Robert brought out the Monopoly iron token that would transport me to another time, I knew this was it.

At first, the light was so strong I could barely see. When the light faded, I saw we were in a cave. The trade, a woman, stood on an altar, belly large with child. She was writing, pen poised in hand, blood dripping onto paper. And she was angry. We'd interrupted whatever it was she was doing.

Her eyes locked on mine for the briefest of moments. The Illuminator, a young, glowing boy, took my hand, and we approached her.

"Trinka," a deep, eerie voice said from the depths of the cave we'd entered. I heard Robert's shouts before I saw the owner of the voice. An evil being. A tall man with skin so pale it nearly gave off as much light as Robert did. But, darkness tugged at the edges, warning of impending destruction.

I tried to pull my hand from the Illuminator and reached for Robert, but he pushed me away just as the man struck him down. In that moment, that never-ending moment when our eyes locked for the last time, I saw Robert's strength, his sorrow, and his love. I gave my unspoken promise to protect what was ours.

Then, he was gone.

As his light dimmed, another light bloomed, and I found myself cradled in the Illuminator's brilliance. We hovered over a cornfield. A young man stared up at me startled, I'm sure, by the vision of a woman floating in the air above him. He shielded his eyes from the light and made the sign of the cross. We looked at one another, both shocked by each other's presence. And I realized then what Robert had done. The sacrifice he'd made.

In a split second, he'd pushed me from harm's way, from certain death, and allowed the Illuminator a chance to find another trade. The light cocooned the young man and I and, for mere seconds, we stood within its glory. Terrified, I stepped out of the light and my

Illuminator escort bore the man away to another time and the only life I'd ever known, while I stayed behind to fulfill my promise.

I sat in the cornfield for many hours.

I wanted to die. I couldn't do this, this crazy journey through time to save the world from darkness. I could've done it, if I knew one day I'd be back at Robert's side. That would never happen now.

I placed my hand on my enlarged abdomen and cried. After a while, the tears stopped, though not the heartbreak. It was still daytime when I wiped my tears on the apron of my skirt and stood. The corn was about a foot taller than me. I didn't know which way was the quickest out of the cornfield, so I simply started walking.

I should've been paying more attention to my surroundings, but all I could think about was Robert. So when I stepped out of the cornfield, I was startled to find myself facing the long barrel of a shotgun. I froze. I'm not sure who was more frightened at that moment. The man holding the gun or me.

"Who are you?" he asked. I told him my name, forgetting to use the colonial accent Robert had made me practice over and over. The man wanted to know what I was doing in his field. For a moment, I thought about turning around, going back into the cornstalks and lying there until I died. But I couldn't waste the sacrifice Robert had made. So, I launched into the story we'd practiced. This time with the colonial accent and dialect.

The man easily believed I'd been traveling on the road with my husband and had been attacked by a band of Indians, that my husband had been killed and I'd walked, not knowing where I was going.

In the end he lowered his gun, told me his name, and invited me in for tea and stew.

And that's how I walked into Sam Darling's life.

An hour later, diary read beginning to end, Liz snapped the journal shut, needing to process what she'd learned. When Merry had entered Liz's life, she'd had a hard time believing the possibility that Merry's story of time travel could be true. When Liz learned that Sidney, her own cousin, was part of some cosmic light brigade, her imagination had grown. Now it was positively stretched thin. *How could all of this have happened in her own home and she'd not known a bit of it until now?* Her Uncle Robert had been a good man, but the words of Aimee Donovan made him out to be some sort of god.

And, her mother had known too. Had even had a piece of the puzzle, the iron trinket from their Monopoly game. The closest Liz had come to that tale was wondering where the heck the piece had gone. But, her mother hadn't known who the woman in the photograph had been. Didn't know about William's mother. Didn't know William was her nephew, Liz's cousin. Didn't know William was Sidney's half-brother.

14 RAYNE

Devon Rayne came into the world screaming. Twice.

The first when he'd emerged from his dying mother's womb. He'd exhaled his first breath into a demanding scream, while his mother's last rattled into non-existence.

The second when, at the hands of another woman, he'd been plucked from one world and birthed into another.

Always one to make the best of his circumstances, Devon had crafted a home in both worlds, the second made infinitely richer with the love of Summer and Molly. But that life had ended in one horrible moment, and he'd spent the last fifteen years roaming the country tying to pretend he didn't exist at all.

He thought of the day he'd lost his family everyday since they'd disappeared. But as he worried the rough newspaper in his hands, the events of that day slammed into him with a clarity he'd thought he'd left in some unreachable place.

Distraught over the sight of his wife and daughter vanishing before his eyes, he'd crumpled into a useless mass near the swing set waiting for their return. But they didn't come back. He hated himself for not being honest with Summer. For letting her think his confusion and oddness was due to a head injury. It was easy to do given she'd found him in such a state.

He'd needed her, then he'd loved her, and he'd continued to lie to her.

Could he have done something more to bring his family back had he been honest about his own origins? Possibly. Though, truth be told, his ability to resolve his daughter's situation was unlikely in light of the fact he'd not been able to reverse his own travel through time.

He played the scene over and over in his head. Never coming up with a way to make it turn out different. Bring them back.

One minute Molly had been proudly showing them how she could pump her legs to make the swing go high, an ability she'd recently mastered. The next moment, she was soaring through the air, her mother screaming, running to catch her as an impossible rainbow surrounded them and wove them right into the sunny summer day. He, only a few feet away, arms reaching, snatching nothing but air. Impotent. Left behind.

The first time Molly disappeared, she'd been eight months old. Summer had seen it; for only a few seconds their daughter had vanished from her crib. Dev ran when he heard his wife's screams. She'd been nearly incoherent. He might not have believed Molly had disappeared as Summer claimed, had he not seen his daughter suddenly appear out of thin air, giggling and cooing in her recently empty crib.

They hadn't known what to do. This wasn't exactly a malady one could call the pediatrician for. A medical diagnosis was unlikely. There was something else at play here. Otherworldly and frustratingly familiar, yet still unknowable.

They didn't let Molly out of their sight afterwards. The crib was moved into their room and one of them was always with her. A few times they caught strands of colors spiraling above the baby's sleeping form like a mobile made of rainbows. But, she didn't disappear again.

Then Summer found Adina or, more accurately, Adina found them. When the tall, mystical-looking woman approached Summer and her baby as they strolled down Derby Street to the pier and told her she could see auras, in particular,

Molly's aura, Summer listened. At last they'd found someone who knew what they were dealing with.

Adina explained how everyone had an aura, made up of many colors though most people's auras spotlighted the strongest hue at a given time. But, when she looked at Molly, she saw all the colors. The rainbow and every hue, too many to know, each one as strong as the next. No wonder they'd escaped from time to time.

When it had grown nearly dark, he'd picked himself off the ground and headed down the street to visit the woman who'd been helping them with controlling Molly's colors. Summer said she had the gift of sight. Perhaps she could tell him where his family was and what he could do to get them back.

The newspaper crinkled in protest as he absently folded and unfolded it. Adina had been waiting for him, silhouetted in the low-lit doorway of her shop. She'd shuffled him into the empty store and before he could say anything, she told him what had occurred as though she'd been there. But of course she knew. She'd predicted it. Despite such a prediction, despite knowing Molly and Summer would go back in time, they'd been unable to prevent it from happening. This time Molly wasn't coming back. And neither was Summer. *The only two people in the world who mattered to me.*

Over the years, he'd punished himself again and again. The argument of why he hadn't done more competed with the question of what more could've been done. The fates orchestrating place and time were bigger than him. Adina had warned him the police would come after him for the disappearance of his wife and daughter. It didn't matter if he stayed or ran, he'd be considered guilty either way. And the girls would still be gone.

So Devon ran. He'd grabbed a few items from his house, money, a jacket, a photo of his girls, and he ran.

The bench sank under another man's weight.

"You all right man?" asked Jerry.

Dev pulled himself away from memories he hadn't let himself indulge in for years. He looked at Jerry, his only true friend in this world. "Thinking. Remembering."

His friend nodded. Jerry was a drifter, too. Drifting away from an unwanted past toward an uncertain future.

Dev straightened the paper to showcase an article, the news it contained nothing short of miraculous. He ran a shaking hand along the top of his close-shaved head. His heart pounded, his face and hands tingled. A few tears slid down his cheeks.

"Bad news?"

Dev shook his head and handed the newspaper to Jerry. "Read it." Dev leaned back against the building, his eyes staring unseeing at the porch overhang.

Jerry's lips moved wordlessly as he scanned the article. "Shit man. Shit."

The corners of Dev's mouth began to prick upward into an involuntary smile.

"Dev. Man, holy shit. Your daughter's alive."

Dev's mouth flew past a smile and went straight to laughter at hearing the words spoken out loud.

Molly was alive.

Molly was home.

15 CRYSTAL

Sophie fell victim to the sedating effects of her own goulash, her rumbling snores overtaking the television's hum. Meanwhile, Merry couldn't stop moving. Her blood jumped in her veins, and she couldn't shake the restlessness that urged her to do something. *Something!*

She wanted to get out. She *needed* to get out. Maybe Salem, the place where she supposedly belonged, would bring her back to herself. She crept past Sophie, who was lost to her reclining chair, and grabbed her jacket off a hook by the back door. She peered outside and after determining that no reporters had snuck to the back yard, slipped outside and gently shut the door behind her.

Merry crossed the yard, stealing past the neighbor's thick bushes and into the next street. She found herself in a small parking lot and darted between two cars, crossing the lot to emerge onto a cobblestone walkway. Merry stood for a moment taking in her surroundings. A large group of brick buildings connected by glass columns loomed before her. Alternating triangular and round roofs topped them. To the left of her the cobblestone ended and another parking lot faced her. The sounds of heavy machinery at the nearby site of the sinkhole reached her.

A few people passed by and she watched them walk a path through a small garden to her right before passing beneath an arch onto another cobblestoned street. Merry followed and found herself on a street crowded with pedestrians. People streamed past her in both directions. It took a moment for Merry to realize more than a few people were dressed in costumes. Witches, pirates. A smile lit her face as she attempted to dodge a rather large pumpkin. "Excuse me."

"Sorry," the pumpkin said as it tilted its plump orange body to make room for Merry to pass, before wobbling on its way. She continued passed carts filled with t-shirts and pointy witch hats.

As Merry rounded a corner, a passerby knocked into her shoulder, spinning her around. The person stumbled by and groaned, a sound echoed by other nearby walkers. Merry took a good look at the throng shuffling toward her. They all appeared to be in various stages of decay. Faces filled with the sallow shades of death, torn flesh, bloodied and ripped clothing. A man turned toward her, his cheek hanging in a flap, exposing rotting flesh beneath. He reached a gray hand toward her.

Merry screamed.

Suddenly, she saw hundreds of bodiless hands reaching for her. They pulled at her, tugged her down into the suffocating dirt from whence they came. She struggled as more hands pinned her arms to her side and pulled her up. Strong arms wrapped around her. She squirmed and kicked her foot out behind her. A man grunted, and she kicked again.

"Lady! Hey lady, stop!"

She froze. Several of the creatures flanked another who held Merry's arms at her side. Now that she'd stopped kicking, he dropped her arms and stepped back. "It's OK. You're OK."

Merry peered at the owner of the voice, shivering at the sight of his bloodied face, fixating on a nail protruding from his forehead. Panic swelled anew. He tapped the nail head. "It's fake." He grinned a somewhat endearing grin. "Zombie walk, you know?"

Merry bit her lip, daring to observe the never-ending stream of zombies as they continued to parade down the cobblestoned street. The man's friend rubbed his thigh, and she realized he must've received the brunt of her tantrum.

"I'm sorry. I didn't realize..."

"It's cool," he said. They rejoined the shuffling mob, a few other passersby stealing glances at the crazy woman she was.

Merry leaned against the brick building behind her and sighed. She wanted to crawl under a rock. Zombies. Laughter, just this side of hysterical, escaped her. She had to get her head together if she wanted to regain her memories.

Merry pushed off the wall and continued along the cobblestones, turning down a side street and away from the zombie parade at first opportunity. It was here she encountered more costumed people. This time they were actors dressed in colonial garb. A crowd surrounded them as the actors reenacted the capture of an accused witch. Merry stood mesmerized.

The actors moved along, snow-balling a larger crowd as they went. She sensed something important slipping away. Merry followed, lured by the promise of a memory. But when she arrived at the meeting house where a large group had amassed to watch the fate of the witch, her lack of money stopped her from entering. She cursed under her breath as the doors shut her out. What she thought she'd gain by watching the reenactment of a witch trial she didn't know, but it seemed significant nonetheless.

She turned and headed back the way she came, dreading joining the zombies again, but she wasn't sure how to get back to Sophie's house unless she retraced her steps. Sophie was certain to know she was missing by now. She'd be worried. As Merry made her way up the street, a shop sparkling with light and brightly colored displays attracted her attention. She paused before the window, a sense of deja vu pressing in on her. Merry gently pushed the glass door open, a tinkling sound announcing her entry, and a young dark-haired woman, dressed in black greeted her with a smile.

"It's nice to see you again," the woman said, followed by a frown and a tentative touch her own neck. "Oh! What happened to you?"

Merry's fingers grazed the angry purple marks encircling her neck, stunned that this woman knew her. She attempted a smile. "Oh, you know us, witches. People are always trying to hang us."

The girl's eyes widened. "Someone tried to hang you?"

"I'm joking. It's..." She paused, searching for a second excuse. On the counter sat a flyer for Salem's month-long Halloween festivities. "It's make-up I was trying out for Halloween. Doesn't wash away well."

The girl smiled, relieved. "Well, it looks good. Authentic."

Merry grimaced. "Thanks."

"Any word on Sidney?"

Sidney. Liz's cousin. She'd been injured. Merry couldn't remember anything but the fact that when Sophie had asked Liz the same question, the answer had been, "She's the same." Merry repeated the answer to the girl who nodded solemnly.

Several people browsed shelves filled with tiny figurines of fairies, gargoyles and other magical creatures. Merry strolled to the opposite side of the store where a wall of round crystal balls perched on glass shelves. The combination of the store's light and the sun streaming through the window drew their colors onto the walls and ceiling. Bells tinkled as more people entered. Someone called Merry's name, and she turned to find Liz pushing her way through the crowd toward her.

"There you are!" she said. "Oh my God, Mer... Molly! You had Sophie in a panic! She's out there looking for you now." Liz dug a phone out of her pocket. "I need to let her know I found you and that you're OK."

"Of course, I'm OK," Merry said, annoyed until Liz dealt a pointed look first at her neck than into her eyes. She mumbled an apology as Liz dialed the phone and gave Sophie the news that her granddaughter had been found.

"How did you know where to find me?" Merry asked.

"I didn't, but I thought you might come to places you'd been before. This is Sidney's shop." Liz touched her arm. "We need to get you back home."

Before she could make an argument to stay out a bit longer, Merry heard her name called out once again. This time by Sophie who was pushing her plump self through the crowd. Murmurs and a flickering movement tugged Merry's attention back to the shelves of crystal balls. She gasped as a familiar scene played out on the surface of every ball.

It was her dream. The dark room, groping hands, and haunted man all coming toward her as though they'd leap out of the crystal and materialize before her. She shook her head from side to side, willing it to stop. But it continued playing over and over. People paused to watch the display, some thinking it a clever trick, some snatching up a ball to buy. But as the scene continued, they stepped back, fear replacing curiosity.

Merry turned away, ready to push through the crowd, get away from her dream, when something even more incredible occurred. She heard her own voice coming from the glass orbs.

"William."

She peered at the largest ball near her, watching as the man was pushed forward by many hands. He shouted for her to run.

"No," Merry said in unison with her disembodied voice. Then, she found herself shouting in stereo.

"Leave him alone!"

Sophie froze a few feet from Merry. The crowd quieted, all attention on the crystal balls.

"Sophie, go!" Liz said. It took another shout, another moment, before Sophie turned and began to push through the statue-like ensemble toward the door.

Suddenly, the crystal balls gave off a blinding light. People screamed. Merry reached for the largest crystal and held it high above her head, then threw it at the wall. It hit the top glass shelf, obliterating it, sending it crashing to the one beneath it.

They collapsed one atop the other, sending the balls rolling through the crowd.

The room filled with color, as though a rainbow had exploded inside the shop. People fled, pushing one another toward the door, knocking figurines from shelves as they shoved their way out. A teen boy knocked a bookstand over. More people screamed. The colors danced and swirled along the ceiling as though they were a living, breathing entity. Merry reached up as a tendril of blue drifted down toward her. Her heart lifted and despite the chaos, a peace settled inside her.

It didn't last long. Liz shouted and grabbed her arm before she could connect with the remaining colors. Merry tried to free herself, but the crystals went dark and silent. The colors vanished.

"Close up the shop," Liz told the stunned girl behind the counter. Then she maneuvered Merry through the broken glass and dead crystal balls. As they neared the front of the store, they found Sophie standing outside looking in at them, tears streaming down her face.

Once outside, Liz hugged Sophie. "Go back to your house."

Before Sophie could muster an argument, Liz implored her to leave. With hugs and apologies, Sophie left, and Liz grabbed Merry's hand and led her in the opposite direction.

16 THE REPORTER

Alex Olivier was getting tired of sitting in front of Madame Sophie's Psychic Parlor. It was a good story—lost girl returned after being assumed dead. So many questions to ask. No one to answer them. It was evident the girl's grandmother wouldn't let them near her. They had to come out sometime, but when? Only the stigma of being the first to leave kept him there.

Aside from some idle chatter, none of the waiting reporters spoke to each other. His colleagues were a naturally suspicious bunch, trusting each other the least when the all-important "scoop" hung in the balance.

While most of the other reporters crammed themselves as close to the entrance of Madam Sophie's Physic Parlor as possible, Alex sat in the news van, watching. As his eyes wandered over the facade for any interior movement, he caught sight of someone running from Sophie Cooke's house to the neighbor's. He opened the door of the truck and got out, pausing to stretch, then walked toward the house to the spot he'd left his cameraman, Joel.

He nodded toward Joel as he walked the few steps over to him. "What's up?"

"I think I saw someone in the back," said Alex in a low

voice. "Looks like they ran into the neighbor's yard. Do you know what's behind this street?"

Joel looked around for a moment. "I think the museum is back there."

Alex nodded. "I'm going to check it out."

"Alex."

"Hey, I'm never going to get anywhere by waiting for something to happen. You coming?"

"You walk away and that's when something happens."

"You coming?" Alex repeated.

Joel shook his head. "I always do, don't I?"

A corner of Alex's mouth turned up in a smile. "Come on, let's get some food." He said it loud enough for his fellow vultures to hear. They could wait for their carrion; he was a hunter.

After turning onto Essex Street, Joel said, "This better not be like the Kirschner case. You'll be back in print and I'll be drawing stick figures in a court room."

"Do you seriously think we're missing something by leaving Madame Sophie's front door for a few minutes?"

Joel frowned.

"Listen, if we don't see anything, we go back to the house. No harm done."

Alex sped his pace nonetheless. He'd made a mess of the Kirschner case, another wait and see report. He wasn't good at waiting. It had only taken a few minutes to step away for a bathroom break for the window of opportunity to open. That being Kirschner himself stepping outside his house to give a five-minute speech about his innocence in the bribery case against him and how he held his legislative responsibility with the highest regard, never stooping to taking money from the local businesses to place votes in their favor. All these blatant lies out there for the taking, followed by a perp walk. And, he'd missed it. *Hell, a man had to piss, didn't he?*

Now, he was placed on missing children stories. He had to admit this one was a bit extraordinary. Not every child came home fifteen years later, having survived a hanging attempt.

Whether self-inflicted or not, well, that was one of the unanswered questions. They rounded the corner to Essex Street, the crowd already thick. October was Salem's busiest month.

"She could be anywhere," said Alex. "Keep an eye out."

"Or she could be in Madame Sophie's house."

"I saw someone, trust me."

"How do you know it wasn't another reporter trying to sneak in the back way?" Joel asked.

"They were running away. And, I'm sure I caught long, auburn hair."

"Well, that's a clincher."

Alex stopped. "If you want to go back, I won't stop you."

Joel hesitated, then resumed walking toward the museum. "Shit Alex."

Alex grinned as they moved on, all the while scanning the crowd for Molly Cooke. They took a left turn into the museum garden where some people lingered on the stone benches. The day grew dark behind them as clouds rolled over Salem.

"Storm coming," Joel said.

"Let's move it then."

They stepped back onto Essex Street and fought a strong wind as they continued their way past the vendor carts and shops. Up ahead, near the corner of Central Street, there appeared to be a bit of a commotion. Several teenaged boys were high-fiving each other shouting "That was awesome!" while several other people were pushing their way through the crowd as if fleeing a fire.

Adrenalin pumped through Alex. He approached one of the exuberant teens.

"Excuse me, can you tell me what's going on here?"

"Some witchy shit, man! The crystal balls all turned on like a freakin' horror movie, and then they exploded and there were these colors. It was wicked!"

"Wicked!" echoed his friend.

Alex looked at Joel standing behind him, who was shaking his head. Before the teens moved on, Alex asked them where the 'witchy' activity had happened. They pointed to a shop at the end of the street, and Alex and his reluctant cameraman headed towards it.

As they approached, Alex scanned the area, finding a cluster of women shouting at one another. Head tilted to one side, he moved in.

Joel, recognizing Alex's signature head tilt as a sign he'd found his story, hoisted the camera to his shoulder, while Alex grabbed the microphone from the side mount.

"Hello. Alex Olivier, FX Five News, can you tell me what happened here?"

Through tears and wide eyes, the women relayed a story of fantastical proportions straight out of a modern-day horror movie. In the end, Alex knew he'd shelve the tape, even though the women seemed sincere in their relay of events.

"What do you think?" Joel asked after they moved on.

Before Alex could answer, a woman emerged from the alleged shop of horrors. Alex sidled up to her and introduced himself, thrusting the microphone in her direction.

She recoiled at the intrusion. Not wanting to lose her, Alex lowered the mike, lessening the intimidation effect while still detecting her response.

"Do you work here?" he asked.

The girl nodded as she attempted to lock the door.

"Some of your customers say there was a stampede of sorts in your shop."

The girl looked up in surprise and dropped her keys at the same time. She bent down to retrieve the keys, but Alex stepped in, making it impossible for her to do so in the small space.

"What can you tell me about the disturbance?"

She looked at him, her large, dark eyes warring with loyalty and the notion of wanting to tell everything. "I... shouldn't."

Alex looked at the sign on the door and paused. This was the same store front that had been featured in the Sidney Kerrington story a couple of weeks ago. Sidney had been shot during a coven ceremony. Now there was a disturbance at her shop.

"Sidney Kerrington owns this shop. Did the disturbance have anything to do with the recent shooting?"

The girl shook her head. "No. No, it was nothing like that."

"What's your name?" Alex asked.

"Candace," she answered.

Alex's eyes flicked toward the window for a second, noticing a bookcase crashed through the glass countertop. "Place looks trashed. Why was everyone in such a hurry to get out?" When she didn't answer right away, Alex grinned. "Some people are saying there was a supernatural event. Maybe a Halloween prank gone wrong?"

"It wasn't a prank. The crystal balls... came alive."

"What does that mean?"

"It means you could see images on the surfaces. And, they were horrible images. Corpses trying to pull a woman through the earth, some tortured man. Merry started screaming at them and she threw one of the balls. Then it got really strange."

Alex lifted an eyebrow.

"The room filled with colors, like a rainbow exploded. Colors everywhere."

Alex forced himself to ask his next question as though it mattered. "I don't see any in there now. Where did they go?"

"Disappeared."

"You mentioned Merry. Is she a customer?"

"She's Liz's friend. Liz is Sidney's cousin. Oh, and talk about a Halloween prank. I thought she'd actually been hung when I saw her neck."

The hairs on the back of Alex's neck pricked up. "Was there some marking around her neck? Bruising?"

Candace frowned. "Yes, a nasty purple bruise. But, she told me it was fake. Halloween make-up that wouldn't come off."

"You said her name was Merry. Are you certain? Does she have long, dark, reddish hair. About 5'5"?

"That sounds like her."

"And, you're sure her name is Merry."

"That's how I was introduced to her."

Now it was Alex's turn to frown. Joel, lowered the camera for a moment to dig in his back pocket.

"Joel," said Alex. "What are you doing, keep the camera up."

"Hang on," he said, producing a folded piece of newspaper. He held it out to the girl, while hoisting his camera back into position. "Does Merry look like the person in the photo by any chance?"

Alex beamed as Candace unfolded the newspaper and studied the two photos on its surface. One, a head shot of Molly Rose Cooke as she left the hospital. Another one of her running into her grandmother's house.

Candace looked up, shock and confusion in her eyes. "This is her. Merry. But, here it says her name is Molly. That's the girl who was missing for like... forever."

"And, this is the woman who was in your store today?"

Candace nodded. "Yes, but I don't understand how that could be. She's been around for weeks. She was living with Liz and Sidney, well until Sidney was shot."

Alex shot a glance at Joel who's smile said, *You were right to leave the grandmother's house. Well played.*

"Any idea where Merry went?" Alex asked.

Candace shook her head. "She and Liz left together. But, I don't know if they were going to Iron House or to the condo."

Alex knew Iron House was the Thompson estate in Danvers. "Where's the condo?"

Candace pointed up Central Street. "It's on the common. Big blue house corner of Washington."

Alex finally stepped back so Candace could pick up her keys and finish locking up the shop. "Thank you and good luck with the cleanup."

Then, he and Joel hurried up Central Street, turned right, and headed for the Common.

17 PURSUIT

"Oh crap," Sophie muttered to herself.

The sight of Liz's red Mercedes sitting in the parking lot behind her house stopped Sophie in her tracks. She knew Liz and Merry were going to Liz's condo, but how would they get to Iron House without a car? She'd take her own if she thought she could get out of her driveway without picking up a few shadowing reporters.

Sophie reversed direction and headed back to the shop, hoping to catch up with the girls. She searched the crowd of tourists, but didn't find Liz's blonde head or Merry's dark, auburn waves. Sophie pushed herself to move faster, her breath getting louder in her ears. She stopped when she reached Center Street's cobblestoned path. What was she thinking? Her old, short legs were no match for this mission. Merry and Liz were probably halfway across the common already. Still, she scanned the crowd once more, hoping to catch sight of them.

That's when she saw the reporter, microphone in hand, and his buddy with the camera on his shoulder. The handsome reporter from FX Five. She'd seen them earlier on her own front sidewalk. They were interviewing the girl from the shop, and it looked like she was talking.

"Crap," she muttered again. There were probably a handful of times when she'd wished she had a cellphone. This was one of them. She'd never had anyone to call before. She desperately wanted to warn Liz to get Merry out of Salem *now*. Sophie edged closer, using the cover of a few women huddled outside the shop, still chatting about the crystal balls.

She was close enough to catch a few words. Close enough to hear the girl talk of how Merry had been around for weeks before today. Close enough to hear the girl tell the reporter where to find Merry. Without delay, Sophie made her way through the throngs of people toward Essex Street. She needed to get to the girls before pretty boy and his camera found them.

After winding their way along cobblestoned streets and sidewalks, past a gothic museum, through a grassy common and up the porch steps of a three-story home, Merry stopped, halting Liz beside her.

"Where are we?" she asked.

Liz looked surprised by the question, but only for a moment, which Merry took to mean she'd been there before.

"It's Sidney's condo. We can hole up here until I know for sure the reporters didn't get wind of what happened. Later, I'll ask Logan and Frederick to get my car. We'll be heading to Iron House tonight."

Merry followed Liz upstairs to the second-floor apartment without another word. When the door was shut securely behind them, Merry spoke. "Liz, what *did* happen?"

"The crystal balls..."

"They were my dreams! Inside those crystals, those were my dreams!"

Liz buried her face in her hands for a moment and sat heavily in a chair by the window.

"Your dreams, your memories, they're all the same. At least I'm pretty sure they are. What you saw, though, in the crystal balls? Those weren't your memories. I mean they were, but they were manifested through Sophie's visions."

Merry sat in a chair opposite Liz. "I don't follow."

"Sophie is a psychic. She has the ability to see the future."

"But, if they're memories, they've already happened."

"True. With you, it gets a bit complicated. When Sophie sees something that will happen to you, well, in essence, it's already happened."

"I don't understand."

Liz shook her head. "I don't suppose you do."

Merry leaned forward. "Help me to."

Liz rubbed her forehead. "I can't."

"You mean *won't*." Merry shut her eyes. Not knowing haunted her. Liz and Sophie were so tight-lipped about her past, that she feared the reason for it. It was bad enough she couldn't remember, but what if what she remembered was better left forgotten?

She seemed to possess some ability to send colors from her body to avert disaster, bring calm. Colors flooded her dreams. Dreams so realistic, she nearly believed they were. The people of the light and the man in pain seemed more than a dream. They felt like life. Her life.

Frustration seemed the only emotion she knew these days.

The window panes rattled under a windy assault. What had started out a gray, dreary day had turned into a nor'easter. It was midday, yet the window that nearly took up an entire wall of the sitting room, showed no hint of day. It wasn't lost on her that the day's wrath mirrored her own vexation.

"Molly, please..."

Liz begged for her to listen. But, all Merry could hear was the roar of her own confusion. The anger at not knowing herself boiled within her veins. A sharp crack sounded outside as a sudden storm descended upon the common. Merry took a deep breath. She couldn't let this anger overtake her. She needed focus, calm. She needed the truth.

Liz shouted for Merry to stop.

Stop what? She thought as she opened her eyes. Liz's worried face was mere inches from her own, her hands holding the arms of Merry's chair.

"Please Merry, you have to calm down. This isn't good."

Merry frowned. "What are you talking about?"

"Humor me," she said. "Take some deep breaths. That's right... slower."

Thunder became a distant toll, the rain receded to a slight drizzle. Liz sighed. "Good. I think it's over now."

"What's over?"

"The storm."

For the life of her, Merry couldn't understand why Liz appeared to be attributing the weather to her. "Liz."

Liz held up a hand, stopping her tongue. "We need to get you to Iron House. You're injured and you need to heal. Let's take this one step at a time, OK?"

Merry stood.

"No."

Once again, surprise reigned in Liz's face. "No?"

"Everyone keeps telling me to slow down, to wait to hear whatever it is I need to know. But, something else, something stronger, is telling me I can't wait. I can't explain it, but my instincts tell me if I wait..." Merry shook her head, unable to finish her thought. She didn't know what would happen; she just knew it wouldn't be good.

The winding line outside the Witch Museum was at least fifty people deep. Once she realized there was no real end to it, Sophie started weaving through the tourists. When she reached the corner gates of the Common, a honk of a car horn turned her attention back toward the museum. The reporter and his sidekick had broken through the human chain and were narrowly missed by a swerving car.

Sophie's heart raced as she realized the handsome reporter was heading to the same place she was. She thought about going somewhere else in an effort to throw them off the trail, but discarded the notion when she remembered they knew where to find Merry with or without her thanks to the girl at the shop. *She'd have to let Liz know about Miss Chatty when she saw her.*

Sophie continued past the gazebo and down the paved walkway, which charted a straight path to Sidney's condo. Her brain sorted through idea after idea on how to stop this from ending badly. None stood up to the test. As she neared the end of the path, she noticed a man standing on the sidewalk across the street outside Sidney's home, staring at the front door. Sophie slowed, alarms sounding in her head. She was certain she'd seen the man before. A hood hid his face, and his hands were jammed into the pockets of his sweatshirt. *So familiar.*

"Mrs. Cooke."

Sophie spun around. Alex Olivier and his cameraman stood a few feet away. Sophie cursed under her breath. She glanced back toward the house; the hooded man was gone.

"Mrs. Cooke," Alex repeated.

Sophie glared at him. "You're following me."

Alex gave a small smile. "I believe we happen to be going to the same place." He looked up, his gaze landing on the large blue house across the street behind them. "I'm Alex Olivier. This is Joel..."

"I know who you are. I've seen you stalking us outside my front door."

Alex shook his head. "Stalking seems a bit harsh."

"And yet, here we are."

"Mrs. Cooke, I..."

"My granddaughter needs peace and quiet to recover."

Alex nodded to Joel, and he raised the camera to his shoulder. Sophie stared at the blinking red light, anger running hot through her body.

"Some say Molly returned before she was found at Gallows Hill," Alex said.

She could play this two ways. Denial or admittance. In the end, both paths would lead to the same place. "Tell your sidekick to shut off the camera."

"Mrs. Cooke, I..."

"He shuts it off, or I don't tell you what you're dying to

know."

Alex nodded to his partner to lower the camera. Sophie only spoke when she saw the red light go dark.

"It's true," she said. "Molly has been here for nearly a month. But, she was confused and thought she was someone else. We didn't even know who she was until a few weeks ago."

"Yet, you told no one. Not your son. Not the police. And, what connection does she have to the wealthiest family on the north shore?"

"This isn't the place to talk."

"Where? When?"

Sophie bit her lip. Liz was going to kill her. "At the Thompson residence, Iron House. Tomorrow. But, not a word in the news before then? OK?"

"Mrs. Cooke, this is not a secret that will keep."

"It is, if you keep it."

"What I mean is we didn't find this out because you told us. We found out from some random shop girl. The information is already out there."

Before Sophie could respond, a commotion broke out behind her. She turned to find Merry storming across the street, Liz close behind shouting for her to stop and come back inside. Merry ignored Liz, her focused glare on Alex. Within a few feet of her mark, Merry shouted at him.

"Go away! Leave us alone and go away!"

Alex stumbled backward as if dealt a physical blow. His eyes glazed and without another word, he turned and started walking across the common, back the way he'd come. His cameraman, turned, confused.

"Alex?"

Alex ignored him, and Joel turned to Merry. He started to raise his camera when she shouted for him to leave as well. In moments, both men were halfway across the common.

"I'm sorry Sophie," said Liz, breathing heavily. "I couldn't stop her."

Sophie, too stunned by the sudden turn of events, said nothing.

"I was looking out the window," said Merry, still shaking with anger. "I felt... saw them coming. Their intentions did not appear honorable."

Thunder rumbled in the distance.

"Oh boy," said Liz.

Sophie glanced up. "Storm's coming back."

"That's no storm, Sophie," said Liz. "That's your granddaughter."

18 IRON HOUSE

The buzzer sounded, indicating the unlocking of the imposing iron gates. Logan drove slowly down the tree-lined lane. Several gardeners worked to rid the vivid green lawns of any evidence fall had arrived, riding large machines that blew each errant leaf into one of several neat piles, which dotted the premises. The gazebo gleamed beneath the afternoon sun, still adorned with late blooming roses.

Merry stared in awe at the still distant, but impressive, residence. "It's beautiful."

"It sure is, honey," said Sophie, wishing her granddaughter didn't sound as though this were the first time she'd seen the place.

After the morning's events, and after calming Merry down, Liz had called for Logan to pick them up to take them to Iron House. The mansion came into full view, and Merry drew a sharp intake of breath. Liz turned to peer over the front seat and smiled. Merry reciprocated with an uncertain upturn of her lips, and Sophie reached across the seat and took her hand. They approached the fountain, which dutifully poured arms of water into the crystal blue pool surrounding it. A mix of hydrangea, mums, and vines adorned the stone veranda, accessorizing the crisp autumn day.

"This is where I stayed before?" Merry asked.

"Yes," Sophie answered.

"It seems I would remember a place like this."

Sophie turned her head to look out the window, focusing hard not to let her disappointment show. She knew she shouldn't have expected the sight of Iron House to have immediately returned Merry to them. Nonetheless she'd hoped for such an outcome. Logan parked the sedan and opened each of their doors.

"Do I pretend I'm Merry?" she asked Sophie as they climbed the steps to the veranda.

"Honey, I'm new at this, too. You do what feels right," Sophie answered. *Who knew? Maybe pretending to be Merry might bring her back.*

Liz placed an arm around Merry, leaned her head against hers and squeezed her into a side hug. "There's no pressure for you to be anyone other than yourself."

Before they'd climbed more than three steps, the large wooden doors swung open. Fred, as elegant as ever, greeted them, breaking his facade of nonchalance to offer a nod and a smile to Sophie, an act she suspected was meant to convey both his concern about Merry and his happiness at their arrival. Sophie's neck and face heated in embarrassment. She shouldn't know so much about Fred's subtle nods and gestures.

Sophie knew she'd made the right decision to bring Merry here when she saw an honest-to-goodness smile on her face, something that had been absent ever since her rescue. She had to give credit to the girl. Not many people could've dealt with what she had and yet still be willing to find a way to make it work. But, that's what Merry had been all about. Dealing with unimaginable circumstances, turning them in her favor, saving what mattered. Fixing problems. Perhaps she could fix herself as well. A piece of her still shone through in Molly.

"It's a bit cool, but there's a fire pit going on the back deck," Liz said. "Is it OK to sit out there? Or do you want to sit inside? Are you hungry? I can have..."

Merry held up a hand to stop her friend's chatter. "It's fine. Outdoors is fine. And, yes, I'm hungry."

Liz grinned. "Great."

She led them through the house to the back veranda, a path familiar to all but Merry. The acrid smell of burning wood hit them the minute they stepped outside. Both Christine and Jonathan sat in chairs near the fire and rose as they approached. Hugs were exchanged all around.

"How are you feeling Mer...Molly?" asked Jonathan.

Merry blushed. "I'm OK. It's Jonathan, right?"

Jonathan's smile faltered. "Yeah, that's right."

"Merry, I'm Christine, Liz's mother," Christine said as she gave Merry a quick hug.

Merry bit her lip. "Did I know you, too?"

Christine nodded. "Yes, you did. And, as you were then you are now welcome in our home. You're among friends here."

Merry looked at each of the faces surrounding her. "I believe you," she said. "And, thank you."

Sophie fought the tears that threatened. "It smells delicious out here."

"I'm starving," Jonathan said, apparently also eager to lighten the moment.

Conversation was lively throughout the meal. Sophie was relieved when Merry started participating. By the time Liz offered to bring Merry to her room, she looked to be a very comfortable guest. It made leaving that much easier.

"I hate to dine and dash, but I should get back home," Sophie said. "Hopefully, the reporters have gotten bored enough to leave."

"I doubt it," Jonathan said. "I'm convinced they're directly descended from the vulture family."

Sophie laughed. "You too, huh? Thought you'd be old news by now."

"It's not as bad, but there are still a few diehards that hang out by the front gate."

"Well, hopefully, they won't migrate down here," Liz said, giving Sophie a pointed look.

Sophie grimaced. Liz hadn't been happy to find out she'd promised Alex Olivier an interview.

"If they come, we'll deal with it," Christine said. "For now, let's focus on Mer...Molly."

"I'm sorry, I know it's hard for you to call me Molly, but it's the only piece of me I remember."

Christine put an arm around her. "Oh honey, I'm the one who should be sorry. We'll all try harder, right guys? It's out of habit, not disrespect."

Merry smiled.

Sophie rose from her seat. "Molly, will you walk me out?"

"Of course," she said and they left the group trailing behind them as they reentered the house and made their way to the front door.

Sophie stepped onto the porch. "Come outside with me for a minute." Once outside, she took Merry's hands. "I want you to know I think this is the right place for you right now. That said, you always have a place in my home. If you never decide to come back, that's all right too. I don't want you ever feeling like you have to do something because of me. This is your time to heal. You need to do what's right for you, not anyone else. Understand?"

Merry hesitated a moment, then nodded. "I'm a lucky person. I know that sounds odd, but it's how I feel."

Sophie smiled. "It's not odd. That's how Merry felt, too."

Jonathan left soon after Sophie, and shortly thereafter Merry followed Liz upstairs. She tried desperately not to stare at her surroundings as though she'd never been there before, even though that was exactly how she felt. When Liz opened the door at the end of a long hallway, Merry hesitated.

"What's the matter?" Liz asked.

"I want to remember," Merry said, "but I might not."

"I know."

"I'm disappointing everyone."

"Me...olly," Liz said, with a tip of her head. "Sorry. That's ridiculous. You can't help what happened to you. You were hung! And, then, well who knows what happened?"

"I probably do, somewhere inside."

"Point is, you've experienced trauma. You're memories will come back, I'm sure of it."

"You sound like the doctor at the hospital."

Liz smiled. "I might've stolen some of his material."

"I wish I could be as sure as everyone else. And, I wish I could make it happen faster."

"It'll happen when it happens. You need to stop worrying."

Merry stepped into the room. "But, you're worried, aren't you? Sophie is too, and your mother and Jonathan. What is it, Liz?"

Liz frowned and shook her head. "I don't think it's a good time to be talking about this. You should settle in, get some rest."

"I'm fine. Look at me. The marks are nearly gone. I have no pain, and the only thing not repaired is my memory. I need to know what it is I'm missing. Won't you tell me?"

Merry held Liz's gaze. She needed to convince her she was ready for whatever it was she wanted to tell her. Even if she couldn't remember, she could pick up where she'd left off, couldn't she? Merry sat down on the sofa, and Liz did the same. "I have dreams. They're like memories. But they can't be."

"Why not?"

"In those dreams, I'm wearing old clothing. I mean, not old, but from a different time period. And I'm cooking in this giant fireplace you'd see in colonial times." Merry rubbed her forehead. "You and Sophie told me that when I showed up weeks ago, I thought I was from the colonial time period. Maybe I'm crazy. Is that what you and Sophie are hiding? That I'm a crazy person?"

Liz bit her lower lip. "You weren't crazy before, and you're not crazy now."

Merry stood up and paced. "What about what happened in your cousin's shop?"

"Everyone saw that. You didn't imagine it."

"And that... what? Makes it normal?"

The smile that had started to form on Liz's lips collapsed into a grimace. "Maybe not normal, but, well, it did happen."

Merry pressed lightly against her neck to stem the dull throb that ringed it like a too tight choker. Her head buzzed with the threat of a headache. Liz was holding back, which was nothing new. It didn't make the situation any less frustrating.

"You OK?" Liz asked.

Merry rubbed her forehead. "Headache."

"You should take your medicine."

"No, it's too strong. It'll knock me out. I don't need it anymore, an aspirin will do if you have any."

"Sure. There should be some in your bathroom." They rose at the same time.

"I'll get them," Merry said. When she came back into the room, Liz left her to rest. Merry watched the door shut behind Liz, staring at it as she listened to her friend's footsteps recede down the hallway. She wished Liz would tell her something. Anything.

Merry stepped onto the balcony and leaned against its stone railing. Brilliant red and orange hues set the horizon aflame. When the stars replaced the sunset, Merry went back inside and dropped herself into the ridiculously over-stuffed chair near the fireplace, losing herself in its comfort.

She shut her eyes and began to drift into that place where limbs settled into a delicious numbness and a mind was left to ponder and dream. Her thoughts filled with images of a man, glorious, strong, and full of light. Impossible blue eyes delved into her soul. She witnessed his laughter, his ecstasy, and his pain. His torment; he was the man who wanted to both save and hurt her.

He was the man in pain.

William.

She roused herself from the disturbing images. Though the man's plight tore at her soul, she couldn't associate any familiarity with him. Yet, she could not deny the sense of loss that pervaded.

One day, she hoped to remember that loss.
To own it.
No matter how painful.

19 SAMENESS

Corinne crossed the cavernous ballroom, her footsteps echoing upon the glittering granite floor. She stopped in front of one of the tall ballroom windows and stared into the everlasting night. There was no telling what surrounded the house. *House? Castle. Better yet, monstrosity. A spectacle, certainly.*

The pitch black revealed nothing. Until the Tall Man decided what those surroundings should be, it remained a dense black tapestry awaiting its master's brush. Corinne tapped her fingers against the window frame. As much as she appreciated the dark beauty of the Tall Man's domain, she wished to be back in the midst of the world above where she could impart her own destruction and enjoy the descent into chaos that would soon be Salem.

Salem first. Then the dark reach of the Tall Man, she at his side, would stretch beyond Salem's borders, slither south into Boston, and creep north to Maine and New Hampshire. Their reign would spread like a cancer across the Americas and further still. Corinne leaned her forehead against the diamond paned glass, closing her eyes as visions of destruction and a damned population played merrily in her mind. She sighed.

Her eye caught the reflection of the most intriguing aspect

in the room. The crystal known as Crimson defied gravity as it floated, suspended halfway between the floor and the ceiling. Vanessa stood beneath it, inspecting the prism, as its colors spiraled within its chiseled confines. At Corinne's approach, she startled like a child caught doing something wrong.

"You didn't know about it at all, did you?" Corinne asked.

Vanessa's expression turned stony. "How could I? You kept it from me."

Corinne circled the crystal, her gaze never leaving it. "Only my mother knew."

"You trusted her with that information?"

"I didn't tell her anything. She took it from me. Stole the thought right out of my head." Corinne stopped her prowling to watch the colors dance within their prison. Oh how she wished to be the one to release them.

Vanessa spoke in a soft voice. "How did you learn about it in the first place?"

"My mother stole knowledge," Corinne said. "My father gave it."

Vanessa's eyes narrowed. "I should've been made aware of this little side journey."

"Why? Because you gave yourself the title of High Priestess? Did you think that carried any weight with me?" Corinne closed the distance between them until they stood eye to eye. "I am the daughter of darkness. All the time you played witch, I was my father's daughter. You may comprehend more magic than most, but you are nothing compared to me."

To her credit, Vanessa didn't back down. She returned Corinne's challenging stare with a sturdy glare of her own. Her mouth tilted upward in one corner. "If you're so empowered, then why is it neither you nor your father can take what's inside Crimson?"

Corinne looked up at the suspended crystal, shimmering beneath the brilliant light of the many chandeliers above. It was true that neither she nor her father had been able to take the power they knew lay within the crystal—power that would enable them to make the world a much darker place. One in which they would reign. They had tried smashing it, burning it, freezing it. Neither abuse nor spell could release the colors. For now, it was nothing more than a decorative ornament.

"You forget I am now a part of this. I am your father's mistress and with that comes privilege, knowledge, and certain gifts."

Corinne sneered. "What he gives can be taken away."

"Perhaps," Vanessa said with a lift of her chin. "But Corinne, there is no reason why you and I should be at odds with one another. We yearn for the same outcome. We believe in your father and want to help him succeed. Surely, this common goal can bind us rather than set us apart."

Corinne considered Vanessa's words. She'd formed an alliance with this woman once before, accepting her role as High Priestess, assisting with her plan to go back in time, which was not a small achievement by any means. They'd worked together to bring William to her father, and in doing so had captured more light than anticipated. Still, Vanessa had inserted herself in Corinne's plans in a way she'd not foreseen. She should've known Vanessa would bargain for her own gain.

She had to admit she'd underestimated the lengths to which the woman would go to satisfy her own dark plans. She'd never imagined Vanessa would do so by sharing the Tall Man's bed. And it looked to be a permanent arrangement considering he'd given her the gift of immortality. That was a long time to fight with someone.

Even so, Corinne couldn't embrace the situation, but she could take advantage of it. She forced a small smile to her lips. "You're right, Vanessa. We both want my father to succeed. I'll do better to remember that in the future."

Vanessa offered a thin smile. "That's all I ask."

Corinne's father entered the room, joining them beneath the crystal. He placed a long-fingered hand on Vanessa's back. She shivered and stiffened at his touch.

"Any progress?" he asked. Vanessa tried to move away from him, but he grasped her arms and placed his cheek against hers, staring over her shoulder at Crimson.

"You seem... upset."

Vanessa pressed her hands against her stomach. "It seems to me that my death was more painful than necessary. But, you enjoy pain, other's pain, don't you?"

"Ah," he said, considering her words.

Vanessa turned to face him, meeting his eyes for the briefest of moments before flickering toward the floor, then to Corinne.

"Pain can strengthen the soul, isn't that right, father?" Corinne asked.

The Tall Man chuckled, his eyes glittering like rubies under the chandelier's light. "I suppose that would be true if one had a soul."

Corinne's gaze and taunting smile settled on Vanessa. "Already ungrateful for your gift, Vanessa? You could've stayed a pile of skin and bones."

If she hadn't known her so well, Corinne might have missed the nervous twitch of her lips, the nearly imperceptible widening of her eyes. But Vanessa covered her fear well and ignoring the question, met Corinne's sneer with one of her own.

"What about William?" Vanessa asked.

"The mark has nearly consumed him since father's last visit."

"I should say so," the Tall Man said with the most imperceptible upturn of the lips.

Corinne addressed her father, meeting his ruby-red eyes with her own. "How long before he finds her? They are so much stronger together. We need to ensure he holds a shred of hope."

"My darling child," the Tall Man said, "it's not hope William needs."

"It's desperation," Vanessa finished, her eyes looking quickly away in an effort to hide her own.

The Tall Man smiled.

William stirred and opened his eyes to the view of dagger-like stalactites hanging above him, poised to strike. He wished they would. Wished they'd fall from the anchor that had held them for thousands of years and snuff out his existence altogether. Though sadly, he knew that would not be the end of him. He'd still live. In the shadows. As a figure made of dust. And, his duties would be unbearable. But, they would be nothing compared to the fact that he'd be lost to Merry forever.

He could sense that other part of him lost and wandering with no purpose. His head throbbed at the effort of being in two places at once. He lay flat on the ground, pressing his head against the too-warm earth and closed his eyes. A hand landed upon him, followed by a voice. "William."

His eyes sprang open.

The earth rolled and grumbled in protest as it birthed the rest of the body that belonged to the hand holding his. A head crowned, and eyes, usually disapproving and accusing, looked at him with sorrow and apology. The earth spat the rest of his mother's body into the room and they stared at one another for a full minute before a word was said.

"You're one of his," William uttered at last.

She shook her head, scattering dirt. "I did not intend it."

"Yet, you are here."

"Aye, and so are you." She stared at his chest, at the place where the Tall Man's mark burned. "You shouldn't be here."

William laughed. "Oh, but I could not say no, could I? Not after the Tall Man marked me."

His mother looked down.

"Are you marked as well, mother?"

She shook her head. "Nay, I made my choice. I signed his book."

William was caught speechless. Whatever feelings he had for his mother, he hadn't expected she would pledge herself to the Devil.

"And, what did you get in return for signing his book?"

A sad smile sat upon her lips. "I only wanted to go home, but Vanessa stopped that from happening. I thought she was sent by him to take me home. I was a fool. In so many ways." She paused then spread her hands, indicating their surroundings. "Instead, I got this."

William watched his mother, albeit a dark, shadowy version of her, as tears spilled and carved shiny paths along her dirt-covered face. "Home. You mean another time, do you not?"

Aimee nodded. "You read my journal."

"I did. You should know Merry found me. She brought me to your time. We were safe. We had a future."

"You were not safe, William."

"Mayhap. But, it felt right, if only for a short time."

His mother's body began to slip back into the earth. She grimaced, unable to stop it.

"Mother?"

"Yes? Son?"

"I understand now."

Aimee frowned.

"Why you could not love me."

Aimee sank further, other hands coming up around her waist to bring her back to them. She looked at William with watery eyes and said in a voice no more than a whisper, "'Twas myself I could not love."

Then she was gone.

William stared at the space she'd filled only a moment before. His mother had sacrificed everything to bring him into the world, and though she'd failed on her part to be a mother to him, she'd been a protector. He couldn't condemn her knowing what he now did. For her sacrifice, she'd been made a part of this dark terrain.

He pushed himself up from the ground and wandered through his underground prison. Several tunnels annexed from the main cave. He'd investigated a few, hopeful at first to find an escape, but only finding dead ends. And the one escape he had found, had been worse than what he'd sought escape from. When faced with the choice of prison, he'd come to yearn for his cramped cell in Salem, where his fate had been dealt by human hands—as misguided as they may have been. Better that than to be at the mercy of the Devil himself.

William wondered what had become of those left behind, those who still lived a life unaware of the truth that had lined the lies of their accusers. And, what of the accusers? Though she had delivered many innocents to the courts, including Merry, Susannah Sheldon had in the end attempted to put a stop to the witch trials. Perhaps bitterness was the rightful owner of his heart, but he could not abide it. Susannah had recognized her wrongs. So should he.

He thought about Rose and Elise. He and Merry had disappeared before their nooses could satisfy their purpose. Could the sisters be safe after such an atrocity? Though he knew Elizabeth Proctor had not been hung, when he'd last seen her, she'd still been imprisoned. He recalled his last visit to her after John's hanging.

Her cell had not been much larger than his, but at least there was room for her to fully stretch her legs as she sat on the floor. She'd peered at him with big, scared eyes, her swollen mid-section pressed against the bars of her prison. He'd brought her bread and milk, which she'd drank quickly, hiding the bread in her skirts for later. He recalled her whispered words. "You have been too kind. Do not let others change you."

It had struck him an odd statement for her to make. Now it couldn't ring more true. Could the Tall Man only change him if he allowed it?

A sensation stirred within him. He connected again with his shadowy counterpart and together renewed purpose to his existence.

Corinne stared up at the Crimson crystal for the umpteenth time. No matter how hard she stared, touched, or puzzled, she couldn't break its defenses or obtain its prize. She knew Vanessa had tried and failed just as much as she. Worse, she knew her father had no more power over it than either of them.

And so it remained in its place, tantalizingly within reach, yet unreachable.

"Take it," came a voice, startling Corinne from her reverie. She'd thought she was alone in the great room, accompanied only by the never-ending night pressing against the surrounding windows. But when she looked downward towards the source of the voice, she knew different.

Her lip curled into an involuntary snarl at the sight of the half-submerged dirt-covered body that was trying to pull itself up through the floor.

"Don't waste your energy. Go back to the hole you crawled out of."

"I haven't lost it, you know. I think it's stronger even. I can hear your thoughts as though you're speaking them to me."

Corinne crouched until she was nearly eye-to-eye with the wretched figure. The one who'd tried to control her by denying her birthright from the day she was born. Katrina English, Trinka, had never been held within high regard in society, but she'd managed to fall below most. To have failed to acknowledge that her daughter, born of her mediocre flesh yet sired by the most powerful dark force in existence, held true potential—the only potential—for a power to rival that of her own father's, was at the very least ignorant. To continue to place her own banal needs above those of the Tall Man's offspring was a transgression not worthy of a simple death.

She smiled at her mother. "You think you've gained something?"

Trinka, ever the optimist, answered, "I know your desires, girl. I've heard his, as well. You're on the right path."

Corinne stood, vacillating between kicking her mother's head across the room and listening. Trinka took her hesitation as an invitation to continue speaking. "Purpose supersedes want. I know that now. It's you. You're the one who must be served."

Corinne's lips turned up in amusement. "And, you would serve me?"

Never would she have thought to hear her mother answer as she did. The years she'd spent under the woman's knowing, hateful gaze had only strengthened her animosity. Exposed and threatened at every turn, she'd lived a miserable existence as a child. Only when her father had visited her in the darkest of nights, the darkest of dreams, had she learned how to protect herself against Trinka's invasive mind. Only her father had told her of her destiny. One in which her mother would be made weak and she would be made stronger than any woman or man alive. Stronger than a god.

And, now her mother, nothing more than a disgraced corpse, nodded her head in agreement to servitude.

Corinne's words came with power behind them this time. "Crawl back into your hole, mother."

As the woman who'd given her life slipped, with much complaint, beneath the marble floor, Corinne reached up and snatched Crimson from its suspended nest. It remained as dark and secretive as the colors it held. But, this time, she had an idea.

She crossed the ballroom to one of only two doors in the room. The mahogany doors soared two stories high. As she neared, they opened inward with a practiced groan. A long hallway stood before her, rimmed with rough stone walls adorned with the wavering flames of torches, a distinct break from the shimmering opulence of the nighttime ballroom. A simple wooden door awaited her entry at the opposite end. With a decisive thud, the doors closed behind Corinne, and she made her way toward the end of the hall.

She stopped before the rough door, running her fingertips along the cracks and grooves time had driven into its surface. It took all her upper body strength to push the thick, wooden door inward. The heavy edge whispered against the dusty stone beneath it. Corinne stood on a platform, an arched entryway flickering in the glow of the torches behind her. She breathed in the dank, mustiness of the dungeon, her eyes taking on the ability to see through the darkness beyond the arch as she descended the uneven stone steps.

William let go of that other piece of him, willing his dusty self to reconvene in the world outside, to find what mattered, and perhaps to save himself in the process. The act of release lightened his limbs, and he settled into a meditative state, seeing his journey as though through a second set of eyes, until the shuffling sound of an approach filtered into his concentration.

He jumped to his feet, severing the connection, alert to the soft padding of feet on the earthen floor as they headed toward him. Corinne's blonde hair practically illuminated the cave as her visage broke through the dark. William's lip lifted into a snarl, and he strode in her direction. He would cower no more. Even though he was imprisoned, he didn't have to be a prisoner.

They paused a few feet from one another. Corinne held out an object between them, and William immediately recognized the crystal that, as a boy, he'd found and hidden in fear of what others might suspect of Merry.

"Take it," Corinne said, the command carrying an unsaid consequence.

"I will not." A damnable twitch rippled across his cheek.

She laughed at him. She laughed at his assumption that he could deny her. She laughed at his impotence and his desire. The crystal she held contained Merry's colors. If he was able to breach its walls, would it bring Merry to him?

Corinne smiled. Somehow she knew what was in his damaged heart. The thought unleashed what little physical strength was left inside him. He marched toward her. She didn't shrink from him as he'd hoped. Instead she thrust her hand out, the crystal extended toward him, enticing, taunting.

William reached for it. The witch held what might be a true connection to the only life he ever wanted. *But at what cost?* Surely, his love, his freedom, couldn't be obtained by the possession of an object that at one time had been associated with Merry. If it was that easy, he imagined she would be standing before him trapped in the Dark Man's lair. It became obvious to him what Corinne was trying to obtain. He dropped his hand to his sides, fingers twitching.

Corinne tilted her head and studied him. "You and I are not so different, William."

He glared at her, saying nothing.

"My mother despised me. Her jealousy of my blood connection with my father turned her love into little more than loyalty. Loyalty to him, not me. Your mother did much the same, didn't she? Swore to protect the child of a man she worshipped, unable to love you because of the sacrifices she had to make for such a promise."

Her words rang true, and it pained William to admit it. Corinne stepped closer, dangerously close. Her warm breath brushed his lips as she spoke.

"One born of darkness, the other born of light. You might say we're a perfect match."

With a feathery touch, she tapped his chest. William covered her hand with his, pressing it flat against his skin. The mark flared. Her dark blood spoke to him. William dropped his head back, eyes closed, relishing in the connection between them. She ran her tongue up his neck, across his lips. He grabbed her upper arms. Her fiery, red eyes stared back at him with raw hunger.

William pressed her against the stone wall. But as his lips neared hers, his roving hand found the object she clenched, and with the slightest touch of his fingertips, a calm surged through him subduing the beast within. He paused, lips poised over hers, staring into her red, demon eyes. His hands wrapped around her neck before she sensed the change in him.

William squeezed her throat. Corinne's eyes dimmed and returned to their normal color as she fought for air. Her hands came up between his arms and with an unexpected strength, she pushed outward. He lost his grip, hands flying off of her. Corinne placed her hand on his chest again. This time there was no exquisite connection, instead she twisted the darkness inside him, sending it tearing through his bones and flesh. William dropped to his knees, his body a well of pain. He lunged at her, the effort feeble and useless. Corinne retreated.

Voices rose up around them. Angry voices. William shrunk

himself up against the wall as hands poked through the ground, reaching, though this time not for him but for Corinne, stopping shy of actually touching her. She laughed as she disappeared into the shadow, leaving William the desperate, tormented figure he'd become.

20 BIRTH

Logan dropped Sophie off a few blocks from her house. She navigated the streets with short, quick steps, keeping her head down, stealing only the smallest of glances at the restoration efforts at the site of the sinkhole. No Tall Man, no corpses crawling around—only men in hard hats shouting directions to other men in hard hats.

Once inside her home, Sophie threw her purse onto the table and sank into a chair. She rubbed her head and sat for a while with her elbows on the table, head in hands. Liz had been less than happy when she'd told her about the promised interview with Alex Olivier, but they both knew it was inevitable that news of Merry's previous appearance would get out one way or another.

Lifting her head, she glimpsed the book Liz had thrown onto the kitchen table earlier. She'd only had time to say that it was a journal written by William's mother when they'd realized Merry was missing and all else had been forgotten. Sophie opened the cover. Careful lettering announced the author's name—Aimee Darling.

Sophie set the book aside to heat some water for tea. Before the kettle whistled, she'd read the first few entries.

Kerrington was Sidney's last name, and this man, Robert, was her father. Apparently, he was William's father, as well.

The whistling kettle went unnoticed for some time.

Day 1 – 17th Century, Year Unknown

I thought my pregnancy was largely unnoticeable, but when Sam invited me into his house and I accepted the tea, but refused the food, he said a woman in my condition shouldn't skip meals. His simple concern made me cry all over again. He insisted I spend the night. Since I had no idea what to do, it seemed as good an idea as any. After all, I needed a place to stay while I figured out how I was going to live out my life in the seventeenth century. Or find some way to get back home.

Sam made up a spare room for me and insisted I lie down. I sat for a long time reliving the events of the last few hours. I couldn't erase Robert's last look. His determination, even when he knew the dark would kill him, to make sure we reached our moment in time. I was exhausted with grief. I yearned for a hot shower. I'd probably never have another. Some time later, I woke up stiff from the straw bed to a darkened room. A candle had been lit on a nearby table. Sam must've come in while I slept. I hadn't known what to expect on this journey, but I hadn't expected such kindness.

I took the candle and made my way through the shadowed hallway and down the stairs to the main room. The first floor was made a bit brighter with several lit candles in the windows, but I still kept looking for a light switch. Sam was in the kitchen, and the smell of something roasting made my mouth water. In the kitchen, a small bird, maybe a partridge, roasted at the end of a spear-like tool in the hearth.

Sam told me that while I slept, he'd arranged a party of local men to travel the road I told him I'd walked to find my fictional dead husband. Needless to say, they didn't find him.

His hospitality, and the fact that he'd made an effort to find a fellow man he didn't know to afford him a proper burial—all of this told me one thing. Sam Darling was a good man.

Day 2 – July 1670

The next day was a ruder awakening than the first. Having to use the outhouse made me want to go back to the world I knew, where toilet paper existed and waste disappeared with a flush. Where I could take a shower whenever I wanted. Taking a bath was a huge event. That didn't stop Sam from lugging buckets of hot water into the house to fill a tub in the corner of the kitchen. It took him several trips to gather the water and another hour to heat it to bathing temperature. While I bathed, a local girl, Mina, washed my clothes. They were still wet when bath time was over, so Sam let me borrow a long shirt of his own. It fell to my calves.

Sam is a farmer. His main crop is corn, hence the cornfield I'd arrived in. He also did the odd carpentry job here and there. I was dying to know what year it was. Robert had estimated we'd arrive sometime between 1680 and 1690, but he was a bit off. Through a series of questions, beginning with "how long have you lived here, Sam?", I found out the year was 1670.

"And, when is the bairn is due?" he asked. I silently thanked Robert for forcing me to acquaint myself with seventeenth century vernacular or I might not of known what the heck a "bairn" was.

"October, end of," I told him.

"Ah, you've only four months to go," he answered. Which then told me what I'd suspected. It was July—in fact, July 3rd, same day as it had been in 1985. Only the year had changed. Only.

Day 3 – July 1670

I've been in Salem Village for three days now.

I'm still trying to get used to sleeping on a straw bed. Sam has been so accommodating, I can't complain. Besides, it's not like I can go to the mattress store and get a pillow-top.

Sam insists I get three square meals a day, but his cooking is atrocious and though I tried to choke down his offerings, he soon saw through my struggle. He offered to bring in Mina to prepare our meals, but I argued that it wasn't necessary. I'd left behind a successful career as a gourmet chef in the twentieth century. This was a challenge I would enjoy.

Sam wasn't convinced I was as good a cook as I claimed. I imagine my asking what each of the iron gadgets hanging from the hearth were raised his suspicions. But my corn chowder in a bread bowl changed his mind pretty quickly.

Late July, 1670

There is no end to the strangeness my life has become. As soon as I hit the six-month mark of my pregnancy, my baby's presence became much more noticeable. My stomach seemed to grow overnight. And, lately I started noticing a strange glow emanating from my belly now and then. It mostly occurs when I'm relaxed and is usually accompanied by a kick or two from William. It's like he's setting off sparks. I'm afraid Sam will notice. What if it doesn't stop? What if one day the glow appears and doesn't end? So far, it's been intermittent, lasting seconds only, but what if it lasts longer?

Robert didn't tell me this might happen. He'd mentioned nothing of it. Could it be that it didn't occur when his wife carried his daughter? He said William would be stronger. How he knew this, I don't know. But, I have no reason to question it either. I'm not the authority on baby Illuminators. Robert may have known, but he's gone forever.

Days like this, I can't get out of my own head. Grief seizes me like a violent boyfriend, holding on and shaking me until I'm bruised from the inside out.

Sam came up to check on me. He sat on the edge of my bed for an hour, silent as he held my hand while I cried. I've come to realize he's my best friend. Across both centuries.

August 1670

I've become adept at the handling of the kitchen despite its cave-man like attributes. That's unfair. It's a step above cave-man, but for all intents and purposes it may as well have been. Sam proclaims my lamb stew the best in the land. He made the mistake of saying it in front of Mina the other morning, and I had to keep myself from laughing as he tried to fix the gaffe, only making it worse. Poor Mina. Sam had only been trying to assure her we were doing well on our own so she didn't need to look after us as much. But his accolades for my cooking were perceived as judgments against her own, and she left discouraged.

"I believe I should stop talking now," Sam had said as she headed back toward her home. I laughed so hard I cried.

Then something unexpected happened.

Sam kissed me. He was a gentleman about it as only a puritan man could be. There was a silence between our laughter and the kiss that was charged with a keen awareness of one another's proximity. And, then Sam actually asked me out loud the question so obvious in his eyes. "May I kiss you?"

I surprised myself when I said yes.

It was a nice kiss, warm and safe. Not like Robert's kisses, electric and charged with sex and danger. When he was done, I asked him for another.

August 1670

What I feared would happen did. Sam saw the baby's light. I was falling asleep in my bed, when he came in. He thought I'd left the candle burning as he'd seen light coming from beneath the door. But, I'd blown the candle out minutes ago, the odor of sulphur still in the air. In the twilight moment between sleep and wakefulness I heard his gasp, heard my name called.

As my eyes opened, I saw the light too. It snapped me awake. I stared in horror at Sam. I hadn't wanted him to see this. I knew he'd worry, and I couldn't tell him why it was happening. Or could I?

He came across the room in two strides and knelt beside my bed, his hands hovering above my belly, the light casting a glow upon them.

"Dear God in Heaven," he said and made the sign of the cross. The baby kicked, causing a hiccup in the light. I started to sit up, maybe if I moved it would go away. But, Sam stilled me.

"Are you all right?" he asked. I told him I was.

"You've an angel inside you," he said. I stared at him, unable to speak. Because he was right, wasn't he? Despite Robert's arguments to the contrary, I'd also aligned the Illuminators with angels. Guardian angels. Who else guided weak humans to better decisions, watched over them in time of need? How could I argue Sam's proclamation?

I peeled the covers back, the light stronger without them, and invited Sam to sleep beside me. He hesitated only a moment, then climbed in and I fell asleep content in his arms while my child made the night glow.

September 1670

I've been here two months now. I am in a world where water is considered toxic and ale is the drink of choice.

There is no running water, electricity, indoor plumbing, or refrigeration. I worry about my child and the risks this time presents. Will he even make it into the world? Will I live?

After affecting the language of this era, it has become my own tongue. We attend church twice a week. The puritan religion brooks no forgiveness. No atonement. No matter how hard they try, everyone here is damned.

At least I have Sam.

He asked Mina to measure me for clothes. I can barely fit into the flimsy excuse for colonial garb that I wore when I arrived. Mina is a talented seamstress and I was so grateful to get some new clothes. It wasn't like going to the mall, but it was something. She's teaching me to knit as well, an activity I never imagined myself doing. But, if I want to stay warm and if I want to keep William in blankets, then I'd better get on it. Truth be told, I've gotten the hang of it pretty quickly. Maybe soon, I can make a pair of socks for Sam. I've nothing to give him in return for his kindness, but maybe I can at least do that for him.

October 1670

The leaves are falling, the days and nights growing cold. I have only weeks to go before William's birth. My due date is October 31st. Halloween, All Hallows' Eve as they call it in this time. There wouldn't be any trick-or-treating in colonial New England. No chocolate or sweets for these children—only fear and shut doors to keep the dead from entering. It made me sad to know William would never know the joy of dressing up and coming home with a heavy bag of candy. My friends used to call me the queen of chocolate. I'd give them all the sweet tarts and starbursts and jolly ranchers and keep only the chocolate. When we became teenagers, they could bribe me with chocolate to keep their secrets. I hadn't had chocolate since I'd arrived. What I wouldn't have given for a smidgen of a Milky Way.

Sam raised an eyebrow when he saw me lugging pumpkins to the front stoop. I'd asked him to get them from his Uncle Joseph who lived up the street and grew them for their seeds and soup. When I told him what I planned to do with them, he raised the other eyebrow too. But, as always, he indulged me and even helped me scoop out the seeds. When we were done, he put them on the stoop as I instructed and lit candles inside them. It reminded me of home. He couldn't understand the tears that poured down my face.

Later on, after dinner, I presented Sam with his socks. He looked at me as though I'd handed him gold instead of some haphazardly knitted socks. What happened next was completely unexpected. He looked at me and asked, "You made these for me?"

"Don't get too excited. They'll probably fall apart the first time you wear them."

Sam smiled and put the socks down on the table. Then he reached across the table and took my hand and said he had something to ask me.

Sam looked at me with those dark eyes I'd come to love and said, "I would be honored to have you be my wife, and doubly so to be a father to your child. Aimee Donovan, will you be mine?"

I thought how much my life had changed since the day

I'd met Robert, then again in ways unimaginable when I'd been sent back in time. But ever since then Sam had been there for me. Robert was dead. I could never go back. And Sam was a good man. A life with him would be a good one for any woman.

I looked at him and smiled. Then I said, "Yes."

Sam smiled and kissed my hand and promised to love me and to love William as his own. Then he said to me, "I take you to be my wife, Aimee Donovan. Do you take me to be your husband?"

I said, "I do."

And, we were man and wife.

October 1670

Today was both horrible and amazing. I was in the kitchen measuring out some barley for our soup when I heard panicked shouts coming from outside. I ran to the back door and flung it open to find George and Christopher, two of the farmhands, carrying a wounded Sam. My head couldn't wrap itself around the amount of blood I was seeing. I couldn't even tell where it was coming from until they reached the kitchen and laid Sam on the floor. George told me they had been working through the cornfield with the scythes, cutting down the spent stalks, a chore they'd done for many years now with no incident.

I immediately knelt beside Sam and pressed both my hands as hard as I could against his upper thigh. Blood pulsed through my fingers. While George continued to tell me how somehow he and Sam had crossed paths and his scythe had connected with Sam's leg, I shouted to Christopher to retrieve the heated pot of water I'd put on the hearth for our soup and to get a clean cloth from the cupboard.

To stop George's distraught babbling, I told him to go find a doctor, though I knew the nearest one lived miles away in Salem Town. Sam moaned in pain, but at least he was conscious. He'd lost a lot of blood, and I honestly didn't know how he'd survive this. The wound required stitches. He probably needed blood. I wasn't sure if either technique was even possible in this day and age. What if I lost him? He looked at me with eyes filled with apology, as though he were failing me. Sam had been my savior. I couldn't let him down. I needed him. I pushed harder against the wound and a curious thing happened.

A soft glow seeped between my hands and the laceration. Soon, instead of blood pouring from the wound, light flowed into it. I dared not lift my hands because I thought, I knew, the light was healing Sam. He looked at me, his fear replaced with the knowledge of what was happening. The bleeding stopped; the skin pulled together and grew firmer, taut. I knew when it was done and lifted my hands as Christopher returned with the kettle and cloth. I took the cloth and dipped it in the warm water, then wiped at the blood, revealing a healed thigh, nothing more to show of Sam's injury than a thin scar.

Christopher called it a miracle. I argued that the cut had not been as bad as we'd thought to which he replied that even so, there should still be a cut.

"You are a blessed man, Samuel Darling," he said.

"Aye. Indeed I am," Sam answered, looking only at me. "I have an angel on my side."

October 1670

Last night, I dreamed of William's birth. In my dream, the dead walked. There was a man, tall and white as snow, both handsome and hideous. But surely evil.

He'd come for William.

I heard him climbing the stairs, calling my name. He wanted my child. He wanted William's light. But, what he wanted would not have him.

Light obliterated the night. It came from everywhere. The houses, the ground, William. And, it sent the dark scurrying.

When I awoke, I made Sam get more pumpkins from Joseph. He cut them and lit them, cut them and lit them until they filled the front yard. When Mina asked why so many, I told her it was to ward off evil during All Hallows' Eve. I wasn't lying.

Halloween 1670

I knew when I awoke that William would be born today. October 31st was my due date, but that was no guarantee. It was no more than a gut feeling. I felt off—nervous and jittery. Terrified.

And, it wasn't only the lack of modern facilities that terrified me. More than once I found myself looking out the window as though I were expecting someone. Was this why the people of Salem Village shut themselves away in their homes on Halloween? Did the dead really walk on this day? Or did they walk for William? My panic increased when Sam came in from his morning chores, locked the door behind him and peered out the window, muttering something about not feeling right in his own skin.

By noon, my abdomen began to glow. No amount of moving would stop it. Sam sequestered me in my room. As the day wore on, I became more uncomfortable. The contractions started right after dinner. Night was coming and the glow increased in strength, until my body was like a human lamp. I began to panic. Mina had gone to summon the midwife, Hannah. If she saw my glowing belly, who knows how she'd react. Not everyone might think I harbored an angel as Sam did.

I insisted that no one but Sam be with me during the birth. A man being present during a birth was unheard of, and the thought terrified Sam. But he agreed, knowing it was the right thing to do. Sam lit the jack-o-lanterns, every last one until the lawn blazed with their light. Candles filled every window, many more in my room so as to help detract from the light coming from my child and to ward off whatever dark entity was out there.

When Mina and Hannah arrived, they fought with Sam over my choice to deliver without them. In the end, Sam won the argument and they agreed to stay until the baby came to ensure our health. Sam pulled the curtains tight against the night and stayed by me as the time between contractions grew shorter. With each contraction, I became more certain William was in danger. My recent dream filled my head with images of the tall, white stranger who had so frightened me. Had it been more than a dream? A warning? I made Sam look out the window between each contraction. Each time, he became less and less enthusiastic about pulling the curtain aside. Finally, after staring out the window for a lengthy amount of time and refusing to tell me what he saw, he told me he would look no more.

When the baby crowned, neither one of us knew what to do, but the baby seemed to. With a bit of pushing and not a little bit of screaming, William came into the world a moment before the stroke of midnight. A beautiful glowing angel.

As Sam held him, the baby's wails transformed into a blissful sleep and the light slowly left him. I wondered if Robert could see him. I wished he could. But, I couldn't deny that William's true father held him in his arms at that moment. Before Sam gave Mina the baby to clean and swaddle, he looked out the window one more time. His relief was visible. Only then would he let William out of our sight. While Hannah came into the room to deliver the placenta and ensure the bleeding was under control, Sam went outside and relit whatever pumpkins had gone dark.

Hannah stayed the night, checking on me every couple of hours. Mina stayed behind to help with the baby. I don't believe either of them wanted to go outside. That night, I slept with Sam beside me and William tucked safely in the cradle at the end of the bed.

November 1670

The next morning, I made Sam tell me what he'd seen out the window the night before. He didn't want to, but in the end, he told me everything. He told me how he'd felt off all day, even before he knew I was to give birth. He'd had an odd feeling, like something awful had happened or was going to happen. He hadn't been the only one who felt unsettled. George and Christopher had both complained of the same sensation. Christopher had even asked to leave early to go home to his wife and children. He'd asked for a pumpkin to take as he rode home in the approaching dark. I watched him galloping across the yard holding the flaming pumpkin at his side and couldn't help but think how much he resembled the headless horseman, with head fully intact, of course.

In fact, all of Salem Town was alight. Upon seeing the lit jack-o-lanterns in Sam's yard, others had gone to Joseph's farm to carve one for their own yards. I thought that may have been the way they did things in Salem Town for All Hallows' Eve, but Sam told me it had never been done. He also said, for all the talk of the dead roaming the streets on this one night of the year, no one had actually seen them.

That changed last night.

In the morning, Sam went into town for more candles, but there were none to be found. Even so, the candlemaker's wife was in high spirits, as she and her husband enjoyed their unexpected increase in income. When he came home, he told me the village was abuzz with news of last night's odd happenings. It seemed our home was not the only one the dead had come to visit.

Throughout Salem Village, people reported seeing people they knew to be dead walking the streets. These had been people of a nefarious sort, convicted criminals and unsavory characters. Some claimed to have seen the ghostly outlines of many as though an army of evil walked the streets. Others who'd carved a jack-o-lantern, but had no candle for it, said they'd lit up during the onslaught of the dead despite the fact that they held no candles. And others, who had not put the pumpkins out, soon put lit lanterns on their stoop to ward off the spirits.

It was obvious that William's light threatened all that was unholy and had brought life to the very beings he threatened. It chilled me to think my child had been in danger of losing his life even as it was being given.

I asked Sam what he'd seen the last time he'd dared a look out the window. He hesitated, then said, "'Twas beautiful at first. All those pumpkins dotting the yard, lighting the night. It was also purposeful. I am not a man who believes in superstition, but I do believe that last night, those jack-o-lanterns served a higher purpose."

"Meaning?" I asked, when he paused for too long.

Sam sighed, then resigned to the fact that he couldn't keep it from me, said, "The last time I looked, I saw them, Aimee."

"Saw who?"

He shook his head. "The dead. 'Twas a line of them stretched across the horizon as far as the eye could see. Hundreds of them. I do believe, were it not for the light those lanterns gave off, none of us would be here today. Including our little William."

He picked William up then, holding his content, sleeping form close to him and gently placed a kiss upon his head. "He's our little light, he is."

Then, he kissed him once more and handed him to me while tears streamed down my face.

When Sophie finished reading Aimee Donovan's journal, her tea was cold and barely touched. From the first word to the last, she'd been oblivious to all around her, which would explain her surprise at the fact that it was dark outside. She'd been reading for hours.

Her granddaughter had told her William had been acting strange, distant, those last couple of days before the witches had taken him back to 1692. Could he have read his mother's journal? It would certainly explain such behavior. Hell, *she* felt strange after reading it. She could only imagine how William would have reacted to discovering such family secrets.

21 AGLOW

It was hard falling asleep in a new place. Though, if Merry thought about it, every place was new to her. She stretched out on the luxurious sheets and willed sleep to come to her. But though her eyelids grew heavy, the promise of thoughtless slumber dangled out of reach. Her body zinged with energy. Her legs wouldn't stay still. A bit of exercise was in order.

Merry walked out onto the balcony, the cool October air enhancing her wakefulness. She gazed into the night, the moon, only a crescent of light, offering little illumination. She leaned across the railing, shaking her legs, trying to rid them of their restlessness. Her eyes turned toward the woods. A sudden, overwhelming urge to disappear within their world overtook her.

Without hesitation, she donned her sneakers and crept through the house, out the door to the verandah, down the steps, and onto the lawn. The crisp grass, already dewy with the night, squeaked beneath her steps. As she neared the woods, the cool night engulfed her. It was too dark to enter. She should've brought a flashlight. Yet, was it her imagination or was the ground glowing? A swath of light cut through the shedding trees, illuminating a path. She followed the shining path as it zig-zagged deeper into the woods, and relished in being outside, unseen, and free.

A gurgling brook joined the path, its soft sounds guiding her further into the woods. Merry halted where the trees thinned. A faint shimmer beckoned from the other side of the brook. She gingerly stepped upon the bare heads of protruding rocks, sucking in her breath as she made a brief slip and the cold water swallowed a foot. With haste, she made it the rest of the way across the skinny creek. Her wet sneaker squeaked as she continued on land for a few steps, coming upon a charred circle, which made a wide void in the wood. The smell of recently burnt wood permeated the air.

A faint glow pulsed beneath the ash and ruin. Merry stepped into the burnt perimeter and proceeded toward its center. She bent down, pushing aside the scorched remains, searching for the source of light. Finding none. The ground beneath the ash was barren. She flattened her hand upon the ground, the light outlining her fingers against the night. The earth vibrated beneath her hand, a faint humming sound accompanying the vibration. A brisk wind tore at the tree tops. This place felt right. In fact, it felt like an answer.

As the light faded, Merry stood, brushing her hands against her jeans. A significant event had happened on this spot. It hung about like a slowly dying flame. She would ask Liz about this place in the morning.

As she made her way back to the house, the sleep that had evaded her now overwhelmed her senses. Once in her room she kicked off her wets sneakers and dropped upon her stomach across the soft bed. Behind her closed eyelids, colors bloomed. They grew and swirled and swallowed her. When she opened her eyes again, it was early morning, the sun working diligently to disperse the night's shadows. A woman approached.

"Merry? Is that you?"

Merry sat on the cold ground, a barn nearby, horses whinnying. Her room in Iron House was no more. The woman ran to her and crouched down beside her. She reached a weathered hand out to brush the hair from Merry's face with coarse fingers.

"Merry?"

The woman was familiar. Merry squinted as though that would help her memory.

"It's Aunt Rose, darling."

"Aunt Rose?" Merry repeated, then looking at her surroundings, asked, "How did I get here?"

"Lord knows, child. I'm only glad you're alive."

Instinctively, Merry reached up to touch the fading bruise around her neck. Rose's eyes followed and she stuffed a fist in her mouth to stifle a cry. She pulled Merry to her, hugging her tight.

"I didn't know what happened to you. You disappeared. You and..." Rose pulled back and searched Merry's face. "But, where is William?"

The age-old question. Even her dreams wanted to know the answer.

"Merry?"

Rose looked worried. She called out again, but her voice sounded far away. Merry realized why as the colors swirled into her vision. Rose stumbled backwards as a curtain of color came between them, filling Merry's limbs with the weight of slumber. When her eyes opened to the sight of her room at Iron House, she had a hard time convincing herself that what she'd experienced had been a dream.

Merry sat up and stretched. Her head prickled as goose bumps riddled her scalp, arms, and legs. Her gaze landed on the large window in the sitting area, the gray dawn suffused with the soft glow of the early morning sun. A shadow fell across the window. She blinked. As the dawn grew brighter, a section of gray grew darker.

Merry eased off the bed and crept toward the window. As she neared, her eyes were drawn from the window to the floor beneath it. Her hands flew to her mouth to stifle a sharp gasp, and she froze at the sight of a man's silhouette cast upon the wood floor. She leaned in closer. The shadow moved.

Merry spun toward the window and grabbed a curtain in each hand, yanking them until they securely met in the middle and blocked out both sun and shadow.

If William had breath to hold, he would have done so at that moment, for there she was. His Merry. No, he corrected himself. Not his Merry any longer. He shouldn't even be here.

As though she sensed him, Merry looked up at the window, brows furrowed. Could she see him? But that was a foolish thought. There was nothing to see. She walked toward the window, worry on her face. William, nothing but dust and shadow, shivered and scattered himself as Merry advanced. Then she pulled the curtains shut, blocking him from her view.

She'd sensed him. And it had frightened her.

In a dank prison, dimensions away, William cried out while outside Merry's window, a shadowy figure made of dust and soul faded into the dawn.

"Goody Chalmers? Are you all right?"

Rose startled, losing her balance as she turned around and attempted to rise from her crouched position.

Susannah reached out and grabbed Rose's arm to steady her.

"What are you doing here?" Rose asked, her face wet with recently shed tears, yet hard with animosity.

Susannah had no illusions that this meeting would be easy. "I came to apologize. For Merry..."

"I suppose you'll want forgiveness, too."

Susannah shook her head. "I could not ask for it."

"Yet, being the Christian woman I am, I should be able to give it," Rose said, jaw firmly set.

"I would not presume such a boon."

Rose humpfed and started to walk away.

"Please, Goody Chalmers, if you never forgive me, I shall live deserving every bit of your loathing."

Rose hesitated, her back to Susannah.

"I only want to say I am ashamed of what I have done. I

regret my actions and the sorrow it has brought upon your home."

"I have no home," came Rose's quiet reply, and then she continued her walk to the barn, the charred remains of her house behind them.

A sob escaped Susannah. So much sadness and loss had been delivered in her name. Apologies were meaningless if the accusations and hangings continued. Others thought Merry and William's disappearance from their nooses was a sign the witch-hunts should end. It was as though the town of Salem Village were waking from a heavy slumber, finally able to see the truth of the witch trials. Susannah had been awake for a while. It was time she made certain the rest of her neighbors, but especially the magistrate, see the truth, as well.

22 ILLUMINATED

Sidney continued to put one foot in front of the other as she'd done for the last million miles. At least it felt like a million. For the last half hour, Luke had kept glancing back at her, and it was starting to annoy her. When he looked at her yet again, she asked, "What?"

Luke slowed and turned around walking backwards while talking to her. "Nothing. Just want to make sure you're doing OK. We've been walking for a while."

"And, I've been keeping up."

Luke's eyebrows pulled together in confusion. "Yeah."

Sidney stopped walking and stood, hands on hips. "Luke. What is it?"

"Probably nothing. I guess I'm surprised at how well you *are* keeping up."

He was right, thought Sidney. A day earlier she'd barely been able to hold her head up and now she had enough energy to run a marathon. Her hand went to the iron token hanging around her neck. Luke noticed.

"You think it's because of that?"

"What else could it be?"

Luke didn't answer right away. Then it dawned on Sidney.

"You think I died, don't you?"

Luke tilted his head. "You're strong."

"Wouldn't I know it? If I died? There would be some, I don't know, interval, wouldn't there?"

"Between time," Luke answered. "That's what I called it anyway."

"Tell me about it," Sidney said, picking up the pace again. Luke fell into step beside her.

"I don't remember it well. I think that might be on purpose. I remember being... nowhere for a little while. It felt good. Real good. Like being in the best dream ever. And then, the light came and woke me up."

"Well, that hasn't happened to me, so I guess I'm still alive."

They walked for another half hour in silence. That's how most of their journey had been. Fits of conversation followed by longer periods of silence. Eventually, Sidney became conscious of a crunching sound and then realized it came with each step she took. She looked down and stopped.

"What is it?" Luke asked.

Sidney's heart raced. She looked ahead, then looked behind her, and her heart sped up even more. She spun in a slow circle. "Luke."

Luke spun as well. "Shit. How did we not notice this?"

A moment ago, Sidney would have sworn she'd been walking through a field of freshly mown grass, bordered by oaks, maples, and birches, boasting their fall colors like a peacock's plumage. But, the grass beneath her feet was brown and brittle, the sky bruised and threatening. The trees lining the horizon looked as though it had been a long time since they'd produced anything but decay, their barren branches poised like arthritic fingers ready to grab the next passerby.

"We walked right into it, didn't we?" asked Sidney.

"We sure did."

Somehow, they'd not noticed the moment they'd left Nurya and entered the Tall Man's dark realm. He'd blinded them to it, had let them get in deep before revealing exactly where they were.

Luke nodded toward the horizon where the trees separated to create an entryway, their upper branches forming an arch that resembled skeletons playing London Bridge. "As much as I'd like not to, we're going to have to go through those."

"How's this going to work, Luke? I was hoping for more of a surprise approach. We may as well have rang the doorbell."

Sidney imagined the Tall Man watching them realize their mistake. She was certain he wouldn't make any blunders like this. They were targets out here in the field. She looked towards the woods and wondered what might be in there.

"It's not ideal, but..."

"But, what Luke? I thought you'd done this before."

Luke wouldn't look at her.

"Luke?" A chill trickled down her spine. "You lied, didn't you?"

Luke shook his head. "No. I've been here before."

Sidney knew then. "You didn't come this way though, did you?"

"No," Luke answered so quietly, Sidney had to strain to hear despite the dead silence that weighed the air around them.

Sidney groaned. She didn't like going into such an important journey, life-and-death important, without knowing all the details and all the possible risks, so she could plan appropriately. But, here she was, here *they* were, neither of them having a clue as to what might come next or how exactly to get where they needed to be to carry out their plan.

Sidney grabbed Luke's arm and spoke in a low, firm voice. "I'll go into the scary forest if you can tell me that you know for sure that's what we need to do. Is it, Luke?"

She almost pitied him as he turned into the unsure sixteen-year-old he'd been when he'd died. Luke nodded his head. "We need to go in there. I'm sure."

Sidney studied him for a moment. "Why?"

"It's the way I came out."

"So, there must be a way in."

"Exactly."

Sidney nodded and they continued walking toward the path

beneath those skeletal arms. "You're also going to tell me the truth about your previous visit to this place," Sidney said. "You're going to tell me everything you know. More importantly, you're going to tell me what you don't know."

Luke nodded.

"For starters, what brought you here the first time?"

Luke hesitated, then in a quiet voice replied, "Your father."

Sidney halted. "You know my father."

"Knew."

"Right. Knew." For a moment, Sidney had given life to the hope that her father still lived in the form of an Illuminator. She'd searched for him, despite being told he'd never made it to the Nurya. At sixteen, a letter had been released to her. In it her father had explained what he was and what she was. And why he'd had to leave. But she didn't know what had happened to him after he'd guided Aimee Donovan through the centuries so that their child, her brother, could be born in a time that needed light. Her father should be in Nurya, but wasn't.

"Why were you here with my father?" Sidney asked.

Luke stopped walking. "We shouldn't talk about this here."

Sidney took in their surroundings, which consisted of burnt out grass, a coming storm, and a waiting forest. "Is the grass listening?"

"Maybe."

He might be right, she thought. The truth was, she didn't care. "We can't go back. And, I need to know. Why were you here with my father?"

Luke frowned, looked at the waiting woods, and then frowned some more. When she thought he was going to ignore her and keep walking, he said, "Give me your hand."

Her automatic response was to do as he said, but she stopped her hand midway to ask why.

Luke gave her one of his up-to-no-good smiles. "I'm going to show you what you want to know."

Before she could pull her hand back, he grabbed it and pulled her close so that their arms were entwined between them.

A splash of light spilled from Luke's hand and flowed up her arm and across her skin, enveloping Sidney. She closed her eyes against its brilliance and saw the story Luke had to tell.

A familiar room, the turreted library at Iron House, filled Sidney's mind. Her father was there. He frowned, a look he rarely wore, as he stared at the iron token in his palm.

A woman of about Sidney's age entered the room. She wore the 80's well, with her hair teased into fat golden waves cascading over her shoulders. Robert shoved the token in his pocket as she approached and wrapped her arms around him. He closed his eyes as he hugged her tight. They laughed as the baby kicked. Her brother. Sidney noticed the pregnant bump in Aimee's otherwise slim mid-section.

"Robert, why don't we stay here. It's so beautiful. It's perfect," she pleaded with him. Robert smiled, laughed, and finally the look that brooked no argument - one Sidney remembered well - took over and the light-heartedness faded.

They kissed for a second time. Her father had become involved with this woman so soon after his wife's death. Of course, he'd had a purpose—to sire a male Illuminator. But by the way he looked at her, his eyes filled with longing and sadness, Sidney knew he'd truly loved her. Perhaps that's how it had been with her mother, as well. Which always brought Sidney back to the thought that she'd been a disappointment to him. She was a girl. She could become an Illuminator, but not produce any of her own. It was an odd math that only males could breed Illuminators.

Aimee cried, and as Robert wiped her tears, he opened his palm to reveal the Monopoly token. They held hands as light cloaked them and bore them to another place and time.

A familiar adversary filled Sidney's vision. Trinka, younger and swollen with child, stood on a crude stone alter. Sidney gasped when she realized the book Trinka was so intently signing was the legendary Book of Souls—The Tall Man's book. It was brimming with the names of those who had surrendered their souls to the Tall Man in exchange for their chosen gift. Trinka halted mid-stroke at the blinding appearance of Robert and Aimee.

Trinka turned as though to complete her interrupted signature, but then put the pen back in its well, wiped her bloody hand across her dress bodice and stepped toward the light at the same time that the Tall Man stepped out of the shadows. Even though it was only a vision, Sidney backed up a step. Her father shouted and pushed Aimee away, enveloping her in his light. She disappeared with a flash. Robert Kerrington forced his light against the Tall Man's darkness, making a hopeful advance until he was overcome. He fell to his knees before the Tall Man. Sidney closed her eyes against her father's vulnerability, but it did no good as the story continued to play behind her lids. Tears slid from beneath them as the Tall Man ripped her father's head from his body as though he was a loosely sewn puppet and Robert Kerrington's headless body dissolved into dirt and darkness, his light doused forever.

The vision faded, and Sidney found herself with her head on Luke's shoulder crying like the little girl she'd been when she'd learned her father had died. It was dangerous to show such weakness on the Tall Man's turf, and she forced herself to suck in the tears and raise her head. Luke's green eyes met her own.

She wiped a straggling tear from her cheek. "Why were you there?"

"Your father needed an anchor to land in the Tall Man's territory. I volunteered."

"Why?"

Luke shrugged. "I used to think that maybe if I did something great, ah, you'll think it's stupid."

"Tell me."

"It is stupid, by the way."

Sidney managed a crooked upturn at the corner of her mouth. "Go on."

"I thought I could get my body back, my real body. Get my life back if I did something..."

"Heroic?"

"Pfft. I couldn't save him. It was my job to get the woman to a trade." Luke stole a glance at Sidney.

"You took Aimee. Made sure she was safe." Sidney took his hand and gave a reassuring squeeze. "You did what Robert wanted. What needed to be done."

Luke kicked at the ground, dislodging a clump of brown grass. "I guess."

Sidney wiped the remaining tears from her cheek and nodded toward the dead forest. "So, you said you escaped through those woods. How did you get in?

Luke pursed his lips and glared at the skeletal entryway. "You're not going to like it."

23 SPROUT

Liz shut the door to Sidney's room. Her cousin's condition remained unchanged since she'd come home from the hospital. Maybe that was good considering the position she was in, caught between two worlds and half alive in each. Liz continued to hope for Sidney's recovery, especially after the incident with the Monopoly token. It must have meant something. She wished Illuminators could communicate more clearly, with words rather than light. With certainty, rather than leaving it up to interpretation.

With a sigh, she headed down the hallway to make sure Merry had survived her first night back at Iron House. As Liz passed the grand staircase, Merry rounded the corner near the library.

"Good morning," Liz said.

"Good morning," Merry answered with a wide yawn.

"Did you sleep?"

Merry frowned. "A bit. I had the oddest dream."

"What was it about?"

"A woman. She said she was my Aunt Rose. She hugged me, and I swear I could feel her arms around me."

Liz stopped at the top of the staircase and tried to ignore

her racing heart. "What else?"

"That was it. She asked me where William was, and then there were all these colors. They came between us and she disappeared."

Liz raised an eyebrow. She was certain it hadn't been Rose who'd disappeared. She started down the steps and Merry followed. "Have you had breakfast?"

"I'm not hungry."

Truth was, neither was Liz. The distractions in her head demanded more attention than her stomach. "Do you want to take a walk? Work up an appetite?"

Merry agreed, and they headed outside into a cloudy, cool morning. Liz led them toward the wood, noticing a significant amount of leaves had fallen during the night, laying a crunchy blanket beneath their feet.

"Must've been windy last night," Liz said.

Merry raised her head sharply toward the canopy. "Yes, I suppose it was. Where are we going?"

"You used to come out here when you stayed at Iron House before. I thought you might like it again."

They entered the wood and Merry stopped Liz with a hand on her arm. "Liz, there's something I need to tell you."

"Another dream?"

"No," Merry said. "I came here last night."

"Here? To the woods? In the dark?"

Merry shrugged. "It wasn't dark. Not really. There was a little bit of moonlight. I followed it."

Liz stood still, despite the surge of alarm racing through her body. "Where did you end up?"

Merry frowned. "I'm not sure. But, there'd been a fire. The ground was covered in ash and I could smell burnt wood."

Liz barely spoke above a whisper. "Then what?"

"Something strange happened. There was a light beneath the ash. I touched the ground. It was vibrating, and humming, and... Liz, are you all right?"

Without a word, Liz charged into the woods, running alongside the brook. Merry followed close behind. When Liz halted, Merry bumped into her, steadying herself by grabbing her shoulder.

"Holy shit," Liz said. They both stared across the gurgling stream at the sapling rising from the midst of ash, its small limbs already twisting into the unique shape of the monkey tree.

"That wasn't there last night," Merry said.

"No, it wasn't."

"But, how..."

Liz turned to face Merry, and before she could think to stop herself, blurted, "You did it."

Merry backed up. "What do you mean 'I did it'?"

Looking back at the mini monkey tree, Liz warred with the decision of whether or not to tell Merry what the monkey tree meant for her. How it was a gateway to another world and how she'd recovered her dormant powers from within. Dumping that kind of information on an amnesia victim seemed like a bad idea.

With one last glance at the monkey tree, Liz took Merry's arm and led her away. "I didn't mean anything by it. I guess your story made me say that, you know, how you touched the ground."

"And now there's a tree growing where I touched it. Do you think it's a coincidence?"

"Oh, yeah," Liz said. "Definitely a coincidence."

A rustling sound came from behind them, and both girl's turned around.

"Does it look bigger than it did a minute ago?" Merry asked.

Liz fought for composure. It was clear the tree had grown at least a half a foot and sprouted another misshapen limb. "Hell yeah."

Merry sat on the mossy edge of the creek, staring across its softly flowing current at the tree, which had grown at least ten feet since she'd last seen it four hours ago.

Out of the dirt, a sapling had risen, sprouted limbs,

expanded its trunk, and grown to the size of a decades-old oak tree in a matter of a day. And, it may have all started with a simple touch of her hand. As she watched, another misshapen limb pushed its way beyond a knotty bump into an arm that reached, not upward, but downward until it hit the ground as though to steady itself against its own growth. A leaf burst from the newly formed limb.

Perhaps the evidence of such an impossible wonder as this tree meant that all those other impossible experiences could also be real. Taking wobbly steps across several protruding rocks, Merry crossed the stream and stood in front of the growing tree. The freshly churned dirt released a smoky, earthy scent. A small breeze stirred the dirt behind the tree, swirling it upward into a tall column. She marveled at how the little cyclone maintained its form and stepped towards it. Whether it was the way the sun hit the column or her imagination, Merry swore the dust took on a human shape—a shape of a man to be exact. Piercing blue eyes appeared within the glittering form and bore into Merry as though desperate to make her see him. The softest of whispers fluttered upon the breeze.

"Merry."

Her heart burst with recognition. She took a tentative step forward. She heard her name again. This time louder, this time "Molly". She turned to find Jonathan on the other side of the brook. When she looked back, the man was gone and recognition faded back into the unreachable recesses of her mind. She turned back to Jonathan. "Did you see him?"

Jonathan frowned. "See who?"

"There was a man. Standing right there," she said, pointing toward the tree.

Jonathan peered around her. "Are you sure? Where did he go?"

Merry couldn't answer either question. Truth be told, she wasn't sure what she'd seen. Dust and shadows. A trick played on her injured mind. She crossed the brook and sat down to watch the tree. "What are you doing out here?"

He didn't answer, instead favoring her with a sheepish grin.

"Liz sent you, didn't she?"

"Don't be mad. She's worried about you."

Merry sighed. "I know. But, I think I'm more than capable of protecting myself."

Jonathan raised his eyebrows. "There was that little problem with the rope around your neck the last time you disappeared."

Merry couldn't suppress a small grin. "Fair enough."

Jonathan sat down beside her. "What are we looking at?"

"Watch," she said, indicating the tree with a nod of her head.

Several minutes passed before anything obvious occurred. Then with a groan of wood against wood, one of the limbs jutting out from the middle of the tree bent slightly upward and grew several inches. Jonathan jumped up.

"Holy shit! What the hell was that?" Before Merry could answer, he came to a realization. "This is that tree, isn't it? The one that burned down?"

"You tell me."

"How the hell is it doing that?" Jonathan asked. Merry patted the ground next to her and he sat down again. "Liz said there was nothing left."

They spent a few silent minutes watching the tree sprout more nubby arms and knots.

"Jonathan, you knew me before. Can you tell me something?"

Jonathan eyebrows drew into a V-shape. "Depends on what it is."

"What happened the night William disappeared?"

"Liz or Sophie didn't tell you anything?"

"No. In fact, they've told me little. All I know is that I showed up weeks ago thinking I was some dead witch from the seventeenth century. That's why the reporter is so interested." Merry picked up a dry leaf and tore at its crackly edges. "They say any more information is too much for me to handle right now, but that makes me think whatever it is, it's too horrible to speak of."

"They're only holding back out of concern for you."

Merry stared at Jonathan. "You know what it is, don't you?"

Jonathan looked at Merry's neck, and she instinctively touched her hand to the fading ring of bruises. All the other injuries and marks on her body had healed. There was no evidence that her body had held hundreds of hand-shaped bruises. No evidence of trauma except for the fading noose's mark around her neck.

"You know," she repeated.

"I do," Jonathan said. "But, I think it's better if Merry tells you."

24 FLOOD

Alex wondered what he'd stepped into. It had all started innocently enough with him driving down the driveway of one of the most prestigious estates of the North Shore, not to mention all of Massachusetts, to talk to a beautiful girl. That's where the fantasy ended.

To say Liz Thompson treated him coldly would be an understatement. He was surprised he hadn't had to scrape frost off the interior windows of the front parlor, the atmosphere in the room was so chilled. Ironically, it was Sophie Cooke who started treating him less like a pariah and more like someone who could be trusted. He supposed she'd pitied him.

The conversation had gone like this:

Alex: So, how is Molly?

Liz: Let's cut the crap, OK?

Alex: Uh, OK. Why are people saying Molly Cooke has been in Salem for the last few weeks before she was found at Gallows Hill?

Liz: Because she has been around for the last few weeks.

Alex: Would you care to expand on that?

Liz: Not really.

Alex: Let's cut the crap, OK?

And so it had gone on. Each bit of information pulled like a stubborn tooth. The whole interview was too embarrassing to show anyone.

I know about as much as when I entered through these gates, Alex thought as the gates opened inward to allow them to leave Iron House. Liz and Sophie had admitted Molly Rose Cooke had surfaced in Salem over a month ago. Except, she wasn't known as Molly then. She'd thought she was Meredith Chalmers, the witch memorialized at Burying Point Cemetery. Sophie had, by chance, met her and had come to suspect she might be her granddaughter, but it wasn't until she'd been found the second time at Gallows Hill that Sophie had known for certain they were related.

Neither Liz nor Sophie knew where she'd spent the last fifteen years or what she'd endured. All they knew, all anyone knew, was that she'd ended up at the end of a noose before being discovered on Gallows Hill.

"Why do you think she hates you so much?" Joel asked, interrupting Alex's internal fuming.

"What?"

"The Thompson girl. She hates you. Or did I imagine the stink-eye she fixed on you?"

Alex waved a dismissive hand. "She doesn't hate me."

"Sure seemed that way."

"She hates the attention, the media. It's not personal."

Joel grinned at him.

"What?" Alex asked. "It's not personal, man."

He chose to ignore Joel's knowing grin, paying exaggerated attention to the act of pulling into traffic. The story was too convenient. Alex was young, but he'd done enough investigative interviews to know when he wasn't being told the whole truth.

As if he could hear his thoughts, Joel said. "They're lying."

"They're *hiding*. They're telling some of the truth, but not all."

"Yeah. So what do we do now?"

"We—" Alex slammed on the brakes. "What the...?" As

though the sky had opened up, thousands of hailstones the size of dimes bounced off the car with tinny staccato pings. More alarming to Alex was the sudden and complete absence of sight. It was as though a white blanket had been tossed over Danvers—the fog sudden and thick. The hail grew to tennis-ball size, denting the car hood and smashing spider-web cracks into the windshield. "Shit!" Alex's shout was drowned out by the abrupt onslaught of heavy rain.

The screech of brakes behind them gave little warning for the hit that followed. The metallic grind of car against car faded into the background as Alex was whipped forward. The seatbelt halted his forward movement, the momentum of the hit throwing him back against his seat. He looked at Joel, also belted in.

"You're bleeding," Alex said. It wasn't a big wound, just a small gash along his hairline above his right eye, probably from the camera that had been sitting in his lap a moment ago. Joel raised a shaky hand to his head and pressed, wincing as he did so. The sounds of heavy rain and pelting hail invaded their space once again as though the world had been a totally silent place moments ago.

"Are we floating?" Joel asked.

Alex looked out the driver side window, coldness sweeping his body at the sight that greeted him. A minute ago, they'd been driving down a road. Now they floated in a river. The car spun, the left rear colliding with a tree. Sheets of rain pummeled them. The windshield wipers did little more than create a miniature rainstorm. Water trickled into the car, soaking their feet. Other cars floated past them, helpless against the tide. At least for the moment, they were safe from the current, as their progress was halted by the tree.

"We should get out. Try to get to higher ground," Joel said as he pulled on his door handle.

"Wait!" Alex shouted. Joel followed his gaze out the passenger window.

"Oh hell no," Joel said as another vehicle rushed towards them, clipped the backend and dislodged them from the tree.

The car moved forward like a boat leaving the dock. Panic strove to gain the upper hand on Alex's nerves. They needed help. And fast. He pushed a button on the dash. The car thumped against a metal pole. An emergency dispatch worker answered Alex's call and asked for their location.

Alex peered out the side window at the now tilting pole. "We're somewhere on Hobart Street. In Danvers."

"What's your emergency?" the voice crackled through the faltering connection.

"There's been a flash flood. We're trapped in our car," Alex answered, aware of the shakiness in his voice.

The dispatcher inquired as to how many people were in the car, whether anyone was injured, if it was still raining, to which Alex gave one syllable answers; two, no, yes! The rain grew torrential and when asked if there were downed wires, Alex exchanged a nervous glance with Joel. He hadn't thought beyond the obvious danger of the rising water. The deluge made it impossible to see more than a few feet in any direction.

"I don't think so, but I can't see much in this monsoon," Alex said. She advised them to stay in the vehicle and told them help was on the way. *It doesn't feel that way*, thought Alex as their car-boat gathered speed. They spun and bounced off other vehicles and grazed trees, fences, and mailboxes. The water was up to their calves now. Alex gripped the useless steering wheel. Joel grabbed the dash with white-knuckled hands. A jagged flash ripped through the downpour. Whether lightening or the dreaded downed wire, he didn't know.

Joel leaned forward, squinting at the windshield. "Alex?"

The naked fear in Joel's voice froze Alex. The dispatcher's instructions droned unheeded as he followed Joel's alarmed gaze.

Merry jumped up from her mossy seat on the ground as though electrified. Every nerve in her body tingled. Her skin chilled as a cloud erased the sun's warming presence in a swift coup, and the day turned dark with an impending storm.

Jonathan stood up beside her, following her gaze upward.

"I didn't know it was going to rain today."

Merry sensed more than rain in the storm clouds. She sensed *danger*. Her pulse raced, her muscles twitched. She stalked off in the direction of Iron House. Jonathan ran up behind her, turning her around with a touch on her shoulder. "Hey, what's going on? Are you all right?"

Merry looked to the sky. She replied, though how she knew the answer she gave was a mystery to her. "I'm fine, but someone else isn't."

Jonathan tilted his head, his eye and mouth curving toward one another in question.

"Something bad is happening, Jonathan. Don't ask me how I know. I just do." As soon as she said it, fat raindrops crashed through the dwindling fall canopy.

Jonathan took her elbow and steered them forward. "Let's get back to the house."

They walked, then broke into a run as the rain grew heavier, sending down a flurry of droplets and multi-colored leaves. Merry skidded a few times, Jonathan steadying her as the leafy floor grew slippery. By the time they broke the wood's edge, the rain was a blinding sheet of white. Merry held her hands up in defense against the stabbing torrent, and an odd phenomenon occurred.

Though the downpour continued, it didn't touch Merry. It was as though a shelter had been carved from the storm. Jonathan continued past her, but stopped and paced back, stepping inside the rain-free sanctuary. "What's wrong?"

Merry swept her arms around them, then poked at the wall of water surrounding them. "Don't you see this?"

Jonathan's mouth dropped open, and he too poked at the curtain of rain. It squirted as though he were trying to plug a hole in a dam. "What the...?"

The sense of danger returned ten-fold, jolting Merry's nerves, and sparking the need to move. Merry darted through the deluge. "Come on!"

They did their best to hold each other up as they made their way across the lawn and up the veranda stairs to Iron House.

Once inside, their shoes squeaked as they sped across the tiled floor to the great room. Merry grabbed onto the molding of the wide doorway to keep from sliding past it. Jonathan did the same. As they stood panting and dripping, Liz, Sophie, and Christine stared at the two of them with unadulterated surprise. Liz's mouth snapped shut first. "What happened to you two?"

Merry's gaze flew from Liz to Christine to Sophie. They were fine. More than fine. They were unaware of any potential threat. *How could they be so oblivious to the danger when it gripped her so?* Merry opened her mouth to speak, but instead sucked in her breath and pulled her shoulders together to fend off the icy cold trickling from her skull down her back. Her gaze flicked to the window. The rain had waned to a drizzle while the sense of impending doom had swelled to epic levels.

"I have to... I have..." Merry mumbled before spinning on her heel and racing down the hallway to the front door. The sounds of her friends in pursuit echoed behind her, and for a moment she snatched an image from her broken memory—angry, excited men shouting and chasing. Relentless. Another chill slinked down her spine. She turned and shouted, "Stop!"

A piercing pain erupted behind her right eye. She clamped her hand over it, panting. No one reached her. No one moved. All three women and Jonathan stood about ten feet from her, motionless, their faces filled with frustration and confusion. Merry didn't know what was wrong with them. But she did know a more pressing matter waited outside, so she bit her lip against the pain and pulled the door open, leaving her friends behind.

The rain had died down, but the wind stepped up, whipping Merry's hair into her eyes as she ran down the steps onto the pavement and down the driveway toward the iron gates.

As quick as it came, the downpour ended, dissipating into an unimpressive drizzle. But, Joel and Alex barely noticed as their attention focused on a spot about 100 feet away. The water bubbled and churned as though a large creature were rising from beneath it. The churning soon took on the form of a wave, though not any wave. A *tidal* wave.

"How is that even possible?" Joel asked.

"I don't... it's not," Alex answered. The dispatcher's voice crackled back into the car and into his consciousness. Alex shouted. "Where's the fire department? There's a freakin' tidal wave in the middle of the road!"

"Sir..." the dispatcher managed to utter before the crackling gave way to dead air.

"What do we do now?" Joel asked. Before Alex could answer, another movement caught his attention. He meant to only spare a glance, but then he couldn't look away.

"Oh, shit."

"Is she crazy?" Joel asked. He fidgeted in his seat, snatching his camera from the floor.

A middle-aged woman in a car on the opposite side of the road opened her door and pushed against the water. It acted like a rudder, slowly spinning the car to the right, its rear bumper nudging against the headlight on Alex's car. The woman deposited one jean-clad leg into the street water, which climbed up to her knee. She froze, one foot planted in the watery street, body turned to exit the car.

The woman looked in their direction, her face ashen, her lips trembling. She moved her other leg, inching toward the water. Her gaze locked on Alex's. He shook his head side to side. *Don't do it.*

A rushing noise gathered and built into an ominous rumble, dragging Alex's attention to the impossibly huge wave that had begun to roll toward them. A shrill scream yanked his focus back to the woman. Alex froze. A hand came out of the water and wrapped around her calf, then another emerged. And another. They tugged at her. She gripped the steering wheel to anchor herself, but slipped forward nonetheless. The woman pleaded. "Ayudame!"

"Joel," Alex said in a strangled whisper. "Point your camera over here."

"I'm getting the tidal wave," Joel answered.

More hands rose out of the water. Alex thought he could see dark shapes lurking beneath the surface. Soon hands covered the woman's entire leg. She slid to the edge of her seat and fumbled for the seatbelt, trying to secure herself inside the car. Her awkward position only put her in further danger of falling out. Alex cracked his door open, Joel swinging the camera toward him at the sound.

"What the hell are you doing?" Joel asked in a shrill voice. "Dispatch said to stay in the car."

What was he doing? Alex wondered. If he stepped out in the water, the hands would get him too.

"Por favor..." the woman said with pleading eyes. Alex slammed the door shut and pressed the button to lower his window. Her car had slid closer to theirs. Maybe if he could lean out, he could reach her, pull her into their car or onto the roof, anything to get her away from those hands. The window slid down halfway, stopped, then fell another inch, and stopped again. The dash lights flickered, dimmed, and shut down altogether.

"Shit," Alex said as he watched the hands clamber over one another like a game he'd played as a child. Six to ten hands vied for a piece of the woman. He pushed against the window. Nothing. He pressed his hands against the top of the window. It gave about a half an inch.

"Give me your camera," Alex said to Joel.

"What? No..." Joel argued, then stopped, eyes widening at the sight of the corpse-like hands climbing over the woman. He handed his camera to Alex, who proceeded to butt the back of it against the window. A chunk of glass broke out, then another. He smashed down on the sill to get rid of the jagged remains, then pulled his jacket off and laid it across the window.

The woman grimaced in pain as the tugging hands grew more insistent, their grip tighter. She held onto the doorframe, her other leg still pressed against the floor. Alex placed his hands carefully on the windowsill and hoisted his body through the window. The woman stretched one arm out to him. He did the same. Several inches still separated them.

The dull roar of rushing water turned both their heads. Alex's heart jerked inside his chest. The tidal wave crawled toward them at a slow, controlled, almost taunting pace. Other stranded motorists had abandoned their cars and were attempting to outrun the wave.

"No! No!" Alex shouted as a young man was pulled under the water by many groping hands.

Another man, older and burly, stopped to fight off the hands clambering up his legs. This time a head and torso followed a set of hands out of the water. The woman beside him screamed, and Alex's stomach dropped at the sight of the decaying and grotesque being. It attached itself to its victim, wrapping its arms around the man's waist. Alex snapped his attention back to the woman. She pushed herself out of the car, one leg balanced on the doorstep while she leaned forward. They touched fingertips. Alex leaned out further, dangerously top heavy on the window frame. Joel grabbed onto his legs, and he stretched further, managing to grab her wrist.

More screams erupted around them as people succumbed to either the corpse hands or the tidal wave. Alex stayed focused on the woman. He grasped her other hand, and they made a human bridge between their cars. Alex stared into her large brown eyes, wide with fear. "I'm going pull you to my car. Get on the roof, OK?"

"Si, yes" she answered with a quick nod of her head. Her eyes grew wider. Another set of hands latched onto the other leg. "Prisa!"

With Joel's anchoring, Alex managed to leverage himself a bit out the window, and he wrapped his arms around her upper back. She flung her arms around him, her grip surprisingly tight. Alex hauled her toward him.

The stench of fear rode on the wind and assaulted Merry. Wickedness loomed ahead. A surge of energy ignited her bones, and she ran faster. At some point, she became aware of the splashing sounds her feet made against the pavement, which was fast disappearing beneath a layer of water. The front yard of the Iron House estate now resembled a lake; water covered the land as far as she could see.

She sighted the barred gates of Iron House and slowed until she stood ankle deep in freezing water. *What was she doing?* The icy stream trickling from the base of her skull down her back remained. The sense of impending destruction held fast. An urgency without direction consumed her. She was so lost.

So lost.

A rustling wind pressed at her back, brushed her bare arms. Merry sucked in her breath. Flecks of golden dust shimmered and swirled, forming a cocoon around her. She closed her eyes, her muscles calmed. Peace flooded her veins, pushed back the fear, and strengthened her resolve. Returned her purpose. Her eyelids fluttered open. The golden dust spun around her still form, then exploded outward, sparkling against the bruised sky until it faded from sight.

A hand landed on Merry's arm, and she startled.

"Molly." Liz said between breaths. "Where are you going?"

Merry looked into Liz's face, lined with concern. The storm renewed itself, casting out fat raindrops from swollen clouds. "Can you open the gate?"

Liz must've seen something in her eyes, because she didn't ask any more questions. She pulled her phone from her pants pocket and in a moment was asking her mother to open the gate. "I'm coming with you."

"There's danger..."

"I'm coming," Liz said with finality. The creak of iron against iron greeted them as they ran with increasing difficulty through the deepening water. Merry spared a look behind her, but didn't break stride. Liz didn't either. A shriek followed by a loud splash came from behind her, and Merry stopped and turned to find Liz on her hands and knees. Merry walked toward her as Liz pushed herself up, then caught her as she lost her balance and fell forward once again.

"My foot is caught," Liz said, holding onto Merry's arms.

They looked down for the source at the same time. Liz screamed first. Merry froze at the sight of a decaying hand latched around Liz's ankle. When Liz tugged her foot upward, the hand pulled back down.

Merry's mind circled around to one of the few memories she had. One she'd rather forget, but in light of the current situation, it appeared she was meant to experience again. She tugged Liz forward, but the hand held tight. Another corpse-like hand joined the first, then another. It took everything Merry had not to run away.

"Get off, get off me!" Liz shouted, stomping her free foot on the hands rising in the water.

Merry looked toward the open gate. A deserted car floated past sideways. Not-so-distant screams pierced the beat of the pelting rain. She extricated herself from Liz's grip and stepped away from her.

"Help me!" Liz screamed.

Merry's blood thrummed; her thoughts coalesced. The day took on a green tint, at first the color was weak against the gray-black of the storm, then strengthened to a brilliant hue. When she realized it was coming from her own skin, she stepped backward as if to get away from the color, but it moved with her. Instinctively, she placed her palms upon the surface of the water. Green spiraled off her body and flowed from her skin. The color blossomed outward like emerald fire, rippling along the surface, diving beneath, and saturating every inch.

The rain stopped. Clouds disbursed. The hands fell from Liz's leg and dissolved beneath the water's surface. Liz stumbled backward several paces, her open-mouthed stare fixated on Merry as color continued to surge from her. The earth acted like a thirsty sponge, absorbing the flood until not a drop of moisture remained. The newly revealed sun dispelled the final leftover swirls of green.

Merry raised her rather ordinary-looking hands up to her face, inspecting them before her legs gave out, and she dropped to the dry pavement. Liz crouched next to her, placing a tentative hand on her shoulder. Merry looked into Liz's eyes, which were filled with worry, relief, concern, and pride.

"What's happening to me?" Merry asked in a small voice.

Liz smoothed the hair off her face, and pulled Merry into a hug. "Thank you."

Merry's limbs were heavy and unresponsive.

Liz pulled back. "I'm going to call my mom. She'll help you back to the house."

"You're leaving?"

Liz nodded toward the open gates. "I need to see if anyone out there is hurt."

"I'll come..."

"No, Molly," Liz said, giving her a crooked smile. "You're one of the hurt ones."

Liz's gaze dipped to Merry's neck. Fresh worry entered her eyes. Merry reached tentative fingers to her skin, wincing at her own touch. "How?"

"I don't know, but your neck looks almost as bad as it did a couple of weeks ago."

Liz called her mother and assured Merry someone would come to aid her in a few minutes. Then, with one last quick hug, Liz jogged toward the gates, leaving Merry alone with her confused thoughts and unanswered questions.

The look of relief on the woman's face was short-lived.

As soon as she lifted her unanchored leg toward Alex's car window frame, a corpse shot out of the water and latched its gray, rotting arms around her thigh. Alex nearly dropped her. They screamed together. His terrified gaze locked onto the demon's maniacal face. The creature regarded him with sunken, leering eyes and a black-toothed grin.

"Jesus Christ," Joel said behind him. He tightened his grip on Alex's legs and pulled. The tug-of-war lasted mere moments. A flash of green light tore across the scene like a nuclear blast. The woman fell to the pavement, which was suddenly bone-dry. Alex nearly fell on his head as she dragged him down with her. Joel helped pull him back into the car, and Alex allowed himself to lean his head back against the headrest, calming his breathing for a few seconds. Then he opened the car door and stepped out into what was now a sunny afternoon. Aside from the battered cars haphazardly strewn along the road and on lawns, there was no sign that a flash flood had been there, let alone a tidal wave. Not a remnant of water remained.

Alex sank down next to the woman. "Are you all right?"

Tears rolled down her face as she answered, "Si. I think so."

Alex nodded toward her leg. "Is your leg OK?"

The woman reached down and rolled up her pant leg. Dark hand-shaped bruises covered her calf and shin. The woman gasped. She reached to touch her injured leg, but Alex gently took her hand. "Help is coming. Sit still until they get here, OK?"

The woman nodded. She placed her hand over his. "What is your name?"

"Alex."

"I'm Linda," she said as she pulled him into a tight hug. "Gracias. Thank you."

After reminding her to say still, Alex stood and surveyed the area. People were getting out of their cars, inspecting the damage, and wondering out loud what the heck had happened. A woman stood about ten feet away staring at him. Liz Thompson.

Alex jogged to her. "What are you doing here?"

"I came to help."

"Always rescuing people, huh?" he said, immediately regretting his words.

Liz glared. "I see you're unaffected."

Alex held his hands up. "I'm sorry. I... that was stupid of me. It's good of you to try to help."

One corner of Liz's mouth lifted.

"In my defense, I did just go through a traumatic situation." Her mouth lifted a little more. "What happened here?"

Alex ran a hand through his hair. "Damned if I know. We

were caught in a flood. They're not kidding when they call it a flash flood. Happened in no time. Then there was a tidal wave."

"A tidal wave?" Liz asked with an incredulous tone.

He relayed the events of the last twenty minutes, ending with the creature leaping out of the water moments before a strange green light blasted everything away. He showed her the hand-shaped bruises on Linda's leg. Then Joel, who'd been walking through the scene with his camera, shouted for them to join him near a gathering crowd. He met them halfway.

"Looks like two dead," Joel said. Liz's hand flew to her mouth.

Alex placed a tentative hand on her shoulder. "You don't have to look."

Liz pushed in front of him. A large man lay face down on the pavement. Another younger man lay a few feet away. Both bodies were in an advanced state of decay as though they'd been dead in the water for weeks rather than minutes. A hand-shaped bruise tattooed the younger man's face like a permanent slap.

An ambulance and a fire truck pulled up, followed by several police cars. Alex made sure an EMT stopped to help Linda. He reached for Liz's hand to pull her away from the scene. She startled and snatched her hand away.

"Sorry, didn't mean to scare you," Alex said.

"You didn't," she said like a defensive teenager.

"Joel and I are going to hang around. The studio is sending a van."

"You can handle a news story? After what you went through?"

Alex shrugged. "I won't lie. A shower and a warm bed sounds a lot better, but the show must go on."

"Show. Dead people."

"That's not what I meant. I..."

"I know what you meant," Liz said, as she started walking back through the crowd, away from the dead. "Forgive me for not sticking around for the entertainment. I'm going home."

"Liz, wait," Alex said, jogging after her. She slowed her pace but didn't stop walking. "I was hoping I could ask you something. Those bruises—the man who found Merry said she had the same kind. Is that true?"

Liz's skin flushed. Her hands clenched against her thighs. Before Alex could explain that he only wanted to help, she turned her back on him and walked away.

25 GHOST

A dim light broke the night, and Susannah slowed as she neared the homestead of Mary Herrick. Candles still burned in the windows at this late hour. She crept as silently as possible towards the home, mindful of the hound that lived in the barn. Once she reached the broad side of the house, she settled beneath a window. Her warm breath plumed into the cool night air. After several minutes, the space above her grew a bit darker as the candle in the window was extinguished.

Susannah rose into a crouch beneath the window. The moonlight played between the clouds, casting shifting shadows. It was a ripe evening for a haunting. She dared a peek through the window. Goody Herrick carried a candle as she walked towards the stairs. Susannah guessed it would take her several minutes to make it upstairs to her bedchamber, given the slowness of her gate. She glanced up to the sky. The moon needed to cooperate with her in order for her to pull off what she hoped would be a deterrent to the witch trials.

She pulled the delicate muslin from around her shoulder to cover her head. If her mother knew she'd taken the large square of sheer cloth meant for her summer shift, she'd be less than forgiving. Susannah didn't care if she had to wear wool all summer, as long as her plan worked. Bent in half, she darted several yards from the house and dropped to the cold ground, her eyes on the second-story window.

Then, she waited.

Soon, the flickering approach of the candle appeared in the window. As Mary settled it onto the sill, Susannah popped her head up, the sudden movement snapping Mary's attention in Susannah's direction. Susannah rose, the muslin floating about her in the slight breeze, moonlight shimmered upon the fabric. She turned in a small circle, the fabric fanning out around her. Goody Herrick threw the window open and called out in a tremulous voice. "Who is out there?"

Susannah startled the silent night with an eerie moan. "I am the ghost of Mary Easty."

"What do ye want with me? I've done ye no harm. Go away! Leave me!"

Susannah screamed. Goody Herrick stopped her chatter and froze like a statue framed in her window, her gaze locked on the ghostly apparition come to give warning.

Susannah spoke with an airy, yet strong, voice. "Salem Town has succumbed to lies. There are no witches in Salem Village."

"Why do ye tell me this?"

"You must tell the others before all their souls are damned to Hell."

Goody Herrick shook her head and backed away from the window. "Promise me you will tell the others! Or your soul will be condemned as well, Mary Herrick!"

Mary rushed back to the window, her hands clamped upon the sill. Susannah repeated her demands and after a few moments, received the answer she wanted—a stuttered, terrified agreement to warn all in Salem Village that the witches were no more. Nay, that they had never been. Satisfied, Susannah began to back away, across the field. The moonlight disappeared, shrouding her in darkness.

The next day, Mary Herrick described how the ghost of Mary Easty had visited her to give warning before disappearing right before her eyes.

26 TRAPPED

Merry shivered within the blanket's soft, warm embrace. She pulled it tighter, unable to quell the tremors racking her body, and risked a glance at her onlookers, Sophie and Christine, who sat nearby watching her with unshielded concern. Frederick brought her tea. She'd thanked him even though the thought of drinking or eating made her stomach lurch. She understood the desire to feel useful. *Hadn't that need driven her out into the storm?*

"We should call the doctor," Sophie said.

"N...n...no," Merry said through chattering teeth.

"He can come to the house. You won't have to go anywhere," Christine said.

"I... don't...n...need..."

"But your neck," Sophie said, her hand going to the base of her own neck.

When she'd returned to the house, Merry had first changed into dry clothes. As she peeled off her wet shirt in the bathroom and tossed it in the tub, she caught sight of her disheveled state the mirror. She approached slowly, lifting her chin to better view the mottled bruises encasing her neck. Earlier in the day, they'd been all but gone. Now they stained her skin as though freshly planted.

"Does it hurt?" Sophie asked.

Merry's hand instinctively went to her throat, but she stopped just short of touching the injured area. "A bit," she answered, recalling the sharp pain her earlier touch had caused.

"I don't understand. The bruises were basically gone," Sophie said. "Have the others come back too? The handprints."

"No. Only this."

Frederick poured Merry a cup of tea. He winked as he handed it to her, and it did more to warm her soul than the first sip of the hot liquid. She blew into the cup, sending ripples across the tea's surface. "Where's Jonathan?"

"He's with Sidney," Christine answered. "He became nervous after you left. He wanted to make sure she was all right."

It didn't surprise Merry that Jonathan worried Sidney could be harmed as she lay unconscious upstairs. So much oddness surrounded Merry. So much oddness *was* her.

Christine took her phone out for the tenth time. "Still no word from Liz." She paced as she pressed the screen and held it to her ear waiting for her daughter to answer.

Merry wondered if Liz was all right, sensed that she was, and then wondered how she could know such a thing. "I shouldn't have let her go by herself."

"Well, you were in no position to do otherwise," Sophie said. She moved from her seat to sit beside Merry and rub her back. The shivering had taken to intermittent fits of shaking, and Sophie's touch helped to reduce them further.

Christine lowered the phone, brows furrowed and lips pressed together.

Merry stood, her body aching with the effort. "If you don't mind, I'd like to talk to Jonathan."

"You should rest..." Sophie said.

"I will. After." Merry smiled at her grandmother. Sophie squeezed her hand, and she and Christine escorted her to Sidney's room before heading back downstairs to wait for Liz.

Merry tapped her knuckles lightly against Sidney's door before opening it. She found Jonathan sitting in the chair next to the bed, his head tilted back, staring at the ceiling. He stood when Merry entered.

"Molly."

Merry closed the door behind her. "I hope I'm not intruding."

Jonathan hugged her. "You're all right." Merry nodded her head against his shoulder, then stepped back.

"I'm sorry. I should've gone outside with you," he said, his gaze sliding back to Sidney. "I just needed to see her. I wanted to make sure."

"Make sure of what?"

His mouth opened, but no words followed as his gaze landed on Merry's neck. He took her by the arms and steered her toward the chair he'd recently occupied. "You're hurt. What happened out there?"

Merry fidgeted. It was a good question. She wished she knew the answer. She did know, however, that she couldn't tell Jonathan about the hands that had emerged from the water or about the colors that came out of her. She looked up at him. "The front of the property and the street was flooded. Cars were floating by like boats."

Jonathan lifted an eyebrow. "How did your neck..."

"It finally stopped raining. The water drained away." Merry avoided Jonathan's gaze and studied Sidney's still form. Her thick, long hair fanned out upon the pillow, her face smooth and calm as she breathed slow, steady breaths. "What did you think would happen to her?"

Jonathan ran a hand through his hair. "I don't know. With all the weird stuff happening, I... I just don't know."

Merry approached the bed. She was supposed to have known Sidney before. Yet this woman was another blank spot in her mind. Another face forgotten. Sidney appeared healthier than Merry expected. Her skin, though pale, glowed despite the lack of light in the room. Pink bloomed upon each of her cheeks, and glossy white-blonde curls surrounded her face and draped across her shoulders. "What is wrong with her exactly?"

"Did Liz tell you anything?"

"She said her cousin had been injured, and she was in a coma." Merry moved closer. "She looks like she's sleeping."

Merry reached a hand towards Sidney, but Jonathan snatched it away before she could touch her. They locked gazes, Merry's questioning, and his filled with chagrin. Jonathan barely uttered an "uh" when the door opened and Liz, dripping wet, entered.

"What are you guys doing in here?" she asked.

Merry dismissed Jonathan's strange attempt to keep her from touching Sidney and hugged Liz. Her chilled, wet skin started Merry's shivering all over again. "Jonathan was worried about Sidney. But you're fine? Nothing... else out there?"

"I'm fine," Liz answered. "Is Sidney all right?"

"Yeah, sure. I mean..." Jonathan answered, indicating her still form.

Liz brows formed a concentrated V. "What did you think would happen?"

"I don't know. With all that's going on... I mean, the way Molly reacted to the storm. I thought maybe Sidney was in danger."

Liz folded her arms, shivering. She spared a glance in Merry's direction. "She's in another place."

"And, she's dying in both. She's not safe, Liz." Jonathan also glanced at Merry as though gauging her reaction. For Merry's part, she didn't know what they were talking about.

"Don't say it. Don't even think it."

Jonathan threw his hands up and shook them at the ceiling. "I can't help it. It doesn't do us or Sidney any good to pretend it can't happen."

"Well, it does me good to assume it hasn't."

Jonathan sighed.

A low, dull ache started to take hold of Merry's head. "Liz, what did you see outside? Was anyone hurt?"

Liz took a deep breath, her voice cracking as she answered. "Two people died."

"No!" Merry's hands flew to her mouth.

"Died? How?" Jonathan asked.

Liz recounted how she'd found Alex and his cameraman around the corner from the house. She told them about the flooding and the tidal wave. "Two men left their cars. They drowned. They drowned in the street."

"Jesus, how deep was the water?" Jonathan asked.

"It wasn't just the water..."

Merry finished Liz's sentence in a hushed voice. "It's what was in the water."

Merry stared into the fire. Flames leapt and wood crackled, warming her skin and senses. She glanced at Liz, then back to the fire. After taking a hot bath, Liz had joined her on the plush sofa in front of the fireplace. They'd sat in silence for the past few minutes.

"Molly," Liz started.

"There's so much I don't know," Merry said as she watched the spiraling flames wind themselves around fat logs of wood. "I'm not even sure I want to know. None of this makes sense. My head aches with all of it. But, it doesn't matter. I don't have a choice. I have to know. I can't *not* know."

"Molly."

"Don't you see? Whether or not you or Sophie or Jonathan tells me whatever secrets you're hiding, those secrets are going to find me."

Liz pursed her lips and stared into the flames.

"So, I'll tell you one of my secrets." Liz turned her gaze towards her. "You saw what I did out there. The color that came from me? Came out of me? It happened before."

"When?" Liz asked.

"At the hospital."

Liz tilted her head back in thought. "The hospital. The day the glass blew out?" Merry nodded, then Liz said, "The day the sinkhole appeared."

"Yes. I knew something was wrong. I saw the sinkhole in my mind. I saw a man, an evil man, and I grew angry. I wanted to hurt him for what he was doing. But, also for what he'd done, and I'm not even sure what that was. It didn't matter, though. The glass blew out, color flew out of my hands, and I stopped him. Exactly like I stopped those corpses today. After the hospital, I thought whatever this is, whatever these colors are, I don't want them. But after what I saw today, I think I *need* the colors."

Liz chewed on her finger, not making eye contact with Merry.

"What happened out there, Liz? Those hands in the water—they're the corpse hands from my dreams. But, I didn't dream them, did I?"

"Probably not," Liz answered with a miserable look on her face.

Merry sank back against the sofa with a sigh. "And you still won't tell me why these events are happening."

"Well, I don't know why they're happening either."

"But you know what's behind them, don't you? You know what led to this."

Liz pulled her knees to her chest and propped her chin upon them. She stared at the hearth, ignoring Merry's imploring gaze. Merry rose and paced the length of the room, bouncing on her heels every few steps. Cooped up. That's how she felt. Hidden away, kept like Rapunzel in her tower.

That was unfair.

Today, Liz gave an interview she didn't want to give. All for her. The Thompson family had taken her in, not once, but twice. She told herself they were trying to help. They didn't want to keep her from learning who she was. On the contrary, they desperately wanted her to remember.

Why then, did she feel trapped? Her pacing brought her to the window. She gazed out upon the manicured grounds, disappearing into dusk. Merry picked up the fairy cross stone from her night table and sat down on the cushioned window seat, her legs shaking as if in protest to her stillness. She warmed Liz's gift in her hands, rubbing her thumb over the pronounced cross. Up, down, then left to right.

The buzzing in her veins weakened to an acceptable hum. She no longer wanted to jump out of her skin. Merry leaned back against the window, its cool glass tempering the dull throbbing in her head, and continued to rub the stone.

"Liz?"

"Yeah?"

"With all that happened, you haven't told me how the interview went."

Liz joined her on the window seat. She picked at a microscopic thread at the seam of the cushion. "Not great." She glanced at Merry and grimaced. "I was sort of a bitch."

Merry grinned.

"I didn't tell him much. He knows you were here before, and that you thought you were Merry Chalmers." Liz stared at her, and Merry knew she was hoping that by saying the name, Merry Chalmers, that she would remember *being* Merry Chalmers. "Anyway, it turned into a pissing contest."

"And you got mad at him again," Merry said. "For asking more questions when you found him at the flood site."

"Yeah, Alex probably didn't deserve that. I mean, I'd be asking the same questions. Heck, I *am* asking the same questions. He saved a woman, which was pretty decent of him."

Merry turned her head toward the window so Liz wouldn't see her smile.

"I know you're smiling, Molly. I don't have to see your face to know that."

Still smiling, Merry said, "You called him by his first name. You always call him by his full name. He must've been *really* decent for you to forget his last name."

"Do you want to hear about the interview or not?"

"There's more to tell? Seemed to end fairly quickly."

Liz admitted she hadn't told him much beyond that Merry had been in Salem for a few weeks before she disappeared and was found again. "You're as mysterious as ever."

Merry shook her head. "I don't want to be mysterious. And I wouldn't be if you told me more about what happened before

I was hanged."

Liz cringed. "I hate it when you say that."

"I'm tired of being the only one who doesn't know what's going on."

"I know."

"Liz, it doesn't have to be like this. You can tell me everything. You can..." Merry paused as Liz began to shake her head. Her calm receded, frustration edging its way back to the forefront of emotions. Frustration, sadness, and anger clashed and spurred a deep need for the truth. Merry turned her face toward the window, her angry reflection greeting her. "Something's happening, growing, becoming... I don't know what, but it's bad. I can feel it. I can feel it like a cold wind or a burning flame. It's unpleasant and wrong and I need to do something about it. I *must*."

"Do what? About what?"

"I don't know! I need you to tell me what happened, Liz. Then, maybe I'll know what's coming. What I need to do."

"But, I don't know everything that happened. You left. I don't know what happened while you were gone. I only know I waited here worrying you were dead and then you were found, and I knew I was right to worry."

"Of course, there are incidents I'll only know by remembering. But, everyone else is keeping secrets about what happened before I disappeared. Sophie won't even tell me about my father. My own father! I can't take much more. I'm coming out of my skin, Liz."

"Calm down, Merry," Liz said, with a nervous glance out the window.

"And, you keep doing that!"

"What?"

"You keep looking out the window like you're expecting Armageddon."

Liz hugged her knees to her chest and said nothing.

William's dusty shadow settled on the balcony to watch Merry sleep. She didn't know who she was. She didn't know who he was or what they had been. What they might be again. Yet, when he'd wrapped himself around her during the storm, that buried part of her had responded to him, and he'd sensed her true being.

Despite the darkness inside him, he dared to hope that maybe there *was* a way to reclaim the life that had been his. Theirs. So he watched Merry sleep and hoped her dreams were the same as his.

He was with her again. The blonde, blue-eyed man who stirred a need so raw, that she couldn't understand how she could survive without him. He was her heart and her breath. Her life.

He lay beside her. His kisses penetrated her soul. His touch, his touch... Merry woke, a few tears dampening her pillow. Weak threads of light penetrated the leftover night as the sun pushed itself up over the horizon. Merry lay, watching the threads grow into wide arms as morning gained the day.

A low rumbling snore startled her. She sat up to find Liz curled into a tight ball at the other end of the sofa. Though they'd argued, Liz had asked to stay in Merry's room for the night. Haunted by the morbid images from the day's events, she didn't want to be alone. Despite her frustration at Liz's refusal to tell her about her past, Merry agreed, sharing the same need for company. Liz anchored her as much as an untethered ship could be anchored.

The fire had dwindled down to glowing embers. Keeping her movements small so as not to wake Liz, Merry rose from the sofa and picked up the poker on the hearth. The heft of the tool in her hands sent a skip in her heartbeat. She stared at the long, cold piece of iron as though it were more important than a mere object with which to stoke a fire. A sense of recognition nagged at her mind. Of course she must have used such a tool before. That was all this was, wasn't it?

She looked to the balcony as though for an answer. The sunlight was stronger on that side of the room, distinct rays of light pouring through the glass of the french doors, pooling into natural spotlights upon the wood floor. Dust shimmered in the sunlight. The poker slipped from Merry's hand and landed upon the hearth with a clatter. Liz stirred on the sofa.

Merry crossed the room and pulled the balcony doors open. Dust swirled and dipped as cool October air blew into the room. The dust swelled, then settled, glimmering. Waiting. Merry pressed a shaking hand into a sunbeam, and the dust breathed.

The glimmering particles swelled and merged into what appeared to be the shape of a hand. The sunlight blinded Merry for a moment as she stepped forward and for the brief moment following the sun's glare, she thought she saw the nebulous form of a man. Her stomach fluttered; her mouth went dry. The sunbeam wavered as the shimmering hand aligned with her own. She fought the urge to pull back, but then the dust hand pressed against hers with a feathery touch. Her hand glowed with the connection. Her breath came in shallow gasps.

"Merry?" Liz's groggy voice came from far away.

The dust fingers weaved between her own and a tranquility flowed from hand to heart, settling her pounding heartbeat, calming her erratic breathing. Images flooded her mind.

Her mother's frightened face... a bouquet of yellow daisies on a freshly turned grave... a boy... a friend.

"Merry!" Liz's panicked voice sounded in her ear.

Merry dropped her hand. Dust and light dissolved, leaving nothing but patchy memories and confusion behind.

27 MEMORY

With vivid recollection, as though she were back in that very moment, Merry was four, swinging through the sweet summer air, the ocean's scent from the nearby harbor filling each breath. She pumped her legs, going higher and higher, and there was her mother, her young, beautiful mother. Happiness overwhelmed her and with that came the colors. They were beautiful.

"Mama!" she called out. "Catch me!"

Her mother ran toward her, the smile disappearing from her face as Merry let go of the swing's chains. She flew from the seat, airborne through the colors. Her mother kept coming, was nearly there. Behind her, Merry caught sight of her father coming out the back door. In the split second before her mother's arms wrapped around her, he shouted, "Molly!"

Then, all she knew disappeared.

And, a new world opened up around them.

Her mother cried and begged her to make the rainbows. To take them home. But she couldn't no matter how hard she tried.

Soft footsteps sounded on the dusty road. Summer took Merry into the cover of some nearby cornstalks.

"Shhh," Summer said to Merry, holding a finger in front of her lips.

They watched as a woman came into view. She glanced in their direction and stopped to peer into the cornstalks. "Hello? Who's in there?"

Silence.

"I can see you, whether you answer or not."

Summer pulled Merry's arms from her neck and in a quiet voice, said, "Stay behind me."

"OK, Mama," Merry whispered, holding a chubby finger in front of her lips. Summer smiled and stood, gently pushing Merry behind her. She stepped into the open, Merry following.

The woman wore a long, drab, brown dress with a white apron. Her eyes narrowed as she stared at them.

"Did you just get here?" the woman asked.

Merry's mother startled. "What?" Merry clutched her mother's leg.

"Your clothes. You're not from here."

"Oh, no, you're right. We're from the western..."

"I mean you're not from this time," the woman said.

Merry's mother went still. "Do you know how to help us?"

The woman stared at them for a moment, then looked past the cornfields toward a small brown house, as though asking the question of it.

"Do you live there?" Summer asked. The woman continued staring off into the distance. Summer asked another question. "What's your name?"

"Aimee Darling," she answered, still staring at the house. Finally, she turned her attention back to them. "I'll trade places with you."

Summer gasped and Merry squeezed her leg.

"I, we, don't want to stay here. We want to go home."

Aimee nodded. "I understand."

"I'm sure you don't want to leave you're family."

Aimee gave a short, sad laugh. "No, of course not."

Summer reached down, pried Merry from her leg, and hoisted her up into her arms. "I think we'll walk down the road a bit." They stepped past the woman and into the road, then Summer turned back. "Is there a farmhouse nearby?"

Aimee pointed across the road. "Rose Chalmers' farm is not far ahead in that direction."

Her mother walked a few steps, then turned. "How long have you been in... this time?"

"Six years."

Summer tensed. Merry squirmed in her arms. "Mama, I want to go home."

She patted Merry's back. "I know honey, me too." Then she thanked the woman for the directions. Merry peered over her mother's shoulder as they walked away, staring at the lady who cried as she watched them leave.

She woke up in the farmhouse, where a kind woman named Rose fed them and then cared for them as both she and her mother sickened. The pain in Merry's belly wouldn't go away. At times, she could barely stay awake. She couldn't make the pretty colors for her mother. She leaned in close as her mother breathed out her last words. "I love you, my little rainbow."

Rose, Elise, and Merry buried Summer in a small, pretty meadow behind the house. Merry laid an armful of bright, yellow daisies on the fresh dirt and said goodbye to her mother. Her energy had returned. While Elise had carried her to the gravesite, Merry now walked back to the house on her own steam. Rose and Elise were a short distance behind her, when she caught sight of the boy, William. He'd visited her, told her stories, and tried to make her laugh when she was sad. She waved. "William!"

He met her halfway. Merry wrapped her arms around his waist and hugged him. "Mama's gone. I gave her flowers."

He hugged her back, then stepped away. "I'm sorry about your mother."

He came back to the house and ate lunch with them. After he went home, Merry fell asleep on a thick, wool blanket near the hearth. When she woke, the late afternoon sun filtered through the window. She watched bits of dust floating and shifting in the rays. She couldn't move.

Her arms and legs were heavy as if only her head had woken up. She called for Rose, her voice small and scared. Rose appeared, laying a rough hand on her forehead. She cursed and told Elise to get fresh water. Merry labored to breath. She coughed up the water Elise gave her.

Merry closed her eyes and thought about the daisies on her mother's grave. Their pretty golden heads making a sad place happy. She smiled as she thought of how her new friend, William, had raced her back to the house for dinner. She thought of her father and his safe, strong arms.

Elise said, "Rose, look."

Merry opened her eyes to colors dancing above her heart. She tried to reach out and touch them, but her body wouldn't work. The loud sound of the wind roared in her ears and she realized it was her own breath.

Tears streamed down Rose's face. "Go home, little one. Your colors are here. Go."

But she couldn't. Rose looked behind her and nodded. Merry's eyelids drifted downward as Elise stepped towards the colors, and with a shaking hand grabbed a tendril of blue and disappeared.

But for a slow side-to-side shaking of her head, Liz sat unnaturally still. "You remember."

Merry felt as stunned as Liz looked. "I do. But Liz, what am I remembering?"

Liz opened her mouth, then snapped it shut.

"Oh no," Merry said, head shaking. "It's too late for that. You can't clam up on me now."

Liz bit her lip. "Do you remember anything after your mother died?"

Merry looked away. She hadn't shared her first memories with anyone solely due to the fact that she'd decided they were merely dreams. How could she remember living in a time long past? Yet, now... now she was certain that her life, at least most of it, *had* been lived in a time long ago. Her stomach grew queasy at the incongruity of her situation.

"I might remember a bit. In fact, I may have remembered since I was in the hospital."

"Why didn't you..."

Merry threw her hands up. They fell to the sofa with a thud. "How could I? I didn't believe they were memories. I thought they had to be some crazy dreams."

Liz covered Merry's hand with her own. "What can you tell me about the dreams?"

Merry let out a deep sigh. She shoved her hands into her hair, holding them to the side of her head as she spoke. "They're bits and pieces."

"But, they're your bits and pieces. Anything could be important."

"I remember Aunt Rose at the hearth cooking something in a large cast-iron cauldron. Soup, I think. No..." Merry stood and paced back and forth behind the sofa. Liz laid her head on the back of the sofa listening intently. "Lobster. We had lobster. I remember their screaming when they hit the boiling water."

"Humph," Liz uttered. "Lobster. Guess you guys were pretty well-off."

"It wasn't uncommon to eat fish with the sea so near."

"What else do you remember?" Liz asked.

Merry dropped her head back to look at the ceiling. "Uh, let's see. I remember horses."

"You lived on a horse farm."

"And a swimming pool." Merry stared at Liz before running to the balcony. Liz followed her. Merry's gaze bee-lined toward to the large swimming pool off the veranda, now covered in a protective tarp for the winter. "*You're* swimming pool."

"Good, good, that's really good, Merry."

"Molly."

"Oh... right," Liz said.

"I'm sorry, Liz. This isn't useful."

"Don't think that! You're remembering. That's *huge*."

Merry tilted her head and pursed her lips. "Only, I'm not

remembering the important details. I still don't know what happened to me before or after I..."

"Don't say it," Liz interrupted. "I can't stand hearing it." She held a finger up, her eyes shining with excitement. "Wait here."

Liz ran into the bedroom and snatched an object from the drawer in the table near the door.

Time was not on her side, thought Merry. She was certain of it, even if she didn't know exactly why. Liz returned to the balcony, one hand never leaving her back.

"What are you holding behind your back?"

She was prepared for more deflection, but Liz offered none. Instead, she held a book out to her. It had a rainbow-filled heart on the cover.

"What's that?"

"It's someone else's memories," Liz answered. With a shrug she added, "I thought they might help you to remember your own."

Merry took the book, running her fingers across the rainbow heart. "Whose memories are they?"

"Aimee Donovan's," Liz answered. "William's mother."

28 ARRIVAL

Merry couldn't believe Liz's offering. She knew it went against her friend's desire to shield her from some hard truths. It almost scared her to open the book. But neither thought could keep her from doing what needed to be done, and so she settled into the over-stuffed chair and began to read.

November 1670

William's a perfect baby. A round cherubic face, pinked cheeks and a tussle of blond hair atop his head. Blue eyes that take your breath away. Such perfection.

I sit by the window as he sleeps in my arms. I look upon the field of pumpkins, frosted by the morning chill. Sam stokes the fire in the corner of the room, filling the space with warmth and light. And I'm so empty.

Where there was once light, there is a bleeding darkness. William was born, and has taken his light with him. I'm left with nothing.

While my body nourished and grew my son, his light kept me alive. Without him, my body cannot sustain itself. I can't sustain his life either. There is no milk in these ruined breasts. We've called in a wet nurse. So I sit and watch as another woman takes my baby in her arms and fuels his life.

Whatever my body gave to William cannot be replenished. I'm losing weight, my skin has become dull and sagging, my hair falls out in clumps when I brush it, and any new growth is the dullest of grays.

This is what people see. This is what I've lost. A bit more of myself decays and dies each day. All this, while my heart turns to stone. While love becomes an idea rather than a reality.

It's a hard thing not to love your child. Knowing you should feel one way, yet feel another. How can I not cherish my son? How can I turn my avoidance into yearning? I hold him and sing to him as I rock him in my arms, but my voice withers and fades until there is only the sound of William's peaceful breathing. Even my tears are silent.

October 31, 1674

William is four today. At this young age, he is already eager to help his father with the harvest. I watch him walk to the barn, his hand in Sam's, and think how different his life could've been.

How different both of ours could've been.

He's a beautiful child. I should be a proud mother. But,

all I can see when I look at him is all that I've lost. Each sunny smile chips away at my heart. Makes me less and less, while he becomes more each day.

I watch Sam crouch down to William's level as he speaks to him, ruffles his hair and smiles with the pride of a parent I wish I could feel.

This child was not only mine, but Robert's as well. Robert, a man I loved, love still, but it's different now. Nostalgic and honoring rather than passion and heart. And, William isn't just any child, but an Illuminator and the last hope for light on earth if I'm to believe what Robert told me. And I do.

I often wished Robert could've seen him. Held him. Loved him. When I watch Sam and William together, I do think his true father has done all of those things. Sam's love for William has never wavered, never hinted there was anything less than blood between them. Thank God William has Sam.

Later, we will have a small cake, and Sam will tell William his favorite story about the time he found a small Indian boy in his cornfield and how he'd filled the boy's arms with ears of corn before sending him on his way, not knowing, but hoping, he would find his way home. How three days later he'd found an arrowhead on his front step. A gift from the boy.

Then Sam will tuck William into his bed, and he'll fall asleep a happy child. And another day, another year, of our misplaced lives will have passed.

April 1676

I don't know why, but William has given to flights of imagination lately. At least that's what I suspect it is. Twice in the last month he's claimed to have seen a child, a girl to be specific, in the woods near the creek where he hunts for newts. William says the girl is three or four years old. Yet, no one nearby has a child that young, and when I asked at church whether anyone's daughter, perhaps one of the Proctor children, has gone into the woods, I'm looked upon as though I'm a madwoman.

I know William is making it all up. I know because he said the last time he saw her, he walked toward her and she disappeared into thin air. I shouted at him, called him a liar. He doesn't need to say much these days to make me yell.

I simply can't have him talking about ghost girls in the woods, not when I know what is coming. What sort of stories will have the capacity to end people's lives. I don't need anyone remembering William and his stories when the witch trials begin.

I may be a horrible mother, but I made a promise.

May 1676

My joints are sore today. It hurts to bend my fingers. I can barely shuck the corn for our dinner. I'm old.

I try to take care of myself in this age when clean water is scarce and diets can weaken rather than strengthen a body. Though I know the colonial diet is not the cause of my declining youth. Robert warned me of the consequences of bearing an Illuminator, but only after he'd filled my body with his child. Only after he'd made me love him.

My hair has grayed. My eyes have weakened. My heart is broken.

Today, I am twenty-nine years old. Sam is forty-eight. We look as equals.

I feel like William's grandmother. I'm not only losing my looks and my health. I have lost my place in time.

Twenty-nine. A milestone year in my place in time. Just another year in this God-forsaken age. Sam still reaches for me in the night. Still makes me feel like a desirable woman. I know better.

The lines in my face aren't fine whispers of old age to come, but deep scars of a life hard-lived. I am old before I am old. Sam doesn't know my true age. He doesn't know much about me that is true. But I was lucky to find him. I've loved him for the kind man he is. For the father he's been to a son who's not his own.

I'm ever grateful for him. I'm only sorry my love can never be like it was for Robert. Never like that.

June 1676

Oh my God, my God, my God. There are more people like me in Salem Town. A mother and child, a little girl. Lost. Like me.

I found them in our cornfield. I'd been walking back from Daniel Rayne's house after exchanging corn for roving when I found the young mother and her daughter a couple of rows into the cornfield. The woman evidently thought they were better hidden than they were. But the important and AMAZING discovery here is that they're from my time. My real time. Or close to it, judging by their clothes.

They spoke like me. Or like I used to speak. They dressed like I used to dress. They were me. Deposited in another time. Lost.

I confess, I offered to trade places with them. Offered to leave William and Sam behind to live their lives without me. She declined the offer.

But I would have gone.

June 1676

I sent William to the Chalmers farm today. That's where the woman and child were heading last. He came back with news that they were staying with Rose and her sister, Elise. The mother is sick. I decided to visit them and renew my offer to trade places. I know she'll die without a trade. So will the little girl.

I'm hoping I can get both William and I out of this time.

Rose wouldn't let me in her house! I could hear the little girl crying. I went home, but I sent William back the next morning, and the next. The woman is getting worse. And now the little girl is sick too. I believe my only chance to go home is slipping away.

Five days later - June 1676

I finally went back to Rose's house and banged on the door until she opened it.

"I know they're dying, Rose," I said through the slim crack of the door.

Rose opened the door a bit further. I almost couldn't hear her when she said, "She's already dead."

"Who?" I asked.

"The woman."

I couldn't breathe. "What about the child?"

Rose's worn face, always filled with a fierce compassion, withered and crumpled. "She's alive, but barely."

Tears streamed down my face. Stupid woman! I'd given her a chance to live and instead she'd run to Rose's farm for milk for her child. Milk, when she could've had life!

All week I'd thought of nothing but going home. It had seemed so possible. Like nothing had since I came to Salem Village. Of course, I'd assumed the woman knew how to get back home. After all, she'd gotten here, hadn't she? But then, so had I. And I didn't know how to get home either.

What if they were as trapped as I was? The thought didn't sit right. The woman had asked about a farm as if she knew that's where she needed to go. Which is why I thought she knew what to do, how to get back.

"I found them in my cornfield, Rose. Who are they?"

Rose hesitated and when she answered, her voice wobbled, not only with tears, but with the lie she told. "She was my niece. My niece and her daughter."

Later that evening I asked William if Rose's niece was the little girl he'd seen in the woods. The one who'd disappeared right before his eyes. He wouldn't answer me. No matter how much I shouted. No matter how I cried. He may not have said the words, but I know the answer. I know.

June 1680

The girl lived.

Elise, Rose's sister, disappeared. Or, as Rose would tell it, she went to Rhode Island to be with her husband's family.

I never told Rose I knew she was lying. I never told her about my own journey from another time.

I send William to their house every possible day. When he should be in the fields with his father, I send him to play with the little girl, Merry. She's a couple years younger than him, and he balked at first, but he was a good boy who listened to his mother, no matter how insane she was.

I knew it was a long shot placing all my hopes on a child so young, but it was the only chance I had and so I prayed and prayed on it. I prayed the little girl would remember her way home and somehow take me with her.

One afternoon, William came running into the house. He was out of breath and sweaty from his run through the woods where he and Merry had been climbing trees. He dragged the poor girl, equally sweaty and out of breath, behind him, her hand clenched in his grip. He held a bloody axe in his other hand.

"Mama!" he shouted. It was alarming to hear him call for me. He never did. It was always Sam. Papa. Why would he call to someone who disregarded him so? It scared me, yet for a moment, I felt a warmth I'd believed impossible.

I bent, only slightly—at ten-years old, he was nearly as tall as I was—and asked him what was wrong.

"Indians!"

My eyes went to the axe. I noticed the leather bands and the feathers. The blood.

"Where did you get that?"

Sam burst through the door then, demanding to know what was going on. He'd heard the children screaming on their way to the house. William told us that three warriors had found them at the creek, that they'd given him the tomahawk. He didn't know why.

"They were friendly, Papa," William said.

"They were scary," Merry said in her little voice. "But I gave them a newt and they liked us." She smiled with a child's pride.

William wasn't to be outdone and puffed out his chest. "I protected Merry."

At that, Merry pouted and said in a not so little voice, "Did not. I protected you!" They argued back and forth and I found myself doing something I hadn't done in some time. It stopped all chatter.

I laughed.

Huge belly-busting laughter. Sam laughed too. And then William and Merry laughed as Sam enveloped us all into a bone-crushing hug.

It was one of the best days of my life.

October 31, 1681

So many years have passed since I arrived in Salem Village. Day after day of church and chores. The repetition is almost a comfort to me. Then, there's my duty. Raise William in the seventeenth century when darkness is at its peak (and it is), wait for William's light to emerge, eradicate the darkness. Go home.

That last part seems highly unlikely as this point.

William is eleven and officially taller than me. Of course I've probably shrunk an inch or two. As with each birthday since his birth, we've carved and lit dozens of pumpkins to surround the house. Salem has taken on this tradition, and I find myself wishing to stop at each home to ask for candy. Half the people would be confused. The other half wouldn't even open the door to me.

Though the pumpkins add a festive touch, there's only fear behind each carving. The flickering candles and grim faces are for protection, not celebration. It's a duty we must endure each Halloween. Each birthday.

Since William's birth, the dead haven't walked. There have been no mass sightings of ghost armies roaming the streets. Still, every time this year, I can sense bad vibes growing in Salem Village. Like a storm that sends a wind, not as warm as the one before it. An electricity pelts the air, permeates the skin, sends muscles into a jittery collusion with an atmosphere they can sense but can't abide.

I hurried home with my small bag of flour. The crops have been dismal this year, not enough rain. But I've managed to trade some cornmeal for flour so I can bake a proper birthday cake, albeit a small one. Still, it's better than cornbread.

Sam has presented William with his own dirk. It's a wicked object, a long, sharp blade ending with the pointiest of tips. Not something I would give an eleven-year old. But, here, in this time, in this house, it's a necessary instrument. Besides, Sam has wanted to arm William ever since his encounter with the Indians in the woods, no matter that he came home unharmed.

William was thrilled with his gift, though his joy turned a bit glum when I insisted he sheath the weapon and give it to me for safe-keeping.

October 28, 1683

I visited Rose Chalmers this afternoon when I knew Merry would be climbing trees with William. It was a warm ending to October and the children were taking advantage, knowing cold and snow would soon steal away their outdoor activities.

I rode my horse, Abby, to Rose's house. I've come to rely on the sweet nag more and more. My knees can no longer be counted upon to keep me upright without significant pain. I'd visited Rose many times since Merry's arrival, fostering a relationship not only between William and the girl, but between their guardians. Today, I planned to culminate their relationship with an important request.

William would turn thirteen in a few days. Sam was buying him his own horse. I planned to secure a future bride who might someday remember how to send all of us to the future.

Rose greeted me with her usual kind smile. I returned it with lips pressed tight together. Between my poor health and a lack of dental care, I'd lost two bottom teeth, front and center. Smiling was an expression I actively avoided.

We sat for tea. I brought some corn biscuits I'd made. Rose provided fresh butter. I liked hearing her compliment my culinary skills. Despite primitive cooking equipment, I made a mean corn biscuit.

"Rose," I said. "I have a question, a favor, to ask."

"Did Merry do something?" she was quick to ask. I listened as Rose rattled off a list of possible atrocities Merry could've committed. Hid a rotten egg in William's bed. Again. Damaged cornstalks while playing games in the cornfield. Let our goats out of their pen. The list went on.

I laughed and told her I didn't care about any of that. "William and Merry spend a lot of time together. They are good friends, have been for many years."

"Best friends," Rose said.

"I agree. Which is why I would like to suggest a marriage between the two of them. When, they're older, of course. But, I don't think either would object to such a union in another six or seven years."

Rose agreed they probably would be fine with such an arrangement. Then she told me that only a day earlier she'd been approached by someone with the same request. And she'd agreed to it.

One day. One day stood between me and a yes. Time continues to be my enemy.

Seven years from now Merry will be wed to Jonathan Parrish. I must find a way to get her to remember how she got here before then. I've tried to get her to talk about her mother, tried to make her remember where she came from, but she seems to have forgotten those earlier days, as any child that young might.

October 31, 1683

On William's birthday, I watched as Merry, Sam, and William carved dozens of pumpkins. As William focused on carving out perfect triangle eyes from a tall, misshapen gourd, Merry slipped a handful of pumpkin guts down the back of his shirt. He froze, leaving his knife stuck in the fruit, scooped up a handful of discarded pulp and gave chase.

I laughed as Sam tried to catch a screaming Merry and a shouting William with no success. William finally threw the seeds just as Merry made the ill-timed decision to look back at him. They splattered across her face and stopped her in her tracks. Sam snuck up on the both of them and tossed a handful of slimy pumpkin guts into William's face. Merry no sooner laughed when she received the same. And then, full-on war ensued. Our yard was filled with laughter and love.

Why wasn't I out there? Why did I watch life from behind these dull glass panes? Why was my first instinct to shout for them to stop wasting the seeds?

At lunchtime, Sam presented William with a beautiful young stallion with a sable coat and a white stripe down its face. Another beauty from the Chalmers farms. William promptly named the horse Gunpowder due to the animal's explosive, fiery nature. He'll be taming that horse for many birthdays to come, if it doesn't trample him to death.

I sat that night, staring out the window; the blood-orange harvest moon so bloated and huge that it looked like it was about to slam into the earth. It's orange glow complemented the yellow, flickering light of the dozens of lit pumpkins in the yard. Sam carved more this year, the year William becomes a man. I can't blame him. I have no doubt the dead will rise tonight.

Sometime around 3a.m., I woke slumped in the seat by the window. Sam's heavy, sleep-laden breathing filled the room. I pushed my body, stiff and aching, halfway out of the chair when a flicker of movement caught my eye.

Every fiber of my body sang with fear. I didn't want to look. The moon had risen higher in the dark sky, bathing the land in a haunting orange glow. Where the road met the horizon, a lone figure walked, his tall, distorted shadow reaching halfway across the yard. I watched as he paced along the edge of the road and our property as though waiting for his prey to come to him. I knew that prey was William even before the man lifted his face toward the house. It could've been a trick of the harvest moon that colored the man's eyes a glowing red, but in my heart I knew the Devil himself had come to Salem Village.

November 1683

This morning, the sun shone as though nothing had changed during the night. When everything had.

Sometime before sunrise the candles in the pumpkins extinguished themselves. Two events happened then. The pacing man stopped pacing and Sam had a heart attack. I recalled my CPR training and pumped life back into him, screaming all the while. William came running into the room and filled it with a light I hadn't seen since his birth.

At the same time, someone pounded on the door with such ferocity that I swear the house shook. It was the tall man from the road, I'm certain of it. I froze in fear, for a moment unable to hear Sam's struggle for life, unable to think beyond the horror that I was certain stood on the other side of our front door.

"Mother!" William screamed as he shoved me away from his father and grabbed Sam's shoulders. The light grew brighter. I stumbled away. Unneeded. I had one job to do. To give and sustain William's life. I'd made a promise. I had nothing else to do but keep it.

I ran downstairs and threw my whole body at the door, pressing it against the incessant pounding of an enraged entity. Me, a mere woman. A broken woman at that. But at that moment, I had purpose. And I made sure the bastard on the other side of the door knew it.

I'm sure William would argue that I'd never shown a maternal instinct in my life, but he didn't see me then. He didn't hear me tell the Devil he would never gain access to my son as long as I was alive. He didn't hear me shout that he couldn't have Sam either. I knew what this bastard was trying to do.

I grew up in the eighties. I'd seen a lot of horror movies.

"You can't have us!" I screamed. But it was more than that. My words were my weapons, my determination, and my shield.

All went silent. No more pounding. No more shouting from upstairs. Then a voice—a not unpleasant, yet altogether blood-chilling voice, came from the other side of the door.

"I will have his light."

I dared to look out a window to the left of the door. The steps were empty. The yard. The road. All empty.

But, I know better.

The Devil always comes back.

I went upstairs to find Sam sitting up in bed, William lay unconscious across his legs. Sam told me he passed out moments earlier. I pulled William off Sam and screamed his name. He was like a heavy rag doll in my arms. I slapped him and his eyes flew open. He looked at me, then at Sam, and we held him as he cried.

I held Sam in my arms all night, my hand never leaving his chest where the glorious thump of his heart assured me he would live. However, the tall man's threat had been heard.

William doesn't remember what happened, well, mostly. He remembers Sam's being near death, but he doesn't remember his own light or the pounding at the door. It was as though the light happened outside of him and protected him from the horror which sought him. Perhaps that's best.

July 1686

I haven't written in years. Why bother when every day is the same as the one before. Still stuck in this miserable place. It's my own fault. I didn't realize what sacrifice was when I said yes to Robert's plan. I only knew the fierce love I held for him. Was it even love? Passion then.

But, today. Today is different. Today, Sam died.

Sam died.

He died. Died.

Saying it, writing it, makes it seem even more impossible.

I loved Sam.

I once thought I could never love anyone like I did

Robert. And, that was true. I loved Sam better. He was a good and honest man. A true man.

Robert! He had a destiny! A mysterious future awaited him. William. Us.

Robert was handsome and exciting. Secretive. All those attributes made it easy for him to pull me along to seek the glory, but not the guts, of what my future held. I can blame myself, and I do. But, I'm not alone in blame.

Now Sam, my savior, my husband, my love, is gone.

Years of a weakened heart ended in a threat made true.

William sits out there, in the field that once held hundreds of lit pumpkins to ward off the evil ready to take his newborn soul. He sits there plucking the heads off the too-tall grass. I feel his grief from my seat by the window. I can hear his heart break. I can taste his tears. For they are my own.

April 1687

I see how William and Merry behave around each other, pretending they are the same as they were yesterday. But, they've changed. I believe they've realized there's more to their relationship than being friends. They're in love.

I know his heart aches when he asks me if I know about her betrothal to Jonathan Parrish. I know I have failed in finding a way home. I know it's time to end his infatuation and make him focus on his destiny. If only I knew what that might be.

Robert had said William would attain the mantel of

Illuminator, but how that would happen or what that would mean was information I'd not been made privy to. Back then, I was too stupid in love to ask those important questions.

So, I tell William the girl isn't worthy of him. He's wasting his time. And, he only hates me more.

1692.

I've done something awful. Unforgivable.

And I would do it again.

I'm going home.

    Merry's thoughts brooked no room for anything other than Aimee's story. If what she read was true, Aimee Donovan had endured a journey beyond imagination. Her words brought her love and fear to life. Merry couldn't begin to comprehend the level of confusion that must've engulfed Aimee's life as she adjusted to a new time, a new love, a new baby. She thought of her strength and dedication to willingly embark on such a journey. To sacrifice her own life for her child's, to battle against darkness itself.
    Against those hardships, Merry judged her own. It was possible her story was a similar one, though with the little she remembered, it was difficult to say. Aimee had known her, had been first to meet her and her mother in another time. She'd grown up side by side with her son, William.
    Merry's dreams had proven to be reality.

29 REBIRTH

William was back in the Tall Man's dungeon. One moment he'd been connected to Merry, the next he'd found himself on his back with hundreds of festering, greedy hands holding him down. For the moment, he was one self and not two. His shadow had been yanked out of Iron House and returned to him, and now these dark beings held onto him. No amount of struggling loosened their grip. He gave up and waited, for he knew what was coming.

Soon enough, a door opened and footsteps descended into the dark cavern. He couldn't have turned his head to see who approached if he wanted to, too many hands dug into his scalp and face, pinning him in place. He didn't have to look to know who it was though. Those footsteps were beat into his soul.

Vanessa's cold voice echoed through the cave. "William, did you have a nice visit?"

William struggled against the hands holding him still. He wanted to do what he should've done the first time this witch had stepped into his life. He wanted to end her.

"Was Merry happy to see you?" Vanessa asked in a mocking tone. She commanded the dead to release him, and their ghastly hands loosened their grip and slithered back beneath the surface. Out of sight, but always close. Always ready.

"Get up," Vanessa said. "We have work to do."

Susannah hurried through the night as though it were alive and about to sink its teeth into her. She'd been scaring people with stories of witches and evil entities for so long, one would think she'd be able to stand a bit of fright herself. But her direction had changed since she'd seen the Tall Man. Since he'd seen her.

What had she done? She'd participated in the creation of stories meant to entertain, which had somehow turned into stories that could kill. Whenever she remembered the sight of Rebecca Nurse, a harmless eighty-year-old woman, hanging like a broken doll at the end of the noose, another piece of her heart chipped away. It had taken William to snap her out of the fugue state she'd let herself succumb to. The one person's attention she'd desired most of all had been given to her, though not as she'd wished, but as she deserved.

Now all hell had broken loose. The Tall Man walked the same streets as she, which brought her back to the reason for her skittish behavior as she raced to her destination, eager to be done with her deed and out of the night's grasp.

The axe she carried grew heavy at her side as she climbed the hill toward a lone tree silhouetted against the fattened moon. Susannah paused, awed by the spectacular site of the harvest moon. It's orange glow cast the hanging tree in an ominous light. The limb that had held strong for many doomed necks, stretched across the moon's face as though daring it to judge its nefarious purpose.

She pressed on, climbing the roughly hewn platform until she stood right beneath the branch. It was another foot or so above her head, which would offer a sufficient angle for her to swing an axe. She backed up as far as she could without falling off the skinny platform and raised the axe above her head. Before putting her full force behind a swing, Susannah slowly lowered it's blade to the branch. Satisfied, she brought the axe back, then swung it forward to land it against the limb with a satisfying thunk.

Susannah smiled until she tried to wrench the axe from the branch. After an awkward struggle, she managed to free its head, but disappointment flooded her when she saw what little damage she had actually caused. The limb was thick, at least twenty-four inches in diameter. It had to be to support as many as six necks at a time.

This would be a long night.

She persevered, sweat pouring into her eyes minutes later despite the chilly evening. After several more swings, she lowered the axe, dropping it to the platform. The palms of her hands pulsed with the threat of blisters. She wiped her sleeve across her dripping forehead, her arms shaky and weak. Susannah placed both hands against the limb to the right of the cut and pushed. The branch didn't budge. It was as solid as if she'd not spent the last twenty minutes hacking away at it.

Perhaps this was a foolish endeavor. The magistrate would simply find another tree or build their own hanging platform. But, that's not what this was about. Not totally. This was about sending a message. She bent to pick up the axe, when a noise from the other side of the hill froze her mid-reach. Footsteps, slow and methodical, headed toward her. She searched the horizon, at first seeing nothing. Then three figures, two men and a woman crested the hilltop, the enormous harvest moon silhouetting them. They looked as though they were carved from the night itself.

Susannah eased herself into the shadows of the hanging tree. Keeping her eyes on her unwanted company, she took careful, quiet steps backward into the brush and continued until she was safely hidden behind a cluster of fir trees. Despite the distance between them, Susannah recognized the slender figure of the Tall Man. Her mind screamed for her to run, to get as far away as she could, but something made her stay.

Possibly, it was the fact that despite stumbling and nearly falling, the second man's gait was familiar to her. As they neared the hanging tree, the moonlight made them visible to her and it was all she could do not to scream out loud. Her heart beat frantically in her chest as familiarity grew to recognition. How could she forget the presence of a man she'd pined after since she was a young girl and mourned so recently?

William was alive. Though, he moved as if he was sick or injured. Susannah thought to run for help, get enough men together to take him from the Tall Man. But would they simply hang another noose around his neck? When she saw the woman beside him, she realized that perhaps human numbers and strength might not be enough to save William.

For, the woman in the trio was certainly Vanessa, which should've been impossible considering she'd been dead for more than a week. She didn't look dead. In fact, she looked stunning, which was a notch above what she'd been when she'd been alive.

William stumbled. The Tall Man reached out to steady him, and Susannah watched William struggle between revulsion and need. In the end revulsion won, and he wrenched his arm from the Tall Man's grip, falling down in the process. Vanessa dealt him a kick to the ribs and told him to get up, but all she got for a reply was a grunt.

The Tall Man's deep, velvety voice caressed the night. "Leave him."

Vanessa didn't kick William again, but she stayed by him as the Tall Man climbed upon the platform.

Susannah sucked in a breath. *The axe!* She'd left it on the platform in her haste to hide. As soon as she thought it, the Tall Man's boot made contact with its iron head. She ducked down as he made a quick survey of the area. For an eerie moment, she swore he could see right through the trees and shadows that hid her, but then he turned his attention back to the tree. Immediately, he found the axe marks she'd made, meager as they were, and he reached one long-fingered hand out to touch them.

"What is it?" Vanessa asked.

"Someone has tried to chop down the hanging tree."

"No tree limb, no hangings?"

The Tall Man laughed. "There are many ways to kill." He placed his hands against the limb and pushed. The branch snapped as though it were a twig and went sailing several feet before crashing to the ground.

The Tall Man summoned William. He didn't move from his spot on the ground. Then the Tall Man turned his hand palm up and curled his long, bony fingers inward. With that action, William's chest jutted out and tugged him up and forward as though he were connected to the Devil's hand.

Susannah stifled a cry as she watched William fight every step that brought him closer to the Tall Man. The air practically crackled with his evil. She had done this. She had enabled this abomination. And, all she could do was watch.

The Tall Man hopped off the platform, axe in hand. He hoisted it over his shoulder and walked around the tree toward the bushes where Susannah hid, William and Vanessa following. For a moment, Susannah feared she'd been found, but the Tall Man continued down the hill, stopping near an outcrop of rocks where the grass turned to freshly turned dirt. Below the disturbed dirt lay the dead witches that had hung from the hanging tree's limb. These souls had not been granted a proper funeral, but had been tossed into the ground. No box, no ceremony. Bodies heaped upon one another, their sins perceived to be so great as to be beyond redemption. Sins that had been placed upon them by the people of Salem.

The Tall Man stepped atop the gravesite. He raised his arms to the sky. "My beauties. Rise."

As soon as Susannah thought nothing would happen, a hand punched through the churned earth. One after another, torn, broken bodies hoisted themselves from their graves. Susannah's stomach churned as a chill breeze carried the smell of death her way. A warm stream of urine trickled down her leg as the witches of Whipple Hill climbed out of the ground and collapsed, writhing and screaming in pain as they relived their own deaths. The Tall Man stood amongst them, an evil grin upon his face. It wasn't enough that he'd killed them once, for Susannah was certain that was how they'd died. It hadn't been William. Of course it hadn't. How could one man cause such harm? It took a demon to inflict such abuse. The Devil himself.

The Tall Man waved one hand, palm down across the heads of the moaning witches. They fell silent. Then, one by one, a shadowy form rose from each body and surrounded the Tall Man. William turned away from the scene, his face twisted with disgust and horror. But, the Tall Man wouldn't let him ignore his apparent duty as he forced his attention back to the dusty figures and told him to take them. The dark forms surrounded William, fortifying whatever darkness the Tall Man had visited upon him. For he took the shadowy hands of two witches and led the coven up the hill.

Vanessa hesitated, staying behind to watch the Tall Man wave his hands over the empty bodies scattered upon the ground. When they'd vanished into the night, Vanessa smiled and he chuckled at her satisfaction. Then, she left to follow William and the trail of dark souls up the hill and out of sight.

The Tall Man followed. Then, with a movement so fast as to be nearly invisible to human eyes, he spun around and threw the axe into the woods. It cut through every brush and branch in its path to reach its destination. Susannah fell to the ground, avoiding the blade as it lodged into the tree trunk where her head had been seconds ago.

She looked up, taking huge gulps of air, to find the Tall Man's red glare piercing her own. Then Susannah ran without a backward glance at Gallows Hill.

Extra innings. Of all nights to be late getting home. Cliff Tobin fidgeted in the left field waiting on Jack to pitch the damn ball, guilty about the fact that he hoped the guy would hit a double and send his man on second home for the win.

The lights had come on over an hour ago at the ball field on Gallows Hill. He should've been home a half hour ago. All he wanted was to be there with his newborn son and wife. But Ashley had encouraged him to get out of the house and hang out with someone besides them. He'd been by their side ever since Connor's birth three weeks ago. Maybe he was driving her crazy. It would be feeding time now and he was sad to be missing it. Cliff frowned. Maybe Ashley had a point.

The crack of the bat was music to Cliff's ears until he realized the ball was headed straight toward him. A perfect pop-up fly. For a nanosecond he warred with the idea of dropping the ball, but the athlete in him couldn't do it, and so he found himself racing to meet the ball. He lost it for a moment in the glare of the lights. His team cheered and shouted for him to get the ball, while the other team hustled their guys around the bases. Or, maybe not? Everyone seemed to be slowing down, looking toward him. Cliff registered their confusion along with his own like an afterthought as he closed the distance between his glove and the ball.

He reached his gloved hand out for the catch, the ball landing with a satisfied thump. Instinctively, he closed the glove around the ball. At the same time his leg connected with someone on the ground, and he fell. *Who the hell did I land on?* He hadn't noticed anyone running toward him.

Cliff fell hard, his body sprawled across a pair of legs. Naked legs. A woman's legs. For a moment, all noise ceased, the only sound his own harsh breath as his eyes traveled up the body of the woman he'd fallen over. Locked onto the glassy stare of her dead eyes. Though she lay on her stomach, her face was turned upward, her neck twisted completely around. He scrambled to get away from the dead woman, only to find himself landing atop another dead woman, this one's chest torn open.

Screams tore loose from his throat and with them all other sound returned. Both teams of men were shouting to call 911, telling Cliff to get out of there. Hands reached out to help him stand and walk away. Cliff turned to look back at the women and realized he hadn't known the breadth of what he'd stumbled into.

This was a massacre. Bodies everywhere. Women, naked and torn. Burned and broken. Dead. A few yards away from the woman he'd tripped over lay another, also torn. And beyond her was a body burnt beyond recognition. They formed a crude circle.

But, where had they come from? The field had only held ballplayers moments ago. As he thought it, someone else said out loud, "They came out of nowhere. Appeared from thin air."

For a moment, Cliff thought he heard a low, hideous chuckle come from all around them as though the night itself found this amusing. A few other men looked up at the sound, as well, but, it was soon drowned out by the wailing of approaching sirens.

30 INTERVIEW

Liz sat in the over-stuffed chair in the corner of Sidney's room and watched her cousin breathe. She'd tried talking to Sidney earlier, but had tired of hearing her own voice.

Liz reached for the remote on the side table and clicked on the television. Gina, Sidney's nurse, said it could help for Sidney to hear her favorite shows. She certainly didn't see how it could hurt. Though as the droning television turned from afternoon talk show to the evening news, Liz pondered the possibility that it could hurt. Reports of a murder and a kidnapped child in Danvers, a shooting in Swampscott, and a street brawl outside of a popular pub in Salem played one after another. Crime was getting worse. Not only that, but these violent acts also seemed to be concentrated in Salem and surrounding towns.

It appeared the bad guys were trying to outdo the massacre at Gallows Hill. And, now the anchorwoman was introducing another story, segueing to Alex Olivier who was reporting from Gallows Hill. As much as she didn't want to give him another minute of her attention, Liz couldn't help but look at the TV screen. There he was, his handsome face a lie to the evil he spewed. *Maybe evil was a bit dramatic.* When she realized she was smiling, she decided evil might be exactly right.

Alex reported the police were still trying to find out how the women's bodies had been transported to Gallows Hill and where they'd been before showing up in the field during an active ball game. Liz didn't know how they were ever going to tie this mystery into a neat little bow. The field had been filled with nearly forty people when the women had appeared. Most claimed they'd seen them materialize out of thin air. There was nothing explainable to work with, and Liz was certain physical evidence was lacking as well. There would be no footprints, no fingerprints, and no tire marks. Their wounds couldn't even be attributed to weapons or human interaction at all.

The only connection they had was Jonathan. Even that was weak.

"These are the same women that a week ago allegedly kidnapped and attacked Jonathan Parrish."

"Shit," Liz said out loud.

"There were twelve women on the night of the attack. Three were involved in kidnapping Parrish and a friend, William Darling. Parrish claims Darling was taken and used in some sort of coven ritual, while he, Parrish, had been knocked unconscious. When he came to and tried to help his friend, well, that's when the odd earthquake struck and he was injured again."

"Please don't fuck this up," Liz said to screen Alex.

"Only ten of the twelve women were found in Gallows Hill Park, leaving the whereabouts of Corinne English unknown. She is also one of the alleged kidnappers. To add more mystery, the police say while there are several William Darlings in the area, none of them match the identity of the man who Jonathan Parrish claimed disappeared with the witches, so he's still missing, as well.

Add to all this, the sudden appearance of Molly Rose Cooke, and the mystery deepens."

Liz moaned.

"Since her return, several people have come forward stating they'd seen her in Salem and even Boston, weeks prior to her being discovered seriously injured at Gallows Hill."

Liz clicked off the television. She was going to have to change the way she reacted to him if she wanted the right story to be told. She took her phone out of her pocket and was about to press Sophie's number when its effervescent ring blasted into the room. She pressed to answer without thinking just to stop the noise, and immediately regretted the impulse as Alex Olivier's voice greeted her.

"Why did you even pick up the phone then?" he asked.
"It rang?"
Alex cleared his throat. "I wanted to get your reaction to the witches at Gallows Hill."
Silence.
"Seriously, if you're not going to answer any of my questions, this call is pointless, isn't it?"
"Oh, definitely."
Alex sighed. He'd wanted to know if Liz was all right after the flood incident. *Why couldn't he just say that?* "So, you're backing Parrish's alibi?"
"I'm not backing anything. Jonathan Parrish has spent the last two days here, either at my cousin's bedside or with Molly. I believe the police are satisfied, why aren't you?"
"Oh, I believe you. I'm curious what he has to do with Molly, you, the witches, and Madame Sophie. It's quite the puzzle."
"You're ridiculous."
Alex snorted. Snorted! This girl made him absolutely crazy.
"I'm going to hang up now," she said.
"You do that," he said to the dial tone.

Liz tapped the end call button on her phone and growled. Then she dialed Sophie and told her about the frustrating conversation with Alex Olivier.
"Boy trouble?"
"What? No," Liz answered. "He's a stupid reporter. Not a boy."

"Still a boy."

Liz couldn't have stopped her jaw from dropping if she'd wanted to. "What are you implying? You think I *like* him?" Liz realized how unconvincing she sounded even to herself. "Can we talk about something important here? Did you see what he put on the news? He connected those dead witches to Merry! Out of our whole interview, the only detail he gleaned was the fact that out of all the people Merry could've hooked up with in the few weeks before she turned up at Gallows Hill was you, Sidney, and I. Quite the coincidence." Liz surrounded the last word with air quotes, even though Sophie couldn't see them.

"You didn't give him much to work with."

Liz chose to ignore Sophie's comment, given she'd scolded herself a short while ago about her attitude toward Alex Olivier. She sat down heavily on an oversized ottoman, her gaze distracted by the bleak, gray view outside the window. It matched her mood perfectly.

"It was bound to happen, Liz. With or without the handsome reporter."

Liz glared at the phone.

"Once Merry's photo appeared on TV, too many people came forward saying they'd seen her weeks ago. That girl who choked. Those two girls who were in the graveyard. The bloggers? I think they were the first to contact the police."

"They also started blogging that Molly *is* Merry Chalmers and that William *is* William Darling," Liz said. "They're a little cuckoo."

"They're also right." A pause stretched into silence. Then Sophie said, "We're going to end up on a reality show, aren't we?"

Despite it all, Liz shook her head and laughed.

"This sucks," said Alex as he pocketed his phone.
"Did she say no?" asked Joel.
"What are you talking about?"
"You asked her out, didn't you? The Thompson girl?"

Alex's face grew hot. He thought he might be turning purple. "Are you high?"

Joel laughed. "Whatever. So, what did she have to say about the witches? Confess all her deep, dark secrets, did she?"

"Hardly. She backs up Parrish's alibi. No surprise there. And, she told me I was ridiculous."

"She called you ridiculous?"

"I'm not proud of it."

"Well, this whole story is ridiculous if you ask me," Joel said. "I mean, how does someone go missing for fifteen years, then show up and happen to bump into her grandmother, make friends, hang out for a few weeks with the wealthiest family on the north shore and then turn up in the woods half-dead with no memory of any of it and a new identity to boot? Too coincidental in my view."

Alex rapped his knuckles against the table. "I don't believe in coincidences."

31 KISS

Liz plopped down upon her bed and stared at the ceiling.

"God, I need to get out of this house," she said to the empty room. Or so she thought.

"Sounds like a great idea. Where are we going?" came a voice from the open doorway.

Liz rose up on her elbows to find Jonathan leaning in the doorframe, arms crossed.

"You too?"

He nodded.

"You can leave anytime."

"I'm a part of this too, Liz."

"Yeah," she said, picking at invisible spots on her bed's coverlet. "I know."

He came in and sat beside her. "I'm picturing some place loud, where you can't hear your own thoughts."

Liz grinned. "I know the perfect place." She got up from the bed and tugged Jonathan to a standing position. "Get out, I need to change."

"I'll let Mer...Molly know we're going out."

Liz hesitated.

"What? You don't think we should take her?"

Liz bit her lip. "I don't know. It might be a bit much for her."

"She probably needs it more than we do, Liz. Have you seen how... I don't know, how wild she's getting?"

Wild didn't adequately describe Merry's recent behavior. More like frantic, like she couldn't stand being in her own skin. "You're right," Liz said. "Go get our favorite puritan."

Free Market was at the end of the pier at Derby Wharf. The pumping base of the dance music bounced off the surrounding shops, and Liz had to stop Merry from dancing in the street. Jonathan paid the cover charge at the door and they stepped into a tightly netted throng of people, making their way to the bar where mixed drink prices paraded across a ticker in red lights. Cosmos were popular tonight, judging by their price. Mojitos were in second place. Liz and Jonathan noticed Merry disappear behind them as Liz turned to hand her a drink.

Liz gawked as Merry disappeared into the crowd, a blur of red on the dance floor. Merry, who'd previously been modest in her clothing and subdued in her actions, now wore a tight red dress and jumped around, hands in the air.

"Where did she learn those moves?" Liz shouted over the music at Jonathan.

Jonathan shouted back. "She told me she couldn't dance."

"Yeah, well, apparently Molly can."

They watched a few more moments until the man Merry was dancing with reached in and pulled her close. Jonathan shoved his drink at Liz.

"Hold this."

Liz had no time to protest, trying desperately not to drop the three drinks she now held. She downed half of her own, before placing the other two drinks on the bar, watching as Jonathan pushed his way into the crowd. By the time he reached Merry, it was evident that she was trying to push away from her dance partner who maintained a firm grip on her waist.

"Shit," Liz said to herself. She held her breath as Jonathan tapped the man on the shoulder and leaned in to tell him something. The man shook his head, but then Jonathan spoke to Merry who also said something to the man. He immediately released her, and Jonathan took Merry's hand and dragged her off the dance floor.

She was laughing when they reached Liz back at the bar.

"What happened there Molly?"

"It was only a dance," she said, reaching for the drink Liz held out to her. She took a large gulp, then said, "Jonathan rescued me." More giggling.

"The guy was a tool," he said. "And, you told me you couldn't dance."

"Did I? When?" Merry asked, and then tapped her forehead. "Oh, you mean before. I don't know why I'd say that."

Merry downed the remainder of her drink and slammed her glass on the bar. She gripped Jonathan's sleeve and tugged him toward the floor. "I'll dance with you now."

Jonathan laughed and allowed Merry to pull him onto the dance floor. Suddenly, she let go of him and ran back to the bar, where she proceeded to gulp half of his drink.

"Hey, slow down, sailor," Jonathan said, laughing. Then, they disappeared into the crowd of moving bodies.

Liz shook her head. "Jesus."

"She certainly stepped right back into the land of the living," a voice said beside her.

Liz turned to find an annoyingly familiar face looking down at her.

"Seriously? You're following us?" she asked.

Alex Olivier shrugged. "Maybe. Maybe I'm following *you*."

Liz snorted. "And, what would be the purpose of that? I'm not newsworthy."

"You could be. You're friends with the recently reappeared Molly, or is it Merry, Cooke. Seems like an unlikely alliance."

"Don't you have any friends?"

He grinned, and Liz busied herself with the straw in her

glass, willing the cooling liquid to provide her with a genius idea on how to get this guy off their back. Turns out sometimes genius ideas were the truth.

"Listen, life has been tough at our house over the last month."

"Your cousin."

"Yeah, and frankly, we needed to get out. None of us can move with you guys constantly around, stalking..."

"It's not stalking," he interrupted.

"You can call it whatever makes it right for you, but trust me, it's stalking."

He laughed, and Liz found herself smiling back. At least he could laugh at himself. "Anyway, it's hard, not having the freedom to go where you want without the worry that thousands of eyes are waiting to watch your next move. We haven't done anything wrong, but it's like we've been put in a virtual prison."

Alex looked down at his own drink then. He stole a sideways glance in her direction. "I guess I never thought of it that way."

"You don't need to patronize me." Liz set her empty glass on the bar and snatched up Jonathan's. Looks like he was going thirsty this round. A hand landed tentatively on her arm, as though asking permission to touch her.

"I'm sorry," Alex said, his voice close.

His breath tickled her neck. *Why did it have to feel so damn good?* She faced him.

A crooked smile sat on his lips. "You're right. That was patronizing. I have thought of it, the loss of freedom. I don't know how to get around it. If it's not me following you around, it's someone else."

Liz dropped her gaze. He was right. It would be someone else, no matter what. She tried to keep the smile off her face when she thought that at least it was someone like him following her around. And, by like him, she meant young and good-looking. She was so screwed.

"Dance?" he asked.

"What? So you can report on my lack of coordination to the press tomorrow?"

"I doubt that's the case," he said. "But, no. How about we forget who we are tonight and enjoy a dance together?" When she hesitated, he quickly added, "I understand if you don't want to..."

The uncontrolled blush creeping up his neck at her potential rebuff was enough to help her decide. He was too damn adorable.

"OK. We'll dance. But, no questions and if I hear a word of this on the news, I will..."

He held his hands up in surrender. "Truce! I don't even want to think of what you'll do to me." He led her onto the dance floor, passing Jonathan and Merry on their way. Jonathan's eyes widened when he saw her dance partner, but Liz assured him with a nod that everything was OK. *Poor Jonathan, Liz thought, he'd come out to let loose and instead he was forced into playing the role of protector.*

Alex proved to be as good a dancer as a reporter—better actually. They danced their way through two heart-thumping songs, and Liz's stress melted away. Of course, the Cosmos helped. The reason didn't matter. A great weight had been lifted, if only for the night. She didn't realize at first when the music slowed, but suddenly she found Alex's arm around her waist, pulling her closer. Her hand found his, and he held it close to his heart as they spun in slow circles.

"You're not uncoordinated at all," he said.

She looked up at him, ready to throw out a witty retort, but his dark eyes stopped whatever was about to fall from her tongue. A tingling sensation drifted from where their fingertips met down to the pit of her stomach and lower. She became keenly aware of the strong beat of his heart beneath her fingers. She wanted to kiss him. And, by the looks of his half-lidded gaze, he appeared to want to do the same. *What the hell was she thinking? It was the easiest way to get access wasn't it? Getting through to her opened up Merry's door and Sidney's door and Jonathan's door. She was the key, wasn't she?*

Liz dropped her hand and stepped away from him. "I should get back to my friends." She left him before he could unleash any more of his charm on her and found Merry and Jonathan at the bar, fresh drinks in hand.

"How was the rot heporter?" Merry asked.

Jonathan translated. "Hot reporter."

"Jesus, how many have you guys had?" Liz asked.

"Enough," Jonathan answered. "Or maybe not enough."

"They're so good," Merry said.

"And, you're so drunk," Liz said. "Jonathan, how could you let her get like this?"

"What's the harm, Lizzie? We came out to have a good time, didn't we? Who needs it more than Molly?"

Merry lifted her glass. "Yeah."

Jonathan leaned closer to Liz and said, "Besides, who knows? Maybe getting smashed will be what she needs to bring Merry back."

Liz frowned. It was as good a theory as any. "OK, but the next round is a coke."

"Fine," Jonathan said, signaling the bartender. "So, what's up with you and Mr. Dashing Reporter? Giving him the inside scoop? Or maybe a little something else?"

"Funny. And no on both counts."

"I'm sure I'll read about it in the paper tomorrow."

"You won't. He promised not to report on our being here tonight."

"Even without the something else?"

Liz slapped Jonathan playfully.

"I want to dance," Merry announced. Jonathan rolled his eyes.

"Go ahead, it'll help burn off some alcohol." Liz said, as Jonathan got dragged back onto the floor. Liz was amazed at the amount of energy Merry had as she danced across the floor, weaving in and out of the crowd, Jonathan running more than dancing to keep up. Energy that didn't know where to go. Merry had only let her colors loose by accident so far, and while she may now know she possessed some extraordinary abilities, she didn't know what to do with them. Liz's heart raced with the hope that with her recent use of colors and the memories that had been returned to her today, Merry wouldn't be far behind.

Alex returned, squeezing past a beefy man to stand beside Liz.

"Looks like your friends are having a good time."

"You promised, remember? You promised not to report anything."

"And, I meant it," he said, his brows furrowing. "Jeez, I could've gone to law school if I wanted to be looked down upon like this."

"I'm not sure reporters are in a much better class."

"What can I do to make you trust me?" he asked.

Liz shook her head. "Why do you care if I trust you?"

He grinned a crooked smile. "I'm not sure. But, I'd like to find out." He'd moved closer somehow. Liz put a hand on his chest to stop his approach.

"Let's start with tomorrow's paper," she said. "We shouldn't be in it."

Alex smiled. "You're on. But, I want a favor in return."

Liz froze, once again aware of the lack of space between them, as she waited for him to state his terms.

"I want another interview. This time without the bullshit. I want a usable tape. I want the real story."

Didn't she want that too? She wanted him to know the truth, or as close as she could make it to the truth, to stop all the speculation and lies. So, to her surprise, Liz agreed.

"Mer... Molly, you don't want to do this." Jonathan shouted the words against the pounding beat that had followed them outside.

She giggled and pushed up against him, backing him against the wooden deck railing surrounding Free Market. Anchored boats bounced upon the waves as though powered by the music rather than the wake. Merry wrapped her arms around his neck and pulled his head down. Her lips vibrated against his ear. "Oh, but I do. And so do you."

Jonathan peeled her arms away, holding them to her side. "Trust me, you don't remember now, but when you do, you will regret this moment."

She looked at him with disbelieving eyes. Jonathan reached out and tucked an errant strand of hair behind her ear and smiled. However, she took the gesture as encouragement and rose up on her toes to clutch his face in her hands. Jonathan made an attempt at another protest, but Merry's soft lips squelched his words.

"Kiss me," she said.

He could blame it on the drunken moment, but he didn't push her away. In fact, he found himself pulling her close, kissing her deeply. Undeniable need permeated his being as their tongues darted and explored. Merry pressed into him. His hands held her face, wove through her hair, pulled her closer.

She froze in his arms, her lips so soft and malleable a second ago, now hard and unmoving. Jonathan pulled back. *What the hell did I just do?* Merry's arms fell from his neck, meeting his confused look with one of horror. He dropped his hands from her waist as though she burned.

"Are you all right? Molly?"

Nothing. Just a horrified stare. When he called her name again, her look turned to one of confusion. Then her face lost all color. She looked like she was going to be sick. But when she spoke, *his* stomach churned.

"Why are you calling me Molly?"

He stared at her for several stunned moments.

"What do you want me to call you?"

She raised her eyebrows as though he were soft in the head. "Merry?"

Jonathan's mouth dropped open, slowly transforming into what he supposed was a goofy grin. Merry was back.

She stumbled back against the railing. "Did you *kiss* me?"

"Uh, well, technically, you kissed me."

Merry's eyebrows and mouth turned down, expressing doubt at such a ridiculous concept.

"Do you feel all right?" he asked.

Merry looked around, taking in the bobbing boats, the crowded club. The DJ introduced a new song amidst spotlights of purple, blue, red. A wash of alternating colors spilled beyond the club and flashed across her face. She pressed a hand against her skull, managing to wobble her stance at the same time. "I'm a little drunk. I... why would I kiss you?"

Jonathan steered her across the deck, through other mingling and dancing couples, toward the street. The turn of events was sobering him up like no cup of coffee ever had.

"Why would I kiss you, Jonathan?" she asked once they were farther from the loud music.

"Merry, do you remember anything from a few minutes ago?"

"Of course I do. I was...we," she began, then shook her head. "I don't remember."

"What about further back? Yesterday?"

She looked at him, her brows furrowed. "There was a storm..."

"That's good, that's good. Do you remember what your name was yesterday?"

"I would imagine it to be the same as today. But, you're asking the question for a reason. What was my name yesterday, Jonathan?"

Damn, he wished someone, anyone, would interrupt them. He wasn't equipped to handle the recovery of an amnesia victim. He fumbled his phone from his pocket to text Liz. In the end, she didn't need his answer.

"It was Molly, wasn't it?" she asked in a hushed voice.
"Yes."

Merry leaned back against the club's weathered exterior and stared into the starlit sky for several moments. Jonathan's thumbs flew across the keypad. *Come outside. Merry's back.*

He looked up in time to witness the puzzle pieces fall into place and transform Molly into the Merry he knew. Then she ran.

The narrow streets of Pickering Wharf grew darker as Merry put more distance between herself and the brightly lit nightclub. The lack of light didn't slow her down. She barely noticed her surroundings until with a painful thump and a squeak, Merry came to a halt. "I'm so sorry." She rubbed her chest. "Are you all right?"

No answer. It was then Merry noticed the unfortunate person she'd blindly run into. The woman before her stood strong as though Merry had not just gracelessly crashed into her. Her pale face, framed by a wild tangle of ebony hair, bloomed before Merry like a moonflower in the night. She peered at Merry with kohl-rimmed eyes. Merry took a step back.

"Oh... I beg your pardon."

Still, no response, except for an unnerving, piercing gaze. Simultaneously questioning and knowing. Before Merry could walk away, the woman opened a door. "Come inside."

Merry, head reeling from both alcohol and realization of self, entered. Her mind spun memories of a life lived.

She was a child on a swing surrounded by rainbows, her joy turning to fear at the sound of her father screaming her name.

She was a child in deep sadness, holding her mother's hand for the last time.

She was a child calling for her Aunt Rose in the night, safe in her arms.

She was a young girl, playing in the cool creek while the summer heat melted all within the usually cool forest. William tossed stones from the riverbank, their plunking noise made her laugh.

She was a young lady, sewing a new skirt in the dim candlelight while Rose braided her hair for bed.

She was of age, meeting William at the monkey tree, realizing for the first time that his presence stirred more than friendship in her heart.

She was a woman in love.

She was desperate, lost, and scared.

She was strong with colors.

She'd forgotten herself. More importantly, unbelievably, she'd forgotten William. But, it was all back now.

"Please sit down," the stranger said. The backs of Merry's legs bumped against a chair, a throne, and she collapsed into it. Only then did she escape her own thoughts to observe her surroundings. She was in a witch shop, like many others in Salem, yet this place was more... more... just more. There was no defining element that made it so. She simply knew. Other shops held objects that promised magic. But, here. *Oh*. Here was a place that *held* magic.

She studied the witch before her. *Preserved*—the word described her perfectly in Merry's mind. Her age was indefinable; her eyes ancient, knowing. She was both young and old, beautiful and horrific.

"Who are you?" Merry asked.

The witch tilted her head and appraised Merry. Then, in a voice deep with wisdom, she asked the question which Merry had often asked herself. "What are you?"

"I might ask the same of you," Merry replied. Her indignation born from defense rather than insult.

The witch chuckled. It was not unpleasant. "I can see your colors, my dear. All of them. Too many for one young woman, I'm afraid. You are unsettled."

Merry's mouth dropped open. The witch lifted a brow, inviting her inquiry. Merry cleared her throat. "I have been lost. More times than any one person should be."

Merry's mind floundered. She needed to leave. Jonathan must be wondering where she'd run off. He'd have worried Liz by now. She made to stand, she *thought* to stand, but remained seated.

"You're in no danger. Forgive me, but I saw right away that you were... you are... a being I've only heard of, but have never seen. Never thought I would."

She bowed her head. "Enfys." The word slipped from her like a prayer. Said aloud in any other place, to anyone else, it might mean nothing. But here, to Merry, it meant everything.

"Enfys," Merry repeated. She'd rejected the moniker not

long ago. Now she wished it back to her, wished it into her soul. If it could help her get back to herself, and more importantly, get back to William, then she would claim it for her own.

I must be crazy, Liz thought for the hundredth time since she'd agreed to another dance with Alex. A *slow* dance, nonetheless. He was a gentleman, she had to give him that. One hand light on her waist, the other holding her hand as they moved in a shuffling circle. But Liz was a bit too aware of the hand on her waist and her hand in his.

Did he pull her in closer? Yes, his eyes, his mouth, much closer. And yet, not close enough. God, she wanted to kiss him. He bent his head, his lips near her ear, his warm breath brushing her skin when he spoke.

"Liz?"

"Yes?"

His hand slipped to her hip and grew firm as he pulled her even closer. Alex brushed his lips against her ear this time. "I promise this has nothing to do with wanting an interview."

She started to ask what he meant, but his meaning became clear as his lips left her ear and he leaned in for what was sure to be the kiss she desired until someone tapped her on her shoulder. Alex stepped back and dropped his hands, sending a glare of frustration to whomever stood behind Liz. She immediately missed the pressure of his hand on her hip. Someone else's hand landed on her shoulder, and Liz turned with her own frustrated glare.

Jonathan stood before her. "Sorry to interrupt, Lizzie. But, Merry's gone."

"What the hell, Jonathan!" Liz spun on him, unsure if she was mad because he'd lost Merry or interrupted the almost-kiss with Alex. OK, if she was honest with herself, she'd admit it might be the latter.

"Listen to me. *Merry* is gone." Jonathan said, waiting for the impact of his words to register. "Merry's back."

"You're not making sense. Is she back or is she gone?" Liz

asked, then her eyes widened. "Oh. Oh!"

Liz pulled away from Alex with an incoherent apology, and then pushed Jonathan across the floor toward the exit. Once outside, Jonathan told her about the kiss, the return of Merry. Afterwards, Liz stood, hand on hip, and said, "Let me get this straight. You kissed Molly and brought Merry back? What are you, Prince Charming?"

Jonathan held his hands up. The door opened and closed behind Liz.

"Where is she?" Liz asked.

Jonathan looked behind her and kept silent. Liz turned to Alex. "Can you give us a moment?"

"I can, but I don't think *that* will." Alex said, pointing past them to the harbor.

Liz looked in the direction Alex indicated and gasped. "Holy crap! What the hell is that?"

Far out in the harbor, a blue-gray funnel touched down on the ocean's surface, connecting it to the immense, dark, swirling cloud at its other end in the sky. It spun and churned, whipping the water into a frothy mass with an eerie quiet.

"It's a water spout," Alex answered.

"Look!" Liz said, as two dark circles appeared on the water's surface near the first spout. Soon they were spiraling, appearing to call out to the dark tubes of air emerging from the thick cloud above. As they swirled closer to shore, several more spouts formed.

Jonathan gripped the railing. "Impossible."

"Or possible," Liz said, tugging on Jonathan's arm as Alex towed her around the deck towards Wharf Street. Others had noticed the odd phenomena and joined them in their haste to distance themselves from the fast-approaching spouts. Liz dared a backwards look to find the sea churning large waves toward shore. Alex yanked her forward, but Liz pulled back. She shouted to Jonathan over the whistling wind. "We need to find Merry!"

"She went this way, I think," Jonathan said, as he ran in the direction he'd last seen Merry run.

"What do you know of Enfys?" Merry asked.

"Legends, stories," the witch answered in a deep, yet pleasing, voice. "A person who holds a rainbow of colors inside them and is also gifted with the powers those colors hold. Frankly, I didn't believe it could be real."

A sudden gust of wind blew trash loose from the barrels outside, sending paper and plastic bags cascading past the shop window.

"It's real. I'm real."

A stream of frantic people ran past, their shouts preceding them. Merry stood. She followed the witch to the storefront window. "What's going on?"

The witch took her arm and led her further into the shop.

"Where are you taking me?" Merry asked, pulling her arm free.

"Can't go out that way, you'll be trampled."

The shop was lit only by several small lamps, offering more shadow than light. Merry banged her shin into the protruding leg of a cupboard. They reached a door, which opened onto an alcove. The witch looked out first before opening it and shoving Merry back into the night.

"I think your particular skills are needed now."

"I don't... "

The witch pointed toward the harbor. Merry turned, the wind whipping her hair into her eyes, stunned by the unbelievable site of water spouts, five, six, eight of them. While they roused the sea into a frenzy, mayhem reigned on the wharf in the form of hundreds of people fleeing restaurants, clubs, and boats. Dread froze Merry in place. Liz and Jonathan were somewhere in that wild crowd of fleeing people.

"You must use your colors. Stop this madness," the woman said.

Merry pointed toward the ocean. "What can I do against that? I can't control nature at that level."

The woman smiled, crow's feet creasing the corner of her eyes. "Nature has no part in that."

"But... " The answer came to Merry before she asked her question. Mingled with the tang of low tide came an undercurrent of malignancy. Like a festering wound, it spread its disease from the black cloud-filled sky to the spoiled ocean calm to the rotten scent on the wind. This was the Tall Man's doing. The witch must have seen recognition in her eyes for she nodded her head and nudged Merry forward.

Merry swallowed. Her muscles tensed. Another spout formed. And another. As though in answer, energy surged inside her, urgent for release. She pulled her heels off and dropped them by the door. Shouts and screams alerted her to a mass of people who'd left the main egress from the wharf and now funneled their way toward her. Merry darted across the lane only to find herself swallowed in a throng of people frantically exiting a restaurant. More than once she was spun around as she fought the flow of the pack. She made her way past the restaurant and finally had a clear path to the water.

Boats fought their moors as the ocean tossed them against one another. The Friendship, an eighteenth-century trade ship replica docked in the adjoining pier, bucked and leaned precariously to one side. Merry dropped to her knees at the edge of the pier, but despite the surging tide, she couldn't reach the water. The spouts, too many to count, spun closer to shore, sending a spray of ocean water onto the wharf. The squeal of wood being wrenched apart tore Merry's gaze from the approaching horror. A gale force tore the corner deck of Free Market from the building, tossing it like kindling before sending it crashing into the club. Her heart caught in her throat. She fought the urge to search for Liz and Jonathan and get them to safety. She could only hope they'd found refuge on their own.

An explosion mere yards from her sent Merry falling to the ground. She turned her head away from the heat and squeezed her eyes shut as the pop and crackle of burning boats competed with the howling wind. Merry rose to her knees, shielding her eyes from the smoky air, and jumped into the harbor.

The chill October water pricked against her skin, contracted her chest. Merry pushed through the surface and took a shaky breath of air, free of the smoke hovering above. Another explosion sent her back below the water's surface. A chunk of wood plunked into the water in front of her. Vivid orange flames speared the night sky as another boat burned with the first two. Merry swam upward, her energy no longer contained within her skin, but shimmering above as though she were encased in glowing colors. She funneled her own spout of water, and with a willful push of her hands showered the burning boats to douse the fire before the entire fleet went up in flames.

That done, she focused on the approaching threat from the harbor. Merry attempted to push her colors, all of them, toward the spouts, but the water had acquired a slick, suffocating consistency. Her colors dulled, trapped against her own skin. Merry treaded water, her limbs heavy and her movements clunky. *How did she ever think she could fight this? Fight the Tall Man?* A half-hour ago, she hadn't even known who she was. Now she was neck deep in a wild sea trying to save Salem. The irony of the situation didn't escape her. That she should be Salem's savior, when its own had condemned her to death three hundred years earlier.

A shameful heat rose up her neck, pricked at her temples. A choppy wave pushed her below the surface for a moment, sending brackish water down her throat. She rose up, sputtering, throat burning. The waves grew relentless, each trying to beat her down. She thought of William. She'd promised him she'd come back. She'd promised him she'd find a way to release him from the mark the Tall Man had placed upon him.

Merry lifted her chin. Her pulse sped up, muscles quivering with determination. She shook off the Tall Man's slimy coat of malevolence. Her colors not only shimmered beneath the surface, but above it as well. *Let the waves come.* With a power and speed only her colors could produce, Merry swam out of the pier and into the violent harbor waters.

A spout at least fifty feet wide and a half-mile high spiraled and churned close by. Several others followed behind it as waves crested the lighthouse at the end of the pier. Water droplets speared the air, and Merry ducked beneath the surface for a reprieve against their knifelike attack. Sheltered from the chaos above, Merry focused her energy, her colors responding like poked wasps. Instead of fighting from above, she suffused the water with her colors. A rainbow alighted in the dark water.

The ocean rejected her colors, attempting to thrust her from its grip. Merry broke the surface to find herself in the center of a dark spot, the beginning of another spout. She didn't attempt to swim beyond its growing diameter or fight the spiraling waves. Instead, she lifted her arms and rose up into the swirling winds. A sheath of water surrounded her, creating a cocoon of sorts against the external onslaught of wind and water. With her lower legs still immersed in the harbor, Merry called forth her colors again, sending them in all directions. The dark sea and night sky met in a vivid outburst of brilliant light and color.

For a moment, the spouts, the waves, and Merry were suspended in motion as though time itself had stopped. Then Merry dropped back into the sea. She kicked and resurfaced to a calm ocean, the last of the spouts collapsing. Merry spun in the water, verifying that no threat existed in any direction. Finally, she closed her eyes and let another sense kick in—the one which told her whether danger remained. Nothing.

Then someone called her name.

32 MERRY

Merry swam. Exhaustion consumed her, while the water chilled her to the bone. She pushed on, each laborious stroke bringing her closer to shore, closer to Liz and Jonathan. Closer to home.

A loud, insistent horn blared in the night. Distant sirens accompanied its warning. Her friends waved frantically, calling her name. Merry waved back and swam harder. When she finally reached the dock, Jonathan, with his good arm, and Liz reached down for her and lifted Merry over the wooden pilings and onto land. Liz immediately wrapped her in a tight hug.

Merry held onto Liz as though she'd just returned. And, in a way, she had.

"I've missed you," Liz wept into her neck. Merry hugged her friend tighter. When they finally released one another they were both dripping and shivering. Placing a hand on Liz's shoulders, Merry summoned red and pulled the condensation from them. A thin, steamy veil lifted from their clothes and dissipated into the cool night air.

Merry tugged at her dress, now alarmingly snug, and managed to draw the fabric another inch longer. Liz shook her head, grinned, and nodded toward Merry's attire. "Molly was a bit less inhibited."

Merry gave up the fight with the shrunken material. "Indeed."

Jonathan held his arms up, marveling at the fact that they were completely dry again. "How the heck do you do that?"

"Forget that, Jonathan. It's a parlor trick compared to what she did out there," Liz said, pointing toward the now calm sea.

Merry bit her lip. "You saw that?"

"Anyone with eyes saw that. The entire harbor was a rainbow. It was beautiful, actually."

"But could you see me?" Merry asked.

Liz shook her head. "All I saw were the colors."

"That's why we ran over here," Jonathan said. "We were looking for you further inland when the colors burst. I doubt anyone else saw you afterwards, Merry. They were all too busy trying to run away from the harbor."

Liz grinned. "Yeah, we were the only idiots running toward it."

"That was the work of the Tall Man," Merry said. Liz's grin faded. "Like the flood and the sinkhole."

"What does he want with Salem?" Jonathan asked.

"What has he ever wanted with Salem, but to destroy it." Merry answered.

"Why? It's not like it's some strategic evil headquarters... is it?" Liz said.

Liz's words sent Merry's thoughts in a direction she'd never entertained before. She'd assumed the Tall Man was interested in William's light and her colors for the sake of power alone. But could his quest be for Salem? She and William had thwarted his efforts to destroy Salem during the witch trials. The trials had ended shortly after their hangings. Now the Tall Man had William, and Merry had Salem. She glanced out toward the calm harbor, knowing this wouldn't be the only fight he'd wage.

The sirens grew closer, and Liz suggested they go home. As they headed toward the street, a figure stepped out from a doorway—tall, covered in black, and watching. Liz halted.

"Who's that?"

Merry recognized the witch who'd helped her earlier. "I don't know her name, but she's a witch."

Liz threw up her arms. "Of course she is. Because you attract them, Merry."

"She's friendly," Merry said, then noticed what the witch held in her hands. "Plus, she has my shoes."

"I forgot everything," Merry said.

"You had amnesia," Liz replied.

Merry pulled the cozy, warm Sherpa blanket around her. After soaking in a warm tub and donning pajamas, Merry relaxed into the sofa in her suite where she'd started her morning as Molly. The fire crackled and warmed. Merry reached her hands toward it as Liz and Jonathan sat beside her, worry still strong in their eyes.

Merry gazed into the flame. "I remember now. They burned down Aunt Rose's house, and the children threw stones at me." She raised a hand to her head.

"Jesus," Jonathan said.

"I was injured, but the rocks gave me energy. That's how I obtained the strength to conjure my colors at Gallows Hill."

"Then they hanged you," Liz said, her voice cracking.

Merry looked at her friends. "Not only me. They hanged William, too."

Jonathan looked away. Liz's hand flew to her mouth, not fast enough to stifle a gasp. "My God, Merry. Is he...?"

Merry shook her head. "No. He's alive."

Jonathan exhaled as though he'd been holding his breath. "If he's alive, where is he? Why didn't he come back with you?"

Merry pursed her lips. She found no comfort in the fact that she'd only left under William's insistence and threats.

"Merry?" Liz said.

She stared into the fireplace. "He couldn't come back."

"What does that mean?"

"When I used my colors to free William and I from the noose, we ended up in... a bad place." Merry shuddered at the memory of hundreds of rotting corpse hands grabbing at her, pulling her into the earth with them. "The Tall Man hurt William. He marked him."

"I don't..."

Merry interrupted Jonathan. "William was changed. He could no longer trust himself not to harm me."

Liz placed a reassuring hand on top of Merry's.

"The Tall Man cursed him. I think... I think he made William one of his legion."

"What, and turned him against you?" Liz asked. "That would never work."

"Liz," Jonathan warned.

"Don't even try to shush me on this, Jonathan," Liz said. "Merry, I've never known a man more dedicated to a woman than William is to you. You can't believe he's working with the Tall Man now. If anything, he's figuring out how the hell to get back to you."

"Actually, I agree with you," Jonathan said. "Merry, you can't believe William is a lost cause."

"I don't," Merry said. "But I'm afraid he does."

Merry's voice stuttered. "He once told me not even time could keep us apart." A tear streamed down her face at the memory, and she wished his words into truth. "I guess there is something that can divide us after all."

Liz shook her head from side to side. "No, I don't believe that. You have to convince him."

"I tried, Liz. I tried. You didn't see him. The mark—it changes him." Merry whispered the next words. "I barely recognized him."

"You have to try harder."

"How is she supposed to try anything?" Jonathan asked. "We don't even know where he is."

Liz leaned back against the sofa and sighed. "What about the witch? The one at the harbor? She said she could help you."

"She said she *might* be able to help me."

"Yeah, well. You happened to run into the highest of high

priestesses of Salem. She's like the ambassador of Witch City. If anyone could help you, I'd place my money on her."

"Do you really think she can help? I mean, as far as I'm concerned, Merry is the only real witch in Salem." Jonathan said.

Merry dropped her face into her hands. It all seemed so hopeless. "She called me Enfys."

"What's Enfys? Do *I* know you're Enfys?" Jonathan asked.

"Enfys means rainbow," Liz said. "It's sort of a magical nickname."

Jonathan tilted his head and arched an eyebrow.

"It's what they call me in Nurya," Merry added.

"And she knew that?" Liz asked.

Merry nodded. "She did."

"That's good, right?" Liz asked. "If she knows that, she probably knows more. We could go back tomorrow, talk to her."

Merry agreed, then yawned and stretched.

"Jeez. Sorry, Merry. You must be exhausted. We'll let you get some sleep." Liz rose, Jonathan followed, and after a round of hugs left her for the night.

Though exhausted, Merry couldn't sleep and wandered onto the balcony where she stayed until the wee hours of morning. She'd once resented the twinkling presence of the Illuminators, now she wished for even a hint of them. Merry stared at the woods willing a golden being to step out, wanting a path, any path, back to William. Finally, she gave up on her fruitless desires and went back into the warmth of the room.

Everywhere she looked she saw William. She recalled him bouncing on his toes the first time he'd put sneakers on his feet. His clothing hung in the closet, both centuries accounted for. She ran her hand down the jeans folded on the shelf, recalling how his muscled thigh had felt beneath the rough fabric. Remembering was wonderful, but it was not without pain.

And, the bed. Of course, the bed held many special memories for her. She smiled through the tears and sat down on the floor, leaning her head against the wall.

"I'm so sorry, William," she whispered to the room.

In the nearby woods, among the burnt ground at the foot of a young tree, shadows shifted and coalesced into one, lifting and then spinning into the night sky. Faraway, a man's heart awakened.

She'd left him. Left him in the hands of the Devil. She told herself she'd had no choice. William had threatened her, having been marked by the Tall Man. She'd been weak and had no fight left in her.

She'd left him.

The need for a shower overwhelmed her. She stripped as she walked into the bathroom, dropping her clothes along the way. She turned all the showerheads on. The hot, forceful spray was what she needed to wash away the state of confusion she'd been living in for the last two weeks. *Goodbye Molly*, she thought as water and suds swirled down the drain. True, she'd started out as Molly Rose Cooke, but she'd lived as Meredith Rose Chalmers. That's who she would always be. Who she wanted to be. Two lives, two centuries. One person.

When she stepped out of the shower, raw and pink, she stepped back into her life. As troubled as it was, it was hers, and she embraced it fully. She wrapped the plush robe hanging on the hook beside the shower around her, combed through her hair and walked back into the room.

She froze.

A swirl of dust made visible by the candle light hovered in the corner of the room. Though threat made a small noise in her head, the overwhelming sense of want, need, and hope prevailed. The shadow formed a crude human shape.

She approached the shimmering figure. It stirred, agitated. "Don't! Please don't go."

The shadow stilled. She moved, slower this time, each step closer revealing more than dust and shadow. The outline of a human body came into crisp relief. Then, a lock of blonde hair and blue eyes. Merry gasped. For some time, she could do nothing but stare and breathe. She recalled the shimmering dust that had calmed her and given her purpose during the storm, the dusty hand that had held hers and returned memories to her.

"I forgot you," she whispered.

His voice was hoarse and quiet as though he were unused to speaking. "Not really."

"No, not really. I dreamed of you." She realized she'd done more than dream. "I *saw* you. In the cave."

"You gave me light—you healed me." William smiled, his eyes sad.

"Yes, but... not enough." Merry said, pained by the dusty evidence before her. "I'm not dreaming, am I?"

A smirk appeared on William's face. "Do you mean nightmare?"

She inched closer. "How is it you're here?"

"'Tis an illusion. My body is still trapped in the Tall Man's dungeon."

She reached a hand toward his cheek. "You could shatter my image with a swish of your hand."

Merry pulled her hand away, the sudden movement sending bits of dust scurrying.

"I shouldn't have come," he said.

"I don't want you to leave."

"I've only made it worse. I'm being selfish. 'Twas better you forgot me."

"No, William. It wasn't better. It wasted time."

"Merry."

A tear slid down her cheek. "I don't know how to save you."

William gave her a sad smile. "'Tis not your place to save me, Merry."

She gulped as tears streamed down her face. William's shape wavered and disintegrated into a million pieces of dust and faded into the tenebrous corners of the room, her cries following his disappearing form.

Merry paced the hallway between her room and the library. *Did William truly just appear out of dust?* Nevertheless, the emptiness he'd left in her heart was real. *What have I done? How could I have left him to the Tall Man?* She'd left him alone to fight the curse, the evil, inside him. Both the darkness that tainted his soul and the fire the mark ignited—she was to blame for his torment.

She stepped into the library, the waning gibbous moon slicing a path from the window to the desk, leaving the rest of the room in shadow. Twenty-three years earlier, Robert Kerrington and Aimee Darling had taken a journey back in time from this exact spot. William's father had expected more from his sacrifice. He'd expected a conquest, a vanquishing of the dark that had taken hold in Salem Village, an enlightenment that would carry across the years, strengthening the Illuminators and forever keeping evil at bay.

Instead, he'd started a cascade of events that tore people in and out of time and intertwined all their lives. Robert Kerrington had tried hard to do right for a larger cause. He'd dreamed of an uncorrupted life for William. And Merry had delivered his son to the Devil.

"Merry?"

Merry startled at the sound of Liz's sleepy voice. She turned, catching her friend mid-yawn.

"What are you doing in here? I thought you'd be too tired to move after what you went through tonight."

Merry opened her mouth to respond to Liz, but tears took the place of words, and she instead sobbed into her hands. Liz rushed to her, wrapping her in a tender hug. "What's the matter?"

Unable to speak, Merry shook her head from side to side and sat down on a wide, tufted ottoman. Liz sat down beside her. It took a few more moments more before she'd reined in the tears and could utter a word.

"I saw William. Maybe I hallucinated him."

"What do you mean?"

"I mean he's in trouble, Liz. I left him in the hands of a monster. The Devil! How do I fix that? How can I?"

"Whoa, slow down. You're overwhelmed. A lot happened tonight. Heck, a lot has happened over the past couple of months. You'll get some sleep and..."

"It will all be better?"

Liz released a frustrated sigh. "I was going to say you'll feel more like yourself after resting. And, the you I know thinks her way out of impossible predicaments and fights for her man."

"Really? Because the me I know left her man in an evil place, and didn't fight nearly hard enough."

Liz laid an arm across Merry's shoulders and squeezed. Their gazes landed on the blade of moonlight as they contemplated the situation. Several silent minutes passed. Then, Liz spoke.

"You needed to get strong enough to fight not only for William, but for the both of you."

Liz looked toward the desk, and Merry followed her gaze to the framed photo of Robert, his wife, and young Sidney.

"And, maybe," Liz said in a soft voice, "You're not the only one fighting."

33 HELP

William's world became physical as his roaming, metaphysical self slammed back into his prone body. A soft voice called his name. He opened his eyes to the Tall Man's dungeon. William turned his head toward the source of the voice, recoiling at the nearness of the owner's face so close to his own. He pushed up and sprang backward.

A woman eyed him warily. One of the damned he'd been forced to disinter and lead back to this hell. She crouched upon the dirt floor, as naked and filthy as the makeshift grave that had originally claimed her. William's heart pounded as he realized he recognized this girl from the bar in Salem. She was one of the witches that had put him and Jonathan under their poisonous spell and given him to the Tall Man. His lip lifted in an involuntary snarl at the sight of her, a witch who'd helped orchestrate his own demise.

"What do you want?!"

His shouted demand startled the girl. She leapt to her feet and jumped back to the opposite wall of the cave. He could barely see her in the dim torchlight. Her voice came out of the darkness, shaking and uncertain. "I want to help you."

Help him? Help him! William laughed like the madman he

was. "You want to help me."

"Yes."

William stormed toward her, stopping mere inches from her face. To her credit, the girl didn't sink through the floor to escape his wrath, but stood taller and stronger in the face of it.

"It was wrong of me to sacrifice your life for my own gain," she said.

"You've gained nothing," he said, disgusted by her avarice.

"You're right, but I've sacrificed, too."

"'Twas you're own doing. I had no choice in the matter."

She shook her head. "No, you didn't. And for that, I'm sorry."

William stepped back. There was something in the way she spoke that gave him pause.

"What is your name?" he asked, recalling the fateful day in Salem when she'd refused to answer the same question. This time, there was no mystery. No hesitation.

"Lila."

They looked at one another, gauging their responses. Assessing their value.

"I won't lie to you."

"Why should I believe you?" William asked.

She hesitated only a moment. "Because we want the same thing now."

"I doubt that."

"You don't want your freedom?"

William wanted much more than his freedom, but he'd never admit that to anyone in this godforsaken place. "If you know how to attain your freedom, why is it you're still here?"

"I don't *know* exactly."

"Ahh..."

"But, I think I—*we*—can figure it out. *Together.*"

Freedom. It was a glorious aspiration. It meant so much more than the word could convey.

Lila sat in the dirt, unbothered by her nakedness. "Members of Nurya share your captivity, though in less luxurious accommodations."

"This is luxury, then?"

"You don't live in the dirt as though you're a part of it. You don't need to break its surface to feel air on your skin or light against your eyelids."

William looked around at his dank surroundings, the weak torchlight wavering in its search for enough oxygen to fuel its fire.

"Members of Nurya are below. Does their light still shine?"
"Barely."

William frowned. "You say you wish to help me. How?"

"I've seen your light."

William uttered a small laugh. "My light. 'Tis not much that remains."

"It's enough. Maybe."

"Enough for what, exactly?"

"To escape, of course. You'll need help. There's more light below, and another that can feed yours. Strengthen you. Do you know whose it is?"

William stared at the witch before him, naked in form and desire, covered in the filth of her deeds. She deserved his condemnation. Yet, he almost trusted her.

She stepped closer, her hand brushing against his. His fingers wrapped around a familiar weapon. "Do you know, William? Do you know who the other light is?"

William nodded, afraid to even whisper the words in the Tall Man's lair. But the answer would not be contained within his head. Two words filled his mind. Two words only recently added to his vocabulary.

My sister.

A dull thud sounded. Careful, purposeful steps descended down the stone staircase. Torchlight flickered small and weak at the far end of the corridor. The earth around William trembled, then shifted as it swallowed Lila's legs, then torso. "Move fast, William," she said before disappearing beneath the dirt.

The light grew, casting the face behind it into an eerie mask. Vanessa. Come to usher him off to another of their shared master's horrific deeds, no doubt. She approached with the smile that set his teeth on edge. Sweetness on her lips, malevolence in her eyes. He'd tasted those lips once. In a desperate attempt to save Merry, he'd pressed his lips against hers. He wiped the phantom touch from his mouth and pushed up from the damp, cave floor. He could kill her with his own hands. He *desired* the action. Yet, it would be for naught. The Tall Man had granted her eternal life. Nothing he could do would end her.

Screams erupted as she neared, a woman's screams. Vanessa's gaze didn't falter. Her steps remained steady. The screams grew louder. William fought the urge to put his hands on his ears to dull the noise. Vanessa spoke, but though he saw her lips move, he heard nothing but the screams. He knew then that she didn't hear them. They were happening in his head. And, then, he knew whose they were.

As if it was as natural as breathing, he pushed his other self from his body to go to the screaming woman. But Vanessa leaned forward and placed her hand upon his mark at the same time, and it all went horribly wrong. His dust self ripped from his chest and Vanessa meshed with him. Her shadow and his dust and light soared together into darkness.

They landed in the midst of an expansive dead field, lit by the eerie white glow of a full moon. A body lay at his feet, the dying blond girl from his cornfield. "Sidney."

She reached a shaking hand toward him. "Your light."

He reached down, but Vanessa inserted herself between them. She smiled, though it was wicked. "You needn't help the girl. She's nothing to you."

"Move, witch," he said.

"Let her go. The dark will welcome her." The ground groaned as hands bubbled beneath its skin, fingers poking through.

Vanessa placed the heel of her hand on his chest. Chills cascaded down his body. What light he'd held turned to shadow. The night abruptly fell into a suffocating blackness. Only the smallest pinprick of light remained, and it emanated from the injured girl. She reached for William. She didn't need his light, after all. He needed hers.

William extended his hand toward Sidney, and she clasped it, sending light up his arm. At the same time, he gripped the dirk he'd received from Lila. In the moment it took Vanessa to register the light's threat, William plunged the blade into her heart, sinking it to the hilt.

His sister's light enveloped him, so bright, he could not breath for the beauty of it.

It lasted but a moment before the earth shifted and William found himself back in the gloom of the Tall Man's dungeon, the dying sounds of Vanessa's screams rebounding off the walls. Vanessa lay on the ground, the greedy tongues of the dead licking at her blood pooling in the dirt. His knife stuck out of her chest. He pulled it free and hid it in his pocket. More blood pulsed out of the wound. The dead grew wild, climbing upon her, devouring every drop of blood.

William turned away from the abhorrent scene. Then, he heard his name. He squeezed his eyes shut, hoping to block out what he was hearing, but the voice only grew stronger, and finally he was forced to face its owner. Vanessa stared at him, no longer with unseeing eyes. She pushed angrily at the grotesque beings still licking at her. Her screams sent them scurrying back into the bowels of the earth. And, despite the fact that she must have lost nearly all her blood, that she'd most certainly been dead moments earlier, Vanessa stood.

She ran towards William and before he could react, she leapt and landed a kick to his chest. He fell backward, and hands burst from the ground, pegging him in place. Vanessa stood over him, glaring. "What you did won't matter. The Illuminators are weak and we're strong. They'll all be dead soon."

William strained against the hands that held him. He growled his words. "You're wrong."

Her laughter trailed behind her as she left him, once again trapped in his prison.

34 CASTLE

"Gotta move faster if you want to live."

Sidney could barely keep the pace as it was. Giving what light she could to William had drained her and made escape little more than a fantasy. Luke wrapped an arm around her waist and lifted her to his side, while he ran and supported or, rather, dragged her along.

"Luke, you don't... "

He glanced over his shoulder, increasing the pace. "Shut up and move."

Sidney followed his gaze. The moon had rejoined the night and laid their pursuers bare. Hundreds of hands pushed up through the ground, hoisting decayed bodies to the surface. Once freed from the earth, those bodies moved faster than the dead ought to. Sidney managed to increase her speed, but not enough.

Cold flesh brushed against her as the earth heaved forth another body at her heels. Before it could make an attempt to take hold, Luke leaped over a grasping corpse taking Sidney into the air with him.

He tucked her close to him. "Sorry, Sid." They were enveloped in a storm of glimmering light. When the light ebbed, a new landscape appeared.

Sidney spun, searching the horizon, and then sank to her knees as she realized where Luke had taken them. "No, no, no, no, no."

"Sid..."

Sidney screamed, a tortured guttural sound that tore at her throat and loosed her despair. Luke sank down beside her and as her screams turned to sobs, he put an arm around her and pulled her close. "I'm so sorry, Sid."

Sidney leaned into his shoulder. "You said we could save him."

"We will. I promise, we will."

Sidney lifted her head from Luke's tear-drenched shoulder. "How? How can we do anything now?" She searched the terrain for a hint of the one they'd escaped from. The rolling hills, the menagerie of eccentric homes, and the smattering of Illuminators told her they were back in Nurya. They'd been so close, and now it was as if their journey had never happened. As if they'd never stepped out of the land of light and trekked across an endless field to a wooded horizon.

As if she'd not come so close to saving her brother.

"We're right back where we started from," Sidney said.

Luke sat back on the grass beside her, hugging his knees to his chest. He tilted his head toward her, meeting Sidney's eyes only for a moment. "You know we had no choice, right?"

Sidney studied him. His shaggy hair and slim build screamed boy, while the depth of regret in his eyes whispered man. He'd done so much to help her, and she'd laid failure at his feet. She placed a hand on his forearm. Luke started to apologize again, but Sidney cut him off.

"No, I'm sorry, Luke. I know you were trying to help, and you did. We managed to get William outside. If Vanessa hadn't been there, maybe William would be with us now."

Luke offered a crooked smile, so different from his usual smirk. "You produced some kick ass light for a halfie."

Sidney laughed. "Halfie?"

Luke's smile grew more crooked, his eyes lit up. "Half

human, half light. Halfie."

"Is that right?" Sidney smiled.

"We can go back, you know," Luke said.

Sidney inhaled deeply. "We have to. I can't leave him there."

"Of course not."

"The way you saved us, with your light. Can we use it to get back there?"

Luke hung his head and shook it slowly back and forth. "That was a one way deal, I'm afraid. I mean, don't you think I would've done that instead of trekking across no man's land in the first place?"

"I don't understand."

"Look around, Sidney. Tell me what you see."

Sidney did as he asked. Luke had landed them in the midst of a neighborhood, no two houses alike, and each a testament to what the imagination could build. Sidney rose and held her hand out to Luke. He took it, and they walked together through the neighborhood. As they passed a small, thatch-roofed cottage, then a Swiss chalet, Sidney began to notice something amiss. She stopped before a large glass structure jutting from a hillside. It usually sparkled like a diamond in a sunbeam. Now its panes stared dull and dusty. The other houses stood dark as well.

Her heart quickened. She dropped Luke's hand and jogged along the dirt path, finding one darkened house after another.

"Sidney!" Luke called as she ran farther on.

She stopped running and turned around.

Luke jogged up to her. "What do you see?"

A lump rose in Sidney's throat, her legs shook. "I see... shadows."

"Shadows. In the land of light."

"What does it mean?"

Luke sighed. "It means chaos, weakness, and terror. It means the darkness is coming. It means there's not enough light for acts of illumination. We're trapped in Nurya. The only way out is the old-fashioned way."

"Walking," Sidney said.

"Walking."

They rounded a corner to find more houses shuttered and abandoned, forlorn in the absence of light.

"I shouldn't have even used the light to escape. It was pure instinct, but it was selfish." He kicked at a rock in the road, sending it clattering down the street.

"Well, you saved my life, so I don't think it was selfish," Sidney said. "Plus, we're William's only chance right now, so it wasn't selfish at all. It was heroic, actually."

Sidney smiled at Luke and nudged him with her shoulder. He looked up, an impish grin on his face that disappeared as quickly as it came. His eyes focused beyond her. Sidney followed his stunned gaze to find her favorite home in Nurya, a medieval castle, complete with moat, bridge and turrets lit up like Christmas.

Torches lined the bridge, the reflection of their bright orange flames rippling on the water's surface. More torches rimmed the turrets, and warm, glowing light spilled from every window cut into the stone facade. Illuminators, five deep on each side of the arched entryway, radiated a nuclear brilliance.

Sidney took another glance at their surroundings, dim and nearly colorless. The shining castle all the more dominant with the neighboring homes enveloped in deep shadows. "How?"

Luke looked as perplexed as she was. He stepped onto the bridge.

Sidney grabbed his arm. "Wait."

"You're worried."

"It's so out of place."

"You're wrong. These shadows are out of place." He pointed toward the castle. "That's sanctuary."

A chill stole along Sidney's neck, and she turned. Behind her the shadows grew like black vines strangling their host. Whispers chased the wind. She didn't need to see or hear anything else to believe Luke. She stepped onto the bridge, and together they walked toward a glimmering hope.

The castle was every bit as incredible as Sidney imagined it would be. Colorful tapestries adorned the walls, their muted colors exuding warmth under the flickering light of the torches. Chairs and benches boasting intricately carved finials and legs lined the perimeter of the hall, filled with many, if not most, of the remaining Illuminators in Nurya.

Choice of abode was personal, a fantasy granted. But for Squire Axylus Perri, it was homage to the life he'd planned to live. Just shy of twenty-one years old and obtaining knighthood, Axylus had died when he'd placed himself between an arrow and his knight during the Battle of Agincourt. That was after downing no less than a dozen of the French cavalry with his own bow.

Sidney's first thought upon seeing Axylus was that he was one hot guy. Maybe it was the skintight leggings, which should've been a major turn-off but instead emphasized the sculpted body contained within them. Or maybe it was the way he looked at everyone with the utmost confidence as he spoke, each word chosen wisely. And the way he said those words! His medieval English accent teetered on the edge of comprehension, but rolled off the tongue with an assuredness that guaranteed his audience's rapt attention.

For the last twenty minutes, Axylus paced the center of the hall championing honor, faith, and pushing back the dark to its own realm. Unlike the Tall Man, who wanted to eradicate light from the world, Illuminators simply wanted balance. The light needed the dark—it would be meaningless without it—while the dark only grew darker.

Sidney leaned towards Luke. "I like this guy."

Luke shrugged. "I guess. If you like chivalry and all that."

"Oh, I like."

Luke frowned. "So, you're ready to join the army? In case you've forgotten, your brother is one of the bad guys now."

Sidney turned on him. "He's not one of the bad guys, Luke. He's being *held* by the bad guy. There's a difference."

She must've spoken louder than she'd thought, because Axylus stopped pacing and stood directly in front of her, only a few feet away. He held her gaze with his cocoa brown eyes.

"I fear Luke speaks the truth, my lady."

Sidney bristled. She couldn't let Luke's foolish statement taint her brother's worth. She stood and met Axylus's gaze. "You're wrong."

As if he regretted the words, he said, "Nay, methinks not."

"William is an Illuminator. The strongest of our kind. We have to protect him."

"And we shall. We will make battle and take back that which is ours. Alas, we cannot ignore the fie which has been placed upon your brother's soul."

Sidney stared at the medieval Illuminator. "The fie?"

"Aye."

"No, I mean, what the hell is a fie?"

A rustling behind her, then Luke at her side, saying in a loud whisper, "It's a curse."

Sidney glared at Axylus. "My brother's not cursed. He's a prisoner. We have to get him out of there. We have to..."

Luke laid a hand on her shoulder. "Sid."

She shrugged Luke's hand off and marched toward Axylus until they stood toe to toe. "My brother is not one of the bad guys. He's not in league with the Tall Man. He's fighting. You know that!"

Axylus spoke in slow measured words that resounded with horrible certainty throughout the hall. "The mark of the Devil has been placed upon William. I know not whether he fights. But, I know we will."

35 DAUGHTER

"So, you're saying Merry's purpose is to protect Salem?" Jonathan asked Ruby Violette, otherwise known as the premier witch of Salem.

"I'm saying that, yes," Ruby answered with extreme, if not thin, patience.

Merry, Liz, and Jonathan had descended upon Ruby's Derby Wharf shop as soon as it opened. Despite the thunk of wood being tossed upon wood, the beeping sounds of construction vehicles backing up, and the occasional shout—all of which added up to the industrious sounds of a massive cleanup effort—the wharf exuded an eerie quiet. Police tape blocked off the road about twenty feet past Ruby's shop door. Ruby's assistant managed the few undeterred tourists who'd ventured into the shop, while Merry and her friends stood shoulder-to-shoulder with Ruby in an overheated room, normally reserved for personal readings and not meant to fit four people.

"Ruby, your, uh, highness?" Liz said.

Ruby's heavily kohl-rimmed eyes sparkled. "It's Ruby, unless you want to join my coven. Then you can call me High Priestess."

Jonathan frowned. Merry suppressed a smile. Liz continued undiscouraged. "I'll pass for now, thanks, but why exactly does Salem need protecting?"

One by one, Ruby looked each of them in the eye. "Have any of you been to Gallows Hill?"

"I played softball up there last year," Jonathan said.

"I watched him play ball," Liz said. Ruby smiled.

"I was hanged at Gallows Hill a few weeks ago," Merry said in a quiet voice.

Ruby's smile faltered. "What?"

Jonathan cleared his throat and stared at Merry.

"It's fine, Jonathan. Ruby knows I'm Enfys, remember?" Merry crossed her arms. "The point is, Ruby knows about my colors. She may be able to help."

"How?" Jonathan asked, his tone edged with skepticism.

"I have to get William back." Merry said, anxiety creeping into her voice. After she'd regained her identity and then witnessed William dissolving into dust before her eyes, the desperation that had thus far permeated her being had finally been given a name and a purpose—William.

"You have to stop the Tall Man," Ruby said.

"This is crazy. This whole conversation is crazy," Jonathan said, digging his fingers beneath his cast to scratch.

A tinkling sound announced another visitor, followed by the unmistakable sound of Sophie's voice. "I'm here for my granddaughter. She said she'd be here?"

Merry edged passed Liz, pushed aside the satin curtain and stepped into the main shop. "I'm here, Sophie."

Sophie welcomed Merry into open arms. "You're back," Sophie whispered in her ear. Merry nodded against her shoulder. Sophie stepped back and held Merry's face. "Don't take this the wrong way. But, I'm glad Molly is gone."

Merry emitted a sound somewhere between a laugh and a choked cry. "Me too."

"You have to tell me what happened. Last night and... you know, before." Sophie glanced around the shop. "But, why are we meeting here?"

"It's part of what happened last night." There was the sound of swishing cloth, and then Liz and Jonathan stood behind her, followed by Ruby.

"Hello, Ruby," Sophie said, a touch of scorn in her voice.

"*Madame* Sophie," Ruby answered in a mocking tone.

"So," Liz said in an over-bright voice. "You two know each other?"

"One of us *thinks* she does," Sophie said. Ruby tilted her chin up and stared down her nose at Sophie.

"What does that mean?" Liz asked.

Sophie waved her hand. "It doesn't matter." She beamed at Merry. "What's important is that Merry is back."

"What's important is that Merry does what needs doing," Ruby said.

"And you know what that is?" Sophie asked.

"I know more than you do," Ruby answered. Sophie glared.

Liz waved her hands. "Whoa, hey. This—whatever this is—isn't getting us anywhere."

Merry took Sophie's hand. "We need to work together, Sophie."

"Right. Fine. Why don't you finish up your conversation? I'll wait over here, and then we can go home and talk."

Merry sighed. Whatever was between Sophie and Ruby would have to be dealt with at another time. "Ruby, the Tall Man has something, some*one*, of mine. I need to save him." Liz placed a reassuring hand upon Merry's shoulder.

"My dear, you need to focus on the bigger picture here. The Tall Man could end Salem, could end the world, as we know it. Whatever he has, whoever he has, I'm afraid you're going to have to set your feelings aside to get the job done."

Merry shook her head. "That's not going to happen."

Sophie refrained from telling Ruby Violette that once again her assumptions about a person were wrong. If she thought Merry would set aside her mission to save William in order to save the world, she was astoundingly mistaken. Merry would save William *and* the world. That was her granddaughter.

Of course, Ruby was wrong about many of her assumptions, including her claim that Sophie was nothing more than a charlatan with a knack for saying the right words to needy people. OK, maybe she *was* a charlatan. But, she hadn't always been. And she wasn't one now.

Sophie glanced out the window. She was certain the man in the hoodie had followed her, but aside from a slender blonde woman peering into a shop window across the street and the repair crews at the end of the pier, the area was empty. Sophie turned her attention to the objects on the shop's shelves: wands, runes, and tarot cards. The nerve of the woman to claim that Sophie was a fake. *Just look at this place!* It was all Sophie could do to keep from laughing out loud.

Sophie lifted a wand made of copper, a clear crystal jutting out from one end. She gave it a swoosh before placing it back on the table, all the while keeping one ear open to the conversation happening on the other side of the room.

"I will do what needs doing. But, I won't leave William behind again," Merry told Ruby. Sophie smiled as she removed a clear crystal ball from a perch in the window display. Light stabbed a rainbow into its center. A shadow grew from the colors. Sophie peered into the crystal's depths.

A dark mass bloomed, painting the crystal black. Indistinct forms writhed within the black depths. The crystal warmed as Sophie watched the forms take shape. A single decrepit hand slapped its palm against the interior of the crystal causing a jagged crack to split its surface. Sophie screamed and dropped the ball to the ebony wood floor. The crystal split into two halves, spewing a dark cloud and a thousand tortured screams into the shop.

Merry's skin prickled with the threat of evil a moment before the torments of hell exploded in Ruby's shop. She covered her ears, barely muffling the screams of the damned. Sophie fell to her knees. The black cloud pulsed and grew, suffocating what daylight had filtered into the shop.

"What did you do?!" Ruby shouted at Sophie, then she

shoved passed Jonathan to the back of the store, away from the ever-growing cloud.

"So much for help in the face of danger," Liz said. "What is that, Merry?"

Even if Merry knew, there was no time to answer when, at that moment, the glass in the window burst outward sending shards into the street. Liz screamed and clutched Merry's arm. Tendrils of ebony smoke drifted from the cloud and reached towards them. The scent of dirt mixed with rotting leaves and worse permeated the air. Merry gagged and choked against the onslaught of the foul odor. Liz and Jonathan coughed beside her. The menacing cloud obscured Sophie from her sight, and Merry's internal alarms sounded. Something, or someone, fell to the floor.

A high-pitched shriek erupted behind them, followed by Ruby streaking passed them and into the center of the billowing shadows. A monotone chant penetrated the demons' screams at the same time that a puff of white powder exploded from the center of the darkness. For a moment it looked as if a snowstorm had erupted in Ruby's shop. Powdery flakes drifted down and outward, coating the toxic black mass, bubbling and boiling red as it made contact. The screams drowned within its molten embrace. Merry threw herself to the ground beside Liz and Jonathan, catching brief sight of her grandmother slumped beneath the broken window. A shriek came from the other side of the shop when the spectacle above them burst into a thousand brilliant blue flames before extinguishing itself.

A smothering silence ensued. A heavy sulfurous odor invaded Merry's nostrils. She lifted her head, first noticing Ruby lying prone beneath the display table before her gaze fell upon Sophie's unconscious form leaning against the wall beneath the shattered window. Sophie's chest stuttered against her breath, while Merry's caught in her throat.

Liz shielded her nose and mouth with her arm. "Smells like rotten eggs in here."

"That would be brimstone," Ruby's assistant said as she crawled over to where Ruby lay.

The sounds of glass crunching beneath careful steps drew Merry's gaze toward the ruined shop window where a delicate blonde woman stood outside. Her ethereal beauty was arresting. Unsettling.

Jonathan noticed her, too. "Hey." He pushed up from the floor with his good arm. "Hey, I know you."

The woman smiled, sending warning shivers across Merry's scalp.

Jonathan took a few steps toward the window. "You're the one from the bar. The one who took us to the witch circle."

Warning bells turned into all-out alarm inside Merry's head. If what Jonathan said was true, that meant this woman was more than a witch. She was the one who'd taken William. She was the Devil's daughter.

Anger surged within her. "Jonathan, don't go near her."

He halted, sparing Merry a quizzical look. "But, she's..."

"Dangerous," Merry finished. As she said the word, Corinne's attention turned to Merry, a sly smile courting her lips. Merry's own mouth twitched into a scowl as discovery sparked in Corinne's piercing blue eyes. Her gaze lifted above Merry's head, cascaded downward and back to her eyes, and Merry knew Corinne saw more than an angry woman; she saw Merry's colors.

"Do you like them?" Merry asked.

Corinne tilted her head to the side and raised her eyebrows, grinning all the while. Merry's ire grew into a boiling knot in her stomach. William would be at her side but not for this woman—this evil spawn. She balled her hands against her side and then flexed her fingers as her colors pushed for release. Before she'd even made the decision, Ruby called for her to stop. She ignored the plea and lifted several of her fingers, allowing the coolness of blue to tickle her palm. Too late, she noticed the assured expectance on Corinne's face.

As Merry summoned the strength of the wind, Corinne reached her hand through the exposed window frame and extended her fingers toward Sophie's unconscious form leaning against the wall beneath the window. Her fingertips reddened and then glowed like hot coals.

Merry rushed across the room, part woman, part wind. Wisps of blue churned the air and raced alongside her. Long strands of blonde hair whipped across Corinne's face. She halted in her reach toward Sophie, perhaps never meaning to target her at all, and turned her attention to Merry. A blast of heat hit Merry, slowing her advance. She shielded herself from the onslaught of flames that kindled and blazed within her wind's embrace.

Sweat streamed down her scalp and into her eyes. Merry pushed her colors into the wind, but Corinne's fire only devoured them. Merry's limbs grew heavy and sluggish. She dropped to one knee. On the other side of the wind and fire, Corinne wore a triumphant smile. While fire pressed toward Merry, a stream of colors poured toward Corinne, covering her in a translucent sheen. Still she smiled.

Worried, shouting voices echoed behind her. Someone tried to tug her back from the encroaching flames, which had begun to lick the shop ceiling. The threat against her family and friends gave new life to Merry's conviction. *Her* purpose was righteous. Her purpose meant life, a life with the potential to love and to right wrongs. She'd not suffer the Devil. *Or* his daughter.

Merry rose, pushed aside her hatred and embraced the determination to get back what was hers. *What was the saying? Fight fire with fire?* Merry clenched her fists, squelching the colors, immediately replacing them with her own flames. Holding her hands up, she sent a churning ball of fire crashing into Corinne's inferno.

Corinne's smile faltered, then disintegrated altogether as Merry's flames first mingled, then overcame her own. She shrieked and spun around, creating a flaming cyclone that reached toward the sky. A second later it snuffed itself out, leaving behind a winding ribbon of smoke. Corinne was nowhere to be found.

Merry ran to her grandmother's side, crouching beside her. Sophie stirred, eyelids fluttering, and then snapping open.

"Sophie, are you all right? Is anything broken? Did she hurt you?"

Sophie pressed the heel of her hand against her forehead, pushing her silver hair off her face. "I'm fine," she said before succumbing to a coughing fit. Merry patted her back.

Ruby leaned heavily against the leg of the nearby table, head tilted back as she took deep breaths. She lowered her head a moment, fixing Sophie with an accusing glare.

Merry glared back at the woman. "This isn't her doing."

Ruby's gaze met Merry's, defiant at first. Then she cast her gaze downward, and Merry accepted her silent apology.

"Can you tell us what happened, Sophie?" Liz asked. Sophie attempted to answer, but couldn't get a word in between her coughing. "She may need to go to the hospital, Merry."

Sophie held a hand up, the other fist catching a cough before she managed to say in a hoarse voice, "I'm OK." She cleared her throat. "Need water."

"By the register," Ruby's assistant said, nodding toward the counter behind her. She kept hold of Ruby's hand. "There's bottled water in the mini-fridge behind the counter."

Jonathan scurried behind the counter, while Ruby attempted to stand. The two halves of the crystal lay near Sophie, now nothing more than broken glass. "How did you stop it?" Merry asked Ruby.

Ruby paused in a half-crouched position. "Powdered sulfur, otherwise known as brimstone. Extremely effective in removing an enemy's power."

Jonathan came around the counter, holding two bottles of water. He handed one to Sophie and the other to Ruby. After several unsuccessful attempts, Sophie handed the bottle to Merry for her to open it. Merry gave up shortly thereafter and thrust it into Liz's hands. "I still can't get these open."

Amusement crossed Liz's eyes, as she made quick work of opening the bottle and handing it back to Sophie.

Another crunch of glass sounded outside the open window behind Merry. A hooded man snuck a curious peak into the shop as he passed by. A tingling warmth cascaded across

Merry's shoulders. It continued down her arms, enveloping her like a cozy sweater. She stuck her head through the open window, careful to avoid the jagged shards that framed the opening. She couldn't see passed the bulk of the entryway. Across the street, a shop door opened and an older man stuck his head out and asked if everyone was all right. Merry nodded absently, then pulled her head back in and headed for the door.

"Where are you going?" Liz asked.

Her hand on the door handle, Merry glanced back at her curious friend. "Wait here." She stepped outside, the warm feeling intensifying as she headed in the direction the hooded man had gone. She caught sight of him just as he turned right onto Derby Street. Merry increased her pace, breaking into a jog, only to find him gone when she turned the corner. An unexpected excitement coursed through her veins, announcing his proximity. She continued down Derby, searching the side roads and peering down the other side of Wharf Street. She stretched up on her toes and craned her neck around a family coming towards her and spotted him heading back toward the shop.

Merry ran.

Her heart thumped with promise. For the barest of moments she entertained the thought that this might be some sort of trick. Her senses overruled such treachery. "Wait," she called out. To her surprise, the man halted. She slowed until she stood behind him, taking in deep breaths. Her heart knew whom she'd found.

The sound of running feet came to a sudden stop behind her. A hand touched her forearm. "Merry?" Liz asked.

Sophie came out of the back door of the shop, stepping directly in front of the hooded man. Her mouth dropped open. "You."

"Merry, what's going on?" Liz asked.

"It's all right," she answered as she reached out to touch the man's shoulder. The connection was undeniable. It screamed in her bones. The man turned.

Dark hair, curling slightly at the neck, surprised blue eyes.

She remembered those same eyes filled with fear as time stole his loved ones away.

Fat tears trickled down Merry's cheeks. "Papa."

For a moment, father and daughter stared at one another, taking in each other's existence. The years apart melted away and Devon saw the little girl he'd lost in her eyes, her softly curling auburn hair, darker now, and her mother's straight nose. This woman standing before him was his little girl. Devon's eyes filled with tears. The only thing that could make this moment more perfect would've been if Summer were there standing beside her.

"Papa," she said, and that one word sent him bawling like a baby. She stepped forward and he swept her into his arms, something he never thought he'd have the chance to do again. Finally, he released her, stepping back to look at her again.

"It's really you."

"I knew you the minute I saw you. Before that even," she said.

He shook his head. "You remember me? You were so young when..."

"I don't remember much from that time," she said, then looking into his eyes added, "But even so, I knew it was you. You... you feel like home."

Devon wiped at his eyes and laughed a little. "Jesus, you're going to make me cry again."

Merry giggled and hugged him. Then, she stiffened. "Sophie."

Devon released her to turn towards his mother-in-law.

"Devon," Sophie said, "You're the one who's been following me."

"Yes. I'm sorry. I wasn't sure how I'd be welcomed, and I didn't know you saw me. I hope I didn't scare you."

"It was a bit nerve-wracking, but... oh come here." She held her arms open and walked toward him, enveloping Devon in a tight embrace. "It's good to have you home."

"I'm sorry," he said as they separated. "I'm sorry I left."

Sophie looked upon him with sadness. "You didn't need to."

Devon tilted his head, looked at the ground, then back to Sophie. "I did. I did need to leave."

Merry touched his arm. "She knows about my colors. What I did that day."

Devon's pulse raced. He stared at his daughter. "What you did?"

Merry nodded, her blue eyes sparkling with fresh tears. "I didn't mean to. It just happened. I couldn't control it. Not then."

Devon sucked in a sharp breath. *Is she saying what I think she's saying? She learned to control the colors?*

"I remember your face. I remember how scared you were."

She fell into his arms again, and he smoothed the hair on the back of her head much like he'd done when she was a crying toddler.

Sophie pursed her lips. "I would have believed you."

Devon kissed the top of Merry's head. "No. You wouldn't have. You couldn't. Not then. But, I'm grateful that you believed Molly when she showed up at your door. Thank you."

Sophie frowned. "I had a little help being convinced."

Merry pulled away, wiping at her eyes. "Sophie has visions."

"And a crystal ball," Liz added.

Devon laughed until he realized he was the only one laughing. "You do?"

A woman dressed in black stepped out of the shop door behind Sophie. Her thick eyebrows raised into arched peaks above her eyes, delivering a look of perpetual curiosity. After spending years evading questions, Devon had learned to build walls against such scrutiny. Sophie frowned at the stranger. Devon held his daughter tight to his side as he turned them away and began to walk toward Derby Street. "I've booked a room nearby. Why don't we go there to talk?"

Sophie followed. His daughter's friends trailed close behind. Devon glanced back at the dark-robed woman who watched them from her doorstep.

"Who's that woman?"

Merry glanced back toward the shop. "That's Ruby. She's a witch. I think she may be able to help me."

Devon was about to asked why she needed help from a witch, when Sophie emitted a derisive *pffft* sound. Merry frowned. "You need to tell me what the problem is, Sophie."

"You call your grandmother Sophie?" Devon asked. It didn't necessarily surprise him. She'd been gone so long. Maybe she didn't want to call him Papa either, though she'd done it so naturally moments ago.

"Oh," Merry said, blushing. "It's how I met her. I mean when I came back. I mean..."

Devon held up a hand. "It's OK, Molly. I get it. If you'd rather call me Devon, that's all right, too, you know."

Merry shook her head, "No. You're my papa. I couldn't call you anything else."

Devon smiled and let out a breath.

"But, if you don't mind, can you call me Merry? I'm... I'm not Molly anymore."

Devon's smile trembled on his lips as he struggled to maintain it.

"I'm sorry. I don't mean to take that away from you. It's only, most of my life, I've been Merry. It's who I am."

Devon looked at his daughter, alive and standing beside him. *Did anything else matter?* "I don't mind. I'm just glad you're home."

She leaned her head against his shoulder as they strolled down the street. "I'm glad you're home, too."

36 REUNION

Sometimes two stories can be different sides of the same story. That's what Merry thought as she listened to her father punctuate her tale with his own experience. When she told him of Summer's panic at finding them in the midst of a cornfield and how Merry couldn't make the colors, Devon said, "I saw the colors wrap around you and your mother. It happened so fast. I couldn't get to you in time. I'd rather have gone with you, then be left behind."

"Then, I would've lost you too," she said.

Devon's brow twitched. "You'd always come back before."

Merry lowered her gaze to the carpeted floor, fixating on a worn spot near the window. It looked as though someone had spent hours pacing the small area. The room her father had rented at the Harbor Hotel was small, most of the space taken up by the king-sized bed. She sat on a soft yellow chair next to the bed, while her father perched on the chair at the desk by the window.

Here she sat, feet from her father. *Her father!* In the short time since they'd discovered one another, Merry had experienced exultation, relief, happiness, nervousness, and now guilt. It didn't matter that her mother knew she was going to die as foretold by Adina. Merry had been unable to summon her colors until it was too late, and she was still the reason her mother had never made it home.

A tear spilled down her cheek, and her father leaned across the short space and wiped it from her face with the gentle touch of the back of his finger, a touch instantly familiar. "Don't blame yourself. Don't you dare."

Merry sighed. She couldn't absolve herself from the responsibility. If not for her colors, she and her mother would have never gone back in time. Her mother wouldn't have died in a seventeenth-century farmhouse. She could forgive the child she'd been, but the culpability was hers.

Her father took her hand in his. "How did you survive?"

Merry looked into her father's unwavering gaze, his blue eyes so much like her own. They would spend hours telling one another about their years apart, but she needed to ask him something first. "Do you have colors, too, Papa? Can you do what I do?"

Her father froze. He dropped her hand and sat back in his chair. Merry's hopes grew. Maybe she wasn't alone. Maybe her father could help her sort through the strangeness of what she was.

Devon rubbed his neck. "No, I don't have colors like you. I can't... disappear like you do."

Merry's hopes fell to the floor.

"And, neither did your mother," he added, answering her next question before she asked. He looked so miserable by the admission, that as disappointed as she was, Merry attempted a reassuring smile. She caught sight of her lop-sided effort in the mirror behind her father and quit altogether. "However," Devon began, sparking a small flame of leftover optimism in Merry's heart.

"I don't know how to tell you this," he said, shaking his head.

This time Merry took his hand. "Please, say whatever it is you have to say. We've lost too much time to hold secrets."

Devon's brows drew together. "You're right. I wish I'd

thought the same years ago, maybe I could've done more."

"What could you have done?"

Devon's shoulders lifted into a helpless shrug. "Nothing, probably. But, still. I should've been honest with your mother."

"Papa, what is it? Tell me."

"You and your mother went back in time."

Merry nodded, but Devon didn't continue. He stood and paced before the window, his feet worrying the worn spot of carpet. Finally, he stopped. "I've been through time, too, Merry. You both went back. I came forward."

Merry's face tingled cold and warm at the same time. "What?"

"I was born in the year 1656. I was eighteen and on my way to Samuel's farm when a bright light surrounded me. There was a woman inside the light with me. She stepped out of the light, and when it fell away, I was here. In Salem. In the future."

Could it be? Had her father been Aimee Donovan's trade?

"After learning about your colors, I wondered if something happened when I moved through time. Whether it changed me somehow, whether I passed that ability along to you."

Merry placed a gentle hand on her father's arm. "You've harbored this worry for a long time, haven't you?"

Devon nodded.

"Even if it's true, it's not your fault." She sat back in her chair. "It seems we both have blamed ourselves for circumstances out of our control."

"Another way we're alike, I suppose."

Merry smiled. "Mayhap. Tell me, what did the woman look like? The one who sent you through time."

"Blonde, pretty. Scared. I only saw her for a moment, but I'll never forget the look on her face. I'd never seen such terror in someone's eyes."

William's mother. Her father must have been the unplanned trade—the boy in the field that Aimee exchanged places with when Robert sacrificed himself to the Tall Man. "I think I know who she was."

Devon tilted his head, "How could you know?"

Merry sighed. "It's a bit complicated."

For another hour, Merry told him about Rose and how she'd raised her as her niece. Taught her how to read, how to sew, how to cook a lobster to perfection, how to shoe a horse, and how to ride like the wind. Rose had taught her manners, strength, and compassion. "Rose loved me like a mother loves their child."

Devon's eyes watered, and Merry laid a gentle hand on his arm. "I didn't tell you that to hurt you or to diminish the memory of my own mother. I told you so you know I was cared for and that I had someone who loved me, and whom I loved."

"I remember Rose and Alexander Chalmers. They were good people. My father bought a horse from them, a strong Shire. I'm glad you and Rose had one another. But, why did she change your name to Meredith?"

Merry tried to recall exactly when the change had taken place. But, in the end, she said, "I don't know. I think I remember a game. My doll was Molly. I was Merry." Merry smiled at the memory. "I... I only remember being Merry."

"There must be some reason."

"Maybe it had to do with my history or with my future. Adina told Mom what would happen. Maybe Mom told Rose. Maybe it was Mom's idea? I don't know."

For another forty-five minutes, Merry talked about the boy down the road who'd gone from childhood friend to the man she wished to marry.

"William Darling?" Devon asked.

"Yes," Merry answered. "But, you can't have known him. He wasn't born yet."

"Samuel Darling was my friend. Are they related by any chance?"

"Samuel... that's who you were going to visit when the light brought you here, right?"

"Yes," Devon said, nodding.

"He's William's father. Well, stepfather. Aimee, the woman

in the light, was pregnant with William when she traded places in time with you."

"How do you know this?"

"Aimee left a journal. She wrote about her journey, how she traded places with a young man."

"Me. But why? Why me?" Devon asked, eyebrows knit together in question.

Merry pushed a few strands of hair behind her ear. "I don't think she meant for it to be you. It was meant to be another woman, but something went wrong. The Tall Man interrupted the exchange. At least I think that's what happened."

"What tall man? Molly, I don't..."

"Merry."

Devon sighed.

"Let me finish," she said. "I think some of your questions will be answered when I'm done."

As Merry continued, eventually launching into the topic of her being accused of witchcraft during the Salem Witch Trials, Devon's relief turned to horror. She continued on with all that had happened since leaping off the cliff during her escape. When she reached the point of her capture and trip to the gallows, Merry tried to temper her story, but her father saw through her attempts to spare him.

"What are you not telling me?" he asked.

Merry didn't answer right away, instead asking for a glass of water. "My throat is parched. Maybe you should talk for a while. I want to know about you and where you went after we disappeared."

Devon smiled and shook his head. "There'll be time for all that after I hear the rest of your story."

Merry bit her bottom lip. "Be warned. What I say may upset you. Some of the events... you have to remember the time. Remember how different it was back then."

"Oh, I remember. Trust me."

Merry studied her father for a moment.

"What?" he asked.

"We're alike."

"You *are* my daughter," Devon said, grinning as if realizing that fact all over again.

Merry laughed. "No, I mean that we share the same experiences. We've both lived in two different times, two different worlds. You know how confusing this life can be, how it is to learn something new nearly every hour. Sometimes every minute."

Devon smile turned a bit sad. "I suppose I do." He stood and walked to the window. From her vantage point, the tips of boat masts were barely visible. "Do you remember when we would walk down to the harbor?" he asked. "You loved to practice counting the boats."

She stood beside him and gazed upon the water. It sparkled bold and blue as though it hadn't been the Devil's violent tool a mere day ago. Merry searched for the memory, wishing she could recall any moment before the sight of her father's panicked face as he screamed her name. He lifted a curl from her shoulder, letting it fall from his fingertips. "You were so young. I don't expect you to remember." A small laugh escaped him. "But I can tell you that you always demanded that I carry you on my shoulders on the way back home."

Merry leaned her head upon her father's shoulder. He draped his arm across her shoulders, as they stared at the world they now shared.

The pull of the harbor proved too strong, and Merry and her father walked down to the water. Merry ignored the broken boats and debris floating upon the water, instead choosing to focus on the waves dashing against the pilings. Her father stood, hands jammed into the pockets of his jeans, staring at a distant boat, the sun glancing off its mast.

"What was she like?" Merry asked.

Devon cocked his head toward her. "You know what I'm thinking, don't you?"

"No! I can't read minds. I could tell from..."

Her father held his palm up. "Relax. I didn't mean that literally."

Merry forced herself to calm down. Her father had remained mostly silent when she'd told him about her colors and what she could do with them. Far from being able to read minds, she wasn't sure what he thought about her at all.

"Your mother saved me," he said. "If I hadn't met her so soon after my, ah, arrival, I'm not sure I would've made it."

Merry bowed her head. She knew all too well how confused and scared he must have been. "I feel that way about Liz."

"Of course. We were both lucky." Her father rubbed his neck. He was still a young man, having become a father before turning twenty, but at the moment he appeared weary. "Merry, do you mind if we save the topic of your mother for another time? She deserves our undivided attention, and right now I want to hear about what they did to you in Salem, and the threat you are currently living under."

Merry so desired to learn more about her mother, especially when the only memories she had of her were the days of fear and death that followed their journey back in time. But, at this moment, her father was right. Almost.

"It's not only me who's living under a threat. It's all of Salem. And, then some."

"What do you mean?"

Merry stared at the pilings, each wave trying harder than the first to reach their wooden heads.

"Merry," Devon said, a hand on her arm. "What did they do to you?"

She told him of the stones the children threw at her and the rope placed around her neck. She told him about Rose accusing Sheriff Corwin of burning down her home and denying Merry a trial, of William's attempt to save Merry or at least to die by her side. Tears streamed down her father's face as he listened to the abuses she'd suffered. She squeezed his hand. "Don't. It's over. I'm fine."

His face twisted in misery. "What they did to you." He brushed her cheek with rough fingers. "My little girl."

A young couple who'd been observing the damage the storm had caused snuck a few looks their way. Merry took her father's hand and led him down the pier, settling on a wooden bench sheltered by a nearby building.

"I should've tried harder. Should've figured out how to get back, get to you."

"There's nothing you could have done, Papa."

Devon wiped at his eyes and nodded. "What happened to William?"

Now it was Merry's turn to tear up as she whispered. "I left him behind."

After talking for hours, trying to piece their lives together with words, they sat in silence as the evening shadows spread across the sky. Finally, Devon straightened in his seat and said, "I want to help. Whatever it takes. I'll help you stop the darkness and save the light. Save William."

"This is something I have to do on my own. No one can help me."

Devon stood. "Nonsense. I can help. I will help."

"Believe in me, Papa. That's how you can help."

He delivered a gentle kiss to the top of her head. "I've never stopped believing in you, my little rainbow."

37 WARNING

Merry lay on her bed as thoughts poked and nudged her muddled brain, unwilling to give in to the fog of sleep yet. Words spoken during the day wove themselves into inane dialogue as conscious thought sputtered against the beginnings of a fantastic dreamscape. When she opened her eyes, she realized she'd fallen into a quasi-slumber. The bedside light was still on, and she pushed up onto her elbows, blinking into wakefulness.

"William?" Merry whispered, searching for a squall of dust amongst the swath of light, but there was nothing. *Had she imagined William last night?* She wished she could convince herself that she had. Anger boiled inside her heart. A man such as he, good, strong, and loving, had been relegated to a mere shadow born of dust. Her father had been forced to hide in a land as foreign to him as a different continent. Her mother— her mother was dead. Merry seethed, tears spilling onto cheeks that were hot with anger. She swore retribution for all of them.

When she'd asked William to stay last night, he'd shattered before her eyes. *What had happened to him? Where had he gone? Where had he come from?* When they'd fallen from the hanging tree on Gallows Hill, they'd landed in a dark place filled with dark beings. The corpse hands that had threatened her there now ventured well beyond their dark chamber, appearing on the streets of Salem and Danvers.

Merry tossed the down comforter aside and sat up, toes touching the cool floor. She could no longer wait to get William back; she had to at least try. Quickly, she exchanged her warm flannel pajamas for jeans and a bulky sweater. After tugging on her sneakers, Merry parted the curtain and peered outside. Though not full, the gibbous moon illuminated a path along the side of the house. Determined, she grabbed her jacket and ran out of the room.

The sleeping house didn't stir as Merry made her way through the hallways, down the stairs, and out the back door. Once outside, she hurried down the veranda steps, hugging her coat tight around her as the chilly night air crept beneath the layers. The moon's weak light barely penetrated the woods and after a few hesitant steps beyond its edge, Merry flicked her palm upward, sparking a ball of flames to light her way. Stepping carefully, she wound her way through the trees, soon guided by the gurgling brook. Shadows shivered and parted as the flickering flames cut through the darkness.

The woods were mostly quiet, but for a distant hooting owl and the groan of wood against wood. She hadn't been back to the monkey tree since the storm. A sliver of moonlight highlighted her destination. Her heart pounded in anticipation of the possibility of entering the depths of the monkey tree. She recalled how desperate Nurya had been when she'd last visited. *What would she find this time?*

Merry clenched her hand into a fist, squelching the flames. Night quickly filled in around her, and she was grateful for what little illumination the moon provided. She placed a palm, sweaty despite the chilly air, against the newly rendered bark. It remained unyielding beneath her touch. She pressed both hands against the trunk and leaned her forehead upon the cool, rough bark. The monkey tree would not let her in.

"Please," she whispered. She needed to get to Nurya. The land of light was the only way she knew how to reach the darkness. If she could do that, then she might be able to find the cave where she'd left William. She slapped the tree and backed away. Truthfully, she didn't even know if this *was* the right path to pursue. But, it was the only one she knew. She recalled Adina's words when Merry had left William to the Tall Man for a second time. "Bring the light," she'd said. Merry needed the Illuminators.

A snuffling noise startled her, and she instinctively conjured flames in both palms. The slice of moonlight cast shadows of the monkey tree's young, distorted branches upon the forest floor. Something moved among them. Merry took a hesitant step forward, heart hammering in her chest. A breeze shook the branches above, and the shadows danced into many forms, one of which appeared to be that of a wolf. Charged panting broke the relative quiet that had settled upon the woods, a shadow tongue shaking with the rhythm. She couldn't find the source of its silhouette. The shadow wolf stopped, stock still, head cocked as though trying to listen, and then shook its body head to tail and padded toward the monkey tree.

Merry backed away as the shadow wolf stood on hind legs to its full height, paws rested against the smooth bark, investigating with an inquisitive nose. Another breeze blew up, spurring the flames in Merry's hands into an erratic dance before snuffing them out. A squeak of surprise escaped Merry as the night immediately encased her. It took a moment before she realized that no wind should've been able to douse her flames. They were magic after all, and far more resilient than a man-made fire. Only a magical force equal to or greater than her own could've extinguished them. Merry called upon her red colors to reignite the flames. They wouldn't come.

Panic wasted no time in taking over her thoughts. Using her hands as eyes, Merry inched through the woods towards Iron House. A twig slapped against her leg, and she stifled a scream. After several more minutes of stumbling, Merry stopped before she managed to bash her head into a tree. She took a deep breath, then another. She focused on her colors, summoned red, and soon her palms lit up like dry wood upon a hearth. She turned in a slow circle, examining her surroundings, releasing a relieved sigh when she realized she was indeed alone. Still, she hustled the rest of the way out, the sensation of eyes watching her back never leaving her, even after she'd left the woods.

As she dashed across the yard back to Iron House, a wolf's howl pierced the night. She froze at the edge of the veranda, heart racing, and then made a mad dash for the door, shutting it against whatever followed.

38 TAPESTRY

Sidney strolled along one length of castle wall, her gaze roaming from floor to ceiling and down again as she scanned the sumptuous fabric landscape that covered it. While Axylus drew crude diagrams of attack in the dirt floor, Sidney drifted from tapestry to tapestry. It wasn't until she crossed the expansive hall that she realized the wall-sized covering wasn't solely an incredible work of craft and art. It was a map.

All of Nurya and beyond spanned the castle wall, laid out stitch by laborious stitch. Vivid greens depicted the park and hilly meadows, thin strips of brown wound their way throughout the tapestry representing trails and roads. Lakes and rivers portrayed by splashes of blue. Other colors dotted the scenery; gray rock formations, colorful cottages, and a castle. This castle. Its details were meticulously woven so one could clearly depict the moat, the drawbridge, and each crenelated turret. A thought nudged Sidney's brain. Something about the castle was familiar, and not because she was standing in it at the moment. Familiar from before Nurya, before the light, but she couldn't place it. After a few more moments of fruitless contemplation, Sidney moved on, trailing her hand along the plush wool, tracing the path of a wandering blue stream. Her fingers bumped over a brown welt in the midst of a green forest, then continued along the stream's path until she was met with a wide ribbon of blue, dotted with choppy white-capped waves. Ocean. She retraced the path, worrying the welt for a minute before returning to the ocean.

Sidney stepped back. Then, stepped back again and again, until she stood on the opposite side of the hall, the full tapestry open to her scrutiny. Her eyes practically bounced in their sockets as she scanned the full landscape, finally pinpointing the knot of brown, which had risen up against her fingers. From there, she followed the band of blue to the ocean, then back to the knot. The river disappeared into a small wood, appearing now and then in a stitch of blue. It ended before a slip of green, beyond which the castle sat encircled by a small lake.

Beyond the castle, the tapestry sported many smaller abodes, then a green meadow until the threads faded into the washed out color of dried grass. Gradually, the colors darkened, as though a shadow had fallen across the fabric. But there were no shadows here, not in this part of Nurya anyway. Silver paths bloomed at the edge of the dead meadow and wound through a forest filled with barren, twisted trees until they were swallowed by the black stitches that made up the remainder of the tapestry. The flames of a nearby torch brought their dead branches to life as they distorted into ominous dancing shadows upon the far reaches of the map.

Sidney's gaze flicked back to the brown welt. Had it grown larger? She fixed upon the turret again and followed the tapestry up towards the ceiling. Horses grazed near a stone wall beyond the castle, and several homes grew into a town above that, the ocean hugging its borders. A chill stole across her scalp and down her spine. The brown welt drew her gaze again, and she gasped. It *had* grown. Not only in size, but spindly arms now branched and spiraled out from it. She ran to the wall, pressing her hand against the soft wool. It pulsed beneath her palm. When she lifted it, there were two more crooked brown lines branching from the welt, which was more than a welt. It was a tree. One she knew all too well. Her heart thudded in her chest as she traced the blue path back to the castle.

She closed one eye, and two images arose, exchanging places like a holographic book cover when she tilted her head side to side. The lake shrunk into a small pool, then expanded again. The turrets reduced to one, then back to four. Castle. Iron House. Castle. Iron House.

She dashed across the room to interrupt Axylus, who held the attention of many Illuminators, Luke amongst them. "It's a map," she blurted out, saying it again when her shout went unheeded.

Axylus turned slightly in her direction, and nodded. "Yes, milady."

Luke dropped his face in his hands, while others favored her with sympathetic smiles.

"What?" Sidney asked. Then it hit her. Her cheeks warmed, and she wished she could rub away the red that was certainly filling them. "You already knew."

Many nodded. Some murmured agreement. Axylus said, "Indeed."

She felt stupid and angry at the same time. Stupid, because she was apparently the only one in Nurya who didn't know this map existed. Angry, because no one had bothered to tell her. And, by no one, she meant Luke.

She served Luke an accusing glare. "You could've shared that bit of information."

In his cavalier manner, Luke shrugged and answered, "We had more important matters to discuss."

Axylus placed a gentle, guiding hand on her back. "If you please. Take a seat."

"Wait. So you know it's a map of Nurya *and* Salem *and* Danvers? And you know this castle is Iron House, too?"

Sidney was almost thrilled by the shocked faces before her. But, the fact that she was the only one who'd figured this out scared her more than anything.

"What are you talking about?" Luke asked.

"When you close one eye and tilt your head, you can see it," Sidney said, trying it again to make sure she hadn't hallucinated. Castle—Iron House. Nope, she hadn't.

Luke tried it, along with a few others. None saw what she saw. When Sir Axylus closed an eye and tilted his head, Sidney held her breath. But, he was also unable to see Iron House. Sidney pointed as she strode toward the tapestry. "OK, what about the tree? You can at least see it growing, can't you?"

Its branches had thickened and sprouted leaves as it carved out it's niche in the fabric. She flattened her hand against the thick weave; a branch squirmed beneath her fingers, and she pulled back with a squeal. Then Axylus reached out and did the same, his hand lifting a bit as a new branch formed. "God's thumb," he whispered.

"I guess that means you can see it," Sidney said.

Axylus stepped back and others followed suit. "'Twas naught but a burnt hole several weeks now. I'd thought someone had nicked it with a torch."

"The tree was gone. Burned to the ground," Luke marveled.

Axylus nodded. "I did not make the connection."

"What does it mean?" a woman asked.

"It means, we have a way to watch every move the Tall Man makes," Sidney answered. "It means we have a chance."

William paced, dragging a hand against the rough stone wall. He walked the familiar path of Merry's escape, no longer searching for one of his own. The only way out was up the dungeon stairs and through the door that led into the Tall Man's domain—a path that had proven fruitless and had only made matters worse.

He couldn't even escape his own body right now. Whatever ability the Tall Man had given him that allowed him to soar the skies and appear to Merry was mute at the moment. Unreachable. The Tall Man must have decided he was an unworthy recipient, having fulfilled his own desires rather than those of his master and had cut off his access. He shuddered to think that they shared the same desire with very distinct differences. William yearned for a life with Merry. The Tall Man yearned for Merry's life.

Or her colors to put a finer point to it. Corinne had appeared desperate to obtain the colors within Crimson, which had been procured from Merry when she was a child. Merry's mother had hidden the crystal in her favorite doll where it had attracted and trapped Merry's colors until William had found it and hidden it in Judge Corwin's house. It appeared all attempts to extract them from the crystal had failed, and now both father and daughter sought Merry for her gift. Even if William could escape his body and go to her now, he wouldn't. He couldn't risk delivering Merry right into their hands. Hopefully, he hadn't already done so.

Though Sidney's light had strengthened him, his situation appeared more dire than ever. He stepped into the area where Merry had disappeared into her colors weeks ago. William sank to his knees and grabbed a handful of dirt. He threw it against the wall, then scraped another handful up and threw that. Fistful after fistful, William threw dirt at his stone prison, shouts erupting like a lion's roar from his chest. Finally, he stopped, head hanging against his heaving chest. He wanted to hurt the Tall Man. He wanted to snuff out the Devil's existence. What chance did he have, when the Devil's staunchest enemy was God? What did he, a lowly human, hope to achieve that God hadn't already?

Even with his gifts—one of light, one of darkness—he was no threat to the Devil. William closed his eyes. *What had Corinne said?* A perfect match. She of darkness, and he of light. But, she was wrong. She was darkness, yes. But, he was both darkness and light. He wondered if he could control the repulsive urges the mark forced upon him, could he push them in another direction? The only way to learn the answer was to embrace the mark, to let it come to life. A rivulet of sweat ran from his scalp and down his temple. His heart raced at the thought of letting the mark out, allowing it a toehold. The fear of giving in completely, of losing himself forever, overwhelmed him. He had to try though. For Merry. For his soul.

To reassure himself, William first allowed thin ribbons of light to escape his palms. They seeped out between his hand and the ground, slipping between his fingers, unfurling like smoke on kindling. A smile lifted his lips. Some of the fear left him, replaced with determination. He sat back, his hands on his legs as he watched the light sink into the rubble and dirt. It was time for the other half.

His stomach lurched as he summoned the dark mark. The mark responded, pulsing and roiling as it heated his chest. He fought back the urge to stifle its power and give into his fear. Allowing it to take hold, he gritted his teeth as fire flooded his veins. A need to hurt, to destroy, ran through his mind, tearing all rational thought from him. He fought to hold onto compassion, empathy, and love, but the mark fought harder.

William squeezed his eyes shut and attempted to focus on his light. The darkness inside him rebelled and snatched a bit more of his will away. Spasms racked his body, sending him into a fit of twitches, and he slammed to the ground, landing on his side. He opened his eyes, hoping to find a thought to focus on other than his internal agony, but the gloom offered no solace. Except... a single dot of brightness bloomed inches from his face where he'd sank his own light. Then another dot followed, and another, until a solid patch of light glowed upon the ground. He recalled a similar light marking a trail for Merry to follow back to her colors so she could escape. *Could whatever, whomever, had produced that trail be responsible for this light?*

He reached toward it as his flesh bubbled up and carved a path from the mark toward his throat. William let out a low moan. He needed to reach the light before the mark consumed him completely. He didn't want his sister to have risked her life for no reason. He could do this. He could fight it. He grasped the thread of an image, remembering Sidney passing her light to him. He clung to the vision, nourished it until it swelled and pushed the mark back a step or two. A war raged inside his body. It was up to him to harness its powers and own it, rather than be ruled by it.

William slammed his hand upon the patch of light. It raced up his arm and to his shoulder, cooling the mark's heat until it was reduced from a raging inferno to a dying ember. He curled his fingers into the dirt, dug into the light. Wrist deep, his fingers connected with something other than pebbles and dirt. He pulled back, an involuntary shudder coursing through his body. The earth did the same, as a hand pushed through its crust and reached upward, fingers outstretched. His first instinct was to retreat, get as far away from this hand and the others that would surely follow. Always followed. But, something was different. This hand *glowed*.

Shuffling closer, William reached out and grasped the wrist of the arm protruding from the earth. Its fingers clamped down on his, warm and reassuring. For a moment, they held onto one another, then the arm slipped downward. "No!" William shouted, pulling, losing his grasp, reaching again. This time he held the arm in both hands and yanked, falling backward at the unexpected lightness of the being attached to the arm. A face appeared.

William scuttled close, and peered into the bright blue eyes peering out from a surprised woman's face. A faint shimmer danced upon her skin, brightest upon her cheeks. "Adina?"

"Yes," the woman whispered back. She grasped awkwardly at the ground to keep her head afloat as it were. William reached forward, taking her hand in his.

"Where did you come from? How did you get in?" The thought of rescue subdued the mark further. His buoyant heart leapt at the prospect.

"How do we get out is the real question."

And that ended his hope. She was as trapped as he.

"You're a prisoner too, then."

The ground answered for her as it attempted to suck her down into its depths. William tugged, gentler this time, and she lifted a few more inches, exposed to her shoulders. With some effort she pushed her other hand through and clung to William's with both of hers.

"Can you not escape? You're but light in the end, are you

not?" he asked.

"You pulled me out of this earth. I'm as much flesh and bone as you are at the moment."

She slid down a bit as the earth churned, and he gripped her hands a bit tighter. "The soil is poison to us. It stifles our light, solidifies our bodies, and contains us."

Judging by the spotty brilliance upon Adina's skin, her light was weak at best.

"How many are you?"

"There are forty-three of us trapped in this suffocating earth. We've been here since your return to Salem Village. The night the witches were killed. The night the Tall Man rose."

William thought back to the evening when the witches had sent him back to Salem Village. There'd been so much chaos. The Tall Man rising as witches died all around him. Corinne's beautiful face contorted by the evil she'd so desired as she came to embrace her father's destiny, while her mother lay dead at her feet. Amidst the screams and his own desperate attempt at escape, William recalled a sky filled with light. In solidarity, he'd connected with the Illuminators and they'd launched an attack on the Tall Man, which had released the curse that had bound him and given him time to flee.

"I thought he'd killed you all," William said.

"Some died," the woman answered. "Most of us were taken. We are more useful alive than dead."

"I've heard that about myself," William said. "Though, I cannot but wonder at what it all means."

"The power of light is ten times, a hundred times, more than that of the darkness. Rather than abolish such power, the Devil seeks to make it his own."

William sat back on his heels. He'd often wondered why he hadn't been killed weeks ago. The Tall Man had plenty of opportunity to do so. William had even begged for such an end during his torture. *What purpose did the mark serve if not to destroy him?*

"Do you know how he plans to achieve such a feat?" William asked. "I cannot think how my light would desert me, short of death."

The woman bowed her head for a moment, what little light she possessed shimmered and danced upon her black curls.

"So, 'tis death that ends it all."

When she looked up, her eyes held a profound sadness. "No, William. It's much worse. Death would be too kind."

"Is there nothing we can do?"

A thin smile lifted Adina's lips as she answered, "You can trust Merry. Trust yourself."

"I need more than that."

"No. It's *all* you need." The earth grumbled and shifted beneath them. The ground swallowed Adina up to her neck, and despite William's efforts, she sank further. He called upon his light to give him the strength to free her. "Do not use your light, William. Not yet."

The earth's tug was too strong. Reluctantly, William released her hands. She slipped through the greedy earth as it consumed her struggling body. William locked eyes with her as she disappeared. Her gaze held his until the dirt touched her cheekbones. Then, she snapped her blue eyes shut, gave up the fight, and let the earth have her.

The light glowing upon the ground dissolved into the black earth, leaving William in darkness. He pushed up from his seat on the cave floor and moved deeper into the tunnel. There had to be some way to free the Illuminators. If he could do that, perhaps they'd have a chance against the Tall Man. He couldn't do it with his light alone. Not even after his sister's fortifying transference.

But, he'd been onto something before Adina's hand had popped through the surface of the cave floor. He'd allowed the mark to live inside him, to intertwine with his light, and the light had overtaken the mark. William needed to learn how to harness the darkness inside him and use it for his own purpose.

39 TRUTH

Merry woke with a jolt, the howling of wolves receding alongside her dreams. Liz stared down at her, an amused smile on her face. "Bad dream?"

Merry lifted herself up onto her elbows. She'd kicked her shoes off before getting into Liz's bed, but still wore her clothes, and had managed to deposit some leaves and pine needles upon the comforter. "I'm sorry. I didn't mean to fall asleep."

"It's OK, Merry."

Still numb from sleep, Merry pushed herself into a sitting position and brushed the debris off the bed.

"What made you come to my room?" Liz asked.

Merry rubbed the sleep from her eyes. "Remind me not to go into the woods at night anymore."

"That should be a given. So you went into the woods again last night? Why?"

"I wanted to get to Nurya through the monkey tree." Merry immediately regretted her admission at the eager look on Liz's face. "I couldn't get through."

"Maybe it needs to grow some more," Liz said, attempting a hopeful smile.

"Mayhap. But, that's not all, Liz. There was someone or something in the woods."

Liz arched an eyebrow and tilted her head. "What do you mean something?"

"I'm not certain. As I was leaving the tree, I heard what I thought to be a dog sniffing and panting. I saw its shadow, yet it was off somehow. As though reflected through glass or..."

"Another dimension," Liz finished.

It was Merry's turn to arch an eyebrow.

"Don't look at me like that. There are weirder things to consider when you think about what's been happening around here lately."

"Weirder? You think this is some sort of destiny?"

"Uh, no. Weird means strange, unusual, bizarre."

"Ah... this is one of those words that has changed meaning over time, isn't it?"

"I guess so," Liz answered. "Enough of the English lesson. What was in the woods?"

"I believe it was a wolf. Did you not hear it howling? Chilled me to the bone. It was... weird."

Liz smiled. "I didn't hear anything. But... a wolf?"

Merry nodded. "There's more. I conjured flames to light my way through the woods. An odd breeze came up and extinguished the flames." At Liz's confused look Merry added, "Liz, my flames are magic. They don't exist under the same rules as man-made fire."

Liz's eyes widened. "So, you're saying only magic can counteract magic?"

Merry nodded.

"Merry, what was out there with you?"

"I fear we both know what the likely answer is," Merry answered.

"Wait a minute. Are you telling me that the Tall Man, the *Devil*, was walking around the woods behind my house?" Liz's pitch rose with each word.

"Yes, Liz. That's exactly what I'm saying."

Liz leaned back against the headboard. "This shit just got

real."

Merry leaned back beside her. "Indeed."

After a few minutes of silence in which Merry suspected that Liz, like she, was contemplating the import of the Devil in such close proximity, Merry said, "It may no longer be safe for us here. At least not for me and Sidney."

Liz's head whipped toward her. "What does he want with Sidney?"

"She's William's sister."

"She's unconscious."

"Not in Nurya."

"Merry, we can't move her. She needs care, and I'm not sending her back to a hospital."

"It's possible it's me drawing him here. He has... William." Liz laid a hand on hers. "He has his light. I think he wants my colors."

"I don't want you to leave, Merry."

"I don't want to leave. But, I think it's best if I go back to Salem. To Sophie's."

"But, the Tall Man is trying to *destroy* Salem. And, if he's here, walking around..."

"I'm not sure he's physically here, in Salem, yet. All I felt was a breeze. I didn't see anyone. I sensed someone was near, though not present."

"Dimension," Liz stated. Merry couldn't help but laugh at the serious look on Liz's face.

"Fine. Dimension."

Liz turned, the covers shifting with a rustle. "Really. Think about it, Merry. It seems like Nurya is inside or below the monkey tree. But, it's not. It's bigger than that. It has earth, water, and sky. What if it's a parallel dimension to our world? If that's the case, then maybe the Tall Man is closer than we think. Maybe *William* is closer than we think."

Merry's stomach fluttered at the thought. She had thought she could reach both Nurya and the darkness through the monkey tree. She recalled the darkness lurking beyond Nurya's borders, and had hoped it was a path to William. *Maybe she was thinking of it all wrong.* She pursed her lips, brows furrowed. "It doesn't matter. I can't get into the monkey tree. I can't get to Nurya or any other dimension."

"Not today, but after it's done growing..."

Merry dropped her head back, gazing at the ceiling. "I can't wait for a tree to grow."

"Maybe you don't have a choice," Liz said, adding, "Of course, at the rate it's going, it'll probably be fully grown in a few days."

A few days. Three weeks had passed since Merry had been found in the woods on Gallows Hill. Three weeks and William had been turned to dust. She fought the idea that she'd already lost him. "I still think I should go. I can stay with Sophie. Besides, I'll be close to my father."

"We can bring him here."

"No, Liz. Iron House isn't an inn. You and your family have done enough."

Liz slumped, then straightened. "Fine, I'll come with you."

"No. I don't want to put you in danger. Don't you understand? Look what almost happened to you in your own driveway!"

"So, you're going to leave me here with the Devil?"

Merry gasped. "Of course not!"

A sudden burst of music startled Merry. Liz slapped the top of her alarm clock, instantly quieting the noisy intrusion. "I have to get ready. Boy wonder and his trusty sidekick will be here for the interview in an hour and a half."

Merry hopped off the bed. "I'll give you some privacy."

As she slipped out the door, Liz said, "We're not done talking!"

Merry smiled and shut the door.

Liz paced the hallway as Alex Olivier's crew set up cameras and performed sound checks in her father's library. "Shit," Liz said for the hundredth time.

"Stop panicking," Merry said. "You said you wanted to get something of the truth out there. This is your opportunity."

"It might make things worse."

"It might make them better," Merry countered.

"You don't even believe that."

"Well, I'm sure you're not going to tell the world I came from the seventeenth century and was hung as a witch. That sounds crazy."

They stared at each other for a moment before bursting out in laughter.

Frederick left his post outside the library and walked down the hall to inform Liz they were ready for her.

"You'll do fine, Liz," Merry said as she walked with her to the library.

"Don't come in, OK? I don't want you to get mixed up in this."

Merry smiled. "A little late for that, isn't it?"

"Yeah, for all of us I'd say."

Her mother met them in front of the open door to the library, arms folded, and mouth set. Merry gave Liz a quick hug before heading to her room. Christine took Liz's arm and steered her halfway down the corridor.

"Lizzie, don't panic over this," she said in a hushed voice. "You had the right idea and it's still right. Give them enough truth to stop them looking for a story that isn't there."

"Technically, it is there, Mom."

"Liz."

"I know. I know," she said, putting her hands up in defense. "I promise I won't screw it up this time. I'm going to tell as much of the truth as I can."

A few moments later, she stepped into the library. Alex rushed over to her the minute she entered. "Hi."

"Hi," Liz answered, unable to stop a small smile from touching her lips.

The crew milled about tweaking lights and focusing camera lenses. Alex asked her to sit on the settee near the fireplace.

"We're going to get started in a few minutes. Try to relax."

"Try not to be a jerk." She regretted saying it as soon as the words left her lips. "Sorry, I guess I should take my own advice."

Alex offered a lop-sided grin. "It's OK. I've been called worse."

"Yeah," said Liz. "By me." Alex surprised her by laughing out loud. A small laugh escaped her, as well.

"Better?" he asked.

"I suppose."

It took another five minutes to make sure the light was hitting her at the right angle before they began. Then Alex faced the camera and introduced her, telling the would-be audience Molly Rose Cooke had apparently been in Salem weeks prior to being left for dead in the woods near Gallows Hill. They quickly got up to speed on how Liz had gone out on the harbor on her boat, where she first found Merry.

"What did you think when you saw her at the base of the cliff?"

Liz paused. What had she thought at that moment? All the events that had occurred since discovering Merry at the base of the cliff had obscured those initial moments.

"I guess I was thinking the tide was coming in fast and she needed a ride back to the pier."

"So, you wanted to help," Alex said.

Simple.

"Yes. That's it exactly."

"But, after you brought Molly back to Salem, you stayed with her."

"Well, she was confused. She didn't seem to know where she was and..."

"And, she thought she was Meredith Chalmers, the woman who'd been hung during the Salem witch trials."

Oh, how Liz wished they'd never divulged that little fact. "She was a bit confused, yes."

"So, instead of bringing this lost, confused person to the police or the hospital, you did what?"

Liz tried not to glare at Alex. "She was scared and confused and I thought a hospital or the police might scare her even more. I felt bad for her, so I took her home. I thought she might have amnesia."

"So you decided to diagnose her and decided..."

Liz cut him off with a stony stare. "I decided to be her friend."

A small smile escaped Alex before he asked his next question.

They talked for a bit about Sophie's chance meeting at her parlor and how she'd thought this lost person might be her granddaughter.

"Why didn't she take her in for a DNA sample?"

"She wanted to, but Mer...sorry, Molly, refused."

"Yet, you still didn't bring her to the police."

"No."

"Or a hospital."

"No. Listen, all this seems easy on the face of it. Bring her to the police, check her in at the hospital, but, Merry was a living, breathing, intelligent person who needed help. She was only here for a few weeks before she disappeared. But, while she was here, she was my friend and I don't regret that. Not one bit."

"I.."

"You can sit there and judge my actions, but I know they were right. And, Merry knows they were right."

"Molly."

That one word undid her. Tears streamed unbidden down her cheeks. She wiped at them furiously.

"Are you all right?" he asked.

The question threw her for a moment. *Was this part of the interview? Or was he actually concerned about her?* He looked as uncomfortable as she felt.

He leaned forward and said in a low voice only she could hear. "Do you want to take a break?"

It was tempting, but she didn't think she'd come back if she left. She needed to finish this. So she shook her head and, after dabbing the wetness off her cheeks, continued Merry's story.

40 TITUBA

"The Court of Oyer & Terminer has been dissolved," Susannah said in a hushed voice. "There are rumors that those who've been convicted of witchcraft will have their records expunged. They'll be freed."

Tituba watched her through cell bars, expressionless.

"You'll be freed," Susannah said.

Tituba bowed her head. "Miss Susannah, thank you for bringing me this news."

Susannah frowned. "What is it, Tituba?"

A sad smile barely lifted her lips. "I won't never be free."

"You will," Susannah said, then lowered her eyes, unable to hold Tituba's gaze. "It's..."

"It's what, Missy?"

She forced her gaze back to Tituba's knowing hazel eyes. "A fee will have to be paid by each prisoner to compensate for their stay."

Tituba shook her head from side to side. "I ain't got no money."

"I know."

"Reverend Parris ain't goin' pay for me. Not after poor Betty. And Abigail."

Susannah bit her lip. "He's terribly sore that you recanted your confession."

Tituba tilted her head back. "I shouldn't never said those things. I was weak."

"He was cruel."

Tituba appraised Susannah before speaking in a quiet voice. "I had to recant. I got to right my wrong."

Susannah grimaced. Tituba wasn't alone in the need to right her wrongs. "Don't you worry, Tituba. I'll get you out of here somehow."

"Mayhap you will, child. But, even if there comes a day when I'm standin' on the other side of these bars, and even if I can walk right out of this filthy building and feel the sun on my face—even then, I will never be free."

41 SALEM

In one week, it would be William's birthday. Unless the situation changed quickly, it would be the first time Merry wouldn't spend it with him since they'd met. But, that wasn't what concerned her. October 31st was not only William's birthday, but it was also All Hallows' Eve, the night the dead roamed the earth. The night the Tall Man had sought out a baby nearly twenty-two years ago, depending on what century one hailed from. He'd looked to extinguish William's light before it could take hold. Since then, William had gone on blissfully unaware of what lay inside him. Until now.

She wasn't sure, but based on the recent attacks on Salem and Aimee Donavan's journal, Merry knew she needed to steal William away from the Tall Man's lair before Halloween or all would be lost—and, not only William. According to Ruby, the Tall Man's prize was Salem. And beyond. This puzzled Merry—the Tall Man's yearning to vanquish Salem. *What was it about this city that pulled him so?* On her visits to Salem Town, she'd been enamored with the ships in the harbor, the taste of the salty ocean air on her lips, and the bustle of industrious people—all human delights. *What did the Devil know of such wonders?*

Then, there was her part in this story. She was strong, stronger than ever. But, the Devil had something of hers, the Crimson crystal. She meant to get it back and send the Devil back to his fiery hell.

Merry folded a sweater and placed it into a large suitcase. Alone in the mostly barren closet, hanged the clothing she'd been wearing when she'd first leapt into the future. She ran her hand down the coarse fabric of a sleeve. Next time she wore it, people would think it was a costume.

A knock on the door startled her, and Merry grabbed the outfit off the hanger and shoved it into the bag before shouting for her visitor to enter.

"All packed?" Liz said as she walked through the door.

Merry zipped the bag closed and stood back to survey the room, hands on hip. "I think so."

Liz's attempt at indifference fell short as she answered in a too-high voice. "Great!" She nodded toward the luggage. "I can ask Logan to bring it down."

"No need," Merry answered, not wanting to delay the inevitable any longer. Liz picked up two smaller bags, one full of shoes, the other toiletries, while Merry wheeled the suitcase out the door. They headed down the hallway together. As they neared the library, voices could be heard through the partially closed door.

"How long does this go on for, Christine? We can't take in every stray off the street. First Elise, then..."

"Don't call her that."

"I didn't mean anything by it. I just don't understand why this is our concern."

Merry tried to walk faster and ignored Liz's apologetic look as they sped by the library. Daniel Thompson's voice followed them down the hall. "Ever since your brother..."

"Daniel..." Christine's voice answered in warning. The rest of the conversation faded as they drew further away.

"Sorry about that," Liz said. "Dad's never gotten things around here. He's hardly ever home, so I don't know why he cares so much."

"Don't worry yourself over it," Merry answered. "He's right. Your family shouldn't have to worry about my needs."

Liz grasped her arm, spun her around, and nearly caused Merry to fall over her large bundle. "Stop it. I don't want to hear that from you ever again. This is happening, Merry. It's happening to the both of us. To all of us! It's *not* just about you."

Merry had never seen Liz so annoyed. While she'd worried about the burden she'd placed on others, she often forgot it was not her burden alone. The residents of Iron House had been involved in this before she'd even been born. She bowed her head. "You're right. It's not just about me. Or William. Or even Sidney."

Liz let go of her arm. "Then stay."

Merry stepped back. "I can't. I need to be in Salem."

Liz shrugged. "Fine."

They proceeded down the staircase, Merry's bag thumping down behind her. Logan already had the car out front. He took the bags from them and began to load them into the back of the SUV. Merry hugged Liz and climbed into the back seat. Liz followed, shutting the door behind her.

"What are you doing?" Merry asked.

"You need to be in Salem. Then, so do I."

"What? Liz, you should stay here."

"You can't tell me what to do, Merry. I'm a grown woman. I know the risks. I'm making my own decision."

Logan started driving a slow loop around the fountain.

"Sidney's apartment is empty. We can stay there without anyone bothering us."

"I was planning to stay at Sophie's. The reporters have mostly left."

"And, they'll mostly return when you do."

Merry dropped her head against the headrest and sighed as Iron House's landscape streamed by. *It looks like we're going to Salem together*, she thought.

William focused. As the mark pulsed into life, he

envisioned threads of light wrapping around the twisting darkness. The mark bucked against the light as it attempted to imprison and control it. William's body spasmed, and he fell forward to his knees. The next seizure sent him onto his hands. He gasped for air as the torturing heat expanded from his chest and ran down his arms. William locked his elbows and clenched the dirt with his fists as he fought to retain his conscience, his awareness of self, even as the mark attempted to erase all that made him who he was.

A spot of light, tinier than a nail head, spilled from his fingertip into the soil. It grew, and soon the earth trembled as a glowing head ruptured its crust. The mark pressed harder, and he lifted his hand to smash it down on the Illuminator's head. Several moments passed as his arm vacillated between the commands to destroy and his instinct to save. His true self slid into a hidden place, giving way to the demon inside. His fist came crashing toward the emerging Illuminator, when another hand erupted from the earth and latched onto his. William howled against the light that poured into him and ate at the darkness. He collapsed, his face coming to rest on the cool floor.

Adina stared unflinching, inches away. William lay there panting, while the mark released its hold. Adina pulled herself upward, straining against the earth's grip until she'd freed her upper torso. Finally William sat up and spoke. "Thank you."

"You almost did it, William. You were nearly there," she said in a voice so confident he wished he could believe her.

"Nay. Were it not for your touch, your light, I would've succumbed. Again."

"Don't give up."

He didn't want to give up. He wanted to fight. He wanted to win his release from this dungeon, from this fate, and from the mark. He wanted to live a life, a good life, with Merry beside him. But, it appeared more impossible with each day that passed in the Tall Man's keep.

"William, do you know why your father sent you back in time?"

He thought back to the passages from his mother's journal. "To strengthen the light. With my own, and that of my children. 'Twas a cruel thing he did. Both to my mother, and to me."

"He asked for great sacrifices of all of you. Including himself."

William fixed her with an angry glare. "I was not asked."

"No," Adina said, pebbles and dirt flinging from her hair as she shook her head. "It's true this mantel was thrust upon you. But, it's one you must wear all the same."

"What if one does not wish to accept such responsibility?"

"There are two elements inside you. One is the light you were born with. It will always be a part of you. It is, in part, why you are the man you are today. A good man. A man who loves. A man who fights for what's right."

William hung his head. "Mayhap I once was that man. Now, I am but a wretched beast."

"You are what you allow yourself to be."

William's lifted his gaze to meet Adina's. "How can you say such things, when the mark takes away my will and uses me for the Tall Man's dark purpose?"

To his surprise, Adina smiled. "And now you bring me to the second element. The Devil's mark. Darkness." She slid down a bit, and William grabbed her arm to hold her above ground. "It's like a cancer, a disease eating away what makes you strong. What makes you human."

"And it is winning."

"Only if you let it, William. Sometimes, we can't cure a disease. Sometimes, we have to learn how to live with it. How to manage it."

"I am trying."

"I know you are. And, I believe you will soon do more than manage it."

"You think I can rid myself of it?"

"I don't know, maybe under the right circumstances. But, in the meantime, you can learn to suppress it. Even more important, you can learn how to control it. How to use it to your advantage rather than his."

William stood, unable to contemplate such a possibility. *Could he actually learn how to control the mark? Make it serve him rather than its master? Would he even want to?* In order to wield such a power, he'd have to first accept it.

"Make no mistake, William. The Tall Man means to take your light. Imagine if you took his darkness instead?"

Liz jumped and let out a small shriek at the sound of a loud knock right as she was walking past the front door. She'd been at the condo for less than an hour, and other than her family and Sophie, no one else knew they were there. Merry had left fifteen minutes ago to visit Sophie; she couldn't have gotten there and back already. She must've forgotten something. Liz threw the door open, surprised to find Alex Olivier standing outside the door. *So much for staying under the radar.*

"What are you doing here?" Liz asked, cringing at the edge in her voice.

A faint blush crossed Alex's cheeks. "I was coming to Iron House, when the gates opened, and I saw you leave."

"So you, what, followed us here?"

"You. Yes."

He'd followed her. Not Merry. Not the story. Liz's cheeks warmed. "We've been here for almost an hour. Have you been waiting outside all this time?"

Alex answered with an embarrassed tilt of one corner of his mouth.

"Don't you think that's a little... I don't know. Creepy?"

Alex nodded. "Yeah, it's totally creepy."

Liz's lips twitched as she fought the grin pushing against them. "OK stalker boy. You can come in." She stepped back and pulled the door open wide enough for Alex to squeeze through, then immediately shut it behind him, leaning against it with folded arms.

He turned to face her. "Nice place."

"So, did you think of more questions you wanted to ask me?"

"Just one." His face broke into a sheepish smile that disarmed Liz's attempt at playing it cool. She dropped her arms to her sides, suddenly unsure what to do with them. Alex stepped closer. "I was wondering if you'd like to go out to dinner tonight."

She gripped her hands in front of her to keep them from shaking. *What the heck was wrong with her?* It wasn't like she'd never been asked on a date before. "Tonight... " she started, her voice sounding high and pitchy even to her ears. She cleared her throat and tried again. "Tonight, this week, might be tough. Molly and I have... stuff we have to do." *Like stopping the Devil and his demons from destroying Salem. You know, that stuff.*

"Oh, yeah, well," Alex said. "I know you're busy. Just a few hours on one night, though?"

Liz chewed her lip. "I don't know. Isn't there some rule about reporters..."

"What? Dating beautiful women?"

Liz glanced toward the ground, then back to his face. The line was cheesy, but effective. "OK. But, it's not because of that ridiculous line."

"Bad, huh?"

Liz raised an eyebrow.

"I'll pick you up at 7:00?"

"Or you could wait in front of the house for six hours."

Alex grinned, relief turning to confidence. "Tempting. But, I think I'll come back later."

He stared at her for an awkward moment, until Liz realized she was still leaning against the door, blocking the exit. She reached behind her and pulled the door open.

"See you later." His shoulder rubbed against hers as he stepped onto the landing. He smelled like crisp air and black pepper. Liz inhaled deeply as he descended the stairs. *Damn, she was in trouble.*

42 JUMP

Merry opened the unlocked back door and let herself into Sophie's kitchen. She paused to listen. Quiet. The house sounded barren of life. Merry crept through the kitchen and up the stairs to the second floor, pausing by Sophie's room to see if she might be napping, but the bed was empty. Satisfied, Merry went to her mother's room and dumped out the contents of her bag. She quickly undressed, then put on her seventeenth-century shift, skirts, and to the best of her ability, her corset. She left her sneakers on. They'd be hidden under her skirts and could be helpful if she had to run.

Shoving her clothing into the bag and dropping it beside the bed, she continued down to the end of the hallway. She opened the attic door and jogged up the stairs, zig-zagging through piles of boxes to get to the window overlooking the backyard. From the outside, the window presented a majestic architectural detail. From the inside, it posed a stumbling block.

Many layers of thick white paint covered the window frame and sill. Merry grasped the metal handles at the bottom of the window and tugged upward, managing to do nothing more than strain her shoulder muscles. She looked across the narrow room to the front-facing window, but it looked the same.

Merry scanned the room for a tool she could wedge beneath the window and break the decades old melding of wood and paint. A metal rack stood in the corner covered in old, forgotten coats. She rummaged through the draws of a pot-bellied dresser, nearly shouting with joy at finding a short metal letter opener near a loose stack of letters. Returning to the window, she pried the metal between the sill and frame. She worked the tool to loosen the painted bond, trying to open the window every few seconds. The third attempt elicited a stubborn groan of wood against wood. A few more minutes working the sides of the window, and she was able to lift it nearly two inches.

"Hello?" a voice called out two stories below. "Sophie?"

Merry froze as her father's voice echoed throughout the house. Had she closed the door to the attic? She didn't have time to check. She stabbed at the window frame with a renewed urgency, managing to raise the window a few more inches. Her father's footsteps sounded on the staircase. His voice grew closer as he called for Sophie.

"Is anyone up there?" he called up the attic steps, answering Merry's question as to whether she'd left the door open. She thrust herself against the frame, not caring about the noise she made.

"I can hear you up there. Is that you, Sophie?"

Wood screeched as the sash finally came loose from the layers of paint. Her father had also given up on caution it seemed as his footsteps pounded up the stairs. Merry climbed through the window, steadying herself on the slight incline of the roof. Ignoring the sounds of her father's approach, she focused on her colors. They came in short bursts between her anxiety. Merry took a deep breath and thought of William, of holding him once again. A yearning flooded her senses and a glorious rainbow bloomed around her.

Her father shouted her name, clambering onto the roof as she ran toward the edge and jumped.

"No! No! No!" Merry screamed. She sank to her knees, clutching her hands in front of her chest, begging for the impossible.

Her father grasped her upper arms and tried to draw her into a standing position. Merry shook her head side to side. She couldn't catch a breath. "We have to go back. We have to go back. We..."

"Shhh, Merry!"

This couldn't be happening. Not again. It couldn't. First, she'd unwittingly transported her mother to the seventeenth century and had lost her forever. Now, she'd done the same to her father. Devon had been closer than she'd thought and had latched onto her as she'd leapt off Sophie's roof. He'd followed her to Salem Village, 1692, just as her mother had.

Merry whimpered against her father's chest. "You can't... you..."

"It's all right."

She shouted into his face. "It's *not* all right! You have no trade. You can't be here!"

"Merry..."

"No." Slips of color faded around them, and she wished she'd listened to Liz and had stayed at Iron House.

Her father clutched both sides of her face, stilling her. She had no choice but to return his purposeful gaze. "Merry, I have no trade. But, I have you. I have you, and you have your colors." He beseeched her understanding with his stare. His last words were a whisper. "It's not like before."

Merry looked away, her attention riveted to a last wisp of green as it melted into the gray sky.

"It's not like before," her father repeated, stronger this time. "I want to help."

Merry stared into her father's eyes. They held no fear. Unlike her mother, he knew the risk he'd taken. As frightened as she was to take another step inside this time period, as much as she wanted to spin her colors around them and deposit her father safely in the twenty-first century, time was ever their master. She had to get to Judge Corwin's house and back before All Hallows' Eve or she might lose William forever.

Merry took her father's hand. "We'll have to move fast, and we can't be seen."

"I'll be an extra pair of eyes, then."

As much as she hated to admit it, a lookout would be helpful. She surveyed their surroundings, which were a might different than the environment they'd left behind. For one thing, Sophie's house no longer existed. There was nothing but an empty field behind them and a clear view to the cemetery before them. The dirt road was void of people, though a morose horse stood attached to a cart outside a nearby home. Merry directed her father down North Street, her eyes drawn to the jeans, sweatshirt, and sneakers he wore. Even if no one recognized her, Devon's attire would draw attention like a beacon.

"You're dressed all wrong," Merry said.

"I threw all my clothing away long ago. I didn't think I'd need them again."

A creaking door sent them scurrying past the cart. Keeping her father in front of her, Merry guided him toward the cemetery. There were less gravestones than there were in the future, and these stones stood straight and true, the names of the dead clearly etched into their surface, unworn by time. They darted behind a wide tree in the middle of the graveyard. Merry peered around its trunk and spied a young man climbing into the driver's seat of the cart. He grabbed the reins and with a swift snap, set the horses in motion.

"We'll continue down North Street, after he leaves. It's the most direct route."

"Why did you come here?" her father asked.

"There's a crystal I need to retrieve."

"A crystal? Like the ones your mother used to collect your colors?"

"Yes, exactly. Frankly, I don't know if it will even be here."

"It's important?"

"The daughter of the Devil himself sought it out and stole it from the Witch House." Merry pursed her lips. "It's important."

Once the clip-clop of hooves receded, they slipped out from behind the gnarled tree and with speed and care moved onto the street. Their steps made little noise in the dirt road as they moved passed empty houses. Judging by the deserted town, Merry assumed the majority of Salem Town residents were at church. The sun's mid-level position on the western horizon suggested early afternoon. The streets could be flooded with homeward bound churchgoers at any moment. As they neared the corner of North Street and Essex, Judge Corwin's house came into view.

Merry touched her father's shoulder, halting him. "Let's watch for a few moments."

They sheltered behind an overgrown beach rosebush and peered between the sparse branches. Nothing moved around the home. No children ran about nor were there candles lit within indicating the presence of the home's inhabitants. After several minutes, Merry said, "I'm going to go closer. See if there's anyone inside."

She rose from her crouched position.

Her father placed a hand on her forearm. "What's the plan?"

Merry hunkered down beside him again. "I need to get upstairs to the closet in Corwin's bedchamber, pry up the floorboard and retrieve the crimson crystal."

"How much time do you need?"

"If the floorboard is loose as it was when William placed the crystal there, I should be a few minutes only. If it is not, I may need at least ten minutes."

"Can we agree that you come out after ten minutes? No matter what?"

"I can't leave without the crystal."

"If you're caught, it'll do you no good."

Merry bit her lip. Her father was right, but so was she. She *had* to get the crystal. "I can promise you this. After ten minutes past, if I still have no success and need more time, I will stand at that window." She pointed at the top left window beneath a gable.

Her father nodded. "Fine. But, after ten minutes, if I don't see you at the window, I'm coming in to get you."

She didn't like it, but she had no time to argue. Leaving her father behind the rosebush, Merry dashed across the street feeling like a thousand eyes were upon her despite the silent surroundings. She walked up to the front door as though she were a visitor and not the prowler that she was. She held her breath as she knocked and listened for answering footsteps. None came. Merry peered into a nearby window, seeing nothing within the afternoon sunbeam that lit the dim interior. Glancing toward where she knew her father to be, Merry nodded, cracked open the front door, and slipped inside.

For the second time in her life, Merry stood inside Judge Corwin's house. The acrid scent of burning wood stung her nostrils, followed by a more pleasant odor of freshly baked bread setting a palpable distinction between this home and the ghostly remains of the Witch House. Other than the soft crackle of the embers in the hearth, no other sound greeted her intrusion. Still, she crept to the archways on either side of the entrance and peeked into the rooms, confirming their emptiness. That done, Merry climbed up the twisting staircase to the second floor, freezing when one of the steps elicited a protesting squeak. Other than her pounding heartbeat, she heard no one stir and soon continued her upward climb, albeit with a bit more caution.

Merry peered around the corner of the door way to Judge Corwin's bedchamber. She let out a breath when she saw the bed empty; she'd been afraid someone might have stayed behind. Certain she was alone, Merry quickly crossed the room and opened the closet, immediately jumping back and emitting a startled shout. The young girl inside the closet screamed. The baby she held wailed.

Merry held her hands up. "Shush. All is well. I won't hurt you."

The girl jiggled the baby to quiet him.

"Step out of the closet, little one," Merry said.

The girl took a shuffling step and then stopped, her worried gaze flicking toward Merry.

"I promise I will not hurt you."

The girl hugged her sibling close as she stepped past Merry. They stared at one another for a few moments. "Are you here to put a curse on us?" the girl asked.

Merry shook her head and offered a small smile. "No."

The girl tilted her head and looked deep into Merry's eyes. "Where did you go?"

"What?"

"On Gallows Hill. You disappeared. Where did you go?"

Merry searched the girl's face. "We shouldn't speak of such things."

The girl nodded, eyes big. Merry could only wonder what her imagination was doing with her answer. Merry turned away, knelt in the closet doorway, and ran her hand across the closet floor, checking for an unsecured board.

"What are you doing?" the girl asked.

"I'm looking for something of mine."

"How did something of yours get in papa's closet?"

"A little boy put it there many years ago." Merry nudged the corner of a board. Wood squeaked as she pressed on each plank.

"Papa will be home soon."

The heel of Merry's hand sank, popping a long board up and nearly hitting her in the head. She fell back on her legs.

"Did you find it?" the girl asked.

Merry dove back into the closet, pushed the floorboard aside, and poked in the dusty underneath until her fingers closed around a cool stone surface. Her fingertips zinged upon contact. Merry pulled the crystal from its hiding place. Her hope that it would still be there since it had gone untouched for nearly three-hundred years turned to truth.

She stood, holding the crystal up to the meager light filtering into the room. Her heart pounded with the thrill of the find. This stone was different from the others, its chiseled surface rough rather than smooth. And, it held only one color.

Crimson. A tingling sensation trickled from her fingers and up her arm as she looked closer. At first glance, the crystal had appeared to be a wand of solid red glass, but upon more critical inspection, small eddies could be found as the color moved within the glass.

"It's beautiful," the girl said, her brown eyes wide, her mouth opened in awe. "What is it?"

Merry pocketed it in her skirt, holding onto one of the pointed beveled ends. She leaned down until her eyes were level with the child's. The baby squirmed around to fix her with a curious gaze. "It's a crystal. It's my crystal."

"What does it do?"

Merry pursed her lips. "I'm not certain of its purpose. But, I believe it to have an important one. Now, you'll not tell of this, will you? You'll keep this a secret?"

The girl twisted her mouth as she contemplated her answer. "Papa says you're a witch. I shouldn't make secrets with a witch."

Merry offered a wan smile. She stood back. "Very well. You're a good daughter." She gripped the crystal tight in her fist as she headed to the stairs, pausing to look back before she leaving the room. "I did not harm you or your baby brother. I only came for what was mine. Please remember that kindness."

As she raised her foot to take the first step down the steep winding staircase, a jolt of white heat coursed through her body. Merry lurched and grabbed for the stair rail while still clutching the crystal. She breathed short, choking breaths as fiery needles pierced every bone in her body.

"What's wrong?" the girl asked in a small, panicked voice.

"I don't..." Merry opened her clenched fist to find she held nothing more than pulverized glass. It drifted from her fingers, disintegrating before reaching the ground. Merry doubled over, gripping the stair rail with both hands as her bones screamed and her legs went out from under her. She fell forward, her weakened hands unable to hold onto the rail. Her shoulder hit the edge of a stair, her head the wall as she skidded down the stairs, legs-over-head and crashed onto the landing at the staircase's turn.

"Oh!" the girl shouted. "Are you all right? Miss?"

Merry lifted her head with some effort. She grunted in reply. Unable to get her limbs to support her, Merry dragged herself across the landing and down the remaining stairs, sliding down the last two until she lay face down on the foyer floor. She managed to get to her knees. The girl's ginger footsteps and fussing baby sounded behind her.

"What ails you? Is it a curse?"

Merry crawled toward the door, ignoring the girl as she continued with her questions. Merry reached for the doorknob and with the help of the doorframe, pulled herself up to a standing position. Through blurred vision, she spied her father running toward her.

Then, the screaming began.

43 JOURNEY

The carriage dipped to the right, then lurched forward, jolting Susannah from her seat.

"Blasted potholes," mumbled her uncle from the seat across from her. He pounded on the wall separating them from the coachman. "Gil! Mind the road!"

The carriage righted, Uncle Richard turned his attention to Susannah, his face creased with concern. "You all right there, Susannah?"

"Yes, Uncle." Susannah straightened her skirts and settled herself upon the tufted seat inside the carriage. This luxury would take some getting used to. She'd convinced her mother to allow her to spend the winter at her uncle's house in Boston in order to gain experience in the fine art of being a young lady worthy of a wealthy suitor, or someone at least a pinch above her current station. In return, she would help with the household chores and take care of her two young cousins, James and Patience.

Her mother was thrilled with the arrangement, but Susannah cared little about a suitor, wealthy or otherwise. Her efforts to stop the witch trials had had great effect. Rumors of Mary Easty's ghostly warnings had spread, curtailing more than a few accusations. The Court of Oyer and Terminer had been dissolved. Though the trials might continue, spectral evidence would no longer be allowed. The courts would be hard-pressed to convict anyone of witchcraft without the lies and imaginations of so-called witnesses. Still, Susannah had one more wrong to right, which was the real reason why she sat in a carriage headed for Boston.

With the money she would earn working for her uncle, she'd be able to cover Tituba's jail fees. Reverend Parris boasted he would not pay for her freedom, that she deserved to rot in jail for her lies—lies he'd beaten out of Tituba, then condemned her for telling them. Those untruths had freed her from his wrath, but chained her to a prison cell. Susannah released a frustrated sigh. From the Reverend's hands to Tituba's lips, an evil had been visited upon Salem Village.

Brushing aside the sheer curtain, Susannah peered out to the calm streets of Salem Town. Church service ended a bit later here than in Salem Village, and only now, as the afternoon sun began its descent, did families filter onto the streets. As they rounded the corner of North and Essex Streets, Susannah spied an oddly-dressed man assisting what appeared to be an injured woman. They trundled along in an awkward crouch-walk and disappeared behind a line of bushes as though not to be seen.

It can't be.

"Uncle Richard, stop the carriage! Please!" she shouted.

To her uncle's astonishment, she leapt onto his bench and pounded on the wall to gain the Coachman's attention. While she yelled for the carriage to stop, her uncle attempted to physically stop her banging, which ended in an awkward wrestle that was wholly unsuccessful. The horses whinnied in protest at the sudden stop. As the lumbering wheels silenced, she broke free from her uncle's grasp, but a child's scream froze Susannah's hand on the door handle. The horses spooked, rocking the carriage and tossing Susannah to the floor. She landed with a "humph". Her uncle shouted as Gil steadied the horses, and Susannah scrambled back to the bench.

She yanked the door open to find several townspeople who'd been making their way home from church standing nearby, staring passed the carriage. Susannah stood tiptoe on the step of the carriage and peered over the roof, her uncle telling her to get back inside all the while. Judge Corwin's house sat on the other side of the road, a young girl, about age ten, stood in the open doorway, red-faced, wild-eyed, and screaming. The solemn walk home from church grew chaotic as people ran toward the sounds of a distressed child.

Susannah scanned the area where she'd last seen Meredith Chalmers, but saw no one. Movement further down the street caught her eye, and she glimpsed a flash of auburn before Merry slipped from sight around the corner of a large saltbox home.

The defiant cry of "Witch!" indicated someone else had noticed those auburn locks as well.

Susannah leapt out of the carriage and climbed onto the bench beside Gil, still engaged in the business of controlling the two powerful horses.

Susannah pointed in the direction Merry had gone. "Sir, we must help a friend. She's around the corner. There." Susannah must have stunned Gil with her sudden appearance and demands, judging by his open-mouthed stare.

"Make haste!" she shouted.

Shocked into action, Gil snapped the reins, and the horses spurred into motion. As they rallied into a fast-paced trot, Gil spared Susannah a glance. "You shouldn't be up here, Miss."

Susannah pointed toward the corner she'd last seen Merry. "Turn there."

Their carriage easily overtook the small group of returning church-goers who'd also spied Merry. The door creaked open behind Susannah and she turned to find Uncle Richard leaning out, glaring at her over the carriage head.

"Susannah," he said over the pounding hooves and grating wheels, "I must insist you get back inside at once!"

Before she could respond, her uncle ducked back inside

and slammed the door shut. At first relieved, she realized why he'd given up his fight so fast as the carriage turned sharply down the street. "Hang on, Miss," Gil said. Susannah gripped the wing of the carriage with one hand and the box with another and tilted with the turn, trying not to slide off the narrow seat altogether. Inside the carriage, her uncle could be heard yelling words not meant for a young lady's ears. She would have a hard time convincing him to let her stay after this.

Susannah scanned the area for any sign of Merry. "Slow down."

Gil pulled back on the reins, slowing the horses' gait. Susannah jumped up at a quick movement to their left. "Over there!"

Gil steered the carriage toward Merry and the man holding her up as they moved at a crippled pace. She didn't recognized the man from this distance. As they drew closer, Susannah cupped her hands around her mouth and shouted Merry's name. At the same time, her uncle yelled for Gil to stop. Despite Susannah's imploring look to continue, the old servant couldn't disobey his master. The carriage came to a gradual halt. Susannah leapt from the seat and ran as soon as she hit the ground, impervious to her uncle's shouts.

Susannah shouted as she ran toward them. "Stop, please!"

The man stumbled to a halt, Merry collapsing against him. He caught her, turning toward Susannah as he did. He held Merry's unconscious form, her head cradled against his chest, auburn curls fluttering in the breeze. Susannah took a step closer. "I can help."

The man tore his worried gaze from Merry and studied Susannah's face. She gestured toward the waiting carriage, at the same time noticing her uncle stomping in their direction. "My uncle's carriage. We can take you to Boston. You'll be safe there."

"Susannah!" her uncle shouted.

"Please, others have seen you. They will follow."

The man's gaze darted from Susannah to her red-faced

uncle to Merry. He hoisted her into his arms and nodded his assent to Susannah. They headed to the carriage only to be intercepted by her uncle. "Young lady, you will get in the carriage, and you will get in now!"

"Yes Uncle. I'm sorry for this, but I must ask a favor," Susannah said, hoping the desperation in her eyes would soften the glare in his. "My friends need help. Can we give them a ride to Boston?"

"I will not tolerate such rash behavior in my household!"

Susannah bowed her head and summoned as much chagrin as she could muster. "Of course not, Uncle. I am truly sorry."

She peeked from beneath her lashes. Her uncle's color faded to a less alarming pink. He scrutinized the man, his gaze fixing for a moment upon the strange metal teeth coursing down the center of the man's odd coat. Then he tipped his head toward Merry. "What's wrong with her?"

The man gripped Merry tighter. "I'm not certain. She passed out. She may need some food."

Uncle Richard frowned and rubbed his stubbly chin. He raised an eyebrow toward the man. "What's in Boston?"

"Beg pardon?" the man asked.

"Boston. Susannah said you needed a ride to Boston. Do you have family there?"

The man's face perked up as though suddenly remembering. A small smile appeared on his lips. "I believe I may."

"You don't know?" Uncle Richard asked.

The man cleared his throat. "I've been away for a few years."

"Ah, well then. What are their names? These relatives you may have in Boston?"

"Rayne. My cousin, Bran, lived there with his wife, last I knew."

"And you, sir, are?"

"Devon Rayne."

Susannah gasped. "Surely, you're not the son of Fergus Rayne?"

"Aye," Devon answered, his eyes alighting. "Is he still alive, do you know?"

Susannah answered with a stuttering "yes" while trying to comprehend the fact that a man who'd been missing for twenty years stood in front of her. Even stranger, she'd found him with Merry. In fact, he seemed protective of her. She nodded toward Merry, pale and still in his arms. "But, how did you come to know Merry?"

His answer nearly knocked her off her feet. "She's my daughter."

44 BOSTON

The jolt of wooden wheels on cobblestones woke Merry. She didn't open her eyes fully, not because she didn't want to, but because she couldn't. Her limbs bore the consistency of a sodden sponge, drenched with fatigue, and her mind didn't fair much better. Was she seeing Susannah Sheldon or had her visage somehow manifested in Merry's subconscious? A deep hum vibrated against her head. Muffled words followed. Her father's voice penetrated her murky awareness. Merry tried to speak, tried to manage some form of communication, but colors swam across her vision, numbed her heavy limbs, and she soon succumbed to blissful sleep.

When she awoke later, it was not in a trundling carriage, but in a feather bed that felt like heaven beneath her. A little girl sat on a small wooden chair next to the bed. She scooted closer and announced with a demure smile, "I'm Patience." Merry attempted to smile back, certain her lips had barely moved. This lack of encouragement did nothing to sway young Patience's monologue. "Susannah is my cousin. She's come to watch over me and my brother. His name is James."

So, she hadn't imagined seeing Susannah, thought Merry. Managing a smile, she said, "How nice."

"'Tis nice," Patience agreed, bouncing in her seat once before reeling in her exuberance and folding her hands in her lap like a decorous young lady. She couldn't stay still, though, squirming like an excited puppy. She leaned a bit closer than proper and whispered, "Papa says Susannah needs a husband." A giggle escaped her, and she clapped a tiny hand against her lips as though to shove it back inside.

Merry laughed, immediately paying for the act as minuscule knives stabbed into her forehead above her left eye. She sucked in her breath and clutched her head. "Where am I?"

"You're in Susannah's chambers. I wanted to give you my bed, but Susannah insisted."

Before Merry could ask her question in a more direct fashion, Susannah entered the room. She gently ushered her young ward off the chair and out of the room. "Hush, now Patience. Miss Meredith needs her rest, not your gibberish."

Before she disappeared from sight, Patience turned and gave a small wave and a large smile to Merry, who wiggled her fingers in response. It was all her body seemed capable of.

Susannah stepped closer to the bed. As their gaze connected, guilt and anger passed between Merry and Susannah as though it were a physical thing. Merry focused on her former accuser but sensed no animosity. "Where are we?"

"Boston," Susannah replied. "You're in my Uncle Richard's house."

Alarms screamed in her head, tingling her wooly mind. *Boston. Why was she in Boston?* "I need to get back to Salem."

"You're in no condition. Even if you were, I'm certain it would be most disastrous for you."

Merry tried to piece together a coherent thought. Tried to retrace her steps. She recalled finding the crystal. She'd placed so much hope in the object, expecting it to be the key to their plight. After all, if the Devil wanted it, it must be powerful. But it had turned to dust mere moments after she'd found it, and in the process she'd been weakened. Incapacitated. Susannah placed a hand under Merry's head and lifted her, at the same time bringing a cup of warm ale to her lips. Parched, Merry took a few sips, instantly wishing for bottled water instead. Susannah eased her back onto the pillow. "I'll leave the ale here in case you want more."

Merry blinked, fighting against the threatening slumber. The few minutes of consciousness had taken its toll. "Why are you helping me?" she asked, her voice sounding far away.

Susannah tucked the blanket around Merry's shoulders. "Because you're mine to help."

Someone knocked. Liz ran the short distance from the kitchen to the door, ripping it open. It slammed against the small table to the side of it, sending her keys to the floor.

"Mer..." her words died on her lips at the sight of Alex Olivier. She tried to recover her disappointment that Merry wasn't standing on her doorstep, but he noticed.

"Not exactly the hello I was hoping for," he said.

She was still wearing the jeans and t-shirt she'd had on when he'd stopped by earlier to ask her out. "Alex, I'm so sorry. I didn't forget." She had. "Something's happened, and I got completely distracted."

"Is everything all right?"

"I honestly don't know, but it doesn't feel all right." She stepped aside. "Please come in."

The scent of black pepper and fresh air whispered to her as he entered. It couldn't distract her from her worry though. She tried to tell herself Merry was fine, that she was visiting her Dad. But she hadn't been able to get a hold of either of them. When she'd called Sophie, she was at the grocery store and didn't know where Merry was either.

Alex studied her. "You don't look well."

Liz forced her clasped hands apart and dropped them to her side, which quickly became awkward. She grasped the back of a dining room chair and leaned forward. "Merry's missing."

Alex frowned. "Again?"

"At least the last time I had an idea of where she was."

Alex's frown turned into open-mouthed shock. "What do you mean you knew where she was?"

"I... I mean when she... what?" She was making a mess of things. "Of course, I didn't know where she was. I was a kid when she disappeared. I'm talking about after she came back. The first time."

Shaking his head, Alex said, "Listen, I know this is complicated. But, I'm here as a friend, not a reporter. What can I do to help?"

She wanted to tell him he probably couldn't do anything and at the same time hug him for his sweet offer. Before she could do either, her phone rang. "Sophie! Did you find her?"

"I just got in," she said.

Alex's intense gaze followed Liz as she walked around the room, phone to ear.

"She's not here," Sophie said. "But, I think she was."

Liz stopped pacing. Her heart sank before she even heard Sophie's next words. "I found a bag with her clothing in it upstairs."

"Maybe she left them behind when she stayed with you?"

"I don't think so. There's more. The door to the attic was open, and so was an attic window."

"Maybe the window was open already and blew the door open?"

"It wasn't, Liz. And, the window was opened high enough for someone to climb through."

Dead silence followed, interrupted only by the clicking of the telephone line. Then, Liz said, "High enough for someone to climb through and jump."

Her body trembled head to toe. Eyes still closed, Merry reached out to push away whoever was shaking her, her quivering arms connecting with nothing but air. Her eyes shot open, and she popped up to a sitting position. Her teeth rattled, and her body quaked.

"Papa?" she called out, her voice barely reaching above a whisper. Something shifted in the dark. The familiar sound of flint struck against steel preceded a spark, followed by a flame that pierced the shadows. The flame illuminated Susannah's faced as it danced its way toward Merry.

"You're awake," she said in a hushed voice. "I wasn't sure if you'd ever wake."

Merry's voice wobbled as a spasm racked her body. "How long..." she managed to say before a tremor flattened her to the bed. Shadows flickered over Susannah's worried face.

"Three days you've been asleep," Susannah answered her half-articulated question.

A moan escaped Merry as another wave of tremors cascaded down her arms. Her fingers shook, and she lifted her hands to the ceiling not a moment to soon as the energy, which had been coiled inside her for days, sprung from her fingertips. The colors filled the room, cocooning them in a shimmering rainbow. Susannah tilted her head back, eyes scanning her brilliant surroundings as she spun a slow circle.

The tremors stopped. The heaviness in Merry's limbs lifted. She stood amid the spiraling rainbows as energy vibrated beneath her skin. No longer too much or too little. She was... perfect.

"What is this?" Susannah asked.

It's me, Merry thought. She turned to face Susannah. "Where is my father?"

"He is your father, then?"

"He is," Merry answered.

Susannah pursed her lips and shot a worried glance toward the door.

"What is it, Susannah?"

She sighed and turned toward the door. "Follow me."

Anxiety built up inside Merry like a puddle after a rainstorm. She followed Susannah's shadowy figure, the candlelight barely breaking through the night-ridden hallway. Three days she'd been asleep. Three days her father had been without a trade. While the rest had strengthened her, she was certain it had not done so for her father. Once again she was on the other side of time with a parent destined to die. She bit her lip to stifle morbid thoughts as Susannah led her down the stairs.

The embers in the hearth leant a soft glow to the parlor and enough light to see a blanket-covered form lying on the floor before the fireplace. Merry stopped. "He's not... "

"No," Susannah answered before Merry could say the dreaded word. "But, he's not well. He fell unconscious here earlier. We thought it best to leave him near the warmth." She added a couple of logs to the hearth, stirring the embers until they latched onto the new wood and licked flaming tongues up their sides. "Do you know what ails him?"

Merry swallowed the lump, which had formed in her throat. "Aye." She knelt down, touching her father's shoulder, and giving a small shake. Nothing. "Papa," she whispered. She leaned in close. His weak breath puffed against her cheek. She had to get her father to the future. Merry stood and faced Susannah. "I need to get him home. Will you help me lift him?"

"You can't go to Salem Village, Merry," Susannah said. "It's too dangerous for you."

Merry knelt at her father's head. Heat radiated from him. His face was beaded with sweat. She shoved her hands beneath his shoulders. "I have to. Now, please, take his legs."

Susannah bent and grasped Devon's ankles. "How are you going to get him home? You can't carry him."

"I need to get him to a high place." With some effort, Merry lifted her father's torso. His sleep-heavy weight pulled her forward until she hunched over him. "Lift his ankles."

Susannah dropped his legs and stood back.

"You said you wanted to help me."

"I do. But, first I want answers."

"There's no time," Merry said. She could leap through time, but was no master of it. Like everyone else, she was at time's mercy as it plodded forward one second after another.

Susannah ignored her pleading. "I want to know what happened at Gallows Hill. I want to know what the colors are."

"Susannah, my father is dying!"

"And, how is Devon Rayne your father? He's been missing for nearly twenty years!"

A choking snore broke the night hush. Both girls froze. Merry would need to resort to commanding Susannah to help her before anyone else joined the fray. Before she could respond, Susannah said in a muted tone, "I want to know what happened to William."

The poignancy of the request shocked Merry into inaction. She lowered her father gently to the floor. "You still care for him," Merry said, her tone a mix of astonishment and accusation.

Susannah's face crumpled. "The Tall Man has him." Her fist flew to her mouth as she stifled a small cry.

All the recriminations, all the guilt she wanted to throw at Susannah's feet, fled from Merry's mind. "How do you know this?"

Susannah sat on the bench, her gaze on Devon's still form. "I saw him. Them. Together. On Gallows Hill. I'd gone there thinking I could stop the hanging if I chopped the offensive branch from the hanging tree. I made little progress before the Tall Man arrived. William was with him. And, that nasty woman, Vanessa."

"Vanessa? But, she died in William's cornfield."

"She was with them. I am certain."

Mayhap William had misjudged what he'd seen. He'd admitted the scene was one of chaos.

Tears slid down Susannah's face. "William was not himself. He tried to fight, tried to disobey, but the Tall Man's abuse won."

Fists clenched, Merry struggled to contain her raging colors. She needed to remain focused. William. Salem. With that, she realized the best approach to take was to be honest about herself. She lifted her arms, palms up and unfurled her fists. Like the smoky start of a fire, her colors drifted toward the ceiling. Susannah's gaze transfixed upon the display.

"These are my colors," Merry said. "They are a part of me. They always have been."

"They're beautiful," Susannah whispered, her gaze following the undulating coils of colors.

"They're also powerful. They give me the ability to manipulate the elements. And to travel through time."

Susannah's eyes widened into two bright blue saucers. "You *are* a witch."

This time Merry couldn't keep the accusation from her voice. "You've claimed such before."

Susannah bunched her skirt in her hands. She had the decency to look Merry in the eye as she said, "'Twas no truth to it. Only jealousy." Her face flushed, but she held Merry's gaze. "To be caught in a lie seemed worse to me than letting others suffer. But, when William told me about the angels, I grasped the chance to right my wrongs. I know I can't fix it, but I will do what I can to end the witch hunts."

Merry raised an eyebrow. "Like trying to chop down the hanging tree?"

Susannah dipped her gaze toward the floor. "'Twas foolish, I know. But, I also scared Goody Herrick into thinking she saw a ghost who warned her the witch hunts should end." Susannah stood and took Merry's hand. "The magistrate is listening. And, so is the governor. The Court of Oyer and Terminer has disbanded. Spectral evidence is no longer allowed. There is even talk of freeing the convicted, provided they pay their prison costs."

Merry absorbed Susannah's words with fascination. All this in a few weeks' time. Perhaps there could be a better ending than she'd thought.

Susannah continued. "Patience told you I've come here to find a husband. But, I've come for another reason. I plan to use my savings to pay Tituba's fee."

"You would free Tituba?"

"She only told stories at our requests. We were bored and relentless. She doesn't deserve her fate."

"No one did."

"Aye. 'Tis true. I cannot change what has happened, but I can try to better the outcome for some."

The truth of Susannah's conviction permeated Merry's senses. The woman standing before her had caused much of her turmoil, but she'd also unleashed the truth inside Merry. Finally, it appeared Susannah had released the truth inside herself, as well.

Merry took Susannah's other hand and stared into her eyes. "You are right. The Tall Man has William. I am doing what I can to save him. And, not only him. I believe on All Hallows' Eve, William's birthday, The Tall Man plans to take to the streets of Salem and claim the souls of all who dwell within its borders. He means to become powerful enough to make hell on earth."

Susannah's hands trembled in Merry's. She bit her quivering lip. "Merry, today is All Hallows' Eve."

45 FATE

The crystal taunted, shimmering invitingly, yet holding tight to its contents. Corinne rubbed her thumb across its rough surface, worrying the knot of glass where the color pooled and darkened. It scratched her skin, but she only rubbed harder as she fought the temptation to slam it against the marble floor.

She leaned her forehead against the window, able to see as clearly as if there was daylight outside rather than eternal night. The land beyond the castle pulsed. While her father assembled an army, she was tasked with safeguarding the crystal.

"You're bleeding," a voice said from behind.

Corinne stiffened. She looked down as her blood dripped from the crystal's tip to a widening red pool on the floor below. Vanessa stepped into view, a smug expression on her face.

"Oh, don't pout, Corinne. I'm sure daddy will bring you back a t-shirt."

Corinne held back the glare burning to come alive, delivering the bite in her words instead. "And, I'm sure he won't bring you back at all." She smiled at the telltale twitch of Vanessa's lips. The one that said she stressed about her fate, as well.

A rumble filled the cavernous ballroom as the earth beneath them roiled with the movement of thousands of the Tall Man's soldiers. Corinne peered out the window as the earth's surface rippled and cracked, and the first of many hands grasped for purchase. The dead began the arduous task of hauling their bodies to Salem in time for Halloween. Her father had sought William since his birth, nearly twenty-two years ago. A light born during All Hallows' Eve, the darkest of nights, threatened the darkness like no other. But, he was a threat no more. Now, he was the Tall Man's weapon.

Vanessa stood beside her. "Make sure you're ready when we bring Merry back. We'll have to act before she can react."

Corinne shrugged. "I'm not worried about rainbow girl."

"Sometimes a little worry is good. It keeps you sharp."

Corinne turned from the sight of the grotesque corpses overtaking the landscape and walked back to the center of the room. She lifted her hands and released the crystal. Blood snaked a path from her thumb to her wrist and then elbow as the air snatched the crystal and floated it back to its home midway between floor and ceiling. As soon as it reached its destination, the crystal burst. Corinne screamed and thrust her hand up to shield her face as hundreds of shards flew outward. Before the broken pieces could reach her, they were pulled back to their home where they coalesced into a glittering band of crimson.

Vanessa came running up behind Corinne. "What did you do?!"

Corinne glared at the spectacle. Even the dust-sized pieces of crystal held stubbornly onto their crimson charge. "I didn't *do* anything."

Panic edged Vanessa's voice. "Well then, what happened?"

"You saw the same thing I did."

Vanessa pursed her lips. "What do we do?"

Corinne spared Vanessa a glance before turning and leaving the witch to contemplate the ruined crystal. Something was off—Corinne had felt it as soon as the crystal burst. She looked back, emitting a derisive laugh as Vanessa scooped the bits of crimson crystal from the air and deposited them into a pocket in her cloak.

"What do you think you'll do with those?" Corinne asked.

Vanessa glared at her. "I'll fix your foolish mistake."

Corinne returned her glare until Vanessa averted her eyes and resumed collecting the remaining shards. Vanessa was to accompany the Tall Man to Salem, while Corinne had been instructed to stay back and guard Crimson, but there was nothing to guard anymore. And after all, Corinne was her father's daughter, and she wasn't about to be left behind.

46 TREMORS

Susannah grunted as they half lifted and half dragged Devon's motionless form toward the stairs. Merry had tried to wake him with a shake and even a slap to the face, but he'd not responded. She'd pressed her hand over his heart and released her colors. His faint pulse had strengthened, but he remained unconscious. There was no time to secure a ride and get back to Salem. They would have to jump here, in Boston.

"Explain why we need to go to the roof?"

Merry blew a straggling lock of hair out of her eyes. "I don't know. It's how the colors work. I need to leap through them."

Susannah slowed, nearly causing Merry to shout at her to move faster until she heard her words. "But, Merry, you only fell a few feet before you disappeared from Gallows Hill."

Merry, who had already backed up two steps of the main staircase, fell against the tread at the revelation. The platform beneath the limb that their nooses had been secured to stood only two or three feet above ground. Her heart raced at the prospect of saving her father without having to jump off a roof. She wasn't afraid of heights, but she'd had her fill of death-defying leaps.

"Help me get him up a few more steps." They'd labored

midway up the staircase when Merry asked Susannah to help her prop her father up as best they could. It was an awkward task, but at last Devon's warm forehead lolled against her shoulder. Merry wrapped her arms tightly around his waist. Susannah hovered close by, still helping to support him.

"You must go back downstairs now and stand as far away from us as possible." Susannah took one step down, then ran back up and threw her arms around Merry's neck. She almost fell over between Susannah's assault and her father's weight.

"I'm sorry for everything," Susannah whispered. "Find William. Live the life you both deserve."

As Susannah released her, Merry stared at the girl whose lies had changed both their lives in so many ways. Her heart lifted as she said the words she never thought she'd say to Susannah Sheldon. "I forgive you."

Susannah dipped her head in gratitude, then jogged down the steps and sped to the far corner of the room. As soon as Merry summoned them, the colors bloomed like a brilliant flower. They curled and spun at the edge of the staircase. Merry dragged her father to the edge of the step, and together they fell forward into a swirling rainbow.

Sophie peeked around the corner of her parlor. Liz and the handsome reporter were still there—Liz hadn't moved from her sentry post at the picture window. Alex stood a hair's breadth behind her, a comforting hand on her shoulder. Sophie palmed the small crystal ball, which usually sat in the center of the round, velvet-covered table.

She'd come to dislike the ball of glass and the ominous prophecies it spun. Upon reflection, she could attribute only one positive vision the ball had revealed—that being the first, when Merry had leapt from the past. Despite the terrifying view of her leap from a cliff, Merry had turned up safe, and her granddaughter had come home. It had been the last good vision she'd received.

The wall beneath her fingers vibrated, the motion followed by a low rumble, as the earth trembled. Liz looked over her shoulder at Sophie as though she'd known she'd been standing there the whole time. "It's getting worse. I felt it that time."

"Me too," Sophie said.

Liz slipped out from under Alex's touch. "Give us a moment?"

Alex shoved his hands into his pants pockets. "Sure. I'll wait outside."

After he left, Liz spoke with urgency. "We should go to Gallows Hill, Sophie."

Sophie tucked the crystal ball into her generous coat pocket. "It's not a good idea, Liz."

"How do you know?" Liz asked. She'd asked it twenty times before, but Sophie refused to tell her what she'd seen on the face of the crystal ball. Not because it was awful, but because it was *vague*. All Sophie was certain of was that whatever the ball was trying to show her wasn't good. There had been fire and screaming. Screaming was never good in her experience. She'd seen Merry and Ruby in the vision, but that had no chance of coming true since Merry was still missing. She thought that as long as they stayed put, maybe they had a chance of thwarting the future.

Liz held her hand out and wiggled her fingers. "Give me the ball."

"No, Liz."

"Sophie! You can't expect me to stare out a window until Merry returns! We have to do something!"

"What do you propose we do, Liz? I can't make a time-traveling rainbow, can you?"

"We're not even certain she went back in time. She might have... gotten lost."

Sophie fixed Liz with one of her "really?" looks.

"What if Ruby's right?" Liz asked.

Sophie tried hard to keep her face from twisting into a grimace and attempted a nonchalant look.

"Why is your eye twitching?" Liz asked.

Sophie dropped the facade. "Right about what? She hasn't told us why Merry needs to go to Gallows Hill." Sophie threw her arms up and stalked to the kitchen. "And we don't even know where Merry is!"

The front door banged open, and Liz and Sophie spun around. *Uh oh*, Sophie thought at the site of Alex's flushed, panicked face.

Alex pointed beyond the open door. "Something's happening out there."

A rumbling, louder this time, followed his words. Liz rushed past Alex, halting on Sophie's doorstep to take in the late afternoon scene on Salem's streets, which were already packed with costumed party goers. Even with the dangerous weather phenomena Salem had recently experienced, the streets were busy with people well into their celebration of Halloween. In all likelihood, the spike in odd occurrences and the discovery of the bodies on Gallows Hill had only served to draw more people towards Salem than they might have repelled.

A thin, jagged crack had formed in the section of concrete outside Sophie's door. With all the festivities out here—the carnival on the wharf and the general loudness of the happy party-goers—the low rumbling went entirely unnoticed. Liz held onto the doorframe as the earth jolted beneath the stoop. Alex steadied Sophie.

"Stay here," Liz told Sophie as she ran toward Essex Street, Alex on her heels.

She skidded to a stop as they rounded the corner. Essex Street was already crammed with visitors. She tripped over a dislodged cobblestone. Alex caught her, holding her a moment longer than necessary. A woman a few feet in front of her tripped and Liz followed her accusing gaze toward the ground where several other bricks protruded.

Liz took Alex's hand and dragged him into the Halloween celebration. "Come on."

She peered through the many feet parading along the street and soon found another cluster of uprooted bricks. She'd traveled this street often enough to know that this was not its normal state.

"What are we looking for?" Alex asked.

She pointed toward the bricks. "I think those bricks were lifted by the tremors."

They pushed through the thickening crowd, finding a line of displaced cobblestones every six feet or so. They followed the path until the cobblestones ended, then picked it up again in a crooked half-inch crack in the pavement after crossing Washington Street. The crowd had waned at this point, most of the celebration behind them. Liz became aware she still held Alex's hand. She slipped out of his grasp, her face heating as she stared back at Alex's questioning gaze. "I don't think we'll lose each other now."

He smiled as though her words meant something more. Liz ducked her head and stepped in front of him. "Let's see where this ends."

They walked on in silence, passing a large group of tourists lined up outside the Witch House to hear ghost stories within its candle-lit rooms.

"How far are we planning to follow this?" Alex asked.

Liz stopped and surveyed the area behind them, then looked down the street, the dark crevice in the pavement resembled a scar beneath the bright afternoon sun. "A little bit further, if that's all right. I want to see something."

After walking around a slight bend in the road, Liz stopped again. "It's odd, isn't it? The line is exactly in the middle of the road. If the road curves, the crack does too."

Alex followed Liz's finger as she pointed out the curving break in the street. "It's almost like it's following the road," he said.

Liz nodded. "Like a subterranean GPS. And it's heading straight for Gallows Hill."

The first action Merry took when she realized they were back in 2010 was to pull her father into a small side street. They were surrounded by brick homes, all several stories high, and all decked out in fall colors. Jack-o-Lanterns sat on stoops; their glowing smiles welcoming the costumed children climbing their steps. Under the frowning scrutiny of a watchful mother as she escorted her children, Merry tugged her father into an alleyway.

His sluggish response filled her with more hope than was warranted, but his wakefulness was a good sign.

"Papa, can you hear me?" she gently tapped his cheeks, trying to make him focus. "Papa?"

He attempted to swat her hands away. It was a welcome change from his near-death state. "Can you hear me?" she asked.

Devon's eyes opened with a vacant stare. His breath came in fast gasps. Merry pressed a hand against his too-warm face. He shuddered, but when his gaze landed on her face, an awareness seeped into his eyes. He managed a hint of a smile and said in barely audible voice, "You're better."

"So are you," she answered. Relief flooded her veins as her father scrutinized their surroundings.

He pushed out of his slump into a sitting position and leaned his head against the brick building behind him. "Where are we?"

"Still in Boston. Different century."

"We're back?"

Merry nodded. "We're back."

Devon straightened, eyes widening. "You have to get to Salem."

Merry pressed a hand against his shoulder to keep him from rising. "Take it easy. You're in no shape to go anywhere yet."

Her father reached up and placed his hand over hers. "I didn't say 'we'. *You* need to go. Now."

"I can't leave you!"

"You have to, Merry. This is bigger than us."

"But..."

"Listen," he said, with a strength that exceeded his obvious state. "I'll be fine. I've been in worse spots than this over the last fifteen years."

Merry stared into her father's eyes. She knew he was

capable of taking care of himself, but she couldn't get rid of the fear that if she walked away, she'd never see him again. He gripped her upper arms; his gaze bore into hers. "William needs you. *Salem* needs you. Now, go."

She surveyed the rows of brick houses lined along a grassy median. *Would one of these homeowners take her father in?*

"Go, Merry."

She backed up a few steps. It occurred to her that even if she did as her father asked and left him, she had no way to get to Salem.

"Why are you hesitating?" her father asked.

Merry straightened her back. "I'm not leaving you in some alleyway. And how am I to get to Salem?"

With some effort, Devon reached behind him and drew a wallet from his back pants pocket. "Sorry, I wasn't thinking." He extracted several green bills and thrust them toward her. "Here's $200. Take it. We'll get you a cab to drive you back."

Merry raised her chin. "A cab can take you back, too." She wasn't certain what a cab was, but if it could take her to Salem, surely it could take her father, as well.

Devon dropped his hand in defeat and turned his head. Merry crouched down before him. "We will go together."

Devon let out a frustrated sigh. He pushed against the ground in an attempt to stand. Merry grabbed his arm and wrapped another around his waist, helping him get upright. He breathed a heavy sigh, but otherwise appeared more stable than he had been only minutes earlier.

They stepped out of the alleyway onto the cobblestone sidewalk, her father leaning on her. The late Boston afternoon assaulted her senses with an amalgamation of crisp October air, burning wood, car horns, and the chatter of boisterous children. She turned to her father as a frog and several princesses ran past them. "Now, where do we find this cab?"

47 FIGHT

"Can you see this?" Sidney pointed at a thin rainbow trail leading away from Iron House.

"See what?" Luke asked.

Sidney traced the colors along the tapestry until they ended just short of the ocean and faded into the wool. "She's in Salem."

"Who?"

"Merry." Sidney stood back, puzzled why she was the only one who could see some images in the tapestry where others couldn't. She startled when Axylus's deep voice sounded right near her ear.

"Merry. Enfys?" he asked.

She nodded, and stepped forward to retrace the path the colors had taken. "She left Iron House, here." A faint glow of muted colors shimmered in the general location of Salem. Sidney laid a finger upon it. "And ended up here. Salem."

"You know this, how?" Axylus asked.

"Her colors. They left a trail."

"And, you can see this trail?"

"Yes, like I can see Iron House," she said, then at Axylus's quizzical look, added, "My home."

"Ahhh, your home."

Luke pushed into the small space between her and Axylus. "Where you still are. Sort of."

I'm here and I'm there, Sidney mused. She looked at Luke's grinning face. "That's why I can see both places, isn't it."

Luke shrugged a shoulder and lifted an eyebrow.

"Milady, your ability to track the Enfys will be most helpful when we go to battle," Axylus said.

Sidney grinned. She didn't think she'd get tired of being called *milady*. "It will be hard to drag that tapestry along though, won't it?"

Axylus gave her an amused look. "You will monitor the landscape from here, of course."

Sidney's smile froze and then disappeared completely. "You want me to stay behind while you go to rescue my brother."

"How will that even help?" Luke asked, making Sidney proud as he spoke up in her favor. "She can't communicate with us."

The Illuminators were able to speak into one another's minds through images, a talent they used when something needed to be communicated to everyone in Nurya. Just as she couldn't dissolve and light travel on her own, Sidney didn't have the ability to mind-speak. She had to be a full-fledged Illuminator before those skills kicked in. But, that didn't mean she couldn't fight. "I'm going with you."

"Luke, you will stay with her and communicate what she sees."

"What? No! I'm going to the fight. You need me! I'm..."

"You are needed here more," Axylus answered in his infuriatingly certain voice. The cavernous room seemed to shrink in around them as panic gripped Sidney. She had to get back to her brother.

"There must be some other way," she said, hating how desperate she sounded. She stared at the tapestry that had fascinated her a moment ago, now an albatross.

"What's that?" A woman asked. Sidney thought she used to reside in the modern glass house on the hill. Her gaze followed the woman's pointing finger toward the far end of the tapestry where the fabric grew dark. The crowd which had gathered wandered en masse down the wall to get a closer look. It appeared as though many tiny brown insects were crawling through the wool. Bit by bit, they broke from the darker end of the fabric and slithered into the area Sidney had dubbed the dead zone when she and Luke had stepped from the green grass of Nurya into the dead landscape that led to the Tall Man's dark forest. The insects, no bigger than the head of a pin, clambered over one another making an undulating escape from the forest.

Sidney gasped. She gripped Luke's arm. His eyes rounded as understanding hit him. "Shit."

"Luke," Axylus warned.

"Sorry, what do you say? Shite? Either way, this isn't good."

"Would you care to elaborate?"

"After we saw William, the Tall Man set his minions on us—corpses, hundreds of them. They came right out of the ground," Luke answered, scrabbling at the air with clawed hands. He pointed toward the bubbling pool of insects. "I'm pretty sure that's what's moving up there."

Hundreds of heads tilted upward to watch the brown wave form a thin line, wider at the base. Sidney pointed a finger outward from the line and followed its trajectory. "I'm sure that's what's moving there, as well." The path led straight to Salem. To Merry. "They're headed for Salem."

Murmurs broke out amongst the group, but Axylus only allowed them a moment before raising his arms and turning to face everyone. "Kinsman, it is time for us to leave the castle."

48 ESCAPE

Thirteen shining heads breached the dirt floor of William's prison. He paused in his work to breathe in a lungful of damp, cave air.

"Thank you," Adina said, her voice igniting a whispering echo.

"Ye may not thank me after tonight," William answered.

"Be strong, William."

Adina worked to free her upper torso from the densely packed soil. Two Illuminators had already managed to extricate themselves from the ground, while a third sat at the edge of a hole and tugged on his leg. William looked down upon a head of matted silver hair, a faint glow peaking from beneath the debris tangled in it. A softly-lined face stared back at him. Her voice cracked on each syllable, and he wondered when she'd last used it through such a human mechanism. "This is your purpose."

Purpose. Too simple a word for what he'd been through, for what he had yet to do.

"It appears we are all in this purpose together," William said.

Several more heads crowned, and William moved across the

cave floor to help unearth them. He scraped at the soil, freed shoulders, tugged upward, and then let the Illuminator continue their luminous birth as he moved onto the next newborn.

Seventeen, eighteen, nineteen. They kept coming. Nearly half the captured had breached their prison. Adina helped the silver-haired woman climb out of her hole, while other freed Illuminators assisted their companions. William dug his hand into the ground and sent his light downward, calling the buried Illuminators to him. A hand pushed through the earth. A chill coursed through William as he realized the hand belonged to one of the Tall Man's demons. When her head breached the earth, he saw it was the witch, Lila. She blinked the dirt out of her eyes and turned her pleading gaze upon him. "Release me, William. I'm begging you."

William recoiled from her reaching hand. He glanced at Adina, who nodded toward Lila. *What could he do for this wretched creature?* Adina nodded toward Lila's outstretched hand again, and William realized what she was suggesting. "It won't work, Adina."

"Do you know that? Forgiveness can be a powerful thing."

William recalled how Lila had tricked him into joining the witch circle, which had ultimately led to his captivity. More recently, she'd furnished him with his knife so he could defend his sister against Vanessa. He touched his fingers to Lila's, then clasped her grimy hand in his.

She looked up at him with grateful eyes.

Light flowed from William and sped up Lila's arm, quickly covering her shoulders, neck and head. She shivered and then smiled, and William saw her as the girl she must have been before turning to the Tall Man. Lila reached for another hand pushing through the dirt, and William's light continued through Lila into the newcomer. Lila's hand slipped out of William's as she and the other prisoner rose up from the cave floor, and she and her companion shared looks of euphoria between them. Before dissolving into shimmering bits of light, she tilted her head to the side and whispered, "Thank you."

William stared at the ground, trying to sort out what he'd just witnessed. What he'd done. Just as his sister had given William her light to strengthen him, William had shared his light. With it, Lila and another damned soul had escaped the Tall Man's prison to ascend to a better place.

"How is this possible?" William asked Adina.

"Light can fill many a dark place."

A thought scratched at the back of William's mind. Hope glimmered. Then, another hand reached for him, and he let go of the distracting ideas swimming in his head. There was still much work to do. He grasped the glowing hand and tugged another Illuminator to freedom. More Illuminators roamed the cave, pushing their light into the ground, aiding in the call to their brethren.

After another half-hour, William stood back to count. *Thirty-eight.* The Illuminators lit the usually gloomy cavern with an unaccustomed brightness, and William allowed himself a shred of hope. *Could escape be this close?* Several holes in the ground had collapsed into one larger hole where the remaining Illuminators wriggled and worked their bodies from its grasp. William stepped down the incline to help the last of the prisoners.

Then the earth erupted.

He skidded down the crumbling slope, losing his balance and landing on his hands and knees upon the churned dirt. The ground bucked and buckled beneath him. He called out as a young Illuminator lost his tenuous purchase on freedom and slid back under the surface. William scrambled forward and reached for another hand, but only managed to brush fingertips before that Illuminator was lost too.

Flashes of light erupted and then winked out around him, leaving behind the flickering memories of the Illuminators as they escaped the cave. William attempted to climb out of the pit as the ground heaved beneath him. He grasped for purchase, sliding backwards. A grunt sounded from behind as he collided with a half-unearthed Illuminator. His glow was faint, but William thought if the man could get out of the ground, he'd be able to disappear and reunite with his companions in Nurya. He grasped his arm above the elbow and braced himself against the short wall of the pit. William pulled, the man glowing brighter as more of his body emerged.

Adina's worried face appeared near his. Several Illuminators hovered behind them. The ground rumbled, and other hands, dirty, torn, dead hands, pushed through near their feet.

"Go!" William shouted at Adina. She looked behind her, then at William.

He shouted for her to leave. Shouted at the others who remained. "Get out of here!" With no alternative, and with regret in their eyes, they winked out of existence.

"Remember your light," Adina said. Then she vanished, leaving the cave a much darker place. William refocused, leaning back further for leverage. Corpse hands groped at the Illuminator's exposed torso, at William's legs. Sweat poured down from his scalp, trickling into his eyes. His heart pounded as the earth disintegrated amid the onslaught of the corpses trying to get free. His eyes locked with the terrified eyes of the Illuminator. William's heart skipped and leapt into a jagged rhythm.

The mark thumped into life.

Heat radiated from the center of his chest, raced down his arms to his fingertips. The din of the corpses erupting from the earth made it impossible to hear anyone's approach, but the mark knew. It swelled and burned. William fought against the scream rising up from some primal place deep within him as the Tall Man neared.

"Release me," a deep voice said, and William looked down upon the hands he still held. The Illuminator had extricated one leg, and having managed to yank one hand out of William's grip, scraped at the soil, which held his other leg firm. William's blood boiled within his veins, pulsed and broke through his skin into flaming rivulets. He shouted and gripped the man's hand tighter, both horrified and delighted at the crunch of his bones. The man howled and, abandoning his attempt to dig himself free, tried to peel William's hand from his own.

"Your light," he croaked.

The moment froze. A fierce trembling coursed through William's body as he sought to hold onto the light he knew to be his. He grabbed hold of it, and pushed back against the demands of the mark. He could do this. He could fight. The Illuminator pulled back and William let his hand slip away until only the slightest hold remained.

"Don't be so weak," the Tall Man's angry voice reprimanded. The Illuminator wrenched his hand from his grip. William looked over his shoulder, his gaze instantly riveted to the Tall Man's red glare. He doubled over against the surge of fiery heat and lost the thread of light he'd managed to reel in. The Tall Man placed a bony finger under William's chin and with the slightest of nudges raised him to a standing position, his touch giving him the strength to endure the mark's rebirth. The Tall Man looked upon him with pride, gave a curt nod and said, "You know what you must do."

A smile fleeted across his lips, then William turned with grim determination, catching the Illuminator by the neck as he freed his other leg. With a strength unknown to him before, William slammed the man back to the ground. He sank several inches into the earth with the force of the blow. The man screamed, his horrified gaze never leaving William's face as a hundred dead hands pulled him down into the dirt back to the prison he'd nearly escaped.

When it was done, William head his head high under the Tall Man's prideful gaze.

49 RACE

"I can't take you to Salem."

This was the second cab driver that had told them as much. Merry wasn't going to get out of the cab, even if she had to command the driver to take them there. Before she could do so, the grim-faced driver looked over the back of the seat at them.

"It's Halloween, nothing but a train is getting close to Salem. You could try the ferry, but the train is faster."

"Take us to North Station," Devon said to the driver. To Merry, he said, "He's right. We'll get there faster by train than car any day, and especially today. Thousands of people will be in Salem tonight."

Merry ignored the looming anxiety and trusted her father's direction. He certainly knew better than her when it came to twenty-first century transportation. In less than fifteen minutes, they arrived at North Station, also called The Garden much to Merry's confusion. Devon paid the cab driver, and they joined the throng of people entering the large building. There were ten tracks with large, circled numbers above each set of doors.

"How will we know which door to go through?" Merry

asked.

Devon, whose skin had taken on a pale sheen from the effort of traveling through time, no less across Boston, pointed toward a particularly crowded track. "That might be a hint."

The line-up at the track included a large, furry wolf, a caped man with slicked-back hair and blood running down his chin, and a kitten in an alarmingly short skirt.

"I supposed you're right," Merry said.

Devon led the way to a ticket booth, Merry holding tightly onto his arm, where he purchased two tickets from a non-smiling woman sitting behind a glass partition.

He handed Merry a ticket. "We have twelve minutes until the train leaves."

Panic welled up inside Merry, but she pushed it down. Between cab and train, it would be an hour before they made it to Salem. She hoped it wouldn't be too late.

Liz clicked off her cell phone. Alex had convinced his news crew, which consisted of his Cameraman, Joel, to go to Gallows Hill for an update broadcast on the dead witches and the ensuing excavation. He'd also convinced Joel to wait on the part of Essex Street that was still open to cars so Liz and Sophie could catch a ride. There was no way they could drive their cars through town now. "We need to go, Sophie."

Sophie shook her head. "What can we do, Liz? Without Merry, what can we possibly do?"

Liz pursed her lips and shrugged. "I don't know. Ruby's there. What can she do?"

Sophie waved her hand as if swatting an annoying gnat. "Pfft."

"No, pfft. You can't pfft this away, Sophie. Ruby knows something. Maybe she knows where Merry is."

"She doesn't."

"Fine, she doesn't. But, you know something, don't you."

Sophie straightened her back, a now familiar stance that indicated she wasn't giving anything up. "If you want to go to Gallows Hill, then we'll go. Ruby's there already, so I guess it doesn't matter."

"What does that mean?" Liz asked.

"It means... nothing." She shook her head, a look of resignation stealing over her features. "Nothing. It means nothing."

Liz knew Sophie well enough to know that *nothing* meant *something*. She also knew Sophie was convinced that the outcome of her visions couldn't be altered. So far, Liz had seen nothing to contradict that conviction. "If you don't want to go, you don't have to. I can meet Ruby and Alex..."

Sophie threw her chubby arms up in the air. "I'm going! I'm going! Let me grab a sweater."

Two minutes later they were out the door. Liz hoped Ruby was right about Merry being at Gallows Hill. The first night Merry had gone missing again, Liz had spent the night watching the street and common from the living room window at the condo. Her date with Alex had turned into a vigil. Alex had been there when she received the call that Merry had disappeared and had proceeded to spend the next several hours scouring the streets, restaurants, and shops of Salem. When he returned, he'd sat for another hour by Liz's side. Now he was leading their trio to his news van.

They avoided most of the Halloween crowd by circumventing Essex Street. Liz's phone vibrated in her jeans pocket. She answered it, hating the distress in her voice. "Jonathan. Is she back?"

"Not here," Jonathan answered, sounding as anxious as she felt. "How about by you?"

Jonathan had been charged with keeping watch at the Monkey Tree, in case Merry came through it.

"She's not here either. We're heading to Gallows Hill."

"Don't tell me you're listening to that witch."

"No... well yes, but it's more than that. And, stop calling her a witch."

"She calls *herself* a witch."

"Not the way you say it." Liz pressed her hand against her forehead. "Never mind. I'll let you know if I find Merry first.

You do the same."

"Will do, be careful at Gallows... what... hang on a sec."

Liz kept moving, heading up a side street back toward Essex. Jonathan spoke, trepidation in his voice. "Something's happening. The tree's... humming."

"What do you mean it's humming? Like a show tune?"

"Funny, Liz. It's vibrating. I can feel it."

Liz bit her lip. "Maybe you should stand further away."

"Walking away as we speak."

Sophie, Alex, and Liz turned up another side street, finally turning back onto Essex Street near the Witch House. The news van was easily spotted, parked a few cars away. "Jonathan, our ride is here. Keep me posted on the vibrating tree?"

"I will. Be careful, Liz."

"You too," she said.

The blur of passing landscape finally slowed into recognizable terrain as the train pulled into Salem station. The frivolity of the passengers over the half-hour ride, their sheer ignorance of impending doom, had buoyed Merry's resolve to eradicate the Tall Man's threat upon Salem. The train came to a shuddering stop, as the announcer encouraged everyone to have a "Happy Haunted Halloween."

Merry and her father joined the throng of disembarking passengers on the platform, where they were immediately swept onto Washington Street. Even if they'd not been carried along on the tidal wave of people, the live music and excited thrum of the thousands of partygoers would have drawn them in the right direction.

Merry searched for a lurking evil, but despite the plethora of frightening costumes, the crowd's energy did not hold even a wisp of malevolence. Total strangers delighted in one another's creative attire, posing for photographs as they paraded through the streets. The night was one of joyful lightheartedness. In Salem, at that moment, the human hearts of many became one.

Devon stumbled beside Merry. He'd slept through the train ride, his recent travel through time taking a lingering toll.

"Papa, go to Sophie's house. Let her know we're all right, and get some rest."

He opened his mouth to argue, but Merry pulled him out of the path of the streaming crowd to the relative calm of a storefront vestibule. "You can't help me with this," she said, not unkindly.

"That's what you said when we traveled back, and I ended up saving you," Devon said, sounding much like a scolding father, something he hadn't had much chance to be before this moment.

Merry sighed. "You're right. But, it was different then. I'm strong now. Stronger than ever. And, forgive me for saying this, but you are weakened."

Devon hung his head a moment, and Merry wished there were a way to make him understand without demeaning him. "I can do what needs doing. But, worrying about you will only hinder me."

He studied her with pursed lips and frowning eyes.

"Trust me," she said.

Devon nodded his head in quick succession and blew out a breath. "All right. I don't like it, but I trust you, Merry."

With a smile, Merry hugged her father. He placed a light kiss on her cheek before heading off toward Sophie's place. After he'd melted into the crowd, Merry continued walking until Washington met Essex Street. As the crowd thickened, so did her disquiet, and she fought the urge to run headlong into the crush. The lights of the carnival at Pickering Wharf glimmered over the buildings to her left, the sky-high Ferris wheel a marvel. Merry stood a moment transfixed by the spinning wheel as its riders' screams accentuated the evening's festivities.

She turned as the crowd streamed around her, unsure which direction to take. Trepidation pressed upon her like a thick cloud. She took a step backward and stumbled as her foot caught the edge of a raised stone. A sinister-looking wolf reached out a furry arm to steady her. "Thank you," Merry said, looking back to the ground at the offending stone. A shiver stole up her back as she noticed not one, but an entire jagged line of raised stones. *Am I imagining the scent of decay?*

It came then, the wickedness she'd been seeking. The Tall Man's presence sliced through her skin like a piercing blade, dirtying her mind with his vile intentions.

He stood in the crowd as if he were any other reveler. Dressed in a dark suit that hung off his tall frame, wispy white hair fluttering in the breeze—he looked like an ill-dressed funeral director. This evening, even though his eyes glowed like red-hot coals, he failed to truly stand out among the elaborate costumes of the revelers. Yet as others passed by—a winged gargoyle, a purple-headed witch, a dead bride and groom—they all unwittingly gave wide berth to the Devil in their midst.

Merry pressed back into the shadows of the brick buildings lining the street, hand against her chest, heart pounding as though to meet it. *This has to be done.* She knew it. But, all these people didn't deserve to be brought into this fight. Her fight. There had to be some way to get the Tall Man away from here. Her breath hitched as the Devil turned his gaze in her direction. She pressed herself further into the darkness, and though a large group of costumed partygoers stood between her and her nemesis, she didn't trust that her presence had gone unnoticed.

A woman stopped and took a picture of Merry. "Great costume! You look like a real pilgrim."

"Puritan," Merry automatically corrected, but the woman had already moved on to photograph a knight and his horse. Merry moved parallel to the procession, peering between people to try to spot the Tall Man, but he too had disappeared into the multitude. His iniquity remained, hanging in the air like a suffocating poison.

Once again, Merry's toe caught an uprooted brick. This time a man wearing a dark coat caught her. Her gaze fixed on the pale face of the man who supported her. Blood dripped down his chin as he grinned at her surprise with a fanged smile. "Careful there," he said with a wink and released her arm. One side of her lips lifted in an embarrassed smile, but he'd already moved on. Merry observed the cobblestones at her feet, once again finding a broken line of bricks. She didn't recall Essex Street being in such bad repair.

She nudged a stone with her toe, coming to the slow realization that people had unconsciously arranged themselves on either side of the broken line of stones, forming a thin gap down the center of Essex Street. With a turn of her head to the right, Merry followed the divide all the way past the Peabody Essex Museum and to the left, as it continued toward the Witch House. She wrinkled her nose as the odd scent of decay once again assaulted her. Merry frowned and knelt, placing a tentative hand upon a lifted brick, pulling back when it trembled beneath her.

A foot away, a brick shifted, while another pushed upward a few inches beyond. One cautious step after the next, Merry followed the crooked bricks. A woman stumbled as she crossed the imaginary line, and Merry thought she saw a hand dart out from beneath the bricks. She scurried forward, but found nothing.

"Hey," a nearby man shouted. "What the hell?"

Merry looked up. A man stomped on the ground attempting to tamp the bricks back into place. This time Merry was certain she saw squirming fingers beneath the man's boot.

Something tickled her ankle.

Merry leapt backward with a shriek. More hands pushed through the cobblestone. Keeping a safe distance from the searching fingers, Merry knelt and placed her hand upon the cracked street. A pulse of yellow flew from her fingers and coursed through the crack. With a rumble that only someone concentrating may have distinguished from the general din, the earth shifted and bricks pressed and sealed the hands back into the soil.

A man, dressed in a ridiculous chicken costume, crouched beside her. "Did you lose something?"

Merry startled at the unexpected intrusion and leapt to her feet. She spared one last glance at the man and took off running. She ran away from the hustle of Essex Street, following the glow of the corpse trail. A sense of urgency overwhelmed her, and she summoned a bit of wind beneath her heels to increase her speed. She practically flew past the Witch House, at some point realizing where she was headed. Her neck itched with phantom discomfort as Merry raced toward Gallows Hill.

Liz slid the van door shut as Sophie settled into the seat beside her. Alex gave Joel quick directions to Gallows Hill as Joel started the engine.

"Thanks for giving us a ride," Liz said. "We'd never get there in time if we had to walk."

"In time for what?" Joel asked. "The party's downtown. Unless you think more dead witches are going to pop out of the ground."

"You never know around here," Liz answered. She looked out the window as she pulled the seatbelt from its anchor over her right shoulder. Her gaze caught the fleeting form of a woman racing up Essex Street. "Someone's in a hurry."

Sophie bounced in her seat, leaning forward to peer out the windshield at the woman speeding by. "Stop the car!" she shouted.

Joel turned a quizzical face toward Sophie. "We're not moving yet."

Sophie slammed a hand against his headrest. "Well drive then! We have to catch her!"

"Sophie! What—" Liz leaned forward, her gaze on the woman's long skirt billowing up behind her as she ran at a nearly inhuman speed. "Wait, is that?"

Joel, who'd picked up on Sophie's observation faster than Liz, pulled out of the parking spot and began pursuit of the running woman—Merry.

Despite her speed, they caught up with her around a bend in the road. Alex called her name as they pulled alongside her.

She slowed to a jog, and as soon as the van came to a stop, Liz slid the door open.

"Merry!" Liz leapt from the van and pulled her surprised friend into a tight embrace.

"How did you find me?" Merry asked.

"You ran past us. How did you move so fast?"

Merry fought a smile, twisting her mouth as though to stop her admission. "Magic?"

Liz laughed. Sophie leaned out of the van. "Where were you? You had us so worried."

"And where are you going?" Liz asked before Merry could address Sophie's question.

Merry's smile disappeared, and her face grew serious. "I'm heading to Gallows Hill. I think something's happening or going to happen there."

Liz's mouth dropped open. She tried to speak, but too many words fought and failed to gain voice. Merry cocked an eyebrow at her. "Where were you going? And why are you in a news van?"

Finally Liz's mouth cooperated. "We're going to Gallows Hill, too. We followed some weird tremor that cracked Essex Street right down its middle."

"I did too! It led me this way."

Sophie waved Merry toward the van. "Get in, honey. We'll all go together."

Merry hesitated, and Liz planted her feet in a wide stance, hands on hips. She wasn't going to let Merry do this, whatever *this* was, on her own. "Don't even think it, Merry. I know you. We were headed to Gallows Hill without you. It doesn't matter if you ride with us or not, we're all going to end up in the same place."

Merry climbed into the van. "That's what I'm afraid of."

50 FIRESTORM

"Maybe this wasn't such a great idea after all," Liz said.

Merry bristled at the words, though they appeared to be true. Gallows Hill was inaccessible. Police tape still ringed the baseball field where the dead witches had appeared a few days ago. Tall lights, too bright to look at, towered over the park. Within the tape, white-suited men and women poked at the ground, and scooped up samples of dirt. Flashes illuminated the cloudy day as a woman photographed a particular corner of excavated earth; a large, clawed machine stood nearby, ready to dig up more of the land as needed. Three dozen or so onlookers, some in costumes, stood along the perimeter of the park trying to get a glimpse of the witches' graves. News trucks and a bevy of reporters and camera crews convened in an area closer to the excavation site, Alex's among them.

"I told you so," Sophie said, staring at Ruby who looked unconcerned by the obvious impasse.

Liz stepped between the two women. "Ruby, maybe if you tell us why we're here, we can figure out a way around this."

"There's no need," Ruby said with a toss of her head. "I think we're about to get what we came here for."

Merry exchanged a questioning look with Liz, then noticed

Sophie had taken her small crystal ball from her purse. She held it close to her face, peering into the glass, turning her shoulder slightly to block their curious stares.

Ruby cleared her throat, and Sophie lowered the ball, clutching it against her chest. "She may be right," Sophie said, a slight tremble in her voice.

Merry's gaze returned to the taped crime scene. A uniformed officer took a few steps in their direction, pushing his hands out in front of him to indicate they and the other onlookers needed to move back.

"I'm not sure we should stay," Sophie said, her voice rising.

"What's wrong, Sophie? What did you see?" Liz asked.

"Nothing's wrong," Ruby interjected. "She hasn't seen anything in that silly little ball."

"Oh?" Sophie said. "You haven't exactly enlightened us as to why we're here either."

"Here we go," Liz said, eyes raised toward the sky.

"Merry," Ruby said. "You know why we're here, don't you? You can feel the pull. The need. You can feel it, right?"

Merry frowned. She'd certainly been called to Gallows Hill, but now another indistinct need emerged, muffled as though a large obstacle stood between her and the want.

"I do feel something," Merry said in a quiet voice.

Ruby spoke fast. "This is important, Merry. The most important thing you can do. You have the power to end this now. Before it's too late."

"Oh for Christ's sake," Sophie said. "Too late for what? You still haven't told us a damn thing."

Ruby grabbed Merry's shoulders. "Innocents were buried here. They need you."

"Innocents. You mean the witches that were hanged?"

"They deserved a proper burial. Now, they deserve to be freed."

"Freed? How?" Merry asked.

Sophie stood between them, hands on hips. "That's why you brought us here? To ease your conscience?"

Ruby stared down her nose at Sophie.

"What are you talking about, Sophie?" Merry asked.

"Ruby, *the* witch of Salem, claims to be a descendent of a Salem Witch Trials judge—"

"I don't *claim* to be. I *am*."

"Well, there's irony for you," Liz said.

"Ruby, whatever you think Merry can do, it's too dangerous. It's—"

Ruby flung her hand toward the field. "It's necessary!"

Liz joined in the fray, as Merry wandered away to focus on the environment. Certainly, a need sprouted from the excavated area. It tugged at her mind, but only gently, as if it lacked the confidence or the will to hope for a response. Then there was the original threat, which had brought her here. It forced its way into her head, sparking a warning chill down her spine. Behind her, Sophie insisted they leave.

Merry turned as Sophie shoved the tennis-ball sized crystal toward Ruby until it practically touched her nose. "You can *see* my vision."

Ruby swatted her hand away, the yellow orb falling to the ground. Merry's gaze followed, spying Gallows Hill as it looked now on the surface of the crystal before the globe darkened and revealed a swirling mass of bodies. Merry gasped.

Screams erupted around them. The earth trembled beneath their feet, tossing several people to the ground. Sophie danced backward as a groping hand broke the surface by her foot and wrapped gray, sloppy fingers around the crystal ball.

Merry pulled Sophie toward her and away from the corpse who now proceeded to push its body out of the ground. More hands burst through the ground. People ran for the parking lot. Merry's gaze darted to the news trucks. Rather than running from the chaos the reporters stepped into it, cameras at the ready.

"Look out!" someone shouted behind them. Merry spun around in time to see one of the spotlights wobble and tilt, several white-suited people running out of its path. The earth bucked beneath the light, toppling it to the ground, the bulb shattering upon impact. A second light fell, but the bulb remained intact upon landing, illuminating a horizontal path across Gallows Hill, highlighting a scene beyond comprehension. Roiling waves of dirt churned and spewed soil like an angry ocean. Hands clawed at the air as though to keep from drowning. Fear knotted Merry's stomach, anchored her feet to the ground, and glued her gaze to the disastrous tableau.

A fleeing investigator became tangled in the eruption and fell to the ground, screaming as hands swarmed and pulled him beneath the earth until only the smallest speck of his white suit could be seen. A police officer opened fire as several corpses crawled their way toward him, their bodies bursting as the bullets hit. More corpses took their place until the officer ran out of bullets and fled. A reporter backed right into the melee, her cameraman dropping his equipment to help pull her from a corpse's grip, only for the both of them to be sucked beneath the earth.

"Oh my God," Liz said, jarring Merry from her transfixed state.

Sophie's panicked face appeared before her. "We need to leave. Now."

"I need to stop this," Merry said.

"Stop *this*?" Sophie's voice rose an octave.

"I need to try."

"That's right, Enfys," Ruby said. "You can do..."

"Shut up! Shut up!" Sophie shouted, her face contorted and red. Ruby stepped back as Sophie advanced. "This isn't the place or the time!"

"This is *exactly* the place," Ruby yelled back.

"Stop it!" Merry said, and both women froze at her words. Merry shuddered as pain sparked behind her eyes. "All of you, please get to safety. I need to stay."

"Merry," Sophie said, her voice desperate. "Can't you do whatever needs doing from a safer place, too?"

"Come with us," Liz said, grasping her wrist with a clammy, shaking hand.

Merry glanced back toward the taped off area. The tape, no longer anchored, fluttered above the heads of a fast approaching dead army. Without a thought, Merry clenched her fists and then thrust them before her, palms flipped outwards. Fire sprang from her fingertips, hitting the first line of the Tall Man's army. Pitiful cries resounded on Gallows Hill as flames engulfed the first line, then the second.

Merry turned to her friends, still standing behind her. "Go!"

"Where?" Liz asked, her voice reduced to a trembling whisper.

The Tall Man's legion not only approached from the excavated area, but also stood between them and the parking lot. Merry blanketed them with flames and spun back to face the still approaching army, sending a wall of fire at them.

Fire blazed on either side of them. Sweat dripped into Merry's eyes. She shouted over her shoulder to Liz. "Take Sophie and Ruby to the parking lot, then keep going. Get as far away from here as you can."

"I don't want to leave you!"

"Go!"

Merry prayed her family and friends would make it to safety as Liz took Sophie's hand and told Ruby to follow them.

Liz led Sophie and Ruby down the only piece of Gallows Hill that wasn't burning. She knew the fire didn't burn Merry when she cast it, but she was certain it would burn them as it had the dead. She ran as fast as she could down the fire-rimmed corridor toward the news vans and the parking lot beyond, while trying not to lose the older women. Sophie panted heavily behind her. Ruby took up the rear, coughing and sputtering as she ran. The flames dropped lower and lower, the smoke growing thicker as they waned.

Sophie squealed and fell against Liz, shoving her forward. Liz tripped, but caught herself and turned to find Sophie on the ground, a hand wrapped around her ankle.

"Sophie!" Liz screamed as a corpse burst through the soil.

Sophie twisted, swatting at the hand on her ankle as the corpse reached its other hand higher up on her leg. Ruby ran to her, still choking on the thickening smoke and grabbed the leg of the corpse, the three of them linked together like a grotesque human chain. The corpse, a man, turned his attention to Ruby. Liz scanned the area for a branch or rock to use as a weapon. Finding none, she hauled back her foot and delivered a kick to the dead man's head. It snapped back, and he released Sophie, flying back against the flames. Barely a moment passed before he leapt onto Ruby, knocking her to the ground. Small flames licked at his torso and legs as he covered Ruby with his body and pressed them both into the earth. Ruby screamed, her mouth filling with dirt. Liz grabbed her arm, Sophie a leg, as they fought to keep her above the surface.

Another corpse emerged from the fire, reaching with flaming hand toward Sophie. She stumbled backwards and dropped Ruby's leg. The corpse, a woman, piled on top of Ruby and the man. Liz lost her grip on Ruby's arm, scrambling to regain hold a moment too late. She screamed as Ruby and the corpses sank into the ground. Flames licked the wounded earth. Liz's chest heaved with panicked breaths as Sophie scrabbled at the soil with her fingers and shouted Ruby's name

Liz rose, coughing as she breathed in smoke. Sophie stopped pawing at the earth and sat back on her heels, her face ashen. They'd lost her. Sophie said nothing as Liz helped her to her feet. "We have to keep moving."

As they neared the end of the fire line, a noise turned Liz's head. Her heart thudded to a near stop at the sight of a line of corpses as wide as the corridor and three deep a few yards behind.

"Sophie! Run!" Liz shouted over the roaring fire.

Sophie turned, her eyes widening at the sight of the approaching threat and broke into a run faster than Liz thought she was capable of. A hint of relief rushed her as Sophie neared the pavement and relative safety. Liz shrieked as a hand brushed her shoulder and looked behind to find the dead army practically on top of her. She sped up, then slammed to a halt when a beautiful blonde woman stepped out of the flames, her unmarred presence mocking the ruined surroundings, and cutting off any chance of escape.

The blaze began to die down on both sides. Merry looked warily in either direction. Nothing stirred. The crackle of burning bones could be heard amid the fire's shivering light. Liz and Sophie had made it midway toward the parking lot. She didn't see Ruby.

Sounds of coughing, moaning, crying slipped into her awareness. Merry dared to hope they'd seen the last of the Tall Man's army. Then, as though someone had blown out a wick, the fire in front of her winked out all at once. A figure emerged through the smoky haze—tall, strong, and familiar. *William.*

Merry raced across the charred land only to be met by an invisible wall that sent her flying backward. She landed hard, gasping for air as William approached.

Merry turned to her side. The world spun. She dug her fingers into the dirt, trying to steady herself against the dizziness, which seized her head and churned her stomach. William's steps crunched upon the crisp earth and charred bones. Merry squinted into the assault of light cast by the overturned spotlight. Smoke slithered through the evening like a ghostly snake, the acrid scent burning her throat, choking her. With a voice no more than a croak, Merry called out. "William."

Corinne held Liz's gaze, her lips turned up into a knowing smile. With the blonde blocking her path and the dead behind her, she brooked no hope for escape. Still, she had to try.

She stepped toward the woman, dangerously inside her personal space, but the woman didn't budge. Or blink. She simply shook her head with exaggerated slowness from side to side. Liz darted a look over the woman's shoulder. Sophie had stopped running and turned, calling for Liz.

A subtle change in the space behind, registered in Liz's panicked thoughts. A backward glance exposed an empty escape route, the last of the dead disappearing into the ground. Across the field, Liz spied a fallen Merry.

"Sophie! Run!" Liz shouted.

When the blonde turned her head toward Sophie, Liz shoved her, sending her stumbling backward. It wasn't much of a defense, but it gave Liz a bit of a head start as she ran back toward Merry.

Merry rolled to her knees, her head spinning with the movement. She lifted her eyes and pushed to an upright position, coughing as she rose. Her head pounded; her limbs resisted the effort. Through blurred vision, Merry caught sight of William marching determinedly across the field, stomping on the protruding heads of corpses in his path. As he neared, Merry's heart dropped at the sight of his blank and emotionless face, void of anything remotely William. She called his name, but he paid no attention as he strode past. Too late, she realized his distraction.

Liz ran toward her, eyes wild with fear, the Devil's daughter following close behind. Panic gripped Merry when she noticed Sophie had also joined the chase. "No!" Merry shouted, her voice cracking. She glanced at William, willing his gaze to her, but he watched the chase with a wry smile.

The Tall Man's daughter kept a steady distance, in no rush to reach Liz. With horror, Merry realized why. William had effectively penned Liz between himself and Corinne. Liz's face lit up when she noticed William, then faded into uncertainty, mistrust, and finally fear. Merry fought the sick roiling her stomach and reached for whatever magic she could muster.

"William! Stop!" she commanded. He paused, and she dared to hope. William turned his head and locked his gaze on Merry, his expression hard and cold. He turned back to Liz, catching her as she backed away from him. Sophie had nearly caught up with Corinne. Merry rose and ran toward them screaming as Corinne whipped around and snagged Sophie's arm. When Merry was only steps away, a burst of flames shot up from the ground, enveloping William, Corinne and, their prisoners. The flames vanished as quickly as they'd sprung up, leaving behind nothing but spits of fire burning upon the ground and Merry alone, but for the faint sounds of weeping and a distant siren's wail as it approached Gallows Hill.

51 ILLUMINATION

Time stuttered to a halt on Gallows Hill. Merry spun, searching the area for Liz, Sophie, or William, finding nothing but the macabre remains of the Tall Man's Army.

She screamed Liz's name, then Sophie's, knowing there would be no response. The ground trembled, dirt cascading atop the disappearing forms of the corpses as the earth sifted them back into its bowels. Rage inflamed Merry's heart, and she dove for a nearby leg before it disappeared, grasping it in her hand. Its skin shifted as though not attached, and slipped from her grip. Determined to follow the foul creatures back to their master, back to her friends, she grabbed for another, snagging an arm this time.

The earth folded in around her arm, her shoulder. Then a hand wrapped around her leg. Instinctively, Merry twisted around and with a flick of her wrist turned the air into a whip of wind which connected with a satisfying whoosh against her assailant, realizing too late that he was friend, not foe. Merry loosened her grip on the arm that led her downward.

"Alex," she said as the poor man rolled to his side and pushed himself off the ground with a groan. *What was she doing?* She released the corpse altogether, leveraging her hand against the earth to free her arm. But, as her elbow emerged, the hand she'd been holding latched onto hers and gave a sharp tug. Merry's cheek smashed against the ground as she sank up to her shoulder. She struggled as another hand joined the first and yanked. Merry gasped at the flare of pain in her shoulder as the hardening earth threatened to separate her from her arm. She dug into the ground with her feet, pulling herself up an inch or two before slamming back down to earth. Spitting dirt out of her mouth, she tried to focus. Alex had recovered and reached under her shoulders, pulling her up. Merry cried out in pain as the corpse hands jerked her downward at the same time.

"Stop!"

Alex immediately dropped her and stepped back, a glazed look in his eyes. Unfortunately, her command had no effect on the corpse hands that were now breaking through the earth and wrapping around her waist. More grabbed her legs and pulled her downward. Earth crumbled and reformed around her, locking her legs in a hard-packed embrace. Her head pounded, her vision blurred. For a moment, she considered letting them take her—that had been her first intention after all. Even though her friends had disappeared in fire, the rational part of her suggested she'd not survive a trip through the suffocating earth. A hand caught her hair and yanked her head back.

With a scream to rival a banshee's, Merry thrust her free hand into the dirt and poured whatever colors remained inside her into the earth. The ground around her rippled blue, yellow, red. A dead hand grabbed her wrist, releasing her at once. Merry blinked away sweat and dirt. Her stomach lurched at the effort to use her colors one more time. The ground heaved, loosening her arm and legs from its grip. The earth bulged and grew into a small hill beneath her. Pebbles and dirt fell down the growing mound. The hands let her go, unable to hold on any longer, and continued their journey downward. Finally, the earth stilled. Merry, propped up by the bed of dirt, stared into the evening sky. She took a deep breath and promptly coughed out smoky air.

A familiar face came into view. "What the hell was that?" Alex asked. "And what are those things?"

How much had he seen? Merry wondered, her brain scrambling for a lie.

"Are you all right?"

"No," Merry said in a barely audible voice. Her attempt to stand sent her sliding down the slope. Like a cat, she landed on her hands and knees. She coughed up dirt and saliva, while Alex patted her back. The ground spun beneath her. Merry swayed and rolled right into Alex's arms. She tried to stand. She had no time for weakness.

"I think you need to lay still."

"Help me stand," Merry said, ignoring the worry in Alex's eyes.

"I don't think it's a good idea," he said, even as he helped her to do so. Supporting her with an arm about her waist and a hand clenching her forearm, they began to walk toward the parking lot. Merry ignored the tightness of Alex's grip upon her freshly bruised arm. Blue and red emergency lights danced upon the landscape. Police searched the field for the fallen, some their own.

"Liz."

Merry snapped her head up. "Where?"

"I was going to ask you that. Where did she go? Last I saw, before the fire, she was standing next to you."

The surge of hope that Liz hadn't disappeared into the flames was replaced with the sickening memory of William's grisly satisfaction as he stole Liz away. The truth that William might be lost to her forever turned her stomach further. The harder truth that she needed to focus on the bigger picture, the Tall Man, forged a place inside her head and pushed aside the painful need to rescue William. She focused on her determination to save her grandmother and best friend and to ultimately end the Devil's plans for Salem once and for all.

The vibration had turned into a verifiable tremor. A thin ribbon of light seeped out from beneath the monkey tree.

Jonathan stepped closer.

Suddenly the wood around him lit up as though the sun had not only switched places with the half-moon, but had landed at his feet. He shielded his eyes from the nearly painful brilliance that consumed the monkey tree. What appeared to be an amalgamation of bodies moved within the brilliant glow. The light billowed and then burst from the tree in a smattering of many bits of twinkling radiance. Jonathan stumbled backwards as the lights raced passed him, instantly registering that these must be the Illuminators Liz had told him about. He watched as they charged a path toward Iron House and wondered if Sidney was among them.

Sidney.

Jonathan took off after the light stream as it whipped its way through the woods. The brilliant trail rendered his flashlight redundant. Onward he sped, the distance increasing between them. He pushed harder, but was no match for the speed of light. As he stepped out of the woods, the flood of light blanketed Iron House in a warm glow before zipping into the night sky in a purposeful path toward Salem.

As he ran toward the house, Jonathan fumbled in his pocket for his phone and pressed *Liz*. Nothing. No ring. No voicemail message. He tried again with same results. He uttered an expletive and shoved the phone back into his pocket as he raced up the veranda steps and into the house. He passed Liz's bewildered father on his way up the main staircase.

"Jonathan?"

"Gotta see Sidney," Jonathan answered, not breaking his stride.

"Did you see the light? Did we have an eclipse or something?" Mr. Thompson called after him.

"Or something," Jonathan shouted as he reached the top step and jogged down the hallway coming to a halt halfway down. The same glow, which had emanated from the monkey tree, now seeped out from beneath Sidney's door. Mr. Thompson skidded to a stop behind him.

"What is that?" Mr. Thompson asked.

In answer Jonathan resumed his race down the hallway, Mr. Thompson on his heels. As they neared the door, the light receded. By the time they opened the door, it was gone altogether.

"Sidney?" Mr. Thompson asked as though she hadn't been unconscious for weeks and would answer him. The hopefulness in his voice crushed Jonathan.

Sidney lay in bed. *Nothing new there.* But, her wan complexion, slack muscles and weak breath had resolved into nearly rosy cheeks and a strong, steady breath. Whatever the light was, it had improved Sidney's state and left a shade of hope in Jonathan's heart.

Merry eased out of Alex's grip, her strength overcoming the effects of William's attack. They picked their way across the freshly churned field. The flashing blue and red lights of the emergency vehicles added a surreal edge to the scene. Alex jogged ahead to meet Joel who'd made his way across the field, scanning the aftermath with his camera. Merry paused a moment, taking in the scene. Several people were being loaded onto stretchers, but the Tall Man's army had taken others into the earth and had strengthened their numbers.

She tilted her head back and noticed a shower of stars arcing across the sky, casting the half-moon in a golden glow. She sucked in her breath as realization hit.

Too late.

The Illuminators' twinkling light streamed downward, heading straight for Gallows Hill. Straight for Merry. Alex must have noticed the light too, for he turned and shouted her name. Then he ran toward her. But, the Illuminators moved faster, cloaking Merry in a shimmering cocoon and whisking her away before she could even think to move out of their path.

52 AWAY

Merry landed with a thud amid a shower of glimmering stars that reassembled themselves into glowing humans and immediately organized into a golden fortress—Merry their ward. The unexpected and sudden journey had taken her breath away, and she spent a few moments simply trying to breathe. After a few successful exchanges of air, Merry approached the sentry. To her surprise, the Illuminators parted and let her pass through their radiant barrier with nary a word. And she stepped into a world better left unseen.

Her arms grew numb, tingly. Her neck throbbed with phantom pain, as she stood stunned by the landscape before her. Though the Illuminators' light burned fiercely behind her, it did little to lift the dark veil that lay over this dead land. Her foot crunched upon the hardscrabble earth, tufts of grass and weeds struggled for life amid the arid crust. Tall, black rocks jutted from the ground like misshapen teeth. In the distance, a dark wood rose up, fronted by ancient gnarled trees. Their limbs were poised like bony hands that had clawed their way out of the earth, ready to defend whatever lay within their woods.

Amid the tableau, a writhing crawl of light and dark receded and advanced as Illuminators battled the Devil's army. Shouts and screams from both sides attained a constant crescendo. If there was a more horrific setting than the battle-scarred Gallows Hill, this was it.

A figure stepped toward her, shedding his light to reveal a solid well-built young man dressed in the garb of a medieval knight. He addressed her with a nod of his head as though they'd always known one another. "Enfys."

"Where are we?" Merry shouted over the din. "Who are you?"

The handsome knight drew closer. "I am Axylus. We've taken the battle to the Devil's doorstep." He glanced toward the battle, then back to Merry. "Your colors are needed if we are to win this war."

Bravado and fear emanated from the man in equal measure. It was nothing short of how Merry felt. *Who was she kidding?* Fear was definitely winning at the moment. "You need me?" she asked. "It looks like your team is doing well on their own."

Axylus observed his fellow light beings as they thwacked their enemies back into their dirt home. He then fixed Merry with a serious gaze. "The true battle has not yet begun."

Merry's stomach sunk at the thought. She surveyed the area. A break in the trees formed an arched entryway into the forest. *Was that the way to the cave where she'd left William? Did it lead to Sophie and Liz?* She started across the field, but before she could take more than a few steps, Axylus wrapped a steely grip around her arm and stopped her. "It's a trap. You cannot help your friends that way."

"How do you—" Merry began, before remembering an Illuminator's sole purpose was to steer people from the wrong path. She stared into Axylus's chocolate eyes and asked. "How then?"

He nodded toward the line of golden sentries behind them. "They block the path to Nurya. When the time is right, we will allow William's entry on our own terms."

"And, when will that time be?"

Axylus tilted his head as though hearing something other

than the din of fighting. Then, he tipped his head toward Merry and said, "I suspect it will be soon enough."

"Tell him there's movement at the tree line. Something big." Sidney shouted out commands to Luke who then communicated her words to the collective sense of the Illuminators. She hated being stuck at the castle, but it appeared she'd managed to be useful so far.

The tapestry pulsed with a life only she could see. Through her sight and Luke's mind, they'd conveyed Merry's location at Gallows Hill. Luke said they'd found her, and she was safe with them. But, Sidney wasn't so sure. The Illuminators were supposed to bring Merry to Nurya, but it appeared they were well off course. While some Illuminators had returned to keep the shadows at bay, most of them had gone to the Tall Man's domain, their location evident in the rapidly twinkling lights across the dark end of the tapestry. Merry's colors sparked into life in the midst of the vile land.

"What are they doing? I thought they were coming back here."

Sidney looked toward Luke for an answer, and found him studying a barren spot on the tapestry. She knew avoidance when she saw it. "Luke. They're coming back, right? Look at me, Luke."

He spared her a glance, but his twitching brow told her everything.

"They're not coming back, are they? Not for me, anyway," Sidney said. "And you knew, didn't you?"

"You're more help here than on the battlefield," Luke said in a barely audible voice.

"Oh, thank you, Squire Axylus. Don't you have all the answers."

Luke faced her. "Sid, he's right. You're not one of us. Not yet."

"I'm enough."

"You think you are."

Sidney's facial muscles tightened. "I *know* I am. Is anyone else prepared to sacrifice himself for William? Oh, they'll fight, but they're not fighting for my brother. Axylus doesn't care if William lives or dies. They're fighting for the greater good. The light. Only, they don't realize that William *is* the light."

Luke crossed his arms and studied Sidney. "What do you mean by 'sacrifice'?"

Merry emulated Axylus's focus on the forest entrance and tried to ignore the desperate fight moving ever closer to her. *Did he expect her to wait for the fight to reach them and not to do what she could to rescue her friends?* She had to trust him, trust his Illuminator instinct. She also knew an Illuminator didn't always tell the whole story.

She surveyed the field for a path void of corpses that could take her safely to the other side, but found none. She'd have to make one. A quick glance assured her Axylus's attention was on the battle, which was growing more contentious by the minute. Merry closed her eyes and pushed her gnawing fear aside, stuffing down thoughts of Liz, Sophie, William, and the possible harm being done to them. Merry then rebuked the nagging concept that she was too late to save William.

She concentrated on the colors buzzing beneath her skin. Even though she'd spent a lot of energy on Gallows Hill, she'd rebounded faster than ever. She suspected the crimson crystal had a hand in that. She could now sustain and renew her colors with a speed and strength unknown to her before. Merry needed to get to the other side of the field. She thought about using the earth to create an elevated path away from the hands of the corpse army, but the thought of getting so close to them again didn't appeal to her. Fire was too risky. Wind—*could she fly?* Liz had suggested the possibility once, but out of all her abilities, it seemed the most far-fetched. Still...

Merry closed her eyes and focused her energy on collecting the slightest of breezes to carry her across the field. Within seconds, the stench of the dead grew ten-fold carried on the air-current Merry summoned. Eyes watering, she doubled over coughing which only made her draw more of the foul odor into her lungs. She didn't lessen her efforts, drawing more wind, however malodorous, toward her. The trees shook, branches snapped and flew like arrows from a bow onto the field, skewering more than a few of the corpses. Her feet left the ground.

Strong arms wrapped around her thighs, pulling her back down to earth in short order. Merry fell back against Axylus, then spun and pushed him away. He barely moved, but she stumbled backward. "What are you doing?"

"What are *you* doing?" he yelled, his formal address lost in the heat of battle. "I told you that is not the way!"

"I have to do something!"

Axylus shook his head in exasperation. "Oh you have, Enfys. You've knocked on the Devil's door."

"I should never have agreed to this," Luke said. Those were the first words Luke had spoken since they'd left the castle.

"You're doing it because you know it's right," Sidney answered.

"Maybe." Luke shot a crooked grin her way. "Or maybe I know how much it'll tick off Sir Knighty Knight."

A small smile escaped Sidney. "Squire."

"Whatever. Does it matter now?"

Sidney shook her head. "No." They'd nearly reached the end of the bridge and cleared the moat. Sidney stopped and looked back toward the castle, then studied the dead grass and lurking shadows. Luke did the same.

"We haven't even gone that far," Sidney said, her voice wavering.

"Darkness creeps in when there's no light," Luke said.

"Poetic."

"It's the truth." He kicked at a clump of grass; it gave off a burnt odor. He looked up at Sidney. "Are we doing this or what?"

Sidney held her hand out, and Luke took it in his own, clasping her fingers in a too-tight grip. His eyes darted toward Sidney.

"It'll be OK, Luke. I promise."

A corner of his mouth lifted in a less than confident smile, but he relaxed his grip. Then, in a flash of light, they were on their way to the battlefield.

A roar erupted, from earth or creature, Merry was uncertain. It was as though sound itself had ruptured. Her gaze snapped toward the tree line. Corpse after corpse unfolded from the shadows and poured onto the field. Their numbers appeared endless as they spilled one after another into the midst of battle. Though the Illuminators' light was strong, they were quickly becoming outnumbered. Another movement tore her terrified gaze from the disaster she'd set in motion. A figure stood beneath the arching trees. Merry's heart leapt at the shock of blonde hair—Liz—then plummeted as two familiar figures, the Devil's daughter and William, joined her. *The Devil's daughter and William.*

"Get them out of there!" Merry shouted to Axylus as she pulled the malodorous wind into a spinning tunnel. "The Illuminators! Call them back!"

Axylus fixed her with a stare more fitting for an enemy. She didn't have time for his stupid pride.

"Now!" Her final shout spurred him into action. In moments, the field fell to darkness while light bloomed behind her as the Illuminators fell back. Merry shot her hands forward, fingers spread as she sent the wind, like an army of whirling dervishes, to the battlefield. Though the corpses still surged forward, their efforts were greatly hampered by the whipping wind.

"Well done," Axylus said in her ear. "We must head back to Nurya."

Merry pointed toward the tree tunnel where Liz and William stood. She didn't see Sophie. "I can't leave without them."

"We won't," Axylus said. "They'll follow."

But, Merry wasn't listening. The hands of the dead had fallen away the last time she'd inserted her colors into the ground. Not sure what would happen, Merry pictured what she hoped would become a protected path across the field of the dead. Then, she stomped her foot on the ground, and she was off.

Colors raced across the field, knitting themselves into a multi-colored path too cheerful to lead to the doorway to hell. Merry ran fast, then faster, as her colors carpeted the ground with a rainbow a few steps ahead of her. Desperate faces peered up from beneath the translucent trail, mouths rounded in hollow screams as they grappled for purchase. But none could touch her.

The twisters were dying down, and those corpses who'd been distracted started to notice the girl running on top of a rainbow. They changed direction and headed for the gap between the unfinished path and the treed entry.

Sweat poured down Merry's face and back as she pressed harder both physically and mentally to complete the path and reach Liz and William. Seventy yards to go. Sixty. The roar of the dead perforated her concentration as they clustered in front of her. Fifty yards. Merry arced the path upward, out of their reach. Forty yards. They climbed atop one another like a tower of ants, threatening Merry's approach. Thirty yards. She saw Liz clearly, sensed the fear rolling off her. Twenty yards. William grabbed Liz and lifted her as though she were a doll. Ten yards. Liz screamed as William heaved her into the awaiting sea of corpses.

Merry leapt.

She grabbed for her flailing friend, managing to clasp hands, her attention faltering for a moment as William leapt to grab Liz as well, though his hardened stare spoke of an opposite intent. Merry hooked her leg around Liz's as gravity pulled them downward. Before they met the hungry hands below, Merry wrapped them in her colors and whisked them away.

53 OBSIDIAN

Merry held tight to her shaking friend, maintaining the cocoon of colors until she was certain they were safe. They'd returned to Salem, landing in the middle of the Halloween celebrations on Essex Street. People scuttled around them, snapping photos and commenting as if they were part of the festivities. Merry tried to erase the image of William, the man she'd known in the most tender of moments, throwing her best friend into a pit of monsters. She hugged Liz. "Are you all right?"

Liz gripped Merry's shoulders, and despite the tremors racking her body, spoke in a strong voice. "I'm fine. I'm fine, Merry."

"I'm so sorry. William..."

"Don't. You can't think about that now."

Liz was right, of course. But she hadn't sensed the evil coming off William. She hadn't known there was nothing left of the only man Merry had ever loved.

"Where is Sophie?" Merry asked.

"I don't know. We got separated. I tried to keep us together, but Will..." Liz ducked her head. "Sorry."

"Tell me what happened, Liz. Quickly. I need to know."

Liz nodded, took a deep breath and continued. "William

had me. The blonde had Sophie. We were at Gallows Hill and then we weren't."

"I saw them take you into the fire."

"Then we were in some, I don't know, some sort of dungeon. Like a cave. It sounded like the place you escaped from. There were bodies everywhere, snakes, everything you never wanted to see. Ever." Liz took another breath. "That's the last time I saw Sophie. William took me outside. It was so dark and surreal. I think the trees were alive, ready to grab me if I tried to run. Then you showed up, and... well."

She wanted to ask Liz if William had been pretending, if he'd told her of some plan to escape. But, she knew the answer already.

"Merry. William isn't William. You should know that. You probably do."

Merry knew, but it didn't make her feel any better.

Merry lifted the curtain of colors to the sound of applause. A crowd had gathered, creating a circle at least four deep around Merry and Liz. A menagerie of creatures cheered and clapped, but through the noise, she heard only one voice. Through the crowd she saw only one face.

Towering over a scantily clad woman thrusting a red pitchfork in the air as she cheered, the Tall Man stared at Merry with burning eyes and in a scratchy, deep voice said, "Enfys."

No sooner had Merry's gaze locked onto the Tall Man than her attention was torn away. A loud rumble consumed all sounds of revelry, shaking the ground as though the earth were enraged. A nervous lull ensued. Then the screams began. Merry couldn't find the Tall Man in the quickening panic.

"What's happening?" Liz asked as she steadied herself against Merry.

"Nothing good I'm sure."

Another rumble rolled through the night.

Liz twisted around, still holding onto Merry. "It sounds like it's coming from the Common."

Merry held tight to her friend's hand as they made their way to the Common. Most of the crowd ran from the area as they forged towards it.

Streetlights lit up the end of Essex Street outside the Hawthorne Hotel. They gave up hope of crossing the street against the evacuating crowd, and came to a standstill as they neared the Witch Museum. Across the street, the spiked iron fences of the Common had transformed from guardians of the pristine landscape to captors as a crush of people bottlenecked at the exits. Several people who'd tried to escape by climbing the fence were instead impaled; some screamed for help, some were beyond such needs. The previously light-hearted celebration had turned into an all out nightmarish pandemonium.

"This way," Merry said, tugging Liz behind her as they passed beneath the statue of Salem's Founder, Roger Conant. They pressed up against the boulder that supported his bronze effigy to allow several terrified teens to pass. Merry wasn't sure if the blood on their faces and clothing was real or part of their costume. She turned to Liz. "Maybe you should wait here."

"Not this time," Liz replied while pulling Merry across the street toward the corner entrance of the Common. The bright lights of the food trucks made it easier to find the holes in the crowd they could slip through. Merry made sure not to lose their connection as they shoved their way through. Finally, they were on the other side of the fence. The smells of popcorn and cooked sausage lingered in the air, though mostly overwhelmed by the stench of sweat and decay.

Following the same strategy as they had outside, Merry and Liz slinked along the right-side fence until the crowd thinned and they were able to move deeper into the Common. Both women halted.

"Oh my God," Liz said.

Straight ahead, a spotlight atop the gazebo exposed a large hole in the ground out of which crawled corpse after corpse. The dead pursued the screaming humans fleeing the scene. Anyone unlucky enough to be caught was dragged back toward the crevice. A haze had settled upon the Common. The ground steamed, especially where it had opened up, and the breeze carried the crevice's heat and the unpleasant odor of burning flesh.

Corinne stood inside the gazebo, the soft lights and haze outlining her in an eerie glow. She lorded over the scene like a proud mother. Her gaze found Merry's, her mocking smile evident across the distance. Anger superseded fear in Merry's heart. Energy soared through her veins like never before. She would take them all down tonight, starting with the Devil's daughter.

Corinne swung her arms up and the corpses, all of them, turned their attention towards Merry.

Merry dropped Liz's hand and ran at them. The colors consumed her, transforming her physical being into light and speed. She met the first corpse and stepped on its head, smashing its face into the dirt, using it to launch her into the churning sea of the dead.

She landed in their midst and before the corpses had a chance to react, she slammed her hands to the ground releasing a rainbow wave that flashed outward to consume the Tall Man's army. Screams filled the night, now coming from the corpses rather than the innocent. She pulled her colors back, stood, and observed the obliterated army. The well-manicured Common had been transformed into a ghastly array of rotted body parts. Merry turned, her gaze locking onto Corinne, whose mocking smile twisted into a worrisome grimace as Merry climbed the gazebo steps and stalked toward her.

"You have someone of mine," Merry said as she took the last step.

Despite the brave face, Corinne's voice shook. "Don't you mean several someones?"

Merry's lip twitched. Corinne didn't know the man called William, the man she loved, no longer existed. A breath caught in Merry's throat, and she clenched her jaw to stave off the hurt that threatened. She needed to focus on her grandmother and Salem.

Corinne tilted her head. "Poor rainbow girl. All out of

colors?"

Merry turned her despair into power and purpose. "I have enough for you."

And she did.

Merry reached down through the pain swimming through her body and summoned her colors once more. She sank into a crouch and screamed as colors erupted from her, tearing her clothing, rattling her teeth, and skewering her to earth and sky. A violent tremor shook the ground and air alike, vibrating in ever-widening rings of color.

In the last moments before the gazebo blew apart, Corinne's smug look transformed into a satisfying mix of astonishment and fear. Then, the wood splintered into a million tiny spears that found their way straight into Corinne's heart.

Merry stood, wobbly and worn. She tore the tattered remains of her dress from her body. Her chemise clung to her, riddled with sweat and dirt. Nothing of the gazebo remained, but a circle of torn earth where it had once stood. Even less evidence of Corinne had endured the explosion.

The Common had transformed from fair ground to battleground in moments. Destruction, largely her own, was everywhere. She searched for Liz, finally spying her stunned and unharmed near a large oak. Relief swam through Merry, though she knew her work was not yet done. She still needed to find Sophie. She took a step in Liz's direction and stumbled. She'd expended so much energy.

The space between her shoulders tickled with the phantom touch of someone's watchful eye. She spun, finding no one behind her and lost her balance altogether with the effort. Strong, wiry arms caught her inches from the ground, but brought no relief as Merry stared directly into the boiling red eyes of the Tall Man. He clamped unkind hands beneath her shoulders. She scrabbled to her feet, twisting in an effort to get away, but the world spun and morphed into another landscape before she could find purchase.

Merry stood knee deep in rotted corpses. The Tall Man had

deposited her in the middle of his battlefield, empty but for the dead and Merry. Without the Illuminators' light, a gloom had settled over the field. The air was heavy with the stifling stench of decay, the sky a week-old bruise, green-yellow with a propensity for pain. Her name floated across the sea of bodies, a moan upon the lips of the dead as they took their final breaths.

What had she been thinking? She'd wasted her energy on revenge and forgotten her purpose. She ignored the throbbing ache between her eyes and climbed atop the nearest cadaver to scan the area. The wooded fortress bordered most of the field, a dark threat waiting for those who dared enter. But, to her right the field lifted into gentle, rolling hills, green with life, a soft, promising glow on the horizon.

Merry looked back to the clawed archway where William had done the unthinkable. *Not William,* she reminded herself, *not William.* The mark he'd warned her about had turned him into someone who would steal her grandmother and harm her best friend. Sophie was somewhere beyond the tunnel, Merry was sure of it. And, so was William, whatever he'd become.

Hands raised, palms up, Merry called for her colors. Aside from the slightest of twinges in her muscles, nothing happened. Not even the tiniest tendril of color appeared. *Odd,* she thought. Before Crimson, she'd have been crippled with pain and exhaustion long after what she'd done on Salem Common. But, aside from a slight headache and achy limbs, she was strong, which made her lack of power all the more troubling. Merry gingerly stepped forward and began to make her awkward journey upon the limbs and heads of the dead using nothing more than muscle and grit.

Why had the Tall Man left her out here? Why not finish her? Merry wondered over this as she stumbled, tripped and pushed her way through the jumble of towering stone and thinning layer of bodies toward a lush meadow. Sweat coated her neck and dripped between her shoulder blades. Each step unearthed a sulfurous odor, and she fought against the constant urge to vomit. Merry leaned against the sharp-edged outcrop of a charcoal rock, and her heart stuttered for several beats. She snatched her hand away, breathing heavy, staring at the pitch-black surface as recognition dawned.

The bench at Iron House, the draining of her powers—all caused by a stone like this one. Obsidian, Liz had called it. She dropped to her knees, pawing through the bodies, shoving aside rotted arms and legs, until her hands hit the hard ground. "No," she murmured. The path to and from hell was paved with obsidian. That's why she couldn't summon her colors. That's why she was weak. Thinking back to her first encounter with the damaging stone when she'd passed out, she was glad she was conscious and able to move at all. Crimson had served her well.

Merry rose and continued her laborious journey upon the backs of corpses, avoiding direct contact with the rock as much as possible. As she neared the last few bodies between her and Nurya, Merry turned to look at the threatening black tunnel that served as the entryway to the Tall Man's domain. For a moment, she contemplated changing direction and slugging her way back to the ominous, gaping entrance, certain Sophie was somewhere inside that nightmarish place.

As she waffled on her decision to follow Axylus's earlier advice to bring the fight to Nurya, the pitch-black tunnel shifted, shadows mutating the trees' arthritic branches into twitching fingers eager to grasp a trespassing victim. Merry took several steps forward. "*It's a trap,*" Axylus's words echoed in her mind. The shadows grew into a glow, then a radiance that could only mean one thing.

A league of Illuminators gathered at the entrance and apparent exit of the Tall Man's domain. And in their center, stood a figure which caused her heart to hope.

54 MONSTER

His roar rattled the creaking branches above and shook the ground below. Corpses scattered as William jumped to catch Enfys before she could get hold of the screaming woman he'd tossed to the monstrous crowd. But Enfys was faster, and her colors faster still. William jumped up, attempting to reclaim his quarry, missing her by mere inches as she disappeared behind a curtain of colors. Instead, he fell into the pit of the dead.

Something inside him shifted. In the moment before they'd disappeared, he'd seen something familiar in Enfys's eyes. Something that had been inside him once, too. Hands greedily pulled him downward. He recoiled at the cold touch of so many desperate corpses. Rage dissolved into disgust. By the time the ground swallowed him, disgust turned into realization. The torments of regret awaited him in his dungeon. William landed on his hands and knees upon the dirt floor. The dank cave was a welcome refuge after journeying through the earth escorted by so many dead. He hung his head in shame, indulging a moment of self-pity, before lifting his eyes toward the person who now shared his prison.

"I'm sorry," he said, voice cracking. He spit dirt from his mouth.

The figure stirred, but said nothing. William walked across the cavern and crouched before her. "Sophie?"

Sophie's tear-streaked face lifted, and his heart cracked at the sight of her distrust. Her voice shook when she spoke. "What are you?"

So many answers flitted through William's mind. *I am broken. I am ruined.* "I am a monster," he finally answered.

Sophie nodded in agreement.

Debris sifted down from the cave's ceiling. The walls shook. Sophie peered out from under her hands, sheltering her eyes from the dust. "What was that?"

Another boom rattled the dungeon before William could answer. He extended a hand to Sophie. The fear of the unknown must have been stronger than her fear of William as she barely hesitated before taking it and allowed him to help her stand. He led her through the dark cavern to the stone steps, which led to the Tall Man's abode.

The shaking grew steady until it became a constant tremor. Jagged shards of rock fell around them. Torchlights flickered and blew out. Sophie cried out as an avalanche of stone caught her shoulder. She stumbled into a rough wall. William knew, unlike him, it was impossible for Sophie to see in the darkness. "Are you all right?"

"I think I'm bleeding."

He drew her close as they neared the stairs. "We're almost there."

The shaking stairs made for difficult navigation. Sophie groped the wall to her right as they ascended. Halfway up, a quake ripped through the cave, tearing down the ceiling behind them. Sophie screamed. The stairs they'd climbed crumbled to dust.

"Run!" William shouted. They scrambled as the staircase collapsed behind them. They'd nearly reached the landing when Sophie slipped. William caught her arm, slick with blood, and held her in his tenuous grasp as her feet dangled above the gaping darkness below.

The monster inside awakened. Heat threaded its way

through his veins. The staircase shifted, rocked by another tremor. Sophie's arm slid through his grasp. William gripped her elbow as she flailed. And all the while, fire raged inside him.

"William!"

William. The name bounced inside his head. A pinprick of light. The monster kicked and spun. He loosened his grip and breathed in the light. A hand, then another wrapped around his arm.

"William!"

Light bloomed in his eyes. Cooled his burning veins. A woman screamed. William fought for his mind as he stared into Sophie's terrified eyes. She was losing purchase on his arm and sliding downward. William reached and hauled Sophie up and over the broken staircase.

She collapsed against the rough stone wall, but William stood and tugged her upward. "We have to move quickly."

Her breath came in heaving gasps as she tried to keep up with William. The quake had twisted the frame and jammed the door. He banged the door with his shoulder several times before it opened. The corridor to the main room was a shambled mess of cracked walls and uneven floor, and still the earth shook. As William pushed open the door to the ballroom, a screeching cacophony of wood, stone, and glass obliterated all other sound. William pulled the door shut against the flying glass and sheltered Sophie with his body as dirt and pebbles rained upon them.

An eerie silence followed.

"Is it over?" Sophie asked.

Though the draw of his master was strong, William sensed something, someone else, too. Somehow he'd managed to save Sophie despite the darkness inside him. He'd used its strength and had held onto his light.

Sophie stepped away from him and looked at his feet. William looked down too and saw the glow seeping beneath the door, illuminating the ground beneath his feet. He shoved the darkness down further as a smile dawned on his lips.

William wrenched the door open and stepped into the blinding brilliance of the Illuminators. He reached a hand back for Sophie. Once again, she trusted him enough to place her hand in his, and they slipped through the doorway together. The ballroom was unrecognizable. Chunks of granite had fallen from the ceiling, some creating gaping holes where flames soared through while others buried themselves into the marble floor, sparking an intricate web of fissures across its surface. William and Sophie made their way along the perimeter where the floor seemed most stable. Their steps crunched upon finely ground glass, in some cases sand, as they walked toward the windows, now open to the outdoors. And freedom.

Sweat poured down William's face, neck, and back. His skin tightened with the fiery heat as he carefully guided Sophie around a flaming hole.

"It's hot as Hell," Sophie said, releasing some nervous laughter.

William looked back and smiled.

They took a moment to lean on an empty window frame and breath in the relatively cool outside air before stepping over the sill onto the forest floor. The total darkness outside the ballroom windows had lightened as though dawn was on the horizon. The ground beneath them shone, forming a glimmering path through the tree tunnel. They followed it, walking fast, and then jogging in short spurts as they passed beneath the eerie wooden claws of the trees.

Light clustered near the tunnel's end, manifesting into a multitude of golden humans. As they approached, William spoke two words. "Take her."

He briefly glanced at Sophie as several Illuminators encased her in a radiant wave and sped her away to the safety of her home. At least he'd done something right today.

And, now here was another chance to do good.

The figure, though distant was unmistakable. Merry, stranded in a sea of dead. So near escape, she turned, her gaze burning into his soul. *Keep moving*, William thought. *A rainbow cannot survive in darkness.*

William took several steps toward the decomposing battlefield. Fire erupted in his chest. He pounded a fist against his heart to stave off his vile hunger. The surrounding Illuminators fortified his light, aiding him in his fight against his monstrous nature.

"We can't leave her," William said.

Adina shimmered into view before him. "Of course not. We need her."

William nodded while selfishly thinking, *I need her.*

"The mark makes it impossible to take you with us. There's too much darkness inside you," Adina said not unkindly. "Your light is also strong. You have to hold onto it."

"I understand."

Adina smiled. "I believe in you, William."

Then she and the rest of the Illuminators shifted into a band of light and sped across the darkening battlefield.

55 INTENT

Was it her imagination or was it getting harder to see? Merry squinted into the gloom, which had gotten thicker over the last few minutes. Or was it the unexpected brightness of the gateway that made it *seem* so much darker on the battlefield? Merry tried to reach out to get a sense of William as he stood at the tunnel's entrance, but, like her colors, her senses were dead in this environment.

Something shifted beneath Merry's feet. She shrieked, tearing her gaze away from William's distant form and stumbled backward, tripping over the body behind her. Her heart leapt at the sight of a league of Illuminators racing toward her. She blinked in an attempt to rid her vision of the lingering blotches of bright light. There was another movement, then another, and soon the entire battlefield writhed.

"Leaving so soon?" a voice, too close, said behind her. Merry spun and came face to face with her captor. If only she'd kept moving. She was so close to Nurya. The minutes she'd spent debating which direction to go had stolen her ability to escape. The nearness of the Tall Man, blood-red eyes boring into her own, sent her stomach into a wrenching spasm. Merry doubled over and wretched.

A bony hand wrapped around her neck, much like the noose that'd nearly taken her life weeks ago, and lifted her. Merry scraped at the Devil's grip, legs kicking at air. He snarled into her face. "You killed one of my children." If Merry were able to speak, she would've remained speechless. *Children?*

The Tall Man shook her and threw her to the ground. Merry landed upon a corpse eager to embrace her. She managed to scramble a few feet on hands and knees before a hand clamped around her ankle and drew her back. The Tall Man had grown impossibly taller. He lifted her like a cat lifts a mouse and dangled her above outstretched, hungry hands.

"You killed my daughter. I told her to say behind, but children never listen, do they?" A wry smile told Merry he cared more for her punishment than he ever did for his child. "But, there is a way to redeem yourself, even gain your freedom, however short-lived."

Upside down, dangling by one leg, she had little choice but to wait for his offer, knowing full well she'd never make a deal with the Devil.

The Tall Man smirked. "Corinne found Crimson. She had this uncanny ability to find objects, events, people—like you, like William."

He gave Merry's ankle a twirl, spinning her like an entertaining toy. Dizziness threatened as the morbid landscape spun beneath her. All the while, the Tall Man laughed.

Black dots swam before Merry's eyes. "What do you want?"

He steadied her and shoved his face close to hers. "Your colors, Enfys."

As the black dots dissipated, Merry saw the Illuminators were close, lighting up most of the field behind the Tall Man. If she could keep his attention on her, they all might have a chance. She forced herself to hold his gaze. "What would you do with my colors?"

The Tall Man chuckled. Each breath brought a word. "I'm no fool."

A bellow erupted from William, born of animal-like despair. The Tall Man held the only person he truly loved in any world.

"Help her," he shouted to the Illuminators who were already fast on their way to Merry.

He grasped his dirk in his right hand. Given to him as a child to protect against evil, he meant to put it to the test. William ran straight into the heart of an awakening army of corpses that considered him brethren. *Hold onto your light*, a voice whispered to him. He did his best, fighting against the fire that ignited and rippled through his veins. William gave voice to his light, a thundering, gut-hollowing shout meant to push back whatever stood between him and Merry.

Still, the fire inside kindled and sparked. *Remember your light.* He pressed onward, trampling the rising bodies before him as he closed the gap between him and Merry, who dangled like a puppet from the Tall Man's repulsive grasp.

The mark's monstrous pull grew stronger as he neared the Tall Man. He was a man divided. Good propelled him forward, evil pulled him toward his quarry.

Renewed terror gripped Merry as a wall of corpses rose out of the ground, blocking the advancing Illuminators. The wall crashed to the ground like a ferocious wave, sending tremors cascading across the field. Light punched holes through a mound of corpses, but not enough to break through the prison. The Tall Man's satisfied grin stained her peripheral vision, but another sight held her attention.

A lone figure ran atop the bodies, lithely dodging groping hands. Again, Merry tried to distract the Devil.

"You can't have my colors. They're gone."

His blood-red eyes measured her. "They're suppressed. I can't have you wreaking havoc in my home now, can I?"

Was the Devil threatened by her? Hanging upside down was taking a toll on Merry. Still dizzy from spinning, Merry fought the increasing sensation of light-headedness. "How am I supposed to give you my colors?"

Her gaze shifted behind the Tall man. William slashed at

reaching hands, his knife glinting in the sparse light as he struggled to breech the corpses that trapped them. William had closed the gap between them enough for Merry to witness his struggle between his desire to save her and the mark's claim.

"He's strong, isn't he?" The Tall Man's words brought her attention back to him.

"You don't need him," Merry said with a pleading voice. "I'll give you the colors. Just let him go."

The Tall Man cocked his head. "I'll have your colors. But, William? I already own him."

A blaze surged in Merry's peripheral. She peered around the Tall Man. William no longer fought against the hands. Instead, they carried him like a burning, fearsome idol. Merry cried out. Her vision blurred with tears born of anger and loss.

Hold the light,
Remember the light.
Hold the light.
William pushed onward.

As he neared, the Tall Man turned his way and offered a knowing grin that both enraged and encouraged William. The monster within threatened. The need to destroy grew strong.

Merry's face—beautiful, terrified, and defiant. Threatening. A bellow erupted from William, born of gruesome intent. He rose on a sea of hands, a flaming ambassador of destruction, knife poised for the kill.

But then the anguished cry of a love remembered crashed through the consuming flames and kindled raw need. Using the strength and speed of the mark, William made a slight change in direction and careened toward the Tall Man. A mix of fire and light, he leapt and thrust the knife toward the neck of his master. The Devil spun, grabbing William's hand and directing it and the knife into Merry's side, finishing what the mark had intended to do.

William caught Merry as the Tall Man dropped her, and light spun up and carried them to Nurya.

Am I dead? That was Merry's first conscious thought upon opening her eyes. She coughed, and warm, thick liquid pooled in her mouth. She swallowed and choked, sending a red spray skyward. Pain tore through her side, and Merry's hands connected with a hole. Panic set in as her hands slid through the slippery wetness that could only be blood. *Her blood.*

Merry tried to move, but her limbs fought the effort, dead weights anchoring her to the ground. She glanced toward her right arm and then spun her head to the left as she realized she was pinned by many corpse hands. Merry tried to move her feet, but they too were restrained. Her gaze finally landed on the source of the ever-increasing pain cascading through her body. Another wet cough escaped her at the sight of the gash in her side and the pool of blood that continued to pour from the wound.

She lifted her head to evaluate the damage, but instead her eyes landed on a familiar face not far from her own. She called out, her voice barely a whisper. "William."

William moaned, then arched his back as a tremor overtook his body. He opened his eyes, bloodshot and unfocused, and Merry recoiled against the hands which held her. William tore at his shirt and screamed as he fought against the mark's poisonous claim. A violent convulsion jerked his body, flipping him to his side so that he faced Merry fully.

Merry attempted to speak, but instead ended up spitting blood. William's chest was a river of boiling scars wending their way down his stomach and up his neck. He panted, his face twisted in pain. A fat tear slid from his eye down his face and splashed onto the ground. He reached a blackened hand toward Merry, and that's when she realized they were in two different lands. While she was still a prisoner of the Tall Man's, William had made it to Nurya. Only three or four feet separated them, but it might as well have been miles.

War raged around them, light and dark shifted in equal measure. Merry tried to get a glimpse of who was winning or losing, but the effort weakened her. The edges of her vision grew blurry. Nearby William dug his hand into the grass-covered ground and pulled himself a few inches closer to Merry. Another spasm racked his body. She tried to meet his hand, but he was too far. Merry's vision shrunk to pinpricks of movement. William's tortured shouts were the last sounds she heard.

56 CRIMSON

"It's like they're determined to die together, isn't it?" Luke said. "Jesus."

"Yeah," Sidney said, watching from a nearby hillside as William struggled against the evil inside him. Merry lay at the edge of the Devil's battlefield a few feet away, held in place by the decaying hands of the dead.

A battle had been reignited by the Illuminators' theft of William and attempted rescue of Merry, Enfys. Sidney and Luke had arrived in time to see it all go wrong. Though the Illuminators had been able to rescue William, they'd not been able to stop the momentum of his attack on Merry, which the Tall Man had finished for him.

"So, what's the plan?" Luke asked.

Sidney glanced once more at the battle, both sides focused upon each other's destruction. Meanwhile, Nurya would not tolerate William's dark mark, and he'd been thrown into his own personal battle as the mark fought for survival.

William was dying before her eyes. Merry, too. She could only heal one of them.

"William," Sidney said as she slid onto the ground beside him. The turn of his head was slight, but his eyes locked onto hers. She took his hand, their fingers meeting with a bit of spark. Sidney threaded and curled her fingers around his and sent every ounce of her light into her brother.

His eyes widened, and he struggled to pull his hand from hers. But she held fast, continuing to send healing light into him. His struggle continued though no longer against the light flowing into him, but against the dark that fought its entry. His eyes rolled back until only the whites could be seen. Sidney watched in horror as his body seized and thrashed against the ground. A low moan escaped him, building to a roar as a dark liquid pooled beneath him.

Sidney nearly broke their connection as she instinctively pulled her hand back and away from the seeping liquid. She gagged at the foul stench that permeated the air. Tears blurred her vision as the light left her. She cried not for the light lost, but because her sacrifice appeared to have been all for naught. She hadn't saved anyone.

William bled out at an alarming rate. Sidney cried as she watched her brother die before her eyes. She didn't break their connection, holding tight, pushing what little light she had left into his dying body. His eyelids fluttered and one last moan escaped him before he fell silent. Eyes closed, blood spilled. Blood that pulsed and pushed itself further from the body it had filled only recently. Blood that rose into the air, swirling, breathing. Sidney's breath caught as she realized it was not blood, but the darkness, which had consumed William. Her light had freed the Tall Man's mark from William's body. At least she had managed to free him from his curse.

Sidney extricated her hand from William's to reach out and thrust her last bit of light into the dark swirling mass. The dark mark wrapped itself around her hand. It crept up her arm, seeking another host. With dread, she realized that indeed all her light had left her. She'd intended to finish off the darkness once and for all, but instead it was consuming her.

Suddenly, a hand shot up and clamped around her forearm. She cried out until she realized the hand belonged to William. He wasn't dead. In fact, he was very much alive as evidenced by the light that surrounded them and ripped the dark mass from her flesh. It hovered above them, exploding into a thousand scraps of darkness, a blemish against the dusky sky, before blinking out of existence altogether.

William crouched down beside her. William. Not dead. Not weak. His eyes held strength and purpose. His body, no longer feeble, was shrouded in light. Sidney smiled and gazed into his light, hers no more, as the realm she'd come to love faded and pushed her out forever.

William watched as his half-sister first took on a ghost-like consistency, and then disappeared completely. She'd sacrificed her light for him. Rid him of the Tall Man's mark. Made him whole.

A strength he'd not realized in a long time came over him. He looked across the field, spotting Vanessa walking among the dead. Merry lay just inside the Tall Man's domain, chest heaving with desperate breath. Blood spilling from the gash the knife, *his* knife, had made. William ran, closing the distance between them, leaping back into Tall Man territory, over grasping corpse hands, and fell onto the mass of bodies. He crawled over the remaining, squirming body that separated them and reached out for Merry, slipping in her still-warm blood.

"Merry."

She looked at him with apologetic eyes as though her dying was her fault. When the truth was, it was his and his alone. Her hands lay limp against the gaping wound in her stomach, a weak attempt to stem the flow of blood. She tried to speak, her voice unable to make it past her lips. Tears flowed down his face as he reached a shaky hand toward her wound. He had to fix her. His life was nothing without Merry.

The sound of laughter, so incongruous to the landscape, crawled along his skin, the hairs on his arms prickling up in warning. William turned toward the source. Vanessa reveled in his suffering as decomposing corpses reached up toward her in a final effort to make her one of them. She kicked them aside like a horse's tail flicks away flies.

"Tsk, tsk, is she dying?" She spread her arms, presenting the carnage around them. "All this fighting for the same ending we've wanted all along."

Her mocking tone undid him. Despair threatened to ruin him. Vanessa smiled.

A flutter of movement caught his eye—a shimmer of crimson. Merry moaned beneath him, and William's breath caught. Vanessa noticed too late.

Out of Vanessa's cloak, crimson shards rose, releasing the dark color each held within. Crimson was loose. And, it was heading home.

Colors undulated and spiraled in a determined path straight into Merry's open wound. She arched her back, her face contorted in exquisite pain as blood and flesh reversed their death march.

Vanessa charged towards Merry, her efforts to snatch Crimson from the air futile. William stood, slamming his arm into Vanessa's chest, sending her flying backwards. A wall of light rose behind her as she soared through the air toward Nurya. The Illuminators, as one blazing army, reached for the witch. Their dazzling embrace proved too powerful. For a moment, Vanessa struggled against them and then went stock-still as the Tall Man's dead reached for her. Their rotting bodies silhouetted against the brilliance of the Illuminators as they climbed atop one another and wrapped their festering limbs around Vanessa. She screamed as their hands climbed first up her legs, then around her hips, her waist, her chest. Her screams died as the dead consumed her. She sank beneath their weight, sliding back into the ground with them.

Yet, another scream replaced Vanessa's. William spun around to find Merry, whole, alive, and sprinting across the field of dead, colors streaming behind her. The Tall Man, her quarry. And she, his.

William ran after her. "Merry!"

As he plunged through the bodies, William realized the Devil's territory no longer claimed him. No more fire. No more anger. No more nefarious desires. Indeed, the mark was gone. He was filled with nothing but light.

The Tall Man eyed the colors, which followed Merry, with a keen hunger. Still, Merry ran toward him so fast there was little distinction between her and the colors. She was a speeding rainbow, and she was delivering what the Devil desired. No match for her incredible speed, William yelled her name again, his voice straining. But, Merry kept running, closing the gap between her and the Devil.

A howling wind tore through the forest, sending skeletal limbs swaying and scraping against each other. The Tall Man's white hair whipped about his head as he looked behind him. Three swirling cyclones ripped through his wood, snapping any tree in their path. They burst from the wood like angry dogs and made their way straight for the Tall Man. He lifted is arms, and the cyclones stalled, but then the earth shuddered beneath his feet and tossed him in the air where he was caught in the arms of the spinning wind. Still Merry ran.

The Tall Man flailed, then disappeared within the twister. Merry slowed. The other cyclones joined the first and expanded in size and strength, spinning its prisoner faster and faster. William had nearly caught up with Merry when the twister burst into flames. The burning mass grazed on the dead as it rotated toward them. The heat hit him like a wall, and William stumbled backward. Within the flames, a face appeared, as wide and long as the twister. Pointed chin, flaming hair, curved horns, crimson eyes. The Devil's true form.

The cyclone dipped low until the Devil's countenance poised before Merry. Her hair whipped behind her as the Devil exhaled flames in her direction. She fought them with a wall of water. He squinted his blood-red eyes, and opened his mouth as though to say something or perhaps send more fire her way, but Merry didn't give him a chance. With a guttural scream aimed toward the night sky, Merry dropped to the ground and released her colors. They raced up her body and into the sky like a gas flame.

The Devil lunged for her, attempting to encase the colors

within his flaming self. But, the colors arced big and wide, encompassing the land as far as one could see. The cyclone died as fast as a snuffed candle. The colors pulsed and vibrated, the outer red band rippling downward until it was the only color left. The world turned a deep, shining red.

Crimson.

For a brief moment, the Tall Man's lanky figure silhouetted against the sky. Then, as his edges wavered, a flame shot out of the ground and winked out in one swift move, leaving spiraling smoke where the Tall Man had stood.

As the crimson light faded, Merry turned toward William. He took two steps before falling to his knees. She closed the gap. Reaching out, she touched his hair and trailed her fingers down his cheek. He leaned his face into the palm of her hand. She knelt down, and William wrapped his arms around her, folding her into him. And there, among the silent and still corpses, they held each other tight.

57 RELEASED

A wave of light washed across the field as the Illuminators swept the landscape and erased the perpetual gloom. Whatever corpses the fire hadn't consumed, sank back into the ground. Lush, green grass sprouted in their place.

William whispered in Merry's ear, his breath soft and warm. "You're alive."

Reluctantly, Merry leaned out of his embrace. She took William's face in her hands and laid a whisper of a kiss upon his lips. "You're you, again," she said in a tone of half-statement, half-question.

William brushed hair from her face and tucked it behind her ear. He avoided her gaze for a moment. "The mark is gone." Then he looked into her eyes. "But it's not over, Merry. We need to go to Gallows Hill."

"Gallows Hill is in ruins. There's nothing there."

William pursed his lips. "There is."

Ruby's words came back to Merry then. *"Innocents were buried here. They need you..."* Merry stood. "I need to find Sophie first. And Ruby."

William rose. "Sophie is safe. The Illuminators delivered her back home."

"And Ruby?"

William's brows furrowed. "There was no one else. Only Sophie and..."

He looked down, and the image of William tossing Liz into the field of corpses filled Merry's mind. Heat crept up her neck and filled her cheeks. They would have to talk through the things they'd done later. She held a hand out to William. "We go together."

William searched her face, and she knew him well enough to know he was looking for the disappointment he expected to find. But the disappointment was in his eyes alone. Merry's heart broke at his self-condemnation. She nodded toward her outstretched hand and he clasped it in his own.

"We need to go back," William said, then specified, "to Salem Town."

Merry smiled and spun a rainbow.

They landed at the bottom of Gallows Hill, facing the hanging tree as morning dawned over Salem Harbor. "Something's different," Merry said. It took a half a moment for her to realize what that difference was. The limb which had held many nooses, hers included, was nothing more than a splintered nub sticking out from the tree's trunk. Merry recalled Susannah telling her how she'd tried, and failed, to chop down the limb. "How?"

"The Tall Man," William answered. "Snapped it like a twig. Mayhap the only good thing he ever did."

Still holding her hand, William led the way beyond the tree, down an incline, and to an outcrop of rocks. The grass gave way to churned dirt. "How did you know to come here?" Merry asked.

William's face clouded over. Whatever memory had been dredged up, he was not about to share.

"What do we do?"

William crouched and placed his hands upon the dirt. He looked up at Merry. "You've already done your part—you brought me, my light, here. Now I have to do mine." With that, William pressed his hands into the dirt and released his light.

Merry gasped at the beauty of its radiance. It raced to cover Gallows Hill in a rippling ocean of gold. Soon, the earth, rocks, and even the hanging tree, were covered in the brilliant glow of William's light, and he, at the center of it all, shined the brightest. New life bloomed in the dried autumn grass. Faded foliage took on a brighter hue.

Light pooled into circles upon the surface of the dirt. Then the illuminated spheres—Merry counted twenty—lifted from the ground, elongated into luminous ribbons, and rose up into the sky until they loosed their tether to the earth and soared past the softly lit clouds. Merry's breath caught. "Beautiful."

The light faded to a soft glimmer, first from William, and then as it dissolved into the ground. Eventually, only the furthest edges glowed, and then they too receded. William stood, brushing the dirt from his hands. "Now the light is where it truly belongs."

He faced Merry. "These lost souls have been released from their prison. The Devil has no hold over them or Salem anymore."

"But, your light..." Merry looked across the hill, to the hanging tree. The despair she'd experienced earlier had dissipated, replaced with a hopeful peace.

William followed her gaze. "The light was never mine. It was theirs. It was Salem's."

Merry turned to him, head tilted. "I don't understand. What about the line? Won't the Illuminators die out without—"

"Without my progeny?" William looked away as he shook his head. "'Twas a burden I knew I could not fulfill. I saw what it did to my mother. What sense did it make to take her good intentions and twist them into the very darkness I was meant to fight?"

"But, how?"

"The light has exclusively taken our own—those descended from the male line of Illuminators. But such rules only favor the dark. You cannot sustain a balance if you shut out all but those in the bloodlines. Evolution does not move as quickly as corruption."

"And the Illuminators' numbers will dwindle, while the dark grows."

William nodded and cleared his throat. "When I was trying to find ways to escape, a witch appeared. She was pitiful, but she was also repentant. She tried to help me escape. She gave me a weapon; helped me realize my sister was the key. So I tried something." He crouched and scooped a handful of dirt. "I tried something, and it worked."

"What did you do, William?"

William tilted his head and stared into Merry's eyes. "I shared my light with a condemned soul." He tossed the dirt back to the ground and stood. "And she shared that light with another, so they both might leave the darkness behind. I began to wonder, if my light could be spread as such, could it stretch further? Could it feed the very earth and the souls it sustained? Could they then become Illuminators?"

"There's no need for a bloodline. The light could come from anyone."

Merry studied William. "So, you're no longer an Illuminator?"

William achieved a half-smile. "Mayhap one day, hopefully far from this day."

Merry reached out and slid her hand down William's forearm, lacing her fingers in his.

A being shimmered into human form beside them, then another, and another. Adina, Axylus, and...

"Luke!" Merry said, recognizing the sullen-faced boy.

He held up a hand, palm facing out, in front of her. "Hey, you kicked a—you did good, Enfys. Real good."

Merry stared at his hand still poised before her face. "Thank you."

Luke wiggled his hand. "You're supposed to slap your hand against mine. It's called a high-five. Like, we shut the Devil the Hell up... yeahhhhh."

Merry smiled and tapped her palm against Luke's, and he finally dropped is hand. "Needs work. Ask Sidney to teach you when you get back."

"Sidney! Do you mean she's not in Nurya anymore?"

"Nope. She did her thing and went home." Luke tried to deliver the news with a smile, but Merry noticed the sadness in his eyes. She'd gained her friend. He'd lost his.

"It's best, Luke," Adina said. "She saved many with her sacrifice today."

"Sacrifice?" Merry asked.

"She gave me all her light. She saved me," William said, eyebrows furrowed.

"She was a true warrior," Axylus said, pride in his voice. "Even if she disobeyed my orders."

"Dude... " Luke began.

Adina interrupted whatever argument they were about to start, and addressed Merry and William. "Well done, the both of you."

Merry stepped closer to Adina, stopping short of asking the clairvoyant what fate awaited them. Adina smiled one of her intuitive and radiant smiles. "Your future is your own to make."

Merry glanced at William and nodded.

He took her hand, pulling her back toward him. "I believe it's time for us to go home."

Merry beamed. *Home. William.* A future she thought they'd never have. She looked into William's eyes. "Yes, let's go home."

Bathed in the Illuminators' glow, Merry and William found themselves thrown from the peaceful hillside into the aftermath of the embattled twenty-first century Gallows Hill. Even here, the effects of William's light could be seen—torn earth mended and covered with a fine growth of grass; the scent of fire replaced with that of crisp autumn leaves and cool dawn. Though a fair sight better than when she'd left it, the scattered sheet-covered bodies overshadowed any improvements.

Merry counted five bodies. She recalled the reporter and

cameraman that had been pulled into the earth by the Tall Man's corpses. Two bodies lay near their van a few feet from the parking lot. A body in a white coat lay at the excavation site, and two other bodies were already in black bags and being loaded into an ambulance. William bowed his head. Merry took his hand.

"You gave the victims of the witch trials peace," Merry said. "I hadn't realized it was their despair I felt earlier. It's gone now."

William nodded toward the bodies and slipped his hand from her grasp. "I gave *them* death." He turned and headed toward the road. Merry sighed and jogged a few feet to catch up with William's determined stride. She took his arm and pulled him to a stop. "You will not take blame for the Devil's doing, William. You didn't kill any of those people."

William avoided her gaze.

Merry tried to place herself in his vision. "If anything, blame me. I should've stayed with you. I should've..."

William seized he shoulders. "Nay Merry. You did right. Had you stayed, we would've both been lost to the Devil and the world would look a might different."

Before she could argue, a voice shouted her name. "Merry!" She spun around to find Alex jogging in their direction, Joel close behind.

"Alex!" Merry threw her arms around him and they hugged for a few moments.

"Are you all right? What the hell happened to you? That light..."

Merry released Alex and stepped back. "I'm fine. I'll tell you about it later."

Alex raised his eyebrows and Merry added with a teasing smile, "If Liz let's me."

His eyebrows drew together, forehead wrinkling. "Have you seen Liz? I haven't been able to reach her all night."

The last time Merry had seen Liz, she'd been on the Common taking cover behind a large oak tree, scared but unhurt. "She's fine."

His forehead smoothed. Merry then introduced William to both Alex and Joel.

Alex shook William's hand. "You're William? The guy who disappeared with the witches?" Without waiting for an answer, Alex launched into his next question. "Did you guys see them? The lights?"

"What lights?" Merry asked.

Alex pulled Joel in closer. "Show them, Joel."

Joel turned the back end of his bulky camera toward Merry and William and they crowded in to watch as ribbons of light, twenty of them, streamed from a patch of sparse wood beyond the ball field at Gallows Hill. Tears blurred Merry's vision. "We did see those as a matter of fact."

"I don't know what it was, but after everything that happened tonight, these lights brought peace to this place. You can feel it, can't you?" Alex asked.

Merry took William's hand and gave a gentle squeeze. "Most certainly."

A few minutes later, they piled into the news van. It took another ten minutes to wind their way through the maze of competing news vans and emergency vehicles before they were on their way downtown. More emergency vehicles and news trucks crowded the streets near the Common. Blue and red lights pulsed through the gray morning light. Merry straightened in her seat and peered out the window; her wide-eyed, open-mouthed shock stared back at her in the glass. Salem Common showed little sign of the corpse's siege. The crater had sewn itself up. Grass, unusually green for November first, sprouted anew. The effort to pick up the rubble from the destroyed gazebo was underway, though Merry was certain most of it had been reduced to dust. The unfortunate victims of the iron fence had been removed, along with pieces of the fence.

Merry slid the door back from the van before Joel brought it to a complete stop in front of Liz's apartment. She ran upstairs and knocked, but no one answered. Their next stop was Sophie's house. When Merry stepped through the front door, it was so quiet she thought the place also empty. But in the kitchen she found Liz, her father, and her grandmother at the table. Liz's upper torso stretched across the table, head upon her folded arms; Sophie snored, chin on chest; and Devon, who'd been looking out the large window to the backyard, turned when she entered.

"Merry!" Her father shouted, standing so quickly he sent his chair back into the wall. Sophie's head snapped up, drool flying. Liz groaned. Merry let herself get wrapped up in her father's arms. He kissed the top of her head. "We were so worried."

Devon released her into Sophie's arms next. William, Alex, and Joel entered the room. "Welcome home," Devon said as he shook William's hand. Alex made his way to Liz, gently nudging her shoulder. She swatted at him several times before lifting her head. She blinked, still groggy with sleep. Merry smiled as Liz's brain caught up with what she was seeing. She leapt out of her chair to join the reunion, hugging Merry tight. "I thought you were dead. When that beast took you..."

Over Liz's shoulder, Merry spied William lurking in a corner of the kitchen, arms crossed and avoiding eye contact. Merry separated from Liz, and they both turned in his direction.

"William," Liz said. Merry couldn't blame her for not welcoming him back with open arms after their last encounter, but her heart broke for William.

He raised his gaze toward Liz, a slow blush creeping up his neck. "I don't expect you to accept my apology, Liz, but I am truly sorry for my actions earlier today."

Sophie made her way to him and pulled William into a hug. "Thank you for saving me, William. I know it was difficult for you."

Liz took a tentative step closer and took William's hand. "That wasn't you, William. I know. It wasn't you." A corner of her mouth lifted. "Besides, we're family. You'll have to try harder than that to get rid of me."

William rubbed his face. His eyes glistened as he pulled Liz in for a shared hug—Sophie in one arm, Liz in another. He glanced at Merry, their gaze connecting for a moment before he looked away. It appeared others would forgive William easier than he would forgive himself. The mark was gone, but its stain remained. Later, when they could be quiet together, she'd help rid him of it completely.

58 DIVIDED

William splashed warm water on his face and watched it drip down his reflection. The pale face looking back at him appeared worn and neglected. It had been a while since he'd felt human. He'd burned, scarred, and burned again. He'd soared among the clouds and drifted in sunshine. His skin had experienced the intolerable touch of fire. His body had sustained a thousand poisoned bites. He'd subsisted on the most meager of meals and rations of water, his throat a constant flame to be doused. Yet, he stood whole. A man. Topside and amongst the living.

The low voices of conversation coming from down the hall sounded foreign after his weeks of desolate captivity. If not for those voices recapping last night's events, he might be tempted to believe he'd hallucinated the entire ordeal. He ran a finger down the pink, raised skin that trailed from his neck and down his chest before disappearing beneath his shirt.

He wanted his life with Merry to be how it was before—before the hangings, before torture, and before Hell. He didn't want to acknowledge it, talk about it, relive it, or remember it. He recalled their time at Iron House, their ability to love with abandon. He wanted that back. He wanted that back and nothing more. He grabbed the hand towel and wiped his face dry, then yanked the door open to join the reunion in Sophie's living room.

"I can't believe she's gone. I should never have let her get involved," Merry said after learning Ruby had been one of the covered bodies at Gallows Hill. Having freshened up and changed out of her tattered sheath into jeans and a sweater, Merry sat beside her grandmother on the love seat in her small living room, clutching her hand.

Sophie squeezed Merry's hand. "You couldn't have stopped her."

"I could have."

"Well, yes, technically you could've told her to lock herself in a closet for the night. But Ruby was in this the minute she knew you existed."

"Is that why you tried to keep us away from Gallows Hill? Why you were fighting with Ruby?" Liz asked.

Sophie leaned her head back against the love seat. "Lord knows Ruby and I never saw eye to eye, but I didn't want her dead."

Liz's hand flew to her mouth. "Did you see her death in the crystal ball?"

Sophie squirmed. "Not quite. I saw us—you, Ruby, and I—running past a wall of fire. When the smoke cleared, I only saw you and me. I knew it was bad, just not..." Sophie sighed. "The thing is, Ruby would never have believed me if I told her. She thought I was a fake who made up the fortunes I told my clients. And, for a long time I was. Sometimes I wish I still was."

Merry hugged Sophie. "It seems we all have some unwanted traits inside us." Merry sensed William's presence before lifting her eyes to meet his uncomfortable gaze. He looked away immediately.

They spent another couple of hours recapping the night's events, filling in the gaps of what had occurred during their separation, and counting the deaths attributable to the Tall

Man's quest for Salem. Merry apprised them of William's cleansing light and assured them that the Tall Man no longer had a hold on Salem, or on William.

Before leaving, Devon hugged Merry and spoke so only she could hear his words. "Your life begins now, daughter. This is your time."

She hugged him back. "*Our* life begins now. It's your time, too, Papa." He kissed her forehead and though he smiled, Merry sensed a certain sadness behind it.

Morning was in full bloom when Alex pulled up to the gates of Iron House to drop off an exhausted Liz, Merry, and William. They found a jubilant Jonathan waiting in the foyer. "She's awake," he said.

With renewed vigor, they raced upstairs. Liz gasped aloud at the sight that greeted them. Sidney sat in the chair by the window, her skin and muscles once again taught and strong, her hair thick and healthy. She turned to them with a broad smile.

Liz ran to embrace her. "Sidney!"

William took Sidney's hand. "Sister." She stood, a bit shaky, and hugged her brother. William pulled away, still holding her arms. "I never thought... I'm honored to be your brother."

"Yeah?" Sidney said, a sly smile upon her lips. "Well, you owe me big time."

It was the first real laugh Merry had heard come from William in a long time.

Sidney's eyes snapped to Jonathan. "So, Jonathan was the first person I saw when I woke up. That must mean something." Her voice sounded stronger than it should have after having gone unused for so long.

Jonathan grinned and then shrugged. "I care?"

Sidney laughed. "I like this new Jonathan."

"Well, I like the old Sidney."

They shared a look between them, and Merry smiled. She hugged Liz, holding onto her friend tight. "I love you, you know."

Liz squeezed her back. "Even when it's weird and ugly, life

is perfect."

They stormed the kitchen for a hearty breakfast, then, despite the vast quantities of coffee, exhaustion set in and one by one they made their way to their beds to get some much needed rest.

William dropped Merry's hand as they entered their suite. He wandered toward the large window in the sitting room and stared out, clutching the sill. "I watched you from this window."

Merry shut the door with a click. "I sensed you."

"You feared me." He spared a glance toward her.

"I didn't know who I was. I had no memory of you."

William looked back out the window. "I know."

Suddenly, Merry didn't know where to look. "I'll draw you a bath."

She left him standing at the window looking more uncomfortable than he should. She sat at the tub's edge and opened the faucet, adding a bit of soap. The cascade of water brought back memories of sharing the bath with William and the utter honesty of their love. *Had they lost that?* She didn't doubt William's love, but did he? Too little sleep and too much angst flooded Merry's eyes with tears. She let them come. She cried for the victims of the witch trials, the people who'd lost their lives then and now; for Ruby, who'd wanted to help and had ended up dead; for Sidney who'd risked so much and had given up the light she cherished; for William, who's soul had been compromised; and for her mother. Happy tears came, too—for Sophie and for her father, who she'd been reunited with against all odds.

Merry shut the tap and wiped her tears away. When she returned to the bedroom, William lay on his back on the rug in front of the fireplace.

"William?"

He didn't answer. The firelight danced across his face, revealing the worried creases present even in sleep. Merry crouched down beside him and smoothed a dirty lock of golden hair off his cheek. She sat, leaning her back against the sofa and placed William's head upon her lap, her hand moving with the rhythmic rise and fall of his chest. A slow smile crept along his lips and he opened his eyes. "Are we in the meadow?"

Merry smiled down at him as she'd done many times in their secret spot amid the tall grass. The meadow seemed a lifetime away. "Wouldn't that be nice?"

William shut his eyes and sighed. "Aye."

"William?"

He grasped her hand. "I'm sorry. You were right to fear me."

"It's over," Merry said, though the Tall Man's destruction clung like a heavy mantle to her shoulders.

William sat up and placed a quick kiss on Merry's cheek. "Of course." He then jumped up and headed to the bathroom. "I'm going to take that bath."

Merry noticed he didn't walk as tall as he had before. His gate was slow, shoulders a bit slumped, and eyes to the ground—not quite broken, but not whole. She looked away, staring into the flames, the door gently shutting a moment later. The fire crackled and spit as the flames touched pockets of moisture. Merry couldn't help but be reminded of the track of fire which had raced across William's body, turning him into a human torch. Now watching the flames curl and unfold as they licked against the logs, Merry saw violence and torment instead of peace and warmth.

She picked up the poker and jabbed at the logs, tamping them down into the ash-covered stone. She slammed the iron against wood and stone over and over, needing to kill the spark that gave life to fire, threat, and memory. At first, the flames leaped at her touch, filling their lungs with air, and expanding their glowing chests. Merry doubled her ferocity, and they succumbed to her wrath, dwindling into smoke and embers. Strong arms encircled her waist, pulling her back from the hearth. The poker fell from her hand with a clatter. Warm breath whispered against her neck. "It's over. I love you. It's over." The words fell like song upon her mind.

She twisted in William's embrace, burying her head against his damp chest. He smelled of soap and fire. When her racing heart calmed and her breath slowed, Merry leaned back, her eyes settling on the faint remnants of the mark's desecration. She traced a finger along its path. "Will it fade away completely?"

William stilled her hand. "I do not know."

Merry stood on her tiptoes and pressed her lips to his for a brief moment, then whispered against them. "You're home now."

She kissed him, her tongue slipping past his lips. William pulled her closer. Merry ran her hands down his chest and gave the towel wrapped around his waist a tug. William broke off the kiss and clutched the towel. His words came through heavy breath. "I need to finish washing, Merry."

Merry released him. "I understand." And she did. She understood the need to rid oneself of the taint of death and the Devil's touch.

While William bathed, Merry undressed and snuck into the bathroom to find him resting his head against the tub's edge, eyes closed as he soaked. After a long, hot shower, she emerged pink-skinned and scrubbed clean. She wrapped a towel around her under William's watchful gaze.

"The water must be getting cool."

"'Tis good to be out of the flames." He frowned as soon as he said it, then mumbled, "I'll be in shortly."

Too exhausted to delve into the meaning of his words, Merry left him. Moments later, she lay beneath the down comforter and fell into a dreamless sleep.

William soaked until the water grew cold and dark with dirt. He then took a long, hot shower to rid himself of the inner filth, which still clung to him. He emerged from the shower with shriveled skin, but could not wash away all the torment. It would take a bit more doing to remove it, if at all.

By the time he emerged, Merry lay fast asleep, buried

beneath the fluffy bedding. His heart swelled with love and the possibility that their life might actually start now. Then his brow furrowed against the improbability of ever leaving the mark's scars behind. William bent and laid a kiss upon Merry's cheek and left to find another bed.

Merry bundled the down comforter tighter, discouraging the cool November morning air from touching anything other than her face. Though her breath cast a visible plume into the air, the comforter kept her warm as she curled her body into the cushioned armchair on the balcony. The pink underbelly of the cloud-covered sky hid the morning sun as it pushed over the horizon. Sparsely attended branches bridged the space between sky and land, and a frosty kiss cast a sparkle upon the fading lawn.

She'd slept soundly, aware only of the moment when William had placed a soft kiss on her cheek. This followed by the click of the door as he'd left the room and another click as he found another bed for the night. Merry closed her eyes, reaching out with her ability to discern the intentions of those nearby. Even through the walls, she picked up William's inner turmoil. A tormented shout startled Merry from her inspection, and she gripped the chair's arms, the comforter baring her shoulders to the elements. The shout settled into a groan, then silence. Merry's heart calmed and she reached out again, sensing William's fear, anger, and despair.

She fought every urge to go to him. He needed time to sort through his experiences, to relinquish the past, and allow himself to live. She'd only spent minutes in the Tall Man's lair, and even now she vividly recalled the unrelenting terror and the constant fight against the dead. She could only imagine William's struggle to adjust from such horrific captivity to a life free to live as his own.

Merry pulled the comforter tighter and shuffled into the bedroom. She froze at the sound of William's door opening and closing, held her breath as she stared at her door, waiting for it to open. Waiting for William to come back to her.

Instead, she was met with the sound of his footsteps receding down the corridor.

59 WANT

Merry dressed and headed down the hallway in search of William. She'd not let their harrowing experiences make them strangers. Before she reached the staircase, she ran into Liz coming down the hallway from her room.

"So, you're up early, too," Liz said, yawning. She linked her arm through Merry's as they headed down the stairs. "How's he doing?"

Merry shrugged a shoulder. "He's struggling."

"Yeah? I'd be struggling too if I'd spent the last month with the Devil." Liz rubbed Merry's shoulder. "He needs time, Merry."

"I know," Merry answered, but she wanted him now. Wanted him whole again.

"Fortunately, time is finally on your side."

They heard voices as they reached the base of the staircase. Merry peeked into the living room to find William and Sidney sitting on the sofa, talking. Merry's heart warmed at William's smile. He listened intently as his sister told him what she remembered about their father. Liz came up behind Merry and touched her shoulder. She tilted her head toward the kitchen. "Let's leave them alone."

Merry nodded, sparing one more glance at the reunited siblings and followed Liz in search of breakfast. They settled in the nook and nibbled on warm corn muffins. "William didn't sleep in our room last night."

"Where did he sleep?"

"In the next room. I think he's having nightmares."

"Why wouldn't he be?" Liz asked, taking a swig of coffee. "I was in—I can't even believe I'm saying this—Hell for less than an hour, and I'm having nightmares. Did he tell you anything about his captivity?"

"Not yet."

Liz put her mug down. "Maybe it would be a good idea for you and William to disappear for a while."

Merry's gaze locked on Liz's. Alarm pricked her skin.

Liz's mouth dropped open. "That was a bad choice of words. I mean you should get away. Together. *In this century.*" Liz dropped back against the padded bench. "Merry, they saw us last night."

"Who?"

"Everyone! We're all over the internet." Liz dug into her pocket and pulled out her phone, tapped it a few times, then shoved it across the table to Merry. She picked it up and stared at a photo of her and Liz standing in the middle of what appeared to be a shimmering rainbow.

"They don't know what they saw, and you could argue the rainbow was some camera glitch or photo-shopped. Except that's not the only photo. Lots of cameras caught us." Liz reached over and took the phone, tapping it a few more times before handing it back to Merry. "There's even video of the explosion on the common."

It was like watching one of Sophie's visions on the crystal ball, only anyone could see this.

"The video has gone viral. Which means a lot of people have seen it. Alex said they're already setting up news crews at Sophie's house, and they're coming here too."

Merry folded her arms across her chest. "I fought for Salem. Not to hide from it."

"It won't be forever, Merry—just until this dies down a bit. Besides, you and William need some alone time, don't you think?"

Merry stared out the window, lips pressed together. "William wants to get to know his sister. His family."

"Sidney will be here when you return. We all will."

"My father."

"He'll be here, too."

Merry shook her head. "He won't. He's going to hide again. My return didn't free him from suspicion. I have no proof of where I've been. My mother is still missing as far as the authorities are concerned."

Liz leaned forward. "I didn't think of that. He'll come back though, won't he? Or you'll know where to find him?"

"He'll find me, and he said if I got a phone like yours, we can call one another." Merry's gaze went back to the beautiful fall day outside the window, bereft of last night's abuses. She wished she could say the same for herself. "It's not perfect. But we'll be separated by miles rather than centuries. That's an improvement."

"You always look on the bright side."

"People died last night. I can't be sad about *my* life, Liz. I have you, and William, a father, and grandmother. I wasn't sure I'd see any of you again yesterday."

Liz squeezed into the seat next to Merry, hugging her tight. "We have each other." She sat back and added, "But, don't feel guilty about being sad about some things. You have every right, Merry."

He found Merry over the crest of the small hill behind Iron House. She sat upon the dried grass, hugging her knees to her chest, gazing toward the sparkling bay. He slowed, taking a few moments to watch her. A light breeze played with her hair; she swept it from her face and placed the strands behind her ear, the wind promptly releasing them.

For weeks he'd yearned to be free of his unnatural prison, to be *human* again. Though he'd been burned to ash and lived as dust, here he stood on a hill pining after the woman he loved. The same hands that now yearned to caress Merry's face, to love her, were the same hands that had tossed Liz to the dead and wielded a knife aimed at Merry's heart. He'd sustained unimaginable torture and had not only survived, but showed no physical scars. There was no reconciliation. His mind repelled the memories that wouldn't leave. They were impossible. Improbable. His.

"I know you're there," Merry said. She glanced over her shoulder, smiling, and patted the ground beside her.

Turning around and running back to the house was no longer an option, so William dutifully sat beside her. "I suppose you always know when I'm near."

Merry's face flushed. "Liz calls it my spidey sense."

"Spidey?"

"It's a reference to a man who's been bitten by a spider, and..." she stopped, waving the thought away. "Never mind."

William pulled his knees to his chest. "'Tis freezing out here."

"It's warm in the sun."

William rubbed his arms and tilted his face skyward. "I yearned to get out of the flames. Now, I can't get warm."

She leaned in to him, rubbing his arm. "It *is* November in New England."

Despite his trepidation, he smiled down at her. Her smile faded from her lips. "Why didn't you stay with me last night?"

He tore his gaze from her lips and stared across the lawn toward the patch of sparkling blue water on the horizon. "I have nightmares."

She tightened her grip on his arm. "Maybe you won't have them if we're together."

"They always come."

She let her hand fall away from his arm, and he immediately regretted the loss of her touch. He chanced a look in her direction, and the sadness in her eyes ruined him. She looked away; it was her turn to stare at the horizon. "Liz suggested we leave Iron House for a while."

"And, go where?"

"Her family has a house on Cape Cod. They're having it prepared for our arrival."

"You agreed to this."

She studied him with serious green eyes. "There are compelling reasons for us to leave Salem for a while. I was captured on camera last night. Reporters are stalking Sophie, and it won't be long before they set up camp in front of Iron House."

"I see."

"No, you don't. Liz thinks you and I need to be alone, without these distractions, to get back to where we were before."

"And, you believe that's possible?"

Merry tilted her head, eyes widening. "You don't?"

William tore a clump of brown grass out of the ground and proceeded to shred it. "Of course. I didn't mean..." He threw the grass back to the ground and leapt to his feet. "I told Jonathan I'd meet him at his barn, take Spirit for a run. I'm late."

Like a coward, he left the truth hanging between them and sped off to an imaginary appointment. *Why couldn't he tell her about his nightmares?* About his inability to fully believe he was actually here, alive, and subject to the human condition. About his fear that he was *not* hallucinating his life, but that he was truly in it and faced with a future all to his own making. The predictability of an unrelenting doom inside the cave was less threatening than a wide-open future.

He could sense her gaze boring into his back as he made his way toward the low, stone wall separating Iron House from the Parrish farms. He was a fool. He was scared. Though he'd escaped, the remnants of Hell clung to him.

Thankfully, the barn was empty of humans when William walked in. Spirit bobbed his head as William approached his stall, then stilled beneath his soothing touch along the bridge of his nose.

"Shall we ride?" William asked Spirit, earning an agreeable

head bob in response. He saddled the horse, his hands recalling the motions as his thoughts wandered to Merry. He wondered if she still sat on the lawn waiting for his answer to her question. He was an idiot. All he'd done to get back to her, and he'd left her without answer.

He led Spirit from the stall and onto the practice well, where they raced from one end to the other. Back and forth over and over, the breeze of their movements turning the cool day into an icy wind. Spirit galloped with the joy of reunion. Finally, nose dripping, body numb with cold, William led the horse back to the stable. As he wiped Spirit down, Jonathan and a stable hand entered the barn.

"William!" Jonathan hugged William and patted his back hard. "What are you doing here?" Before William could answer, Jonathan asked the stable hand to take over rubbing down Spirit.

"He runs hard as ever," William said as they walked toward the barn doors.

"We've kept on him while you were away."

Away. The word seemed a woefully inadequate description of the last few weeks of William's life.

Jonathan stopped at the open doorway. "What are you doing here, man?"

William shook his head and leaned against the rough doorframe. An uneasy silence passed between them.

"Listen, I know what you went through wasn't easy, but Merry loves you. She loves you like nothing I've ever seen. And, you love her. It's that simple."

William frowned. "It's not. You can't imagine what I've endured. What I've done."

"Fair enough. But, it's gone now, isn't it? The mark? It's gone."

"'Tis gone, yes. But, I'm not the same man."

"So?"

"So, Merry deserves better."

"I don't know, that might be true," Jonathan said. "But, the fact is, Merry only wants you."

60 CLOAKED

Merry shuffled along with the rest of the sometimes silent, sometimes chanting crowd as they wound a path from Gallows Hill to Ruby's beloved shop on Pickering Wharf. Liz, Sophie, Jonathan, and William walked beside Merry, none of them distinguishable from the other cloaked figures. Alex had warned them they'd be recognized and swarmed by reporters. But after Merry insisted she needed to honor Ruby's sacrifice before leaving for the Cape, Liz had gone to Sidney's shop and brought back four hooded cloaks. Now, they blended in as Sidney said they would. Unfortunately, she couldn't join them, still weak from her extended bed rest.

They moved along, the chanting continuing like the low hum of a beehive. Merry didn't know what the witches were saying, but found comfort in the lulling rhythm. They'd been walking for a half-hour already, but at their slow pace the trip would take another half-hour before they reached Ruby's shop. Liz had arranged for a car, packed and waiting with Merry's and William's luggage, to whisk them off to the Thompson's Cape house as soon as they arrived at Pickering Wharf. Merry glanced at William, reaching out to give his hand a squeeze. He peered at her from beneath the hood with sad eyes, his lips set in a grim line. She'd told him he didn't need to come. He didn't know Ruby, but he'd insisted on joining them. Merry knew he blamed himself for the mayhem and death that had been forced upon Salem on Halloween night. She also knew it would take time for him to let go of his self-imposed guilt. *If he ever did.*

Liz whispered in Merry's ear. "Merry, look."

Merry followed her pointing finger toward a crowd of onlookers as they neared the Witch House, immediately spotting her father. She eased her hood back a bit, and her father's searching gaze locked upon hers. He nodded, and Merry knew it meant goodbye. Earlier, when they'd said their farewell at Sophie's house, he promised he'd get word to her on where he was, and that he would come back for Thanksgiving. Still, it was hard to let go of him so soon after their reunion. She wanted to run to him for one last hug. Instead, she nodded back and held his gaze until their parade of witches had passed.

61 NEW

"It's smaller than I expected," William said moments after they'd entered the Thompson's beach home. The cedar-sided structure was large, though nowhere near the scale of Iron House, and not as large as some of the homes they'd driven past on their way here. The house stood on a corner parcel of land that jutted toward the blue horizon; the neighboring homes visible, but not too close.

"Cozy," Merry said, as she strolled through the foyer into a great room warmed by turquoise and sand hues. The ceiling rose two-stories, a railed corridor encircled the floor above. Wide-paned windows framed a spectacular ocean view. "It's beautiful."

William stood beside her, and together they gazed upon the white sand beach fenced by an outcrop of rocks on both sides. The frothy ocean water rushed to the shore, spraying geysers into the air as waves crashed against the jetties. William shivered. "Aye, beautiful, but 'tis as frigid in here as it looks outside."

Liz had made sure the heat had been turned on before they'd arrived, but there was still a slight chill in the air. Merry spied a pile of firewood stacked beside the large stone fireplace at the other end of the room. "They've stocked us with wood. Why don't you start a fire while I try to put together some dinner for us? Then we can unpack."

The white kitchen lay beyond the dining area, well-appointed but not overwhelming. Merry sat on a cushioned window seat near a row of paned windows and pressed one of the few names on her phone. Liz answered before the first ring had completed.

"You're there?"

"Yes, we arrived a few moments ago."

"Good. Now lose the phone and make my cousin a happy man again."

"I wish it were that easy."

"It might not be easy, but I have faith in you, Merry. And in William."

Merry bit on her thumb.

"Merry?"

"I'm still here."

"Go get your man." The phone clicked and Merry said Liz's name twice before she realized her friend had hung up. She rose, sighing, tossed the phone into a drawer filled with kitchen towels and focused on finding some food.

A short while later, she returned to the great room to find a roaring fire in the fireplace and William sitting before it, knees tucked into his chest, staring into the flames. She went back to the kitchen to retrieve the platter of cheeses, meats and bread along with two glasses and a bottle of wine. She set the items on the hearth. "I thought it silly to leave such a warm fire."

She poured a glass of wine for each of them. William drained half his glass with one swig. Merry raised an eyebrow. "Thirsty?"

William grinned, and Merry found herself grinning back. Hopeful. William picked some cheese and sliced meat from the plate and leaned back against the sofa. Merry laid her head on his shoulder and gazed at the flames. "I like it here."

William smiled down at her. "It feels like a start, doesn't it?"

Merry smiled back at him. "Yes, like a good start."

William shut the window against the wintry ocean air. The sound of rushing waves, though dulled, permeated the darkened room. He closed his eyes and thought about walking into the night ocean, exposing his wounds to its salty bite, and purging his sins in its icy embrace.

He recalled how Merry had looked at him when he told her he thought it best they sleep apart. She didn't understand why he sought solitude after fighting so hard to get back to her. She didn't understand that his dreams were threaded with the heinous deeds he'd executed in the Tall Man's service. He needed to rid himself of his demons.

The next morning, Merry walked along the sandy shore, the bright morning sun providing some relief from the biting wind as it sent waves crashing against the rocks. William stood a distance away, staring at the sand beneath his feet, his shoulders huddled against the November morning. She called his name when she was a few feet away.

He turned to her, his lips bluish-gray with cold

"What are you doing out here? It's freezing."

"The cold never used to bother me," he answered.

"You just need to get used to it again," Merry said, then added through chattering teeth, "The cold is bothering me as well, if that makes you feel better."

William attempted a grin, but his frozen lips quit halfway through the effort.

"Come inside. I have a fire going, and I've made some breakfast."

Thankfully, William followed and soon they were warming themselves in front of the fireplace with steaming mugs of coffee and bowls of oatmeal.

"You made this?"

"Aye."

William lifted an eyebrow.

"All right. I added warm milk to oats and stirred in some blueberries. Do you not like it?"

William scooped a spoonful into his mouth. "Oh, 'tis good. Mayhap we should let Liz's cook stop by for dinner."

Merry laughed, and soon William laughed with her. The sound warmed her more than the fire. "I suppose I do need more practice."

The house was eerily quiet after their laughter died down. "That sounded nice," Merry said. "It sounded like the William I remember."

William put his bowl down. "I'm trying, Merry."

"I know."

"I fought so hard to come back to you. But, I cannot forget what I've done."

"Perhaps you shouldn't. But, maybe you can make your memories work for you instead of against you. Against us."

He turned to her, his blue eyes stormy like the ocean. "How?"

"I don't know."

William stared into the fire.

"We'll figure it out. You and I. Together." Merry scooted along the sofa until their thighs touched. She laid a hand on his arm. "We're stronger together, don't you think?"

William looked at her, locking is gaze upon hers. "I believe we are."

"Then tell me. Tell me what haunts you so."

William shook his head. "I won't put those images in your head. You saw enough at Gallows Hill, at the Tall Man's gates."

"But, William..."

He grasped both her hands. "Don't do that. Don't say it wasn't me. I know I was an instrument for the Tall Man's evil. It doesn't make the experiences or the memories any less terrible."

Merry touched her forehead to his. "I want to help you."

"I'm not sure you can. The memories may fade in time. But, the mark. I know it is gone, but I sometimes feel the ghost of it's fire flowing through my veins, a cold fire that leaves me with a chill I cannot shake. I don't know how to rid myself of it."

Merry wrapped her arms around his neck pulling him into a fierce hug. His strong arms encircled her, pulled her closer, tighter. He buried his face in her hair, and she whispered in his ear. "Come to me, William. Come back to me."

He visited the shore several more times during the day, braving the wintry chill. Fighting the only way he knew how. Merry tried to keep the conversation light during dinner, regaling him with stories of Liz and Alex's refusal to admit they liked one another.

"She even called him ridiculous."

"Was he?" William laughed.

"Most likely. Most men are from time to time," Merry answered with a playful smile.

She left him alone by the fire that night. He came to her bed sometime in the early morning. She sank against him, his arm wrapping around her as he tucked her into him. She feigned sleep, not wanting to disturb the honesty of the moment. Only when his breathing deepened with slumber, did she dare move. Only then did Merry sneak an arm out from the covers to hold her hand above his body, not touching. She trailed her hovering hand over his head, his heart, then down his body as far as she could reach without disrupting their position. Violet light streamed out from beneath her hand, forming a blanket around William.

She could see his face relax further. The nightmares which lurked a hairsbreadth away from fulfillment, melted into vague thought, never to be realized.

Merry smiled. She harbored no guilt over the manipulation. She would never reveal it. And William would suffer less for it.

In his sleep, he pulled her closer. She laid her head against his chest, the steady thump of his heart the most wonderful sound ever heard. She pulled the blanket around them and fell into the most blissful sleep she'd had in months.

Merry's eyes remained closed as William left their bed. She

heard his soft footsteps pad across the floor, the click of the bathroom door shutting. Reaching across the bed, she rested her hand upon the warm spot where William had slept. Moments later, she rolled onto her back and opened her eyes to the sunlight peaking through the curtains.

Running water broke the silence as William started the shower. Merry left the bed and gently pushed the bathroom door open. As though a memory come to life, she saw William behind the steamed glass, arms braced against the wall, head down as the water rained upon him. He didn't notice her enter the room. Didn't notice her remove her clothing. Didn't acknowledge her until she stood behind him, her hands reaching around him as she pressed herself against him.

As the water pounded down on them, she slowly glided her hands first up to his chest, then downward. William moaned beneath her touch, then turned. His hands cupped her face as he looked into her eyes. His look spoke of the desperation he'd endured and the intensity of his love—everything he couldn't seem to voice. Gently, his lips brushed hers. Merry closed her eyes as he lingered a breath away, then his lips pressed against hers with purpose. His hands were suddenly everywhere, and then he was lifting her, sliding her against him. Merry gasped at the suddenness of his entry, arching her back in delight. He pressed her against the slippery tiled wall, thrusting himself into her as she wrapped her legs tightly around him. Pleasure culminated in powerful, delicious spasms. William joined her with his own release, moaning into her shoulder.

An exquisite numbness consumed her body. William buried his face in her neck, his breath coming hard and fast. Merry's legs refused to support her, and she slid down to the shower floor. William dropped down beside her and took her hand in his, threading their fingers. They sat, heads against the tiled wall, chests heaving, silent and content as the water splashed down around them.

William stood at the ocean's edge gazing out towards the horizon. He'd done so several times since they'd arrived, but today Merry noticed a different attitude in his stance. Gone were the stooped shoulders and hung head, gaze never reaching beyond the sand at his feet. His straight back and searching gaze suggested someone who'd found beauty, yet realized it went much further than could be seen.

She snuck up behind him and circled his waist with a quick hug. "It's a bit warmer today. You're not shivering."

William cocked his head, considering her words. "You are right. I'm cold, but not like I have been." He raised an eyebrow and smiled. "Mayhap you warmed my soul against the elements this morning."

Merry ducked her head, her face heating up. "Incorrigible as ever."

William held her hand and they walked along the shore toward the jetty. "It won't be like it was before. It's not possible."

The words chilled her. *Would he never come back to her?*

"But, I was thinking. Simply because it isn't the same, doesn't mean it can't be good."

Her heart leaped. "It could be better. It will be."

For a fleeting moment, his lop-sided smile made an appearance and Merry knew not everything was lost. She leaned toward him. A few colors escaped and began to weave themselves between their entwined fingers.

"Merry."

"Shhh," she said. She let the colors bloom, cocooning them. For the smallest of moments, the world disappeared. All they had were the colors. And then those too were gone.

William looked at their surroundings, his face shedding his worry for the first time in weeks.

Tall grass rippled in a cool breeze. Another time enveloped them. He turned to Merry.

"You brought us to the meadow."

"Our meadow. I think of this place often. The times we spent here."

"They were some of the best moments of my life," said William, looking into her eyes, as the grass waved in the breeze.

"We can have them again, William. Anytime we want. Our whole lifetime."

He looked down to the ground for a moment, and then locked eyes with her.

"When I was there, in the dark, I became something else. I did things... things I'm ashamed of."

"You..." began Merry, halting as William put a hand up.

"Nay, I have to say this. All that time, in the Tall Man's lair, I wasn't always myself. But, no matter what he did to me. No matter how much he tortured me, how much he tore at my soul, there was one memory I protected above all else. One I wouldn't let him have."

But for the tears rolling down Merry's face, all around them stilled. Even the grass quieted and stood as though waiting to hear William's words.

"It was you, Merry. My love for you."

She pressed her face against his chest, clinging to him as his arms wrapped around her.

"I couldn't let him have that. Not you, Merry. Not you."

She leaned back and looked into his serious blue eyes. "You have my love, my heart, my life, William."

He leaned down and brushed his lips against hers. She opened her eyes and placed a hand upon his cheek as her words danced across the meadow.

"All my time is yours."

62 THE MEADOW

Five years later

Susannah placed her basket on the ground and bent down low to tug a clump of dandelions from the earth, her son happily plucking their fluffy heads from their bodies. The leaves would be a bit more bitter with this yield, but food was food. She smiled down at him and tousled his hair, reveling in the beaming smile he gave to her.

"Don't break the leaves now," she warned.

"I won't, Mama. I'm real careful, see?" He thrust a headless, though leafy, dandelion in her face.

She laughed and gently pushed his chubby hand away. "That's a good boy."

It was a perfect June day, the sun a welcomed warm blanket against her skin. Together they pulled the dandelions from the ground, careful not to crush the leaves or break the roots, which would be used to make a tonic for her husband's sensitive stomach. They moved further into the meadow, finding another cluster of the weeds and continued to fill their basket. When it was brimming, she stood. "That should be plenty now."

Her son wiped his hands on his pants. "It's going to be a good salad, Mama."

"By the grace of God," she said, taking his hand. "Now, no dawdling."

Her son was given to stopping every few minutes to touch a flower or watch a bug crawl along a stalk of the tall grass, which edged the wood. Truth be told, she didn't care as long as he was beside her. He was a gift she never thought she'd be worthy of. He kept up far longer than she'd expected. When he stopped, she tugged a little to encourage forward movement.

"Who are those people, Mama?"

Susannah froze, her head turning, knowing where to look without consulting her child. Knowing who was in the meadow. A gentle laugh rippled across the waving grass, and she saw them. She hadn't been sure they would come back, not having seen them since the end of last summer. But, here they were, hands clasped as they walked through the tall grass to a spot at the top of the hill. Their spot. William tugged Merry toward him, and she laughed again as she fell into his arms and allowed him a kiss.

They didn't notice Susannah, eyes only for one another, and she smiled as her heart lightened at the site of them. Her breath caught, as she thanked God for these two people. These two people who had somehow survived the crimes against them, who's love had been stronger than the pain and wrong that had been inflicted upon them. She thanked God her actions had not been able to destroy this. At least not this.

A small hand tugged at her skirts. She looked down at her child, again cherishing the fortune of someone who'd been given a second chance. "Who are they, Mama?"

She looked up again; William and Merry were lost to the tall grass. She smiled and ruffled her son's hair again. "No one, child. No one."

EPILOGUE

Christianne's skirts swept the tall grass aside as she steadfastly made her way to the meeting place she and Frederick had agreed upon. She scratched at her cheek where the feathered heads tickled her and smiled at the thought of stealing a kiss or a touch, while away from the sharp eyes of her chaperone. She didn't care that this field was purportedly haunted by the ghosts of a witch and her lover. Such stories made it all the more romantic.

"Ouch!" A sharp object dug into the soft sole of her slipper. Christianne stooped to investigate the damage. She lifted her foot and parted the grass. The bright afternoon sun sparked off an object embedded in the dirt. Christianne scraped at the grass and ground to dislodge a bracelet caked in dirt and riddled with time.

"Christianne!" Frederick called from a few yards away. She waved and ran toward him, leaping into his arms. He caught her as though they'd practiced the feat many times before. Indeed they had. She whispered his name against his lips. His kiss lingered. His hands wandered.

"Frederick," she said, pressing her hands against his

shoulders. She stepped away and held up the bracelet, a small charm dangling from its chain links.

Frederick grimaced. "What is this, pray tell?"

"I found it. In the meadow, over there," Christianne answered, waving in the general direction of her discovery. "It's old, isn't it?"

"Practically ancient, I'd say," Frederick answered as he took the silver bracelet and inspected the rough-hammered star charm. "Over a hundred years old, maybe two, if I had to guess."

"Truly?" Christianne snatched it from his hands, a thrill coursing through her veins. "Is it valuable do you think?"

Frederick smiled, and then kissed the tip of her nose. "Not nearly as valuable as you, my dear."

Christianne lifted it against the blue-sky backdrop. The star twinkled as though it were meant to be hanging in the heavens rather than at the end of a rusted chain. An image flashed in her mind of a woman and a man and a love hard won. Christianne clasped the bracelet to her chest, her mind overtaken by visions of the lovers, her soul struck by the depth of their devotion. She gasped.

"Christianne?" Frederick folded his hand over hers, blotting the images from her mind. "What is it, my love?"

She didn't answer right away, unwilling to give up the pureness of emotion that had seeped into her soul. This object had seen love, been through time, and had endured for hundreds of years. She would ensure it would see a hundred more. After a long moment, she looked into Frederick's eyes, as she gripped the bracelet in her fist. A small smile played upon her lips as she brought them to his and breathed. "It's everything, my darling."

Thank you for buying this book! If you would like to receive special offers and be the first to hear news about my latest books, sign up for my newsletter at:
    http://susancatalano.wix.com/susancatalano
I promise I won't flood your inbox - I'm too busy writing!

I love readers! Heck, I am one! So let's keep in touch - join me on:
    Facebook: https://www.facebook.com/TimelessOnes
    Twitter: https://twitter.com/scatu2

One more thing - I would appreciate, I mean really, really, REALLY, appreciate it if you would take a few minutes to leave an honest review on Amazon and/or Goodreads.

ACKNOWLEDGEMENTS

I've had so much support and encouragement to make this book happen, and it's time to say thank you! First, to my three wonderful beta readers who took the time to read A Necessary Darkness and provide valuable feedback that ultimately helped to fine-tune the story. Thank you Antonietta Caputo, Elena Figler, and Barbara Snedeker-Schultz! I appreciate your honesty and enthusiasm! Your input is so important to this whole writing-a-book process. Speaking of process, I'd like to thank my editor, Katrina Diaz, for cleaning things up and my cover artist/son, Christian, for making my book so fetching. I also want to thank my husband, the man who doesn't read fiction, for actually reading my first book! Here's another one, honey. And I must say thank you! thank you! thank you! loyal readers, for your excitement, your encouraging words, and your loyalty. I hope you'll join me for the next book journey— The Green Series!

Cover art and design provided by Christian Catalano

Editing provided by Katrina Diaz

ABOUT THE AUTHOR

Susan Catalano lives in Massachusetts where Salem, known as Witch City, has captured her imagination and inspired her first book series, THE TIMELESS ONES.

You can connect with Susan online at:
https://www.facebook.com/TimelessOnes

Made in the USA
Columbia, SC
30 November 2017